❧ ALSO BY CLAIRE LEGRAND ❧

Sawkill Girls
Thornlight
Foxheart

EXTASIA

CLAIRE LEGRAND

KATHERINE TEGEN BOOKS
An Imprint of HarperCollins Publishers

Katherine Tegen Books is an imprint of HarperCollins Publishers.

Extasia
Copyright © 2022 by Claire Legrand
All rights reserved. Printed in the United States of America.
No part of this book may be used or reproduced in any manner
whatsoever without written permission except in the case of
brief quotations embodied in critical articles and reviews. For
information address HarperCollins Children's Books, a division of
HarperCollins Publishers, 195 Broadway, New York, NY 10007.
www.epicreads.com

Library of Congress Cataloging-in-Publication Data

Names: Legrand, Claire, 1986– author.
Title: Extasia / Claire Legrand.
Description: First edition. | [New York] : Katherine Tegen Books,
    an imprint of HarperCollins Publishers, [2022] | Audience:
    Ages 14 up. | Audience: Grades 10-12. | Summary: In a
    postapocalyptic world, sixteen-year-old Saint Amity joins a coven
    and sets out on a quest to summon the Devil in order to protect
    her village, which is controlled by group of pious elders.
Identifiers: LCCN 2021020598 | ISBN 978-0-06-269664-9
Subjects: CYAC: Witches–Fiction. | Saints–Fiction. |
    Magic–Fiction. | Anger–Fiction. | Revenge–Fiction. |
    Secrets–Fiction. | LCGFT: Novels. | Horror fiction.
Classification: LCC PZ7.L521297 Ex 2022 | DDC [Fic]–dc23
LC record available at https://lccn.loc.gov/2021020598

Typography by Joel Tippie
23 24 25 26 27 LBC 5 4 3 2 1

First paperback edition, 2023

for the women who helped me crawl through it

I

wherever you are

1

My name is unimportant.

The name my dead mother gave me is not really mine, not I who will today be made a saint of Haven. I am not like other girls. My father tells me so. He tells me I am greater than any plain girl walking, and now the other elders say it too. They heard it straight from God.

Never mind what my mother did.

Never mind that there are still some in our village who look at me and my father and my sister—the Barrow family—and wonder if we are Devil-touched, same as Mother was.

Never mind what I did that day five years ago, what I saw, what I said.

No, today marks a new beginning for us Barrows. The elders have deemed me worthy of my true name at last.

But when I wake on this day of my anointing, a great black

bird sits just outside my window. A chill rushes through me. First hot, then cold, it steals away my wits.

This is not just any bird, but a mottled creature with ratty feathers and scaly skin. A jagged toothy beak hanging open, unblinking white eyes like big twin moons. Very still, it watches me, and I watch back.

Mother always told us of the frights, the little creatures sent by the Devil that swarm inside a girl and bring fear, doubt, dark thoughts. They claw and nibble, rake your skin with cold, tie your belly into knots.

Not once did I see a fright outside of Mother's stories until this winter past. For weeks now I have seen them in trees, real and perched and leering. In shadows, skittering. Overhead, fluttering like bats. More and more, they come.

And when they do, death often follows close behind.

And when they come, it seems that only I can see them.

But whatever of my mother's rot lives inside me, it shall not drag me down to Hell as it did her. She brought our family low.

Today, I shall raise us high once more.

"You do not frighten me," I whisper to the bird, and what a lie it is. "Leave us. Go away. This is a holy day."

The bird pecks twice at the glass with that horrible gaping beak, full of fangs that should not be. Its white eyes, so still and bright and clever.

My sister, Blessing, shifts and mumbles in her bed across the room.

Sitting up, I glare at the bird and whisper harshly, "Begone, Devil." Then I strike the window's cool glass with my fists.

The bird flaps away. Our gray cat, Shadow, hisses from her hiding spot under my bed. Shadow always hides if a fright is about. She loses her courage. Her hair stands on end.

Blessing turns over, her voice thick. She sleeps like a stone, my sister, and wakes slowly. "What is it? What's wrong?"

I paint a smile over my racing heart. "Nothing, sister. A fly on the window. I killed it. Rest, now."

She obeys with a grunt, curls up beneath her quilt.

I slip out of my bed and dress quickly—my long white dress with tiny blue flowers, my brown wool cloak, my boots. I quietly climb out the window. Behind our white house with its blue trim, my garden shivers in the morning air.

I close the window and wait a moment to be certain Blessing does not wake again. I stare and hardly breathe. Women and girls in Haven are not allowed to hold or possess or look upon mirrors. Mirrors show God's truth, too mighty for our eyes to bear, and they turn our weak hearts vain. The only mirror I have ever glimpsed is the small square one with the plain wooden frame Father keeps locked away in his bedroom—and this mirror, here, in the dark glass of my window. I take a moment to stare at myself, my skin prickling with shame. There I am—thin and straight up and down, with long brown hair and skin white as river foam and sixteen years of prayers in my eyes. Heart pounding at the back of my tongue, I shake my head and look past the strange sight of my sinful staring self.

Past that thin dark-haired girl are the pale curtains in our window and the flat wool rug. The walls of red and blue flowers painted by my own hand, and my sister's too. Beside her bed, a yellow vase of blue and orange wildflowers. And there is my sister, the younger Barrow, her hair spilled honey on her pillow. Sleep on, sweet Blessing.

I gather a small bunch of flowers and creep through the garden gate on mouse feet. Bell chimes fly on the wind, for every rooftop in Haven has been strung pretty in honor of the winter's dead. There is Elder Joseph's house, across the dirt road. I walk by it and hold my breath. I do not once look at its shivering bells.

Granny Dale's house next, then Benjamin Grainger's, the Abbott house, the Everett house. I turn right onto a narrow road where the oaks arch overhead like raised arms. The Ames house, the Gray house. Nine hanging bells, then nine more, and nine again.

Widow Woodworth kneels at her front steps, where a white wooden cross stands stuck in the ground. Her little girls—Abigail, Patricia—dress the cross with fresh flowers while their mother watches.

I hurry past. I am not meant to be seen before my anointing. I should not even be out of my house.

But Widow Woodworth catches sight of me. Her eyes widen, bright with tears.

"Saint Amity," she whispers, reaching for me with a shaking

hand. "Girls, come. Put those down. Saint Amity will bless us now."

I shake my head, try to step away. "Widow, I am not yet anointed. That is not my name."

"Please, only a small prayer. A tiny blessing. 'Tis all I ask." She and her daughters clasp their hands, turn their faces up to me. Auburn-haired, the girls too small to truly understand. The gaunt widow's cheeks wet from tears.

She has not eaten much since her husband, Clarence, was found in the meadow in January. Limbs splayed, white and limp and strange. All the blood drained from his body, though the elders could find no holes in his flesh.

I glance at the little white cross, then look around at the dim road, the dark windows in every bell-strung house. If an elder sees me bestowing a blessing before my anointing, he could bring word to the others. They might return to their seclusion, ask God to tell them a different name.

What would Father do then?

Such a betrayal would eat away at him from the inside, devour whatever Mother left behind.

But if I leave the widow here, she might tell on me for unkindness.

"'Tis our secret," I whisper.

"We shan't tell a soul," says Widow Woodworth eagerly. "Isn't that right, girls?"

The girls nod. One wrinkles her nose and sneezes.

"Dear Lord," I mutter, "please look upon this family that has lost so much and grant them and their neighbors kindness and mercy as we, the good people of Haven, look to warmer days with hope in our hearts. Protect us from further evil and from the Devil's cruel works. Amen."

"Amen," say the Woodworth girls along with their mother. I rub hasty crosses on their foreheads in the name of the Lamb, God's own son, and hurry away.

Elder Peter sits on his porch around the corner, waiting for me, as he does on every holy day. 'Tis our own small tradition. He raises his hand and smiles. His skin is a pale carpet of wrinkles, his hair only thin white tufts. His eyes are kind, and he never shouts.

"Blessed morning," he says to me, and then my given name, which I pretend was not said. "You are early today. Usually you come with the sun."

"Samuel wishes to pray with me in the meadow before everything begins." I touch my fingers to my forehead, my lips, my chest.

Elder Peter echoes the greeting, his shining eyes on my flowers. "A sunrise vigil. Samuel is good to offer you this."

I glance toward the meadow, which stretches green and fresh beyond the wall. Something twists in my stomach. Not unpleasant, not altogether. A tadpole wriggling through a pond.

As if it heard me thinking this, the wicked bird returns, alighting upon the railing of Elder Peter's porch. It folds its scabby wings and stares at me.

"Samuel is good to me indeed," I say, my voice unsteady. "For God's gifts I am grateful."

"Most importantly, you've brought fresh blooms for my table!" Elder Peter looks up at me with a child's joy. "I love them. They are cheerful as summer clouds." He buries his face in the blue iris petals. "And thank you for freshening my linens yesterday. I was able to find sleep quickly for once."

"What an odd bird," I say lightly. "Don't you agree?"

Elder Peter turns in his creaking chair and looks right at the awful creature, his mouth a mere breath from its open beak. "What bird, child?"

I swallow hard. "It must have flown away."

I grab the flowers from him and hurry inside to find water and a vase, keeping the bird always in my sight. Its white gaze follows me, pins me through the window.

"I am not afraid of you," I say quietly to my hands as I work. "Once I am anointed, God will banish you from this land."

When next I look up, the bird has gone.

"Your gift is a welcome reminder that spring comes after winter, that life comes after death," Elder Peter says as I help him to his feet. He waves his hand at the bells hanging from the scalloped rafters on blue ribbons. Nine golden bells, standing guard alongside the large silver one that hangs near every elder's door. His voice wavers. "Nine men and boys of Haven, all of them gone to God."

"A hard winter," I murmur.

"A distant memory after today." Elder Peter touches my cheek with his wrinkled fingers. "Your anointing will be a celebration. Our people will feel hope again. Spring, and flowers, and a new saint at last. God has spoken, and He has spoken your name. Your father is so proud of you."

Feeling the sting of tears, I fold Elder Peter's hand into mine and press it gently. May God bless this kind old man for saying nothing of my dead mother or her sins.

"Thank you, Elder Peter," I whisper.

A cheerful light twinkles in his eye. He heaves himself toward the steps. "Off I go, then, shall I?"

I watch him shuffle toward the high wall that circles Haven. Never do I see Elder Peter walk so quickly as when he goes to trick the watchmen so I can slip outside the wall unseen. It amuses him to play tricks as he did when he was a boy. Girls are not meant to roam beyond the wall unless a man is with them, but Elder Peter will point the watchmen's eyes elsewhere.

Besides that, I know a place they cannot see.

Samuel showed it to me the day Mother died, so I could watch her run.

A HIDEY-HOLE, WE CALL IT.

'Tis a weak spot in the wooden wall that circles Haven, overgrown with brambles and vines. Many trees stand along the wall, both within and without, but they are thickest here and guard a hollow in the ground.

I crawl into this hollow, find the loose planks in the wall, and squeeze through. Then there is a thick tangle of wire and wood, a second barrier put up in the winter when our men began dying. Blessed every day by the elders, it encircles the wall like a tightly coiled snake, but for all its fearsomeness, it does not seem to scare the Devil.

Samuel makes certain a hidden place in this new barrier is kept thin so I may crawl through it when we are to meet. I hold my breath as I do, hoping no stray nail will catch my skin. In the wild grass beyond, I wait, listening for Elder Peter's voice to sound from above, atop the high wall. He will tell the watchmen stories of God, and they'll be better for his words.

I feel no guilt. I have felt enough guilt.

But this thought is far from pious, so I utter three more Small Graces. I enjoy groups of three. 'Tis a holy number.

Elder Peter's voice drifts down. Time to hurry into the meadow, then. Up and over a slight ridge, then past a gentle rise, and I am safe.

There he is, lying in the soft spring grass, turning over as he sees me: Samuel. A smile on his tanned face, even after all he has lost. His winter pallor has already faded. He works hard in the fields. He hunts and runs. The wind tousles his thick dark hair.

He holds out a small flower—a tiny yellow arnica.

"You give me a flower when I have hundreds," I tell him, joining him in the grass. Side by side, we hide there, half buried in meadow. Green smells come fast. Sage and dirt and dew-damp leaves.

"Ah, but this flower is special," says Samuel, with his gentle smile. "It said your name."

I nudge him. "Flowers do not speak."

"This one did. I came out here early. I prayed for you, that this day may be all you wish it to be. Then I prayed that God might show me the perfect flower, and here it is."

"This humble little bloom?"

"The kind of bloom God loves best."

Gentle Samuel. So serious he is. Other boys might tease

a girl with flower prayers, but no other boy in Haven means what he says like Samuel does. No other boy is quite so soft.

I do not lie: God's fortune shone true upon me when He saw fit to bring me such a friend as Samuel. First, a friend. Now, a someday husband. I see the way other girls look at Samuel. Most of them dare not look at me too meanly, daughter of the High Elder that I am, soon-to-be-saint, but I know they all wish they could—or that I would fall to ruin as Mother did and leave Samuel free for the taking.

He shifts against me, and there is that tadpole again. Not bad, but not good. A feeling I cannot name. It jumps and kicks. I put my hand flat against my belly.

Quiet, little tadpole, and begone. I know not what you mean.

"You have done well," Samuel tells me, after a peaceful quiet. Of course he does not say my hated given name. Dear, good Samuel. To him, my mother's sins are forgotten. To him, I am blameless. "So many trials you've endured. So many have doubted you."

I watch the sun rise and think about pressing my body flat against the dirt. And here I thought we would pray silently together, as we ought to. In such a silence, I could forget the bird I saw. I could forget every last strange creature that has shown its teeth to me these long months.

I could forget that day, what I saw, what I did.

"I deserved their doubt," I tell Samuel sharply, "and the trials too."

"'Twas unjust. No other candidate was made to suffer so."

I almost sigh. "So you have said."

"You disagree."

"I always have."

"Tied to a stake for four days with no food, when the other candidates had to endure only two."

I say nothing.

"The weights you carried, tied to you for weeks. The thistles worn around your ankles! I saw no other girls' legs bound in thorns."

Pride blooms in me. A sin, and yet I hear that awe in Samuel's voice and cannot help myself. Will God forgive me that on this day of all days? Have I not suffered enough in my mother's name?

My eyes are hot. I blink them hard at the gray sky. The prick of the thorns, the ache of my muscles, the pinch of hunger—truth be told, I remember little of those things.

But I remember how they looked at us after Mother ran. My neighbors. Not Samuel, not Elder Peter, not Granny Dale or John Ames, and a few kind others besides them who lean hard on the idea of mercy.

But everyone else. Oh, yes, I remember how they looked at us. Even my father, who has been High Elder since Blessing was born fourteen years past, did not escape their judgment.

After today, no one will ever look at us that way again.

"Why do you speak of this now?" I say quietly. "We were meant to pray, not recount my trials."

"I am proud of you." Samuel draws a breath and touches my fingers. "I wanted you to hear that once more, before the day begins. I wanted to remind you of how good you are. How brave and strong."

He kisses my hand, his mouth hot against my skin. A jolt of feeling shudders through me. No longer a tadpole, but a huge warty toad.

Shy, serious Samuel. Someday he will put a baby in me. Maybe two, or five.

I pull away from him ever so gently. "You are mixing me all up inside, Samuel."

"I'm sorry. I only meant—"

"It is utterly just." I set my eyes upon him. *Listen to me, Samuel. No more kissing of hands.* "After what Mother did, the elders were right to test me. Remember what I've said. All my trials, every moment of suffering, the visions that have plagued me—they have brought me to this day, and I am glad for them."

He catches it on my face, clever boy. "You saw one today, didn't you? One of the Devil's beasts?"

"Only a bird, just this morning. I scared it off quick. After today, all of that will stop. No more beasts. No more killings."

Samuel's eyes move past me. I know where he looks. The House of Woe, some ways beyond, stands fresh and painted blue in the fields. Around it, a charred ring of dirt and brush.

The House of Woe has seen many a body burned this past

hard winter, including Samuel's older brother. Benjamin Aldridge, all of twenty years old. A smile as big as Samuel's, a nature just as gentle.

I turn Samuel's sad, frightened face to me. His chin is narrow and sharp, only a little rough in my palm. I press my brow to his until the grief stops shaking him.

"Nine dead," Samuel whispers then. "And today you saw a bird of the Devil. Is someone else to die, then? What if I am next? My mother could not bear it. I think losing me too would kill her."

"No. Never. Not you. Not anyone." How would my father speak? Like this, steady and unbroken. "Once I am given my hood, and four saints stand anointed in Haven once more, as God said it must be in the Sanctificat, the evil stain my mother left on our land will fade, and the Devil's hold on Haven will end. It has been only in these last weeks, with three saints anointed, that death has stalked us. You know this."

Samuel nods slowly. He watches me as our people watch my father when he speaks. Wide eyes, parted lips. "I do know it."

"After everything I have endured, joyfully and with an open heart, would God not reward me with His gifts? Would He not see that I have atoned for my mother's sins and then, as a sign of His mercy, banish the Devil from Haven with righteous fury?"

"He would," whispers my good Samuel, his eyes alight and fierce. "He will."

I turn away from the black mountain that stands to the west

and clasp my hands around a clutch of tender spring grass. Samuel does the same. He is all hard bones and boy muscle and earnest brow in the grass beside me.

"The Devil has been scratching at the door, oh Lord," I whisper. I came here to pray, and so I shall. "He has visited our home with violence and taken nine souls for his own this winter past. Nine strong men who feared and loved you, oh Lord, including our beloved Benjamin."

Samuel repeats my words, his voice trembling. Does he see every time he closes his eyes the body of his dead brother? The fear in his frozen eyes? The marks upon his flesh?

I do. I see all of them, every night in my dreams.

Bodies found in the meadow's sweet green, flayed and rotten. Bodies strung up along Haven's wall with ropes of thorns.

Deaths the elders have not been able to trace to anyone living in Haven.

"But he will not triumph for much longer, oh God of all that is good." My heart pounds, and my limbs are made of angelfire. Whatever weak thing lives inside me and calls the Devil to my window with beaks and feathers, this day will stamp it dead at last.

"When next he comes with his beasts," I whisper, "he will find me at our gates waiting for him with my three saintly sisters and will fall trembling to his knees. With my blood and sweat, I have washed the stain of my mother's sins from our soil. In me, oh Lord, Your light will shine as the heavens do and burn away all fear, all cruelty, all evil."

The watchmen's first bell is struck, a brassy chime rung from the clouds. This is Elder Peter's secret message to me: *Time to hurry home, sneaking rabbit. Back to your garden.*

I kiss the yellow arnica and press it to Samuel's chest. He holds my hand for a breath—calloused fingers, warm heartbeat—and then I hurry away. Laughter sits on my tongue, the laughter of a godly, goodly girl. The bird's memory is far from me. A joyful thing I am, hurrying home along the secret path Elder Peter has deemed safest. I will be a saint, and I will marry Samuel, and the Devil will release me at last, and my home will be protected, and no one will ever know what strange things I have seen. Only Samuel and God, and they will both forgive me. 'Tis my mother's wicked sight that shows me these things, not my own.

But there is something at my bedroom window, yet another small strangeness. Tucked between the glass and a knot of rosebuds, a strip of pale cloth flutters like a caught bird.

With the flowers of my garden close around me, I tear the cloth free. Crude shapes are writ upon it in a scratchy dark color:

Twenty trees, clustered in a familiar shape. The elm grove by the western wall.

And then a bell, and a single mark beside it. First bell? The watchmen's bell that has only just rung, bringing me in from the meadow?

Then three figures. Girls—long hair, long dresses, joined hands.

And then a word. I struggle to read it, for I am a girl and was not taught the language of God at the elders' feet, as Samuel was. But, foul mother's daughter that I am, I do possess some stolen knowings.

The letters are jagged and messy. I trace the lines with my finger. I speak the sounds: Arr. You. Enn.

RUN

3

I HOLD MY BREATH UNTIL I hear my heart in my ears. A cold feeling trickles down my back.

My wicked brain knows the shape and slope of those letters, though I wish it did not. I first saw them when I was small, when Temperance and I wrote out the Sanctificat's prayers in secret.

This note is her doing.

I clench my fists around the cloth. If only I could crush it into ashes, send it flying. I have worked too hard for this day to be ruined by staring beasts and girls who should know better.

When I was small, I was not always a good child of God, as I am now. I saw my father read from the Sanctificat and wanted to read it my own self. Why should I not? I did not understand then about The World That Once Was and the cunning women who ended it. They read books that were not theirs to read. They defied, they deceived. And there I was, doing the very same. A foolish willful child with tangled hair and dirty knees and my old friend Temperance holding my hand.

In my mother's wild garden that is now mine, we hid and laughed and tried to write words we did not understand. A child's game, we told ourselves. But we knew in our bones that it was wrong.

One day when I was all of six, Mother caught us scratching out prayers in the dirt with our fingers, our heads close and our legs touching. In the dirt before us lay my father's stolen Sanctificat. How clever we were to have snuck it out of the table by his bed. We babbled the prayers aloud. The letters were nonsense to us, but we pretended. We brushed away the shapes when they looked foolish and tried again.

My own sister was small and tiresome. A bald squaller with fat cheeks. Temperance—though her name was different then—was better than a sister. When I first met her at worship, sucking on her thumb and staring with wide dark eyes, I knew she would be mine.

But when Mother found us that day in the garden, she tore me from Temperance's side and took me home. When the door shut, Mother said to me, "Never again, do you hear?"

She began to cry. She held me close, squashed me in her bony arms. I have never been more afraid, not even during my trials, when death crept near.

"If they find you doing such things," she whispered to me,

"they will hurt you." She smelled of sweat, my father's pipe smoke, the herbs from her garden. "Forget those letters. Forget all that you have learned."

The elders would hurt *me*? My little head spun at the thought. The elders hurt the wicked, that was true. But they hurt the saints too, as God commands. I'd seen that with my own eyes. Did my mother, then, see in me that day something worthy of anointing?

Temperance and I never spoke again. I refused to look at her. Not even when she stood at the altar to receive her hood did I raise my eyes to hers. Instead, I stared at the dirt. Ordinary and forgotten amid the crowd that gazed upon her, I fumed. My awful old friend Temperance, a saint? I could not understand why God had told the elders her name. Had it not been her idea to steal my father's book? Had her fingers not carved lines through the dirt, same as mine?

And now, here is this note she has left me. I remember those skinny white fingers of hers, how they moved in the dirt like cottonwood seeds twirling over the river. I would know those letters anywhere.

A dark feeling spills through me. Bones gone, only my anger left, sharp and hot like a sky full of lightning.

The cloth clutched in my damp hand, I push into my garden's deep tangles, where the rosebushes and forsythias grow close and tug at my hair. *Crouch, girl, and hurry.* I dig a small hole. My nose fills with the wet black smell of this earth and the life it holds. Here I once hid with Temperance and choked on frightened laughter and tried to pray with dirty fingers.

Trembling, I blow out a breath. A lump sits in the deep turn of my throat.

What could Temperance mean by giving me this message? Elm grove. First bell. Three girls.

Goodbye, little cloth. I cover it with soil, push down the dirt, pat it flat, crawl out of the bushes.

I should go inside, clean my hands, pray till Father wakes. First bell has rung, second bell will come soon, and then my adornment, and then everything else. Haven will awaken, and the acolytes will beat their drums, and my father will escort me to Holy House, where my hood awaits.

Whatever Temperance means by this note, I fear it can be nothing good. But perhaps she calls me for some rite of sainthood I have never been told, some secret known only to saints and elders.

Or perhaps the Devil has got his hooks in her. A final trial for me to endure—he and Temperance, entwined in godlessness, waiting for me in the elm shadows. They could ruin everything, if I let them.

Elm grove? First bell? Very well, Temperance. Here I come.

I find Temperance in the elm grove near Haven's western wall, not far from the harvest gate.

Beside the grove's largest elm kneels my friend of old. She holds the hands of another girl who sits before her—long red hair to her waist, sharp nose, sharp eyes, freckled skin. Beneath their cloaks, they wear the long white dresses saints wear on holy days, with high lace collars and ribbons at their wrists.

"Just wait a little longer," says Temperance. "Please!"

The girl with red hair, Saint Mercy, glares at Temperance and tears herself free.

Last year, when we were both of us fifteen, was Mercy's anointing. I remember feeling a furious sickness as I watched her. She knelt before my father and lowered her head to receive the ribboned red hood, and I knew that bowed head should have been mine.

I had never hated my dead mother more than I did that day.

"We have waited long enough," says Mercy. In the whispering gloom of these trees, I hear anger bristle in her voice. "She did not come because she is a coward, as I knew she was. 'Tis for the best. None of us should leave Haven until it is finished. Malice was wrong to promise you anything else. I thought you were stronger than this."

Temperance shakes her head. "I can bear no more of this violence."

"We need to wait only a few more weeks. Don't you remember? Malice said—"

"But this is not what I want!"

"And what do you want? Would you rather they find your blood? Wed you to someone you do not love?"

I peek around a rough old elm trunk to watch them, these two girls who should be praying in their homes, asking blessings for the day to come. An ill feeling blooms inside me, carried by the swift drum of my heart.

I want to look away from them.

I cannot look away. The Devil's finger has me pinned to my tree.

"Elias is a fine man," Temperance says, tears cracking her voice.

Mercy laughs unkindly.

My head spins with their words. *Malice*, and *violence*, and *blood*. But if Temperance has begun to bleed, if that is what they mean, then she can no longer be a saint. She must wed her betrothed, Elias Holt, and bear children.

"Perhaps the wind took my message," says Temperance. "We should go find her before it's too late. Malice promised—"

"Malice was playing one of her games. She is testing you. She never meant to leave before this is finished, not even if you bring your little friend skipping through the woods for her. Now, come. Gather yourself. If we are late and weeping, the elders will wonder why."

Mercy rises, and Temperance follows, crying out. A word or a sob? The sound catches in my chest as a thorn snags a hem.

Then Temperance reaches for Mercy, and a thing happens that I do not understand. Mercy steps away—once, twice. She keeps space between them and does not touch Temperance. No, she only pushes her hands through the air, muttering something I cannot hear, but Temperance staggers back as if struck true. Her toe has caught a root, I think, or a dip in the ground.

A strange shadow twists about Mercy's fingers. Or perhaps it is only a thin light? Yes, a trick of the brightening sky come down through the trees.

Then Temperance kneels, murmuring something soft, and swiftly draws her fingers through the dirt. When she rises, she cups her hands as if holding inside them a firefly. Light touches her fingers. It must be the sly shadows, the rising sun. She moves her arms as if to toss a ball to Mercy. I see naught but air—what strange dark dance have they begun?—until a band of shadow snaps around Mercy's body. Her arms now hang stiff at her sides, her fingers splayed. She twists in place but does not move away. Something has rooted her.

I want to run. I must run. Yet here I am, me and my elm, both of us stuck fast.

"We will find her *now*, and quickly," says Temperance, her voice clear and strong. Her sharp chin juts out, a knife of bone under her skin. "There is still time. She is my friend, and yours too."

"Years ago she was your friend," Mercy spits, "when you were both know-nothing children, and then she turned against you, just as they wanted. And she was never my friend at all."

They stare at each other beneath the old giant trees, red-haired Mercy and slight Temperance, moon-white. Her hair is a pane of night-glass down her back.

I remember her lying beside me in the dirt, our small fingers black with mud-scratched letters we did not understand. Her hair so long and dark I knew not where the rich earth ended and my friend's tresses began. I remember tracing one tangled lock against the soil. I remember Temperance looking up at me as I did it, her smile sweet, a spot of dirt on her nose.

There is a quiet snap in the air. Something in the grove gives way.

Mercy stumbles back from Temperance and rubs her wrists, as if they have been bound tight with cords.

And then Temperance rushes to her, gentle, clumsy, like a lamb to its mother. She takes Mercy's face in her hands, and locks her fingers in Mercy's long red hair, and kisses her.

5

I CANNOT FEEL THE ELM beside me or the earth beneath me as I watch them. I am a leaf caught on a spinning wind, punched into the sky.

Temperance's hands on Mercy's face. Mercy's fingers clutching my old friend's cloak. Two saints of Haven, kissing in the elm grove, as a man does his wife. Kissing as Father did Mother long ago, before the Devil took her mind and she muttered his dark stories to anyone who would listen.

Before I found her in Father's bed with a man who was not Father.

Their heads touch, brow to brow. Mercy must bend a little; Temperance is not so very tall.

"If she will not come," whispers Temperance slowly, "then maybe we should leave. Just you and I. We do not need her, or Malice, or anyone. We could run far and fast. We could not look back."

Mercy softens. "You tempt me once again with this."

"I can hunt. You can build fires."

Mercy kisses her cheek, lingers, then steps away. "I went along with this plan to make you happy, though I knew it would end in sadness for you. I knew your *friend* would not come. And now you must see that I cannot leave Haven until it is done. All of it."

"My darling, *why*? It will soothe your heart, and then what?"

"Then my heart will be soothed," says Mercy in a voice so hard it frightens me.

"I think you will bleed forever inside and never be happy," says Temperance. "I think it will change you. I think it already has."

Watching them, I can no longer hide. Darling. *Darling*, said Temperance. The word lodges inside me, pricks open my heart.

When I hurry toward them, they break apart and stare at me, these two girls I have watched every Sunday in their white dresses and red hoods. Mercy's freckled face clouds over, storm crossing sun. She stands a little before Temperance. As if I am the one to be feared!

"What is this?" I say, my voice cracking.

Mercy is very still. Temperance steps around her. On her face, a small smile I remember well and wish I did not.

She calls me by the name my mother gave me. I pretend I do not hear it.

"This is my anointing day," I say harshly, for it seems they have forgotten. "Why are you not at home praying?"

Mercy lifts her chin. "It seems you are not either."

"You found my message?" says Temperance. She reaches for my hand, as if I too will soon feel her mouth against mine, her fingers woven into my hair.

I push her away from me, hard.

Mercy's smile mocks me. "Does the Sanctificat permit a saint to turn violent against anyone but herself? I must have forgotten that particular Scripture."

My blood runs cold against my bones to hear her say such words. Past the elm grove, past the western wall, out beyond the meadows and the woods, stands the Devil's black mountain. Tall and flat-topped, a shadow upon the sky. Somewhere on its sheer slopes perch curved dark horns and eyes that never blink. They watch me now, waiting for me to step wrong just once, to fall as fast as Mother did.

I move away from Temperance. "What did you do just now? I saw strange shadows. You held a light in your hands."

Temperance blinks, then says gently, "I am uncertain what you mean. Perhaps the morning light tricked your eyes."

Yes. Yes, that is it. My eyes were tricked. I say it three times. *A trick, nothing more.* I blow out a sharp breath, my knees weak with relief. "Why did you tell me to come here? You spoke of blood. Have you begun your monthly bleeding?

And yet you have not told the elders?"

Mercy glares. "She has heard far too much."

"I asked you to come because it is time for us all to run," says Temperance, breathless. "Now, before your anointing begins. There are people nearby, in the woods, who can shelter us and take us far from here safely. They are powerful and good. They can teach you things, as they have taught me and Mercy. If we leave now, we can reach them before the drums begin."

I stare at her. Her words come as if from far away. "This is my anointing day," I say again, feeling muddled, and thorny, for I was not muddled until I saw her message and came here. I was happy, with prayers on my tongue and Samuel's kiss still warm on my hand.

Mercy sneers. "Look at her face, how frightened she is. You cannot still think we should bring her to the others. One look at her, and Malice will turn us away forever."

"She will do no such thing," says Temperance firmly. She holds out her hand to me. Her face is kind, but I do not believe it. "I know you have wanted to be anointed for many years, but it is not what you think it will be. If you come with us right now, our friends can save you from it."

"Your friends in the woods," I say. Wild laughter brews in my throat. I swallow it down, my mouth hot and sick.

"Yes. Please. We were friends once. Trust me, as you did then."

"And if I do not come?"

"Then we will stay too, and help you with your sainthood

❦ 32 ❦

as best we can," says Temperance quietly.

"*She* will help you," Mercy says, arms crossed, eyes snapping. "I cannot promise the same."

"This is some Devil's trick," I whisper, stepping away from them. Their words are impossible. They roil inside me, knocking against my teeth. I cover my ears. "I shan't listen!"

Temperance says my loathed name again, my wretched mother's gift. "Hush. Hear me. Malice loves me. She is more a mother to me than mine has ever been. She promised me she would take us all from here if I brought her to you. But we must leave *now*, all three of us together, before everyone gathers for your anointing. Sneaking away will not be so easy then."

What this person named Malice, this false mother, wants with me, I know not. But I know that word, *malice*. I know the Devil deals in it. The very sound of it is wicked.

I turn from Temperance, hands still pressed against my ears. This is a test. A final trial sent by the Devil, or perhaps by the elders. *Tell her to run*, they told Mercy and Temperance. *Tempt her to draw out her weakness. Let us see if she succumbs. Let us see if she is worthy.*

"I am worthy," I say, my voice shaking and pathetic beneath the trees.

"Of course you are," says Temperance. "You must be, or else Malice would not want to meet you."

I knock away Temperance's reaching hands and run. Mercy laughs, spits some crude scornful word.

Spit away, Mercy. I do not fear you. I fear only the judgment of God.

I run home through the shrinking shadows of Haven's roads. Golden bells wink from the rooftops. Cooking fires send up smoke.

"I will stop him," I whisper, a frantic prayer of my own making, a ward against the Devil. "I will save us."

No trial will fell me now, nor any trick or snare.

"Deliver me through the darkness, oh Lord . . ."

Where my mother was weak, I will stand strong.

" . . . that I may see the glory of Your light and rejoice."

But as I slip through my garden's gate, as the second bell rings and the air of Haven fills with golden song, all my righteous thoughts slip from me. Instead, I see them burned into the hot black curtain of my squeezed-shut eyes—Mercy and Temperance, embracing in the trees. Fingers hooked in hair. Eyes shining, mouths pink and tender. Bee and flower. Lock and key.

6

I AM SO QUIET AS I climb back through my bedroom window, boots in hand, that my sister, Blessing, does not at first hear me.

Something moves beneath her blankets. I freeze beside my bed. 'Tis her own hand that moves, I know, for I have seen this happen before. Like a tiny creature burrowing under bracken for food, it seeks and rubs. She's all a-twist, my sister. Even in the gray morning light, I can see the flush pink of her cheeks. She lets out a soft cry.

I hurry to her, place my hand over her mouth, hold her gently down against her pillow.

My sister's blue eyes snap open, twin pools in a field of creamy skin and golden hair. Is she afraid or defiant? I can never tell with Blessing. There is too much of our mother in her sly sweet face.

Finger over my lips, I wait, and so does she. Both of us hold still, hearing footsteps down the hall, in the kitchen. Father is awake, which means it is time for my adornment.

"Have the handmaidens arrived?" I whisper.

Blessing shakes her head. "I did not hear."

I glare at her. "No, I suppose you did not. Hurry—clean your hand and air out your bed. Your smell is everywhere. Pretend that we are just waking up."

I remove my flowered dress and shove it under my bed, don my nightgown once more. I lean hard against the sill and breathe, the air blessedly cool on my cheeks. Shadow mews and leaps outside, eager for mice.

"You . . . you know what I was doing?" Blessing says, hurrying her fingers through her mussed hair.

"I have awoken to it many a night," I tell her, my voice faint, though I wish it could be firm. First Mercy and Temperance in the elm grove, now this. My skin is hot and crawling. "I should have stopped you months ago."

"Have you felt it before too?"

Her careful words sit askew inside me. "Felt what?"

"A strange heat. A gathering of all my insides. An ache. When it comes, I try to ignore it, but I cannot."

My sister is the most wearying creature ever to live.

"You know that to touch oneself in pleasure is to seek the Devil's touch," I say briskly. "Father comes. Quiet, now."

"You won't tell him?" Blessing whispers.

I should tell him, as any godly girl would do, but then what? My father's punishment, and my sister's tears, and our family's day of triumph turned to ruin.

"No, and if he heard you, we will say you had a nightmare."

Blessing's eyes light up with gratitude. I wish I could say the sight of her happiness does not warm me, but it is my fiercest love.

Every waking moment, I worry she will learn what happened that day and the light will forever leave her eyes.

So, then, I will cherish it as I can.

The door opens, and Father sweeps in, his presence clean as the bracing bite of early winter. Long legs and long arms and a broad bright smile, sharp dark features like my own.

At the sight of him, I forget every unordinary thing I have seen today. He pulls me into his arms, and Blessing too, and holds us there. Large hands cup our heads. A happy sigh rumbles deep in his chest.

"My girls, it is a blessed day," he says. Tears choke his voice, as they sometimes do during worship when God's glory comes especially close to him.

"One of many blessed days to come, Father," I whisper.

Two heartbeats, and he releases us, stepping aside to admit my four handmaidens—girls in gray gowns and hooded dark cloaks, all of them younger than I. Thirteen, fourteen, Blessing's age. None of them have yet bled, same as me. I cannot see their faces, for their hoods are pulled low, but I know their names—Mary Everett, Constance Gray, Faith Baxter.

And Rachel Redding, Elder Joseph's only daughter.

I cast my gaze to the floor before her gaze can find mine.

If things had been different those five years past, perhaps I could look at her on this day of my anointing and not see her father's eyes staring out from her face.

They lead me to the kitchen, where our supper table and chairs have been moved aside in favor of a basin of steaming water, brushes, soap, and oils. They remove my nightgown, bathe my skin with brisk strokes of their rags, comb the knots from my hair.

As they work, I imagine the coarse rub of their rags washing me clean of Temperance's words in the elm grove.

Hot water cascades down my back, rushes across the wooden planks of our kitchen floor. Blessing hurries about with our wide broom, pushing the mess out the door and into the garden.

I close my eyes as fresh water rushes over me.

Sainthood is not what I think it will be, Temperance said to me. *Violence*, she whispered. *Malice* and *blood*.

My stomach twists. A hot sour taste rises in my throat as I remember those strange shadows binding Mercy's arms to her sides.

A trial—that is all it was. A test of my strength. Words meant to goad me. Those tricks of the light I saw, they were only some fright sent by the Devil to muddle me. Mother said frights are not real, only evil craftings. That is why they look so terrifying; they know what they are, and who made them, and are frightened by the nothingness of their own selves. I cannot trust what I saw in the elm grove, or what I heard.

Even so, I will tell Father all of it, but only after my anointing. Nothing and no one will ruin this day for the Barrow family.

"As the light of the four saints doth shine," says my father from the corner, his arms upraised, "so shall our own."

"So shall our own," my handmaidens repeat, and then Constance Gray begins the Woman's Prayer.

"Wherever you step . . ." she sings.

Mary Everett follows her. "Whatever you seek . . ."

Then Faith Baxter, her voice sweet as a dove's. "May your tongue hold still . . ."

"May your heart live meek," sings Rachel Redding last of all, tugging her brush through my hair so hard my scalp hurts.

They circle around me, singing and scrubbing, until my skin is raw and pink and my hair hangs down my back in a heavy, shining sheet. Twenty times they sing the prayer as they dry me and oil my skin and help me into the long white dress I shall wear hereafter on holy days.

The dress of a saint.

My breath catches as the thin fabric kisses my hips. When my handmaidens tie the white ribbons at my wrists and throat, I must swallow hard to stifle my scream of joy. Shivering, my bare feet on the wet floor, I hear the slow beat of drums, the heavy chimes of the elders' bells ringing.

Father comes to stand before me. The smile that opens up his face is a twin of my own. His gaze is bright as morning.

"It is time," he says. "All of Haven awaits."

7

MY EYES ARE ON THE tall, narrow white house with the peaked roof that lies at the heart of our village, circled by birch and alder trees already full from spring.

The people of Haven line our streets as I walk toward Holy House, my father and Blessing on either side of me. My neighbors wave long blue and yellow ribbons as I pass them. They ring tiny tin bells and sing prayers from the Sanctificat.

Widow Woodworth and her girls crouch close enough to touch my hem. Granny Dale smiles at me, her crown of white braids tied with blue ribbon. John Ames, hulking and gentle, kneels with crinkling kind eyes and touches his forehead, his lips, his chest.

Past him stands Widow Pruitt, tall and unmoving, her baby son crying in her arms. I should not look at her—I should keep my solemn gaze trained on Holy House—but her scowl pulls at me, sure as a hook, and our eyes lock.

Her mouth moves, as if she will soon spit at my feet. She waves no ribbons, sings no prayers. Shadows paint sallow pictures beneath her eyes. And beside her, her sister Bertha Harding glares just the same way. Even after I pass them, I can feel their eyes on my back. Hungry and furious and full of hate.

Not once have I seen Widow Pruitt smile since her husband, Gregory, was found bloated in the river, his limbs boneless and tied into knots.

Blessing's hand brushes against mine. I move slightly away, though I know she means to comfort me. Not everyone is happy to see Patience Barrow's daughter anointed a saint. Not everyone believes this will save us.

I hold my head high. My blood snaps with a clean cold fire that burns away everything I have seen this morning and leaves me feeling only the light of God.

Glare away, Widow Pruitt. Soon we will all know peace once more, and you will be sorry for your lack of faith.

Tall boys, nearly grown—the elders' seconds, their students and trusted helpers, who serve as acolytes on holy days—stand beside the doors of Holy House, beating drums they carry at their waists. Samuel is among them, but I daren't look for his dear face, lest it soften me. Behind me, a hymn rises from the mouths of my neighbors:

Come to the light, all the wicked and vile.
Show us thy face, come and sit for a while.

Tell us thy story, sing us thy songs,

speak loud thy shame; God shall right all thy wrongs.

Oh yes, oh glory, He shall right all thy wrongs!

Two men open the doors of Holy House. A dark square space. God's own mouth, ready to swallow me.

I look to the words etched into the wood above the doors. The language of God, writ by the hands of our first elders, long dead.

CONCORDIA PER DOLOREM.

Harmony through sorrow, Father told me long ago.

From The World That Once Was, from an age of grief and death, we in Haven have risen from the ashes, chosen by God to escape His wrath.

As I pass beneath the carved words, a prickle touches my neck, like the drag of thin cold fingers. And there before me, atop a polished platform of wood at the center of Holy House, waits a large stone table—the altar of God.

The elders stand around it, dressed in long white tunics and red sashes. Eight men, and my father makes nine. Elder Peter catches my eye. His solemn face cracks with the barest of smiles.

But I hardly notice, for beside him stands Elder Wyatt, his black beard trimmed and stark. He holds my hood in his hands. Cloth dyed red, ties hanging limp from his fingers like a skinned creature. An offering drenched in blood.

My heartbeat floods my mouth. My skin feels like to peel

away from my bones with all the heat blazing inside me.

Then, barefoot, heads bowed, the three saints emerge from the shadows to stand before the altar. My soon-sisters, each with their hands clasped in prayer.

Beneath their hoods—caps of red cloth tied with red ribbon—Temperance and Mercy are still and quiet. Red hair, neat and combed. Black hair, just the same. They could be different girls entirely from the ones I saw in the elm grove.

Watching them—how serene they are, how docile and sweet—a calm rushes through me in quick hot waves that shake my knees.

Yes, those girls in the elm grove weren't these at all. I push from my mind their dark words, their kiss, the strange light in their hands. A Devil's game, clear as day.

What elm grove? 'Tis forgotten. Nothing happened there. A test, easily passed.

Blessing leaves me, taking her place among the others crowding into Holy House. She joins Adam Brinsley, his mother and father just behind him. I know the shape of Adam well. He is tall and narrow as Holy House, with a man's shoulders though he has only just turned eighteen. His eyes are wanderers whose favored path leads always to my sister and the new curving lines of her body.

A thought comes to me, and oh, forgive me for thinking this here, God of all that is good, but I wonder—is it Adam my Blessing thinks of when she sins in her bed at night?

As I kneel at the altar before the elders, I clench my thighs, that hot wet place Blessing touches on her own body but I dare not touch on mine. Someday I will bleed down there. Mother said girls of The World That Once Was often bled earlier than we girls of Haven do now.

"A sign of their corruption," I told her proudly, for it seemed like a thing Father would say.

"No," said Mother softly, looking at something far away that I could not see, "'tis the ruin of war that now delays a girl's blood. What war did to the seas and the air, and to all bodies living and yet unborn. It hurt our bodies most of all: yours, and mine, and Blessing's, and my mother's, and your someday-daughter's too, I fear."

Mother said this in those last days before the madness took her fully, and now she is dead. Dead and gone, dead and wrong.

Someday I will bleed, be stripped of my sainthood, and become a mere low woman of Haven. But today is not that day. The elders' heads circle above me, gray and white and dark. This is my prayer, more than any other:

Hold fast to my blood, oh God, that I may wear my hood for long years and thus keep my home safe from evil.

Then my father begins to speak.

He raises his arms to the ceiling. His hands tremble with a jubilation that I feel bubbling in my own chest.

Today I am my father's delight, his greatest joy and pride.

"People of Haven," he calls out, "we are here today because long ago, The World That Once Was ended."

The people of Haven sway, humming the Song of the Long-Ago Fallen.

"First there was disease," says Elder Zachariah, with his long white beard and watery eyes, "and then a great war that scarred the earth."

Elder Peter chimes in. "God looked upon this destruction and wept, but in the smoke and ruin He found His chosen and told them they would not only live but prosper, if they would do as He told them. And He told them this."

My father looks at those gathered, his eyes brighter than the sun.

"He told them they must build a village, not only with stone and timber but with goodness and piety. They must sow their fields with seeds and their hearts with humility. They must guard their home against evil from without and from within."

Father's gaze falls upon me. I tremble where I kneel.

"They must anoint four saints," he cries. The other elders echo him. "'Four saints, God said. You men of wisdom and valor, listen for My voice, for I shall guide you to choose well. And these girls you anoint shall remind you of those wicked women, those who brought The World That Once Was to ruin with their deceitfulness, their lustful hearts, their thirst for power, their insolence.'"

The people of Haven hiss. They shift closer, crowding near. Though they dare not touch me during my anointing, the room crackles with their desire. Someone behind me wants to strike the back of my head. I can feel the hot bloom of their anger.

My father's voice fills the air. "'Hooded with the cloth of sin, these four saints will remind your people of how the righteous must live in this new world I have given to you, and to you alone! You will allow the sheep of your flock to exhaust their anger and revenge, their lustful depravities, upon the mortal flesh of your chosen anointed!'"

Father gestures grandly at the crowd. "Through this, children of God, you shall be saved!"

"Through this, we shall be saved!" the people of Haven cry.

"The anointed shall bear our sins!" says Elder Daniel, his brow shining.

"The anointed shall endure! The anointed shall be pure!"

"Mercy," declares Elder Peter, his voice gentler than the others.

"Mercy!" cries the crowd.

Kneeling before my father, I cross my arms over my chest. I feel Mercy watching me, but I do not look, I will not look.

Father grips my head in both hands. Another elder pours the holy oil over me. It slides down my face, thick and bitter, and I cry out with joy to taste it on my lips. I burst, I buckle. This is real, this is true. Nothing else matters but this.

"Temperance," says Elder Peter, so kindly I nearly begin to weep.

I clutch the folds of my damp white gown. Mercy and Temperance. Temperance and Mercy. They are nothing to me. I crack open my eyes. There is Temperance's bare white foot. A drop of oil falls on her toes.

Nothing. The elm grove—it is nothing. The shadows, the kiss. They are nothing to me.

"Silence," Elder Wyatt calls out.

The third saint steps forward. Silence is her name. Her father, Nathaniel Goodman, lies neither alive nor dead in her house, confined to his bed after a great fall from his roof. Her mother, Emmy, seldom leaves his side.

I look for Silence's face, which I have not seen in many months, so well does she keep it hidden. But her long fair hair and red hood are a veil. Only on visitation and anointing days does she show herself. Elsewise, she hides in her mother's house and creeps around the village wall to pray for hours in the shadows.

Silence, my father has always said, is the best saint we have seen. The most pious, the purest of heart and blood. "Until you, daughter," he said to me once, kissing my brow. "Until you."

"Amity," says my father now, above my head. He finds my chin with his hand.

"Amity," the crowd repeats, again and again. Their smiles are everywhere, wide and white like a thousand crescent moons.

I rise. The elders touch my shoulders and arms, my neck and brow. One by one they paint holy shapes upon my skin in the slick of the sacred oil. A cross. A cup. A star. They murmur my name. Growl it.

"Amity," says my father, standing with his head bowed.

"Amity!" cry the people of Haven.

'Tis the name for which I have hungered for months, since Saint Amity prior began to bleed and soon after lay with her husband. Now that woman has only her husband's name to call her own. She shouts in the crowd behind me, her belly swollen. Soon she will birth her first child.

My father raises his arms again. The room buzzes eagerly, and then comes the one moment of this day I have long dreaded.

Elder Joseph steps forward. I stare at the ends of his gray hair, which falls in thick waves to his shoulders. Joseph Redding, father of Rachel and two sons, husband of Mary. I could not look at his house this morning, and I cannot quite look at him now. His own knife, which he has taken to wearing at his hip since the winter, as all the men have, stays in its sheath. Instead, he holds my father's knife in his hands. Clean and sharp as if freshly forged. 'Tis only proper, for these cuts to be made with my father's blade.

But, God forgive me, I loathe the sight of this man holding my father's knife. I cannot breathe until he places it in Father's hands, where it belongs. And there is Father's face, smooth as stone, staring calmly at Elder Joseph as if those horrible days five years past never happened. Looking at my father, so brave and good, my chest aches so fiercely that fresh tears burn my eyes.

Then Elder Ezra reaches for my left arm. Elder Wyatt finds my right.

Eyes locked with my father's, I square my jaw and hold my

breath until he smiles, and in that proud gladness, I see my whole self.

The other elders step back. 'Tis only us five—the elders holding me, my father, his blade, and me. Into the tender skin above my breasts he carves the mark of Saint Amity. Two hooked lines, joined by a small triangle.

The letter m, I hear in my head. 'Tis Temperance's voice from so long ago. In the dirt beside the stolen Sanctificat, her fingers draw thin shapes. *M* for *majesty*. *M* for *mighty*.

They are near me, the other saints. With each cut of my father's knife, I hear their breaths, smell the heat of their skin. My sisters in God, watching me bleed just as they have.

When it is done, Father gives his knife to Elder Wyatt for cleaning. My cuts itch as if ants are crawling down my chest, but I feel no pain—no, I will feel no pain at all, only the ecstasy that comes from knowing the Devil will run home like a beat hound because of me. Soon, soon, when my hood is tied around my head.

"Now, Amity, saint of harmony and goodwill," says Elder Joseph, stepping forward, his voice downy-soft, "before you receive your hood, you must first tell us a story of wickedness and sorrow, that we may be reminded of your blood's truth and your determination to fight against it. Concordia per dolorem."

"Concordia per dolorem," answer the people of Haven.

I stare at Elder Joseph's boots, and then at Temperance, who under her hood has gone pale as those nine dead men.

Beside her is Mercy with her sharp narrowed eyes, fiery locks falling down her back. Past her stands Silence, her fair head bowed. Three covered heads, three tidy red ribbons, three faces left bare to face God's judgment.

Elder Peter frowns. A small shadow crosses Father's face, but he says nothing.

No other saint has ever been made to tell a story. They were blessed, they were cut, they were given their hoods.

I lick my oil-coated lips and look straight at Elder Joseph for the first time in years. The sight of his cane startles me, though of course I have not forgotten it and know very well the reason for its use.

"What story must I tell?" I ask him.

Elder Joseph smiles, his eyes petal-pale, pebble-still. "The story of your mother."

A SILENCE FALLS. MY HEART drops dead as a brick.

"My mother deserved everything that befell her," I whisper at last.

Elder Joseph nods, waiting. My father's face is a flat board.

"She tempted you, Elder Joseph, into her marriage bed," I say. Once, recounting for all to hear what vile womb I crawled out of would have made me shrivel with shame. Now, like a well-worn prayer, the words come without a thought. "Again and again, she fouled both my father's house and yours with this sin. She deceived and entranced you, as she did my father."

No more hissing now, no more songs. My neighbors crowded into Holy House are quiet, listening hard. I do not blame them. The horror of this story is like to snatch one's breath.

"And then, when she had tired of you, Elder Joseph, when

the strength of your faith helped free you from the evil she had woven around you, and you begged her to repent with you, she laced your drink with poison root. When you tried to run, she battered your leg and then sat in wait to watch you die."

A quiet stir of sound sweeps through Holy House as the wind does across the meadow. I long to close my eyes, to see those rivers of churning green dotted yellow and white with flowers. But here I stand, calm as rocks, good girl that I am.

"But thanks be to God, our good Lord saved him," black-bearded Elder Wyatt says, prodding me along, "and helped him find the courage to bring Patience Barrow to the elders for judgment."

Elder Wyatt has hurried me past the full truth of that day, which remains locked inside me. I should be ashamed of his pity, but instead I feel a wild urge to embrace him in thanks.

"Thanks be to God," I say. A slight pain tells me I am digging my nails into my palms. Quickly, I unclench my fingers.

"And then what, Saint Amity?" Elder Joseph asks.

Here is where my words catch. I do not wish to upset my sister, whose heart is not so sturdy as mine. She wailed for hours the day Mother ran. Tabitha Grainger and Edith Ames had to drag her back home and wore scratches on their arms for days afterward.

Elder Joseph says again, "Saint Amity? Then what happened?"

"My mother went mad, Elder Joseph. She spoke of visions, things that could not be."

"Devil-woven words."

"Yes," I whisper. Such a knot of thorns sits in my throat. "She yelled them till her voice gave out. Strange stories of darkness. Nonsense and cruelty."

But this is a thing I do not say: Long ago, my mother told other stories to my sister and me alone, all of us safe and squashed in my bed. She painted kind tales with her whispers, full of beauty and light. It was not until very near the end that her stories turned mad and frightening.

"Where did you hear these stories?" my wide-eyed sister would often ask.

I never asked. I did not wish to know. Knowing would strip from Mother's words something fine and secret.

"Angels told me," she would answer, smiling. Or sometimes, "God sent them to me in dreams," and then, later, her eyes full of stars, "The flowers told me, my darlings. The sky and the river, the whispering grass."

"She became a madwoman," I say. Holy House is quiet. Even my whispers come like thunder. "The Devil found her. He found all her cracks and wedged his way in."

Elder Joseph walks slowly around the altar. "And how, Saint Amity, was she punished?"

Behind me, a soft cry rises through the silence. 'Tis Blessing, her voice thick with sadness. I speak loudly to overpower it. She is fourteen now, too old for child's tears.

And if I hurry to the end of this story, maybe Elder Joseph will shut his smiling mouth before it lets loose my great secret, the thing that would make Blessing hate me truly and forever.

"The elders, in their wisdom, tied my mother to the post outside Holy House, beneath the Crying Tree," I say quickly, my stomach gripped in clammy fists. "They read her crimes. They left her tied to the post for two days and three nights, and then brought her to the House of Sighs for some weeks, where the air is cold and black and only men can enter. And then . . ."

Elder Joseph watches me. "And then?"

The memory that rises up inside me feels larger than my body can hold.

It was a chill morning. I was eleven years old, Samuel twelve. From our hidey-hole, we watched through the wall's loose planks, the little rotted hole not much bigger than my eye, as the watchmen and their horses and their hounds chased my naked mother from Haven, out into the wild.

Once, right where the woods begin, she looked back at me. Or so I thought. Child that I was, I told myself she had found my eye watching her through the wall and was frightened by the light of God she saw in me.

What a fool I was then. But no longer.

I raise my head and speak loudly.

"At first they threw stones at her," I say. "She ran. She was quick with the Devil's power. The watchmen picked up their guns and shot her legs. She limped through the meadow and crop fields and into the woods, where the wolves run wild. The watchmen followed her in, and everyone in Haven stood on the wall and shouted and danced and rejoiced in the goodness of God."

Elder Joseph nods, his smile thin as a reed. "A day of celebration it was. A day on which we cast out evil from this home God chose and blessed."

"And then night fell," I whisper, for the story is not finished.

All went dark and quiet across the misting fields that night. I waited by the wall with Father to see that it was done. Near midnight, the men came back, their hounds loping and quiet, tails low between their legs. The men's faces were drawn and hard. They would not look at me. Their gazes slipped and flew. There rose a chorus of wolf howls from the distant woods that made them all jump, and then a piercing wail came and went, fast as daylight in winter.

Then silence. And all those men looking about like frightened pups.

But I cannot say these things, for Father strides forward with a fearsome look. My words catch and fall inside me. 'Tis the whole true ending, but it seems Father does not wish me to tell it. Swiftly, he ties on my hood—the ribbons tight under my chin, the cap of red cloth pulled close against my skull.

Then he lifts his arms and says, "Wherever you step, whatever you seek, may your tongue hold still, may your heart live meek!"

The Woman's Prayer. My sister and I pray it every night before sleep. The handmaidens sang it as they circled around me. The women of Haven, daughters and mothers and aunts, shouted it from the wall as my own mother ran.

And now the people here in Holy House cry it out as one. Their voices rasp and crack. Their words rush in endless circles.

I close my eyes and turn my face to the ceiling. All that I am rises up inside me, a great hot storm cresting in the sky. This is the moment, the last shedding of my mother's rotten skin. Four saints stand in Haven once more. Four saints to banish the Devil and serve God, four saints to remind the good people of Haven what we once lost—and what we could lose again, if we stray from His holy path.

Mercy, Temperance, Silence, Amity.

Amity, Amity. I say the word, then sing it, then shout it, and still the cries of Haven drown out my voice, but I know this word all the same. I have prayed it straight into my bones.

My heart beats as it has not in years, wild and joyous. This is what I have been waiting for, this beaming light rising up in my chest, this power coming down from God to meet the goodness that lives in me. A joining of glories too bright for even the Devil to bear.

My father grips my hand. I lean into him and press my face to his chest. He shouts praise to God, his voice booming in my ears. Around us, the people of Haven stomp and thrash, throw their hands to the ceiling and the sky beyond. The elders shout God's language in voices hoarse with joy. Through the wet ropes of my hair, I see gray Elder Phillip seize Saint Mercy and hold her hard against him. Into her hair he whispers silent prayers, his eyes closed tight, his wet lips atremble. The walls boom and hum.

This is the absolution for which I have long prayed. My family's sin, now redeemed. Our suffering, now rewarded.

Begone, Devil. I pray it through my teeth. *Leave Haven and go hide your scaly face in the foul dirt from which you came.*

Then a shriek outside Holy House stops us all.

I turn with the rest of my people, the air ringing with cries gone quiet.

Widow Heath stands at Holy House's open doors. Never have there been such sounds as her howling cries. Those nearest her hurry away, and others stand frozen and stare, for in Widow Heath's arms lies a body drenched in blood, deep gouges torn across the chest like fresh furrows in the field.

The body must belong to Jeremiah, her son who had just thirteen years to his name. I know this only because the sorrow she wears tells me so.

I cannot look at Jeremiah's face, for all of it has been torn away from his skull.

9

MY NEIGHBORS RUN FOR THE doors of Holy House. Some fall to their knees and pray in harsh wails.

Father grabs my hand and pulls me after him. The light that filled me as I swayed at the altar has gone. I stumble and nearly fall.

There is Blessing, staring at Widow Heath, who has sunk to the ground with her dead boy in her arms. I stare too. I do not understand.

A saintly hood sits on my head. My bones still ache from my long winter trials. Those endless tied-up nights without food, the thorns piercing my ankles, the iron weights bound to me, my voice raw from praying aloud that God might forgive my family for Mother's sins.

And yet, even so, here lies another dead boy.

Father tears my sister from Adam Brinsley's arms, and we

flee for our house, hand in hand in hand.

We are not alone.

My neighbors run after us, fists and voices raised. Not all, but enough to make Father hurry.

"Elder Thomas! What does this mean?"

"Elder Thomas, help us! Please, what does God say to you? Is He angry?"

"God spits on you and your house, Elder Thomas! You offend Him with what you have done today!"

"A girl born from evil is evil herself!"

My eyes and nose burn with tears. This is not possible. I could scream if I were not so afraid.

"Stay here," my father says. A kiss upon my brow, my sister's hand in mine. It is suddenly quiet, the ground under me turned from dirt to wood. Father says more, but his words are far away, and my booming head drowns them out.

Blessing is close. I think I hear her voice. But all I see is this floor before me, the white rug that greets my feet every morning. We are home, though I do not remember coming here. I clutch my knees. I think I am sitting on something soft, and I think these are my hands upon my knees, and I think I hear, from out on the road, the screams of women and the peals of bells.

I find the window. Cheerful midday shines its bright light onto my garden. There is Shadow, stretched out on the sill, tail twitching, eyes closed. Dead boys mean nothing to her.

"Tend to your sister," thunders my far-off father. "Neither of you will leave this room until I come for you."

A door shuts. Such a crash, in this strange spinning world. I stare at the white rug. A red spot marks the place near my toes. I stretch out a finger to touch it.

"Amity?" My sister's voice, near and gentle. "You are shaking. Here." A cool hand on my forehead, another on the back of my neck. "There, now. Breathe slowly. Oh, sister, you're bleeding still." Her softness moves away.

Slowly, I sit up and touch the bony place above my breasts. Now I feel it, yes. A stinging net of fire. Two hooked lines joined with a small triangle. The carved mark of Saint Amity, raw and red.

Heat rushes up my arms, draws my chest tight. I fall forward, but Blessing catches me. I clutch her arms hard.

"I do not understand," I say, my voice all but gone.

Blessing presses a rag to my chest. "What do you mean?"

"I was anointed. They gave me my hood." I touch my head, where sits a ribboned cap of red cloth. "After today, everything was meant to be different. The Devil was to flee from me, from us, but now . . ."

I choke on my own words. I clutch my stomach, my gown.

Blessing catches my wrists. "Amity, please, be still."

"I do not wish to be still!" I push her from me. Hands and knees on the floor, I suck down harsh breaths. "Another boy killed on the very day of my anointing. Brought right to the door of Holy House with my ribbons only just tied!" I curl my fingers, feel the rake of wood against my nails. "A taunt. The Devil *taunts* me."

"It means nothing. Surely Jeremiah was killed before your anointing. Widow Heath must have only just found his body!" Blessing lifts my face to look at me. "And now you wear your hood, and all is as it should be. Isn't that right? I think there will be no more deaths such as this. I think poor Jeremiah is the last."

I blink, letting loose tears. "You don't know that."

"Perhaps Lightluck will know the answer, if we ask him." Blessing folds my hand softly into her own and settles me against her, both our backs against my bed. I huddle beside her, shivering.

"Lightluck," I whisper, and follow my sister's gaze to the door. On the wall frolics a painted lamb with yellow flowers tucked behind his ears. Beside him, three swallows dive into peonies. Below this are straight rows of blue and red diamonds, atop which groups of dancing girls hold hands.

There are four of them, these girls. Painted again and again, four and four and four, they circle the room. Two of them smile—one golden-haired, one dark.

Two of them have no faces at all, only ribboned skirts and heads smooth as newborns.

Mother painted the flowers, the lamb, the birds. She did love animals so.

But 'twas Father who sat on his stool to paint the dancing girls, the four daughters he longed to have. Four daughters, four hoods. Four places at the altar of Holy House, tidy as stitches. My father's greatest dream.

"Good afternoon, Lightluck," says Blessing in her cheerful little voice, just as she did when we were small. "We forgot to say good morning to you, but we hope you will forgive us. After all, today is a most holy day, and our thoughts were with God."

I stare at the lamb. The paint of his gentle face has rubbed away from years of being stroked by our fingers, and Mother's too. I have not touched Lightluck since Mother ran, and Blessing has not dared to when I am near, but I remember well the words of his story. I always will.

"He is a lamb who guards us from evil," Mother said, for when Blessing was small she feared the night noises, and I have always feared my dreams.

"Lightluck the Brave is his name," I whisper. "Tell him good morning and good night. Touch his face when you pass through his door, and luck and light will follow."

Blessing smiles. "You remember! I knew you would."

Suddenly, I can breathe again. That faded face and those yellow flowers bring to mind a different memory. My heart settles back into its cage.

"Mother told us many stories," I say slowly, rising. "But hers are not the only ones in Haven."

Blessing is puzzled. "That is true . . ."

I walk to the door and stare at Lightluck's faded black eyes. "Do you remember the tale of Lost Abigail and the Stolen Relics? From the elders' lessons?"

"I never liked that story," says Blessing, all the cheer gone from her voice. "It frightened me. Mother did not like it either."

Yes, because in its words she saw herself.

"Once, long ago, young Abigail of Haven woke on a bright summer's morning and decided to seek out the Devil. For in the heart of each woman lives his wicked seed, and on each woman's tongue curls his foul whispers. In their weakness, which poisons their every bone, they oftentimes succumb."

"Why do you tell this story?" asks my fearful sister.

I turn to her eagerly. "What happens next? Come, you remember."

Blessing's arms hug her body. So small she seems, with her little frowning brow. "For years, Abigail searched until at last the path became clear to her. A whispering silken voice came to her in a dream. She welcomed it and wrapped it around her body and listened to its song."

"'To find me,' said the voice, 'you must first complete for me the five sacraments of darkness.'" A chill trips down my arms. I follow it. I welcome it. God is speaking to me through my memories of this story, and I will listen. "'The first sacrament is skin. Then fire. Bone. Blood. Palm. Only when these sacraments are honored in my name will I help you find those five relics that have been kept from you so unfairly, wandering daughter.'"

"A book." My sister's voice is shaky. "A mirror."

"A belt. A knife. A key."

"Relics of God meant only for the touch of man," I say, kneeling before her. "A book, full of knowledge. A mirror, which shows truth and invites the sin of vanity."

"A belt," Blessing whispers, "the symbol of men's sovereignty over women."

"A knife," I say, "a tool of power and strength. And a key, to unlock the secrets of God. 'Twas these objects that cursed the women of The World That Once Was. They claimed these gifts that God meant for men alone."

"And this was how the Devil found them, and corrupted them, and brought them low to his kingdom." Blessing shakes her head, biting her lip. "Amity, I do not wish to finish this story."

I ignore her. The story must be finished. Through its words, I am beginning to understand what I must do.

"And so young Abigail walked this ruinous path," I whisper. "But when she brought the five stolen relics to the Devil and looked at last upon his face, she withered in terror at the sight of him and fled home to beg mercy for her sins. But her people turned her away, and in her despair, young Abigail fashioned a rope from which to hang herself."

"But the Devil found her before she could fall." Blessing finishes the tale in a thin hoarse voice. "He dragged her back to his kingdom to sully and crown her, and sometimes, in the early hours of the morning, when the winds are high and the fires of Hell blaze most fiercely, you will hear lost Abigail wail and weep and feel her tears upon your dreaming cheeks."

In the silence that follows the story, we hear the house move around us. The elders' low voices hum from the front room, where they have no doubt gathered with Father to discuss Jeremiah Heath. Beyond our house, people shout orders. Watchmen run for the wall, through the fields, searching for Jeremiah's killer.

A small thing hits the window. Blessing whirls, but in this small quiet moment, I fear nothing. Let it be some Devil's beast, come to taunt me. I will wring its neck.

I touch Blessing's arm, pulling her back to me. "This story tells me what I must do. I wear my hood, and still the Devil comes. A tenth man of Haven now lies dead, an innocent boy defiled."

Blessing pulls away, her blue eyes wide. "Amity, you must think clearly. Did you not hear the story you just told? Abigail was forever lost to evil."

"I am stronger than she was. You saw what I endured in our mother's name, did you not?"

"But 'tis as I said," Blessing whispers, staring at me as if I am something to be frightened of. "You have your hood now. Jeremiah might well be the last of the dead. And then what? You will have sought the Devil for nothing."

"And if Jeremiah is not the last? Can you bear to wait for another death to bring yet more grief to Haven? Can you bear to do nothing but sit and hope and pray for the mercy we deserve? I cannot. And I will not."

I rise and move to the window. Shadow has run off to hunt. My lonely flowers shiver and bob.

Book. Mirror. Belt. Knife. Key.

I will find these relics of God and steal them for my own. With them in hand, I will face the Devil myself and banish him from these lands forever. I will save my sister, my father, my home. The men and boys marked for death, the women and girls the Devil stalks with endless appetite.

I will save them.

I will save them all.

10

I AM LYING IN THE meadow on a white blanket.

To my right is Blessing, smaller than she is now. A child still, flat and knobby. She dozes, sucking on her sleeve. Far too old for such things. Father would scold her, were he here.

But he is not.

Instead, here is my mother. Patience Barrow, on her side in the grass, just as we are. She wears a pale yellow dress with a white collar, her skirts spilled around her legs. She twists a lock of my brown hair around her fingers. I watch her face, trace its soft lines. She showed us how to weave crowns of flowers, and now one sits crooked on her head, blue and white and pink all mashed against our blanket. A loose petal kisses her cheek.

"Once," she says to me, "there was a brave lamb named Lightluck, who on a summer's morn in the meadow—"

"Like this one?" I whisper.

"Like this very one. In the meadow, Lightluck came upon a blue door set flat in the ground." She looks at me, starry-eyed. "A door to the underland."

I whisper it back to her as if, hidden in these grasses, we are exchanging secret prayers unknown even to God. The thought makes me shake with silent laughter. "A door to the underland."

My mother smiles, touches my face, and then says, "Open your mouth, my precious child," with a twist in her voice, as if she too will soon laugh.

I do as she says, obedient girl that I am. She taps one nail against my front teeth. *Tap, tap, tap.*

Mother peers into my mouth. She reaches inside and withdraws a wet black feather. I choke and cough. Her smile is so wide and bright, her skin begins to split like cracked soil.

"Open up, Amity," she says.

I open my eyes.

11

TAP, TAP, TAP.

There above my bed gleam two unblinking white eyes ringed with scabs and thin feathers.

A fright-bird, a Devil's creature, sits on the sill inside my bedroom, pecking the wood to pieces. The window stands ajar. 'Tis the first time one of these beasts has dared enter my house, and the sight of it lights me up with anger, as if lightning has cracked open inside me. I grab the candlestick sitting beside my bed. I will bash the bird's evil greasy head flat.

But then I stop and stare, for in its beak, this bird holds something I recognize. A scrap of cloth, pale and dirt-dusted.

My heart turns cold. I open my mouth to scream, but my voice is gone.

Temperance's message. This horrible creature has found it in the garden and dug it up.

The bird cocks its head, then darts out the open window. The scrap in its beak flaps most strangely.

Candlestick in hand, I climb fast out the window, not stopping to find my boots or see if Blessing has awoken.

That message cannot be found by any living soul. Though no one would know Temperance's clumsy hand as I do, these are the Devil's workings at play, and I can trust none of them. I will kill the bird and burn the cloth it carries.

Or maybe, I think, ducking under the arbor and pushing through my garden's gate, maybe this is the beginning of the dark path I must walk, as Lost Abigail did. If so, I would be a fool not to follow it.

I run after the bird's silent dark wings. We weave through the sleeping houses of Haven, the great hulking barns. There is a breeze. A bell chimes quietly, then another, like two soft yawns.

Soon I see where the bird is leading me: the hidey-hole. A sudden wind clatters the trees, crisp with dregs of winter come back to laugh at us all.

And among the trees, hanging from thick black branches, is my father.

He dangles not from a rope but from a perched flock of birds, so many of them that the trees glisten black. There are no leaves here, only feathers and glinting white eyes.

They hold my father with their beaks and claws. His skin is pulling away from his bones in great ribbons, the weight of him dragging his body down toward the earth, his hair snapping free of his skull in chunks.

I drop my candlestick, a horrible chill sweeping over me. I know now what it was, that pale thing hanging from the bird's black beak.

Not cloth, but flesh.

"Help me, Amity!" my father cries. My name is clumsy on his tongue. Two birds grab hold of his lips, stretching them into a dreadful smile that grows so wide the soft pink flesh of his mouth tears free of his jaw.

When I scream, no sound escapes me. I fall to my knees in the dirt and watch helplessly, no better than poor craven Abigail, as this evil flock lifts into the sky, taking my father with them. Is this the next death in Haven? Here, before my very eyes? I look about wildly, breathless with choked sobs. Why do the watchmen not come? Can they not hear my father's cries?

But then, all at once, a silence falls over me. The skin on my neck and arms prickles with sudden icy cold. My father is no longer screaming, because he is gone. He did not fall to the ground; the birds did not drop him. He is simply no longer there.

The birds scatter and squawk, their eyes now dark and ordinary. I watch them fly north, out over the wall toward the woods.

And then, behind me, the air tightens, as if ready to pop. Someone is there. Someone is watching me.

I whirl around to face them. I lift my face up, and up, and up.

Above me towers a woman, silent and gray, thin and bent, five heads taller than any man I have seen. Her long arms trail to the ground, as if they have sprouted from it. The rest of her drifts formless in the air, disappearing into the night. Wild dark hair to her waist, wide toothless mouth hanging open, and though she has no eyes—that gaping mouth is the only thing I can see on what might be her face—I know she is watching me, waiting for me to speak.

12

So I FIND MY VOICE, press my cold bare feet flat against the ground, and speak.

"Are you from the Devil?"

The gray woman's long neck bends over me like an arm with all its bones gone. Like dead Gregory Pruitt, swollen in the river.

I move away quickly, so afraid it comes out angry. "Do not dare touch me! I am a child of God, an anointed saint." I point west to the black mountain, the Devil's home, ready to snarl at her that she should go back to where she came from.

But then, as she stares at me—if a mouth can be said to stare—I remember how when the gray woman came, the birds' eyes changed from white to black and they flew away.

"Did you tell them to leave? Were they frightened by you?" I swallow hard. "Perhaps you sent the birds away so I would trust you. Well, I do not, and I will not."

She clicks and hums, though I see no tongue in that mouth. Her throat makes rough wet noises, as if someone is scraping out the deepest parts of her body. A tearing-away sound.

My fear tastes bitter as old supper, but I must keep talking. This is the path I have chosen, and I will walk it no matter what I find.

I take a small step toward her. "Do you know of the sacraments of darkness? The story of Lost Abigail and the Stolen Relics?"

She stares and stares.

"There are five relics of God, gifts meant only for men. Book. Mirror. Belt. Knife. Key." I whisper quickly, praying even as I speak of evil that no one will stumble upon me here in the dirt beside the hidey-hole. "Lost Abigail, she honored the sacraments of darkness in the Devil's name and then was able to find these relics, though she was a mere woman. She used them to summon the Devil, and I seek to do the same."

I shut my mouth, my cheeks hot and my body cold. It cannot be so simple, to ask a Devil's creature for a thing and then receive it.

"Do you know where I must begin?" I say instead. Then, my heart pounding faster, "The birds—they held that vision of my father by his *skin*. The first sacrament. Should I follow the birds, then? Is that the way?"

The gray woman's head cocks flat to the right, as if it has bent on a hinge. The unnatural sight of it makes me feel faint, and as if that has opened a door of doubt inside me, my eyes fill with fresh tears.

"That *was* a vision, was it not?" I whisper. "I know it must have been. Is he safe? Tell me."

Then she moves, this gray woman, too fast for me to flee. Her arm stretches out and brushes my shoulder, and all I know is cold. A roar of it down my back and front. Colors fall across my eyes—red and black, the gold of fire, the blue of sky. I hear wild laughter, a howl, a shriek, the chomp of teeth. Too many sounds to name, all slamming against my skull.

Somehow, I find my legs again and wrench myself away, though my feet are heavy as stones. I fall hard on my backside, scramble across the dirt.

The gray woman watches me as if nothing strange has happened. Her mouth opens wider, a vast hole, and out of it drift a few buzzing black flies. Deep inside her throat shines a curve of silver, and though I know it is foolish, I cannot help but lean closer. What is that thing?

Then a hound bays, making me jump. Another comes soon after. Not close, but nearing. A man's shout. A flash of torchlight.

Watchmen are on patrol, more than is common, given what has happened. Certainly no saint is welcome to wander as I have done. And what would they think, seeing me in this state, my hair clinging damp to my neck, my nightgown stained with dirt?

The gray woman's throat clicks, like swift taps of tongue

against teeth, or some night animal stalking in the dark. She flattens herself to the ground, stretches out long like a river eel, and darts away into the shadows.

And I run. My chest is tight, a needle sewing up all the empty space inside my body; soon there will be nothing left but bone and dense meat. Three times I look over my shoulder to see if that gray woman follows me, but there is only Haven, soft with night. My house is far, clear on the other side of town. Much closer is Holy House, its narrow white roof rising from the shadows, circled by trees.

If I am to be caught by watchmen, I had best be caught praying.

13

When I slip inside the doors of Holy House, its vast round room lit as always by the nine ever-burning lanterns of the elders, I see at once that I am not alone.

A girl sits in the room's far shadows, near a bolted door that leads into the elders' workrooms below.

She is crying. Her shoulders shake. She coughs up little bursts of air.

I hold my breath. I know who this is, and finding her here on this strange and terrible night twists a quiet dark feeling deep inside me.

Run, says this feeling, *for after this, everything will change. Arr. You. Enn.*

But it is too late. I must have made some small sound. The girl raises her head and looks at me. My nape prickles as our eyes lock.

'Tis Saint Silence, the third of my new saintly sisters. Not once have I ever heard her speak. Until this night, I have only ever seen her in Holy House on worship days.

The day of her anointing, her mother, Emmy Goodman, sobbed in the gathered crowd. Ecstatic in her devotion, she wept, and many others wept to see her. Such gratitude on her face, even with her ailing husband unable to leave his bed.

"God is good," she cried, her voice ringing above the others. But as she wept and my neighbors joined her, my eyes remained dry and my sight narrow.

I could see nothing and no one but Silence—how slim she was, how contained. A stone unmoved. Her long fair hair, like the dry autumn reeds when they blow golden in the wind. Her pious gaze turned toward her feet.

And on that day—fourteen was I, and Silence fifteen—I thought her just the kind of saint I would someday be. The next week, during her first visitation, she received her blows with neither cry nor flinch. I understood then what it meant to love God with your whole self.

Now Silence cowers in the shadows. On her cheeks are long trails of tears, angry patches of rose pink. She does nothing to clean her face.

As a saint, my duty is to uphold the ideals of womanhood—friendliness, kindness, peacemaking. Amity is my name. I should do as it commands and go to her, offer her comfort.

But Silence is a saint. She is not meant to show her grief to the world. Whatever sadness she carries, she must rise above.

Should she be punished for this weakness I see before me? Or pitied?

The distant calls of watchmen push me farther inside. I quietly pull the doors closed, then hurry toward the altar and kneel.

I glance at Silence. "Come, kneel with me. Watchmen are near. If they find us, we should be praying."

A moment, the quiet around us thick as sleep, and then Silence joins me on the steps. She clasps her hands as I have mine.

"Do not fear, sister," I tell her, "and whatever you despair of, set it free. I am here with you in this place, and God is too."

Silence's lips are red with fresh blood, bitten raw. She stares at my hands. They are dirty from my fall.

I smile, though her bright gaze unsettles me. I wish she would leave. "Shall we pray together?"

Then Silence catches my left wrist and holds it firm.

"Once there was a girl," she whispers, "whose mouth had been sewn shut with black thread. A raven dove out of the sky and offered to pull the thread free with its beak, but the girl saw in the raven's eye a grinning face and knew it was lying, that it would demand in return a gift so rare it would destroy her. And so she clapped her hands over her face and ran until she found a tree in the woods big enough to climb inside."

Silence says this in a quiet rush. The elders' lanterns draw shadows across her face.

A tiny cold feeling blooms inside me.

Long ago, I heard stories much like this one, but kinder, and in Mother's voice. Stories that do not fit well anywhere but in my safe warm bed with her and Blessing beside me.

"A strange prayer, sister," I say evenly. "What do you mean by it?"

I try to move away, but Silence grabs both my hands and pulls me close.

"Once there was a girl," she says, so soft, so quick, "who lived in a hole in the ground. It was deep and dark. Her only friend was the laughing shadow that dropped food to her every night at dusk."

A great terror climbs up my chest. I have a wild thought that soon a body long dead will emerge from the shadows. A body crowned with gold hair like my sister's, a body that once carried me inside it.

"What are you saying?" I whisper. "Stop this!"

Silence draws in a shuddering breath, pulls me into her arms, tucks my head beneath hers. Her heart pounds against my ear, and for a curious moment, I feel safe here in the nest of her warm thin arms.

"Once there was a girl," Silence says, "who on a summer's morn in the meadow came upon a blue door set flat in the ground."

I ice over. I am a frozen river.

Silence must feel the change, for she releases me. I stare at her, prickling all over. I know those words and know them well.

"A door to the underland," I whisper.

Silence's pale blue eyes grow wide. She even flinches. "A door to the underland."

I hesitate. Maybe this is only a bit of strange chance. After all, in my story, 'twas Lightluck the lamb who found the door. In her story, 'tis a girl. Same story, different creatures.

What will happen, then, if I tell more of it?

"A little wrinkled man in a red suit, no taller than a knife," I say slowly, "crawled out of the door and polished its little golden knob with a white cloth."

"He saw the girl and yelped and jumped two feet in the air," says Silence, her mouth hardly moving. There is real fear on her face, stark as bones. It has cleared her eyes, her voice. "She bowed to the little man and said, 'Forgive me, tiny fellow, but what lies beyond that blue door?' And the little man said . . ."

She lets me finish it. "'Well, my friend, perhaps you should open the door and see for your own self!'"

That is the ending. A short tale, one I have never heard uttered by another soul. Not in lessons, not from Temperance when we were small, not from Samuel. My mother spun from this story many others, and none of them have I heard in a voice besides her own until this night. This night of my anointing day, when I have also seen a flock of fright-birds, a gray woman of the Devil, and saints kissing in the elm grove.

None of this is uncanny chance. It cannot be.

"How do you know that story?" Silence whispers.

"My mother told it to me long ago." At once, I wish I had

not answered. Rash, slippery tongue. "How do *you* know that story?"

Silence hesitates. "I was told it too."

Thump, thump, pounds my traitor heart. Did my mother tell other girls her stories and then lie to us that she had not? Well, if that is true, I should not be surprised. My mother was wicked and a liar, and I was a fool to have ever loved her.

"And who told you?" I ask.

"The . . ." Silence bites her chapped lip. Her frightened gaze shifts about. "You won't believe me."

"I will. Speak, now."

She shakes her head. "'Twas only a dream."

"Was it truly?"

"No," Silence whispers after a moment. "*They* told me. The gray women."

Something howls in me, twin storms of fear and wonder. "There are more than one?"

Silence's gaunt face brightens. "You have seen them too?"

"What else have they said to you? Tell me!"

"They tell me stories. Stories I do not understand."

"What are these women? Do you know? Have they told you? Are they from the Devil?"

Silence opens her mouth, hesitates, then closes it. She glances at me with a strange gentle pity, then shakes her head. A tear slides down her white cheek. "They will not stop. I ask them, I plead, but still they come. Perhaps we are both going mad, as your mother did."

Her words cut me open, and I grab on to her, shocked into some blazing meanness. Silence lets out a soft cry, for I have pinched her wrist hard, and I release her at once.

"Forgive me, I . . ." I swallow and swallow. A woolly hot lump in my throat tries to choke me.

Of course Silence does not anger, pious girl. She places her warm hand upon mine. A lock of long fair hair slips down her shoulder.

"Where your mother crumbled," she says kindly, "we will stand tall, no matter how many stories they stuff us with."

But I hardly hear her. Floating gray women, birds of the Devil. Mercy and Temperance kissing in the elm grove. Jeremiah Heath, all red and plowed open. And here I am, Amity Barrow, searching for God's relics meant not for me, but for men. Book. Mirror. Belt. Knife. Key.

A memory settles on me like snow, bracing me. Mercy and Temperance spoke of friends in the woods. A woman named Malice who wishes to meet me.

And meet me she will, whoever she may be. No people are left in this world save for us here in Haven. This Malice, then, must be some messenger of evil, a spider weaving lies in the wild. What I saw and heard in the elm grove was no trick. No, the Devil is showing me right where to go.

I would be a fool not to follow.

14

Two NIGHTS LATER, I AM sweeping the supper crumbs out of Elder Peter's kitchen, but not as carefully as I ought to, for my thoughts are out in the woods.

My quest itches at me. Sacraments and relics, birds and dead men, all of them scattered along a dark path I am desperate to walk, if only I can find the start of it.

I need to speak with Temperance and Mercy, demand they take me to this Malice woman, but from dawn till dusk there are chores, garden tending, prayers, chores again, cooking supper for Elder Peter, as I do every night, more prayers, and Father reading from the Sanctificat by candlelight. Unless I am at home, I am never alone, and after my visitation on Sunday, five days hence, my saintly duties will begin properly. Morning prayers in Holy House, afternoons in the House of Whispers, where I will hear my neighbors' confessions.

Perhaps during visitation, when all of us saints huddle on the altar, I can ask Temperance. I can sneak the question in just before my father rings the bell, ask him to wait, please, if I need to.

One moment, Father, while I ask my sisters about the Devil-woman who lives in the woods.

From the other room come Samuel's and Elder Peter's quiet voices. Samuel being here nags at me like a stuck thorn. Because I am now a saint, because Jeremiah Heath is dead, I cannot even take care of Elder Peter without someone nearby to watch me?

It seems Father thinks I cannot. Impious words sit on my tongue: *Is it not only men who have been killed, Father? All the saints still live, and all the women too. I am safer than you are.*

I sweep a small pile of dust into the yard. I look up, ready to snap closed the door, when I see a shape dart through the air just past the fence. Darker than the growing night, faster than a bird.

I grow still. Is it that gray woman from two nights prior? Or a different one, since Silence said there are many? If Silence can be believed.

I wait, hardly breathing, but the world is still and hushed. My neighbors huddle behind locked doors, afraid, Jeremiah's blood still fresh in their thoughts. I hear nothing but a single cow's tired lowing. The sound mocks me. Then, past where the dark shape flew, two shadowed figures in long cloaks hurry toward the northern wall. They could be anyone. 'Tis difficult to see. But some wild hope rears its head in me. I cannot lose this moment.

Hurrying back inside, I call softly, "Samuel?"

He ducks into the kitchen, too tall for Elder Peter's tiny doorways. I both love his easy soft smile and despise him for not understanding what is happening right outside the door.

"Will you please finish for me?" I whisper, passing him the broom. I sway where I stand, just a little, put a hand to my temple and let my eyes flutter.

Dear Samuel catches me at once. "Careful, there! Are you ill?"

"Samuel?" Elder Peter's thin voice calls out. "Amity?"

"I do feel a bit faint," I say, leaning against Samuel's chest. "Do not tell Elder Peter. He will worry. Forgive me. It seems I have not eaten enough today."

"Of course." Samuel helps me to the door and kisses my brow so gently my chest hurts. "I shall walk you home."

"No! No. Elder Peter still needs his fire built, his bed things settled. He cannot bend well enough on his own. You know that."

Samuel rubs a hand through his hair. "Your father will be angry."

"Certainly not at you. And he will understand when he sees I am ill."

"But it isn't safe."

"It is only just down the road a ways. Go on, now." I give him the sweetest smile I can muster. "And thank you."

Then I leave before he can say anything more. My slow walk to the fence is maddening. Ill girls do not hurry. But once past the fence and its tidy row of trees, I run north toward the wall, keeping to the shadows. The roads of Haven are quiet. Doors locked, windows shut, curtains pulled. The lights of patrolling watchmen float above the distant dark wall.

And two girls, gowned and cloaked, hurry through a door in the wall's northern stretch, unnoticed by the patrolling watchmen coming home. The men walk in, the girls run out unseen. The air moves oddly around their bodies, rippling as it might in high summer.

Peering around the corner of Uriah Brinsley's barn, I watch them run. Above, on the wall, the two nearest watchmen do nothing about the girls running past them down below. Instead, they point their guns at the sky, wave their arms and let out sharp shouts. A cloud of black birds swarms above them. One dives, then another. They make no sound, these birds, and quick as they are, I still see little flashes of round white eyes.

I hold my breath for a moment, gathering all my courage, and then run myself, following the girls' path. Past the torch-light pooling on the ground, through the open door, and out into the meadow beyond. No one above shouts after me. I hear a watchman scream something about bats, then something hard crunch into bone. Maybe one of them has hit a bird with his rifle.

Heart pounding, I find the thin spot in the new barricade,

hiss in a breath as a sharp wire scrapes my arm. I squeeze out, stumble, push myself back up.

And there they are, standing right before me on a tussock of flowered grass—red hair, black hair. Sharp eyes, glad eyes.

Mercy, Temperance.

On Temperance's right shoulder perches a fright-bird, a Devil's creature, all the feathers gone from its head. In their place, a single white eye and gleaming scales.

Beneath her dark hood, Temperance smiles with utter delight. "You've come at last."

Hurry, Amity. Say it now while you dare.

I square my shoulders and stare at Mercy.

"Take me to Malice. I wish to meet her." What else did they whisper in the elm grove? *Powerful.* "I wish to learn her power."

Mercy looks past me with a grin just before something hot and sharp hits my head.

The world flickers black. Someone shoves a small nub like a bean into my mouth, forces my jaws to chew. An awful bitter taste floods my tongue. Heat spreads fast between my shoulder blades and down my back. I choke and fall. I know nothing more.

II

whatever you fight

15

I WAKE IN A WHITE wood. Above me, in a blue sky so dark it is almost black, shines a red moon casting a light like spilled blood.

'Tis difficult to push open my eyes, as if they have been painted over with mud. My tongue is fat and tingling. I cannot feel my fingers, and my head spins even though I am lying flat on the hard ground.

White trees cut across a sky lit sharp with stars. The chill air smells of pine, mud, damp flesh. A wolf howls; a wind whistles. I cannot stand up, but somehow this does not frighten me.

Instead, elated, I laugh. I find my hands amid a sea of bright colors and spinning white trees and wave my fingers around, awestruck.

"She wakes," someone whispers. Booming footfalls ring through my head as if I am a struck drum.

"Leave her," says another. "She will come to her senses soon enough."

Beyond their familiar voices, laughter and music—words I do not know, sung both high and low. The snap of twigs, the pop of fire.

I try again to move. My body is clumsy, made of heavy stones, but I find the earth, press my buzzing fingertips into it, and push.

As I rise, this strange white wood spins along with my aching head. Black spots dance across my eyes. I sit huddled in a crude circle of pine branches. The branches are not large, but when I try to crawl through them, still laughing a little, still wondering at the bright spots of color blooming at my fingers, I am stopped by something unseen.

It is as if these branches have built around me a cage of iron bars, like those I have heard stand tall and unbreakable in the House of Sighs, that dark house at the western wall of Haven where they kept Mother in her last days.

At last, I find the strength to raise my head. A girl moves aside two of the branches with a few soft words of song and a wave of her hands. She kneels before me.

"Temperance?" I whisper. So different she looks, wearing a gown blue as jay feathers. The sleeves are long and loose and slip from her bare white shoulders. Her dark hair is soft with a silver sheen, and as she helps me rise, the warmth of her hands on my arms settles my rocking head.

Beyond her stands Mercy, her dress as deep a green as summer leaves dipped in shadow. She watches me with sharp eyes. Tiny braids hide in the red cascade of her hair, and behind her, the white trees' leaves of blue and red and green and glossy black, their veils of pale flowers, pulse and shiver. They breathe as I do.

I look down, wondering, and cry out when I see the truth. My plain work dress has disappeared, and now I wear a gown as white as the long winter, softer than anything I have touched in my life. The ribboned bodice hugs my torso, and the long lace skirts circle around me like clouds.

Temperance smiles. "Beautiful, isn't it? These woods give you garments from your truest heart."

"I do not know what Malice sees in her, or what you do either," says Mercy bitterly. "She cannot even stomach the bloodroot."

"Bloodroot?" The word feels strange between my teeth. I am not certain I have said anything at all. "What is that?"

As if in answer, a hush falls over the wood. The whirling colors dancing across the twin fields of my eyes grow still.

A woman comes close to us. She wears a fine low-collared gown the color of blood. Roses bloom on her cheeks, and though the set of her mouth is hard, her eyes shine bright as a spring sky. She could be as young as I or as old as Granny Dale, whose house crawls with grandchildren. Her hair is black as the mud that gathers beneath my fingernails when I work in the garden, her skin pale as the white moon I know.

"Here she is at last," she says to me in a voice so warm and rich and kind it brings tears to my eyes. "My name is Malice, little sister. Welcome to the realm of Avazel. Do you know what witches are?"

Temperance and Mercy watch me closely. I struggle to remember my words. "No, but I seek the Devil." A sick feeling washes over me as I say the words, but I swallow it down and look up. "If witches do the same, I ask that you teach me how."

Malice laughs softly. Behind her, Mercy does the same, and Temperance too, as if there has been some grand joke.

"Dear girl," says Malice kindly, "you've let your elders' stories weave dark webs in your mind." She spreads her arms wide. "There is no Devil here. There is only *extasia*."

"*Extasia?*" I fumble over the unfamiliar word.

Mercy giggles behind her hand. Temperance frowns, nudging her with her elbow.

"It's the power we witches use," Malice says. "A beautiful power, full of mystery and light."

I stare at her, my thoughts a jumble. Too many things are happening here that I do not understand. "Then . . . if you are not a woman of the Devil, where have you come from?"

"Ah, yes. Your friends"—Malice nods at Mercy and Temperance—"didn't understand that either." Malice moves closer to me. "What if I told you that Haven is not the only place left in the world where people live and breed and work and die?"

"But . . ." I scratch nervously at my chest, where my saintly mark should be and is not; my skin is pale and smooth. "We are God's chosen. He saw that we should survive when no one else did."

Malice shakes her head. "They really did a number on all of you. Incredible. No, Amity. There are many people left in the world. Not nearly as many as there once were, that's true. War's a bitch. Half the land's spoiled. Everyone's scattered and half alive. Some more than others. But they exist. That's where we witches come from. Other villages. Cities, even. We left our homes and came together to make a coven. And in this coven, we help each other and learn from each other and practice *extasia*."

Coven. Cities. *Extasia*.

Too many words, and not enough room in my head. I do know the word *cities* from my father's Sanctificat readings, and the stories of The World That Once Was, but these other words, they sit strangely inside me, their shapes crooked and frightening. I rub my right temple, listen to the boom of my pounding heart.

"I know it's a lot to try and understand all at once," Malice says, touching my arm. "What if we sit for a while, let you rest? I'll send for food."

"No," I whisper, thinking as quickly as my muddled head will let me. One thought rises above all the others.

If Malice speaks the truth, if there is no Devil here, then I will look elsewhere and never again have to set foot in this strange, spinning wood.

But first I must try everything I can. I must learn more about this power, this *extasia*. Maybe Malice walks with the Devil and does not know it. Certainly this talk of other villages, of people elsewhere in the world, makes me think some malevolent trickster shadow-stalks her steps, too clever for her to see.

"I must ask you this favor," I say. "Help me save my home. Many have died, murdered in awful ways. Perhaps your power can keep such killings from happening ever again."

"Ah, so you are here to save your village." Malice's eyes are keen. "And you think you're the one meant to do that?"

I swallow, find my voice. "I do."

A grin spreads across her face.

"The power whispers your name to me, and has for weeks now. You intrigue me. There might be a place for you here. If you learn from me as the others have done . . ." She pauses, thinking, then slowly nods. "I think maybe we could help you."

I keep my voice even, though my heart beats fast with hope. "And in exchange?"

"That is the exchange. *Extasia* says you should be here. You being here, learning about the power, will make it happy. That's enough payment for me." Her eyes glitter. "Do you have the courage, sister? Do you have the guts to learn *extasia*?"

She watches me, as do Mercy and Temperance behind her. My whirling head aches. I must do this for Haven.

Trembling, I make myself smile, as if she has answered my prayers. "Show me more before I answer you. 'Tis only fair."

Malice gently touches my cheek. "And not enough in this world is fair for people like us. Isn't that true, little sister?"

Then she reaches for me. I take hold of her warm smooth hand and let her pull me to my feet.

16

"My tongue tastes sour." Each word shreds my throat. "The world moves strangely here. It hurts my head."

Beside me, Malice pushes aside a curtain of white flowers hanging from a white tree. At the touch of her hand, the blooms sigh.

"Bloodroot is the quickest way to enter Avazel for those without the power," says Malice, "or those whose power is weak or new. But it leaves a nasty grit behind, both in your mouth and in your brain. I'm sorry for that."

Temperance walks near us, her hand joined with Mercy's. I feel dizzy watching the long coils of their hair sway as they move—dark and red, red and dark. Blue gown, green gown. Lock and key.

"You won't always need bloodroot," Temperance says cheerfully. She is right there before me, yet her voice echoes as if long miles stretch between us. The yellow flower tucked in her dark hair stares at me with a shriveled, mean little face.

I try to push it away, but my hand finds only air. Bright red spots pulse in the corners of my eyes.

"You said we are in the realm of Avazel," I say, coughing. My mouth tastes so foul my stomach turns over. "What does that mean?"

"It's a secret place," says Malice, "a world hidden from powerless eyes. Only we can enter it."

"Powerless. You mean those without *extasia*?"

I stumble over the word once more. Mercy snorts with laughter, as does that grinning little flower in Temperance's hair. I grab for it, my eyes filling with tears.

"Take that flower out of your hair," Malice says sharply. "It's bothering her." Malice pats my arm as Temperance tosses away her mocking bloom. "Keep walking, little sister. The feeling will pass soon enough, and the flowers will stop staring."

My legs are wobbly as a foal's. At a fallen tree, Malice holds out her hand, but I push past her and climb over it my own self. If I want her to help me, I will have to impress her.

"It isn't that we have *extasia*," Malice says, following me. "You can't *possess* a power like that. It's just that we're able to touch it, use it, when most others can't." The choppy rhythm of her words is strange. She does not speak as women in Haven do.

Other villages, she said. *Cities, even.*

My stomach tightens, uneasy. I shake my head a little.

Focus, Amity.

"But what does it do?" I ask.

"Many things, beautiful things." Malice points her finger. "Look over there."

We stop beside a great white tree. I lean against it. The tree's bark is smooth as skin. It pulses, as if beneath it beats a heart. Its leaves tickle my face, and each of them laughs a tiny rough laugh. They shiver pink and green, blue and gold.

Malice cups my chin, not unkindly, to direct my gaze. "Focus on real things, on the women in this wood. They're working, honing their craft. Pay attention. That will ground you here in Avazel, help you find your feet again."

I look where she tells me. A woman with deep brown skin and shorn black hair stands beside another white tree not far from us, her eyes closed and a strange song moving across her lips. Some words I know—*berry, sky, flesh*—but others I do not. They gurgle in her throat, hiss between her teeth.

I stare at her, in awe of her beauty, for I have never in my life seen anyone with skin the color of hers. She spreads her arms wide and rises slowly off the dark moss-covered ground, her bare feet pointed and her gown of sunset colors—orange and red and violet—floating in the air around her. In her right hand, she holds a white branch sanded smooth. When she opens her eyes, they are full white too, like my fright-birds'. Her smile beams.

I step back and fall over a tangle of roots. When I roll to my side, breathing hard, my eyes burst with colors, bright gold and crimson, and I know not where is sky and where is ground.

Malice crouches, helping me sit. "I know it's startling, the first time you see things like this. It was for me too. But don't be afraid. It's just Cunning and her flying spell. A favorite of hers. And look over there. Her name is Furor."

She points to another woman farther back in the trees. Furor is fair and slight with copper hair to her waist. Flowering vines adorn her sky-blue gown. She molds from the dirt a black wolf pup with shining white eyes and a bright pink tongue.

Temperance crouches beside her, watching closely, a look of grave sadness on her face.

Then Furor kisses the pup's furry brow, gazes into its eyes. With a hook she pulls from the pocket of her gown, she spills the wolf's innards upon the ground.

"No need to mourn the pup," croons Malice, rubbing my back. "It was a creature of Avazel, molded by Furor to serve her purpose. It had no will, no mind of its own. It was a tool."

Temperance bows her head over the wolf's remains and begins a quiet song. I would think it a prayer in honor of the slain beast if I was not so afraid of the strange words on her tongue.

The woman, Furor, squats over the mess and moves around each glistening fat piece, peering at it all.

I press the heels of my palms into the dirt. "What is she doing?"

"Furor is a seer," Malice says, watching me closely. I try to swallow my revulsion. "Entrails are her specialty, but she also looks at the stars."

"And Temperance is a . . . a seer too?"

"Not just yet. Someday, maybe. She has a way with animals. When she grows stronger, I think she could walk in them, as Ire does."

I do not know what this means or who Ire is and truly do not wish to know.

But I swallow hard, look eagerly at Malice. "Ire? Who is she?"

"There," she says, tilting her head to the left.

A movement, a flutter of color. I turn and see a woman, white of skin and hair and eyes, wearing green trousers and a long white tunic hemmed in gold. She stands on a felled tree. Her words are part song and part prayer. Words I know—*trap, longing, empty*—and growling, lilting words I know not. As she sing-speaks, bits of darkness peel away from the black sky and flutter down, forming themselves, until they alight upon her head and arms. Soon Ire wears a cloak of crows, their dark feathers all agleam.

"They have bright white eyes, like the birds I saw," I whisper, staring. "But . . ."

"But these birds are healthy?" Malice says. "Yes, it's a funny trick of *extasia*. Some of us can control or walk inside the Avazel beasts, but once they enter the outside world, the creatures start to lose bits of themselves. They change and rot. You have to work quickly. Some are better at it than others."

"Those birds I saw, then—Ire was telling them what to do?"

"Something like that. Not her alone, of course. Even Ire can't fly in dozens of birds at once."

I take a deep breath. "Those birds showed me my father in pain. They were hurting him."

Malice raises her dark eyebrows. "Really? How interesting. We sent the birds to watch you, it's true. To see what you're about. But that vision, that was all *extasia*. It was showing you something it thought you ought to see."

I look hard at her. "Why send them to watch me?"

"I told you. The power whispers your name to me. It has for weeks."

"*Extasia* has, you mean."

Malice nods, her eyes keen. "And the power never lies."

A chill tries to trap me, but I push past its grip. "Why do you think it has told you about me?"

"I guess we'll figure that out together." Malice grins. "Come. There is more to see."

She leads me deeper into the wood and down a hill pocked with stones. At the bottom, crooked huts of white rock stand in a circle, roofed with grass and mud and white branches. Some are built into the hills around us, each hut draped with vivid green moss or fat dark vines or ropes of tiny yellow flowers. One of the chimneys sends up thick curls of gray smoke.

As I watch, the smoke changes. It drifts away from the chimney, takes on a shape.

I stop at once, a sudden cold raising the hair on my arms.

There is a mouth in that darkness. And those are thin arms, long as branches, dragging along the ground.

A gray woman.

I raise a trembling arm. "Is that too a creature of Avazel?"

Malice turns. "What? The smoke?"

I look again, and the woman is gone, the air warmer. I stare for a moment, my heart thundering.

Maybe she left suddenly, or maybe she was never there.

Or she was, and Malice could not see her.

I laugh a little, trying not to cry. I put my hand to my throat. "I think the bloodroot must still be muddling me. I thought I saw my cat from home, stuck up in that tree."

Malice's look is shrewd, but she says nothing.

We enter the smoking hut. 'Tis dim inside, shadows striped with candlelight. Dried plants hang in bunches from the ceiling. Over a low fire, a pot simmers, and at a small table stained brown and red sits another woman, this one with brown skin and shining black hair tied back with a meadow-green ribbon. Around her are roots and mushrooms, long jagged leaves that glisten with oil. She crushes, tears, mixes, then raises her arm without looking up and murmurs one of those strange chants— part song, part plain speaking.

House, beg, join, she sing-speaks. Three words I know, tangled up in others I do not. I listen close, trap the odd sounds in my memory. *Malyatzaf, samdech, grahala, malyodam.*

And suddenly, there is a small sawing tool in her hand that was not there before.

I blink twice, unsteady on my feet. The world seems to tilt around me.

Malice, very near, says, "A summoning spell."

"Summoning?" I whisper.

"Calling something to you that is far away or calling it out of nothing. See the beauty of *extasia*, little sister? It helps us even in small things."

Summoning. I say the word again and again, letting it burn itself into my thoughts. If I could quickly learn such a spell, I could find the five relics before anyone else is killed. Saint Amity's swift salvation.

As I watch, the working woman uses the tool she summoned to cut through a tough thick root. Beside her, in her pot, something bubbles and steams.

Whatever cooks there fills my nose with scents of spring, the green smells that come when the earth is wet and ripe and all my flowers begin to open.

And with my next breath, I smell the sweet richness of bread baking in a stove. I breathe in again, deeply, and my cheeks catch fire. This scent is a different sweet richness, one I know from the mornings in my bedroom after Blessing has touched herself in the night.

Malice laughs, striding past me. "That's a good one, Liberty. Smells just like home. Better than. Cleaner."

The woman, Liberty, glances up with a soft smile. "I do my best." Then she looks over at me. "Is that her? The one *extasia* speaks of?"

"Indeed. Amity, will you eat with us tonight? Liberty has prepared a rare treat."

Suddenly, I boil over with impatience. One too many strange things has happened, and the ropes holding together my mind are fraying fast. If I must learn this power to save my home, if a summoning spell is what I must use, then I wish to start *now*.

"Where does it come from?" I ask sharply. "*Extasia*. You said it is a power of the world. So it is a gift from God, then?"

Liberty glances at Malice. A tiny smile moves Malice's mouth.

"Some think so," she answers.

"And what do you think?"

"When I'm given power such as this, I don't ask many questions."

"I've always thought of us as angels," Liberty says sweetly from her table.

I stare at her, speechless for a moment to hear such blasphemy. "None of you look like angels."

Liberty laughs. "Well, maybe we're new. New angels for a new world."

"What are those songs you sing?" I ask quickly. "The . . . the summoning spell. How do you know it? Is it a prayer?"

Malice moves to clear a second table, stacking bowls, folding rags.

"Spells are rituals of a sort," she says, her back to me. "Each witch writes her own according to what she wishes *extasia* to do."

"It is like praying, then."

"Nothing so empty as that. You pray to your God, and what happens? Very little. Nothing at all, if you ask me. But the power is alive and willful. If you find the right words, it might do as you ask. Then again, it might not. One changed word, one wandering thought, and *extasia* will get bored or angry, or give you something even better than you asked for, or just go to sleep. Rogue, the witch who taught me . . ."

Moving carefully around the hut, I hardly hear Malice as she tells her story. I have found a narrow shelf squashed into the room's corner, sagging beneath the weight of many books. Of course I know what a book is, though I have only ever touched one—my father's stolen Sanctificat, lying open in the dirt before Temperance and me, our dirty fingers tracing each thin page. All other books in Haven are kept in the elders' House of Knowing. There are hundreds, Samuel tells me.

This one, the book that has caught my eye, is a small thing, ordinary and plain and black. Bound shut with a leather cord, it sits by itself atop the others. As I reach for it, the pot's simmering brew pops over the fire, the dried plants shiver where they hang, my fingers tingle as if they carry lightning inside them.

My desperate prayer returns, screaming through my mind: *Book. Mirror. Belt. Knife. Key.*

I grab the book, shove it down into my bodice.

Something slithers across my stomach, then slides around to brush against my back. Something pierces a bit of skin beside my backbone. A narrow, quick touch, as of pinching fingers.

When I whirl around, there is Malice, a pale powder glittering in her cupped hand. She smiles, but her eyes are hard. "*Extasia* says you've had enough for one night."

I mumble an apology, then clutch at my bodice, trying to find the book, but it is gone. Fallen to the floor?

But there is no time to look. Malice raises her hand to her lips and blows the powder at my face. A rosy cloud surrounds me. I choke and cough, suck in something sour. At once I know the taste of bloodroot. I think I shall never forget it.

"Come find us again, little thief, this time without help," says Malice, her lips brushing my ear. "Maybe then I'll know you're worth teaching."

Then, like a feather, I fly off the edge of this red cloud and drift slowly down.

17

I AM RISING UP THROUGH a great thick blackness, my chest tight and hot. After hours of pushing against the black, I burst through to the surface and gulp down fresh air.

Blessing is there, her face framed by the golden curtains of her hair, her creamy skin furrowed with worry.

"Hush, Amity," she says quietly. "You are safe. What a nightmare that must have been."

I blink at her, my eyes afire, as if I have been without sleep for too long. I am in my room at home, I see that now—the white walls and their flowers, Shadow watching, bored, from the bureau, Lightluck the lamb by the door with his faint, faded smile. The window is open to let in the night air. Insects sing in the garden, distant bells chime quietly in the wind.

I am home.

But how?

I find Blessing's hands, hold them tight. "How long? What day is this?"

Blessing frowns. "'Tis Wednesday, very early." She brushes hair from my damp brow. "You look wild with fright. Would it help to tell me of your nightmare?"

"Avazel," I whisper, remembering. Colors and sounds return to me. Smudges of red and blue, muffled cries. A woman flying through white trees. A wolf pup rising from the earth, its insides glistening.

I bite down, taste that awful sour tang. *Bloodroot.*

My back itches. I reach around to scratch.

"What is Avazel?" asks Blessing.

"*Extasia.*" I pat my chest and stomach, reach around to fumble at my back. That soft white gown from Avazel with its trailing lace ribbons is gone, in its place my own familiar nightgown.

And the book I stole is gone too. It must indeed have fallen to the floor of that hut.

"*Extasia.*" The word sounds awkward in Blessing's mouth. "What does that mean? Is it a prayer?"

I am suddenly truly awake. I grab my sister's arms.

"I must tell you what's happened, but you cannot tell a soul," I say quickly. "Not Father, not Adam Brinsley, not even God."

Blessing nods, wide-eyed.

"Saint Mercy and Saint Temperance have befriended women who live in the woods," I tell her. "In a place named Avazel. They are called witches, and they use a power, *extasia*, to do

112

impossible things. It is not a power of the Devil, they say. It is a good power, beautiful, given to them by the world. Some think it is from God. Others do not know. They make miracles with it. I followed them, I saw their home."

"But Amity, Haven is the only—"

"No, *listen*." I silence her with one hand, scratch absently at my back with the other. "They say there are other villages in the world. Maybe Haven is not the only place chosen by God to survive The World That Once Was. Or maybe there are lost wretches out there, saved from death but doomed never to truly know God. I cannot say for certain. But this is the most important thing—these witches, they are going to help me. With words they sing and speak, they craft spells, which are much like prayers, or the elders' rituals on worship day. Some of their words I knew. Others I did not. I saw one witch summon a tool right out of the air. A summoning spell, Malice called it. One moment the tool was not there, and the next it was."

I release Blessing. She stares at me, pale and still with fright. "Who is Malice?"

"She leads the witches. Their elder."

"And these witches," Blessing says slowly, "they did not mind you being in their wood?"

"No, they said *extasia* has whispered my name to them. They have been watching me, hoping I would come to them."

"What does that mean?" Blessing whispers, her voice small. "How does this power know your name?"

"I do not know, nor do they. But they said if I learn about

their power, if I let Malice teach me, they will use *extasia* to help me stop the killings and protect Haven. And if I learn a summoning spell strong enough, I can use it to complete the sacraments of darkness and bring the relics to me. I think all of this means I am on the right path." I catch my breath, watching Blessing. "Do you believe me?"

"I always believe you," she says firmly. Then her gaze goes a little distant, a little sad. "It all sounds like something out of Mother's old stories."

"And you will not tell anyone?" I say, fast, so she will stop speaking of Mother.

"Of course not. But . . . what will you do now?"

I shake my head. "I stole a book from Malice's hut, but I must have dropped it somewhere. I think she knows what I did and got angry with me. She told me if I could find Avazel again on my own, without help, she would begin teaching me."

I rise and begin to pace, thinking. Shadow jumps silently down from the bureau and shows me her belly, hoping for a scratch. I ignore her, instead scratching this awful itch on my back that will not cease.

"Do you think they have written their spells in that book?" Blessing asks. "As the elders wrote God's prayers in the Sanctificat?"

"Perhaps. When I neared the book, I felt a heat in me. My fingers tingled as if my skin held fire or lightning. It was as if something were pulling me toward the shelf on which it sat.

'Tis a book of spells, perhaps, or—"

"Or maybe it is *the* book," Blessing whispers. "The first relic given to men."

"Yes, I suppose the witches could have the book but know not what it truly is," I murmur, thinking, and as I do, a prickle of cold crawls over me. "House, beg, join. *Malyatzaf, samdech . . .*"

Blessing watches curiously from my bed. "What are you saying?"

"Liberty's summoning spell. Hush. *Grahala, malyodam.*" I close my eyes and say the words again. I try to sing-speak as Liberty did, but the words feel strange on my tongue. Ill-fitting.

Malice said that if a witch finds the right words, *extasia* might do as she asks.

I stand still in the dark, staring at Lightluck. I breathe in and out, willing my thoughts calm.

I must use my own words, not Liberty's. But where to even begin?

"*Malyatzaf,*" I whisper, for it is one of the few witch words I know. "*Samdech, grahala.*" I think of what I want—the book from Avazel, here in this room, in my hands. "Home," I whisper, for that is where I am, and then, "Wings," for I would like the book to fly to me, and finally, "Claw," as if I am a wolf dragging my kill to me, to do with as I wish.

"Amity, what are you doing?" Blessing whispers, frantic. "What are you saying? Is that a spell? Amity!"

I say the words all together, front to back, then back to front, and as I do, they come more easily, spilling from my lips like a river down a hill. Heat climbs up my legs and spine. Shadow hisses and darts under Blessing's bed.

I think of that little book so ferociously that my temples ache. I want that book. It should be mine, not theirs. I must protect Haven. Maybe the witches can help me, as Malice says, but I cannot trust her yet. Until I can, I must continue on my quest to find the relics. God spoke my name to the elders, and *extasia* speaks my name to the witches, and that must mean something. I am chosen. I am strong.

I am powerful enough to fight the Devil.

Book. Mirror. Belt. Knife. Key.

Home, *samdech*, *malyodam*, wings, *malyatzaf*, claw, *gra-hala*.

And then, the new words on my lips, I feel something on my back—*in* my back—tear open.

I fall to the floor, the pain swallowing my scream. Blessing scrambles down beside me, holding me against her.

"What is it?" She shakes me a little. "*What*, Amity?"

Panting, I push her away, reach around to my back—and my fingers catch on a lump beneath my nightgown.

A sharp lump poking out from my skin.

Frantically, I loosen the ties of my nightgown, let it fall to my waist.

"What is it?" I whisper, letting Blessing see. "What is on me?"

She lets out a strangled cry. Her hands fly to her mouth.

I stumble to the window, pull it closed, twist around to see what I can in the glass. There it is—a dark pointed lump poking up from my spine and rippling my skin.

Right where I felt that strange sharp pinch in Malice's hut.

Right after trying to steal her book.

"Get it off!" I try to scream, but fear traps my voice in a harsh whisper. "Get it out of me!"

I claw at my flesh, but I cannot quite reach the lump, no matter how violently I twist. A spear of fire shoots up my spine. My skin stretches taut. I shall snap, I shall burst.

I fling myself toward the wall, slam my body and head against the wood. I shall bash this thing out of me if I have to.

Blessing catches me before I can do it again. "Amity, stop! Father will hear! What are you *doing*?"

I rip myself away from her grip, stretch my arm around, dig my fingers into whatever flesh I can find.

"Claw, *malyatzaf*," I recite through gritted teeth. "*Samdech*, *malyodam*, wings, home, *grahala*." I find Blessing. "Say it with me. I summoned it here, now I must finish it."

My sister stares at me for a moment but then obeys. Our whispered voices, frantic and clumsy, mismatched, intone the spell while I dig at my back with shaking fingers.

"Help me," I tell Blessing, and together we tear into my skin. My vision pulses and spins. To muffle my cries, I sob into my fist.

My digging left thumb hits something warm and wet. Torn

skin, slick and hot, and the rough ridges of the book's pages.

I fall forward and retch, black flooding my eyes. Something hits the floor beside me. A wet thump.

"Amity, we did it," Blessing says, her voice hoarse with tears. "It is here."

Shaking, I turn to see what lies there on the rug—shreds of flesh, a pool of blood.

But 'tis only the stolen book from Avazel. How innocent it looks, sitting alone on our rug. Black and dry, small enough to fit in Samuel's pocket. I called for it, and it came. Not kindly, not cleanly, no, but now it is here.

Blessing stares at it, hugging her knees to her chest. "The first sacrament of darkness."

I was thinking just the same. *Skin.*

"Book, mirror, belt, knife, key," I whisper, touching my back with trembling fingers. There is no wound, nothing torn or bleeding. Only my smooth back, cool to the touch, and the sharp ridge of my spine, holding me together.

I glance at the window. Though it is now closed tight and no wind can get in, a slight chill ripples the air, as if *extasia*, watching me, is pleased.

THERE ARE FIVE SACRED HOUSES in Haven.

By the western wall, aligned with the Devil's black mountain beyond, sits the House of Sighs, where sinners who have killed, or stolen, or done some other unholy crime are held belowground in darkness.

The House of Knowing, to the east, is where the elders pray in seclusion when it is time to choose a new saint, where they confer and debate, and where their stores and books are kept.

There is Holy House, of course, in the center of town, where worship is held.

Just beyond the northern wall, between Haven and the woods, stands the House of Woe, in which the dead are burned. After each burning, the meadowland is cleared and the house built anew, painted a fresh bright blue.

And then there is the House of Whispers near the southern

wall—a little red house not far from my father's where people may confess their sins to a saint.

It is in this house that I sit on a small wooden bench with Samuel, below the single high window. Above us, painted gold flowers ring the high red walls.

I watch him, my body drawn tight at every curve and bend. I have told him everything—my quest to find the relics, Avazel, *extasia*, Malice's offer, the book. The first relic given by God to men, first stolen by Abigail, now stolen by me. Every aching bone in me, every throb of pain I can still feel in my back, tells me this is that book.

And now, Samuel sits beside me, staring at the book in his lap, and I wait, my stomach roiling. A square of gold from the window touches his face, painting his dark hair a lustrous brown. If he does not speak soon, I may very well scream.

"Who else knows about this?" he asks at last.

"Only Blessing," I tell him. I have said nothing of the book to Temperance or Mercy, and I will not unless I must.

Samuel blows out a long breath. "I see."

My patience snaps in half. "Will you open it, or will you not?"

"In truth, Amity, I do not know. Do I open the book or leave it closed? Do I keep these wild secrets of yours, or do I run right now to tell your father?"

"You wouldn't," I say calmly, hoping 'tis true. "You love me."

"I do."

"Well, then?"

"But this is madness!" Roughly, he drags a hand through his hair. "A quest to find the stolen relics of Lost Abigail? Women living in the woods? An unholy power that tore open your body and ripped a book out of you?"

"This is how we save Haven, Samuel." I tap the book with my finger. "*Extasia* helped me find this book. The more I learn, the more Malice teaches me, the quicker I may find the other relics, maybe even without pain. And with them in my possession and the witches by my side, the Devil cannot possibly triumph."

"And you truly think yourself strong enough to do all of this? Consort with some woman who may in fact be evil cloaked in goodness? Open yourself up to a power you do not understand? Seek out the Devil as not even the elders dare to do?"

Such scorn in his voice. Glaring, I lift my chin. "I was strong enough to face my saintly trials without fear. I was strong enough to come from a wicked mother and nevertheless be chosen by God and our elders to be anointed." I raise my eyebrows. "Unless you think they were wrong?"

"Of course not," he says quickly. "God speaks, the elders hear."

"So you will help me, then."

"And if, after all of this, you are not strong enough to fight him?" Samuel turns to me, his eyes bright with tears. "If he kills you, or drags you down to Hell as he did Lost Abigail, what then, Amity?" His mouth twists. "You have been my friend all my life. We are to be wed. If you are lost, I do not think I can bear it."

I love him dearly, and yet I am so desperate for him to open the book and start reading it that I could strike him.

Instead, I gently cup his cheek. "Samuel, please. I want to do this. I *must* do this, and with your help, I can do it faster. You can help me read so I may practice and impress the witches with my quick learning. You can help me past the watchmen. Thanks to my mother, God will test me for the rest of my life. This is a chance to prove myself to Him. Haven needs me. It needs *us*." I rub his jaw with my thumb. "Think of Benjamin. This will honor him, avenge him. It will close the door upon your family's grief and let you rest."

Samuel stares at me for a long time, his serious dark eyes looking at my brow, my jaw, my hair. Beneath his troubled, searching gaze, my cheeks grow hot.

Then, with a sharp sigh, he opens the book and gingerly begins turning the pages.

Triumphant, exultant, I keep my face serene and sit on my hands.

Samuel squints at the black letters scrawled on each page. "Some of these words have been marked through. Constance. Harriet. Kendra. Willa. Brittany. Elisabeth. These are names, dates. September fourth. April seventeenth."

What must it be like to look upon words and read them with such ease? Elated as I am, a small, deep-held part of me bristles to watch Samuel do a thing I cannot.

"Elisabeth," I repeat, "like Richard Fairfield's daughter. Though some of those are names I have not heard before."

"Nor I. And then on this page, there are other words, but no lines are drawn through them. These letters are thicker." He runs his fingers across the page. "They have been written with a forceful pen. See how their lines have been gouged deep into the paper? It goes on for many pages. Names with lines marked through them"—he points to the left page—"and then, on the page facing them, the words do not have marks, but . . . I do not think they are names."

I nod at the right-hand page, curled over his thigh. "What do they say?"

"Furor. Storm. Gall. Rampant. Liberty."

My skin prickles. "Those are indeed names. They belong to the witches."

Samuel tenses but says nothing. He turns another page, then several more, then stops. Squints. Frowns. "These words . . . I have never seen them before, nor am I certain how to read them." Then he says slowly, clumsily, "*Zodaasyo. Babacael.*"

Heart pounding, I move closer to look.

"*Niimala. Saldasdire.* Perhaps they are in the holy language? We could ask your father."

"They are spells," I whisper. "Samuel, praise the Lord, this is what I was hoping for! You can help me sound them out, help me read anything I cannot—"

I fall silent. A change has come over Samuel's face, as if

shutters have closed away a window. He bends over the book, squinting, then sits straight and stiffens beside me.

"What is it doing?" he whispers. "Do you see that?"

I peer at the open book. The pages look just as they did before. "See what?"

"The words. They are moving. They are becoming . . ." He shakes his head, his voice fierce. "They are no longer words. They are pictures. Look, there." His finger stabs the page. "A girl wrenching her hair from her head."

All I see are letters, arranged in the shape of some word I know not. Eye. Arr. Eee.

Samuel turns the page, and the next, and the next after that, faster and faster. "Don't you see them? A girl with the head of a bird. A girl with her arms thrown up to the heavens. A girl bent as if she will soon snap in two. A boy—"

Suddenly, Samuel is very quiet. "A boy in pieces. A foot, an arm, an eye, a . . ." He flushes, trails off. "All hanging from the branches of a tree."

I reach for the book. "I see none of this. Perhaps I should hold it."

He jerks away from me and stands. "Do not touch it. Something is wrong with it. We should burn it."

I stare at him. "And risk the witches' anger? Have you heard nothing I have said?"

A soft sound drops between us. Small, hardly more than a sigh, and yet it falls like thunder and shuts both our mouths.

I see it at once—a red circle on the book's page, near Samuel's thumb. Others appear on the back of his hand, on the floor between my boots, on the end of Samuel's nose.

Our eyes meet. We look up.

The walls and ceiling run red with blood.

Samuel staggers back from me. His boots sink into the floor, which has become sodden earth. Red bubbles up beneath his feet. Red drops from the rafters and splatters our clothes. The air is hot and sour, thick with a smell I know, the smell Widow Heath brought into Holy House on the day of my anointing, her dead boy swinging from her arms.

The smell of death.

Samuel flings the book into the shadows, grabs my arm, pulls me outside after him. Fresh air, birdsong. Samuel falls against the sweet little hickory with the empty chair beneath it, ready for the next confessor to wait their turn.

Shaking, I look down at my arms. The blood is gone from my clothes, and from Samuel's too.

I catch my breath and leave him there, creep back to the door and peer inside.

The book lies alone in the middle of the floor. How, I do not know. Did it wriggle itself out of the shadows? When Samuel tossed it away, did it bounce off the wall and fly back? The walls themselves are clean and dry, the floor scrubbed. All that blood gone as if it never was.

"Amity, don't!" Samuel cries from behind me.

He does not understand, but I think I do, though I am not certain I could find the words to explain it to him. I step inside, retrieve the book, press it to my breast. I hold it and breathe.

All is quiet, all is clean. The clouds above shift, and sunlight slides through the high window.

My back to Samuel, my blood still racing from fear, I smile. It seems the book does not like Samuel, good fearful boy that he is.

But I am Saint Amity Barrow, and I seek to beat the Devil, no matter how many lies I must tell, no matter who I must befriend to defeat him.

Whatever words it holds, whatever power it carries, this book knows that in my hands is where it belongs. Mine, and no one else's.

The thought frightens me. I must be honest and admit that.

But I do not think it frightens me as much as it should.

19

THREE DAYS LATER IS MY first visitation day.

On such a day, I should be thinking only of God. I should be praying to Him about The World That Once Was, about how what happened to those fallen people will never happen to us here in Haven, not so long as every visitation day, we saints offer ourselves to our neighbors as the Sanctificat decrees.

Here are the day's rites: the saints sing the Woman's Prayer, a reminder of what all Eve's daughters should be. Then the saints allow their neighbors to relieve upon them their grief, their anger, the shame of their sins. The elders lead more prayers. We all reflect upon the wicked women of those long-ago years, how their union with the Devil brought the world low. More prayers from the elders, a closing song, a solemn silence. The air hot and damp with rage and sweat. Amen.

I have been dreaming of this day since I was eight, old

enough to be brought to visitation at last and see for myself the saints being shoved, struck, stroked, their faces full of calm all the while, their eyes bright with love for God. My tiny heart burst with awe.

Other children cried upon seeing the violence.

I did not. I watched in wonder. All the day after, Mother could not look at me straight on.

Of course she could not. Now I understand why. The light of God in me was too bright for her foul eyes to face.

All of this is true, but—may the good Lord forgive me—here I am, a saint at her first visitation, standing before the altar at last, and I can think only of my stolen book. I go to bed thinking of the words inside it, then wake up thinking the same. Samuel helps me read the ordinary words—recipes for brews, lists of food and supplies, eerie tales written in many scrawled hands.

But the other words, the spell words, he refuses to read again. I do not mind. Those words are for me.

I have not said them with any real meaning behind the sounds. I have not thought of pictures to go with them, or even colors. I want no more books tearing free of my back, not yet. No, I have simply been feeling the words in my mouth. Clumsy and slow, I sound out their letters one by one, as Samuel has taught me.

Amirabah. Pilizaala. Azotcale.

A great noise cuts short my silent recitations.

I look up to see two of the elders' seconds closing the doors of Holy House. An odd thing—on visitation days, we leave Holy

House's doors open to the sunlit world, so God may properly hear the prayers, the songs, the thudding fists. But not today. Today, the doors are locked, the windows fastened shut. Around the room, the nine elder lanterns snap with fire. Dim light, crawling shadows, a thousand glittering, staring eyes. My silent neighbors watching the altar. Stuffed into the room, they are unadorned. 'Tis a holy day, visitation, but not one of celebration.

Still, I have never seen a visitation begin in such booming silence, nor in shadow.

My chest flutters with a small fear. A saint I surely am, but I am also a mere girl, a beast of bone and blood, and that part of me, that animal frailty, wishes desperately to run.

Instead, I press my feet firmly against the floor and bite down on my tongue.

We four saints in our thin white shifts make a tight cluster near the altar, our backs facing outward. Our heads are bare, our hair worn loose. During visitation, a saint must not hide from those who wish to see her.

She must show herself to those who watch and accept whatever comes for her.

I look beyond Mercy's shoulder at our gathered neighbors. My breath stirs the ends of our hair. Red, dark brown, white, and my own, my plain brown. Our heads together, brows touching. I do not look at them, for I fear what I will see. Mercy and Temperance, who saw me in Avazel. Silence, who knows my mother's story.

I try to push their faces from my mind, but then a softness touches my finger. A tiny warmth.

I glance to my left, where Silence stands. Her blue eyes are downcast. Her snow-pale hair falls over her face.

What gown would she wear in that strange secret wood? Temperance's, blue. Mercy's, green. Mine, white as spun clouds.

If I called upon *extasia*, if I knew the proper spell, could I will Silence to look at me? Could I compel her to tell me if that was an imagined touch I felt, or indeed her soft finger brushing mine?

Then Silence begins to sing, her voice hardly more than a whisper.

Wherever you step,
whatever you seek,
may your tongue hold still,
may your heart live meek.

It has begun.

Mercy sings next. She keeps her hands clasped before her in tight fists. Her saintly mark—a single straight line, standing tall, with an upward curve crossing through it. Arms upraised. Begging for mercy, or granting it?

I join their prayer next, then Temperance last of all. Her dark eyes, her thin mouth. Her saintly mark, a straight line down her chest with one triangle at the bottom, another at the top. Opposite banners, balanced scales.

She looks up once and smiles at me, a sad, fleeting thing.

Sainthood is not what I think it will be, she told me in the elm grove.

Well, what does she know, witch that she is? That uneasy turn in my stomach means nothing. That the elders closed all the doors to shut out the sunlight means nothing.

Growls and shouts and groans fill Holy House as the people of Haven begin to stamp their feet, sway their bodies, let their heads hang and swing. The other women in the room join our song, their voices harsh.

I wonder where Blessing is among them, and Samuel, and Father. What will they think as they watch me today? Two keep my secrets locked inside them. All, I hope, will ache with pride to see me bear my suffering in stoic silence. That is not such a wicked wish, is it, oh God?

But when I look up at the ceiling, directing my prayer to the heavens, the words die on my lips.

Shadows seethe in the peaked rafters. A gray woman—no, three of them. Silence was right.

A hand touches my hip, some man I cannot see grasping at me from the crowd. They have begun to surge toward us.

The shadows above split and curl. The gray women's long arms trail to the floor as they dart around furiously like wasps struck from their nest. One of them thrashes her head from side to side. Cold air drops over me, as if with a blink I have stepped back into winter.

Beside me, Silence breathes in sharply. She has seen them too.

One of the gray women dives down to lock eyes with me. In the gaping black maw of her face glitters a teeming swarm of flies. One of her dark hands whips toward me, fingers outstretched.

I stumble back with a cry.

A great swell of sound surges through the room. Someone in the crowd grabs me. Fingers glide down my arm, then pinch my hip.

Temperance drops, knocked flat by a striking hand. Elias Holt, the man meant to wed her, stands over her. He grins to see her fall. Two men grab Mercy, tug her back and forth between them.

Tom Wickens, the butcher, pulls me away from Silence. He holds me to his chest with bulging arms, whispering into my hair as he weeps. A man to be pitied, he is, burdened by so much strength and fierce will. He cannot help his anger, the impurity of his thoughts, the force of his fists, how often they land on his wife. It was women behind the fall of mankind, do I understand? They destroyed The World That Once Was, so in turn, Tom Wickens quite often feels the urge to destroy his wife.

"Will it right their wrongs, Saint Amity?" His words are wet against my ear. "If I hit her often enough, will it erase some of their sins from that long-ago world? Will God forgive me for it?"

Father told me I would be shocked by the confessions I

would hear this day, but what Tom Wickens says steals away my breath. I would have never believed such violence of him, but here he stands, rocking against me, his tearful confession wetting my neck. A saint is meant to be struck, but not a goodly wife.

What would my father do?

"And we shall live ever longer in our hallowed fields," I whisper against Tom Wickens's ear, hoping the prayer will soothe him.

"As the light of the four saints doth shine," he answers, his lips brushing my neck, "so shall our own."

Then he mutters a foul word into my hair, grips my gown, paws my front. Eyes alight with anger, he lets out a small harsh laugh and spits in my face.

Pin your arms to your sides, Amity. Do not clean your face. Bear this, as you have dreamed of. I shut my eyes, breathe in, think of Haven as it once was—peaceful, safe, bursting with flowers and life. Next will come a prayer, a moment to catch my breath, settle my pounding heart. An elder will find me, lead a prayer for those nearest me, then release me, and someone else will grab me, shove me, confess to me, and it will all begin again.

But on this visitation day, no such moment comes. No prayer, no caught breath.

Instead, I am torn away at once by Ester, Tom's daughter, and Hetta and Fanny Jamison, the twins, who are Ester's cousins. They throw me to the floor. My head knocks against it. Red pain blooms behind my eyes as I lie gasping, and the girls above me laugh. They kick and punch, and I close my eyes and bear it. I pray to God that after this day, after cleansing themselves of their anger, Hetta and Fanny and Ester may themselves feel less inclined to sin.

They lift me from the floor by my hair and sleeves.

"You little whore," Ester spits. "What did you say to my father just now? What did you promise him?"

"For how long have you been visiting him?" Hetta twists my hair. "Say it. You lured him into your bed, just as your mother did Elder Joseph."

They throw me back down. I taste blood and turn over. Above me, I see the black sky in that white wood. The fat red moon draws me up by my fingers and toes, urging me up into the cool clean air, and for a moment, I think I hear a voice I once knew crooning to me.

Rise, daughter. Rise and run.

But my mother is not here.

Instead, Father pulls me up from the floor. I swallow blood. A strange tingling heat warms my palms.

"Go on, Amity," he says, his eyes darting around. "Let them see you unafraid."

He worries. I understand why. We are not yet safe from the shadow of my mother, not with death still sitting so thick upon Haven.

I wish I could tell him not to worry. I wish I could tell him of my awful dark work, but he would want to stop me.

And I cannot be stopped.

For a moment, I think Father will now begin a prayer, but no—he pushes me into the waiting arms of Jacob Farthing and Aaron Dale, one of Granny Dale's boys, both of them not much older than I. They slap me and tug on whichever parts of me they can find; they shove me along where they will, until I lose all sense of myself, all sense of up and down. Hissed words, cruel fists, seeking hands. No prayers between the blows, no rest, no end. This is all I know. No room in my mind to think of Father, or books and spell words, or even God.

I should want to bear this for my people, and I *do* want to—it is everything I have worked and hoped for. On desperate knees in my dark bedroom, as Blessing cried into her pillow for our dead mother, I prayed for God to make me a saint. That would make Father happy again. That would calm Blessing's sobs.

But this visitation is not like any I have seen in my life. Abram Watkins strikes my temple. I fall. Rebecca Porter squats over me and spits on my face, again and again. No elders come to lift me to my feet and murmur a prayer over my throbbing head. Only once do I find a brief calm—John Ames, tall and gentle, holds me in his big arms and says into my hair not a confession, but only this: "There, now. Breathe for a moment. It is almost done."

Then I am torn from him, so fast I cannot even see his face.

God? 'Tis the only word I can remember. I turn my face up to the ceiling, as if a light there will warm me. *Are you there?*

But if He is, He does not answer, and I sink into myself. A

boneless, staggering creature, I pass the rest of visitation in amazed silence, shoved here and there until at last the closing prayers are finished and the final bells chime. Night has come.

The men and women of Haven leave my saint sisters and me on the floor, in the corners. Some of my neighbors send quick darting looks at me. Most do not look at me at all. Little Briony Linden wails in her mother's arms, hiding her face in her mother's hair. Her first visitation, I would guess.

My eyes sting, watching her. I can barely swallow my sob.

I have watched visitation dozens of times, perhaps hundreds, and I have reveled in each one. I knew what this day would bring.

But it was not this.

Father carries me home, my body and mind caught in an ill haze. I blame my unholy quest for what has happened. 'Tis a cruel bargain. Yes, go bravely to find the Devil and save your people, but meantime God will not hear you, nor will you feel His light. Here, be anointed, but those evil words you must practice will leave you weak. When visitation comes, it will be darker and crueler than you can imagine. You will feel no joy, no gladness, only pain.

In my dark bedroom, shivering and sweat-damp, I undress with the help of my sister. When I am bare to Blessing's eyes, she covers her mouth and turns away.

"They have hurt you so," she whispers. "Your arms, Amity! And your legs . . ."

"What did you expect?" I stare blearily at nothing. "You

have been to many visitations in your life. It is as it should be."

"No. That was *not* as it should be. That was too much, too harsh. Adam says it is because after Jeremiah, everyone is so afraid. That is why they shut the doors and did not grant any of you rest during prayers." She draws in a shaky breath. "'The meaner the blows, the greater their fear, the gladder God will be, the safer Haven will be.' That is what he said."

Blessing's eyes are wet. There is a sharp sorrowful set to her mouth that stirs in me an absurd anger. I do not want her tears, not do I want whatever wild madness that was in Holy House. I want the visitation I have spent my life awaiting—solemn and severe, yet merciful. My bruises throb, leaving me weak enough for horrible bitter thoughts to slither free. Did I endure those trials for nothing? Having beaten me so soundly, will the frightened people of Haven sleep peacefully tonight? I hope not. I hope Tom Wickens's nightmares are so awful he soils his bed.

I limp toward the window. "Please do not follow me."

"Where are you going? Not to Avazel?"

The worry in her voice makes me ill. Too much tenderness. It does not match my own feelings. "No," I answer. "The garden."

But my shaky legs can barely carry me there. I must crawl beneath the tangled leaves, the tiny knots of thorns, into the secret place where I once hid with Temperance and, later, buried her message.

There, I am not alone.

Silence lies curled on her side in the dirt, knees held to her chest. Her hair shines white in the faint moonlight, and her eyes glimmer with everything that has passed on this holy day. A spot of dried blood mars her fat lip. The scarred mark of Saint Silence pokes up from her collar—four little marks, like stitches, crossing a proud straight line.

I stare, all my thoughts flown far away.

"Forgive me," she whispers. "I love your flowers so. I always have. Is it all right? May I stay, please, Amity?"

Too tired to protest, I simply lie down beside her. We are close in the dirt, my brown hair tangled with her own pale locks, and when she reaches for me, I do not turn her away. She takes gentle hold of my arms and nestles against me, leg hooked over mine. The heat of her body, the rabbit-fast beat of her heart, matches my own and cracks me softly open. My eyes fill.

"Pray for blood," she says at last, soft against my brow. "I do, every night."

How deep and dire is the sadness that carves shadows around her eyes. It settles inside me like winter, sends me shivering. "You pray for their blood?"

"No. I pray for my own."

I should say many things. I should scold her for that sacrilege, for wanting to be rid of her hood before God deems it time. I should send her away, for she should be at home. I should ask her more about the gray women—*how many have you seen? How many stories have you been told? What are they? I think they are part of what is happening. I think they are important. How can we find out?*

But tonight, I am too heartsick for questions. My body aches, my head aches, and my chest is knotted up with tears. I reach for a nearby bloom—a delicate purple pasqueflower—and fold it gently into Silence's fingers.

She stares at it for a moment, then cradles it against her chest and hides her face in the bend of my neck. "My house has been a sad place for years," she says quietly, the brush of her lips making my tender skin prickle. "It will be a little less so now. Thank you, Amity."

Later, the sky still full dark and Silence gone back to her home, I creep back inside and lie awake in my bed. If I hold very still, I can feel her there with me, even alone as I am. Her careful hands on my wrists, her slow sleepy breaths against my hair, her lip smeared black with blood.

20

NEAR DAWN, I WAKE TO a soft rustling noise in my bedroom and open my eyes to see my sister leaning against her bed as she tugs off her mud-crusted boots.

I hardly breathe as I watch her. My eyes burn from my short night of sleep. Was she here when I came back from the garden?

Ah—there, I see. Pillows arranged in the shape of her body, tucked under her quilt. 'Tis a deception well made.

Blessing puts her pillows right, then shoves her boots under her bed, kicks away fallen crumbs of mud, plucks a piece of straw from her nightgown. At last, she crawls under her quilt and settles as she usually does, on her left side, facing me.

But then she looks to my bed, sees me watching, and freezes. One leg under the quilt, one leg out. Blessing Barrow, who never quite knows if she feels hot or cold.

"Where have you been?" I ask her.

"I could not sleep. I was sweeping the kitchen floor."

"In your boots? You have straw in your hair."

Blessing finds the straw and crushes it in her palm. She does not look at me. Her smile is hard and thin. "The kitchen was very dirty."

I sit up. Her voice is too careful. "Blessing, what were you doing? Do not lie to me. What has happened?"

"Nothing. I promise you. Please, can we sleep? I am tired."

So she says—and yet she hides her face, as if ashamed. "You won't look at me," I say. "Why? What have you done?"

"Nothing."

"You were crying when I left you."

She turns away and curls into a ball and tugs the quilt up to her chin so that every other bit of her is hidden from me. "I wish to sleep for a while before Father wakes. Good night."

The next moment, right on the heels of her words, the watchmen's bells begin to ring—a great frantic clamor, first from the southern wall, then from everywhere. Rising into the air like a flock taking flight.

Blessing and I find our boots and cloaks in silence, mud and straw and deceitful pillows forgotten. We know what it means, the sound of those bells ringing madly before the sun rises, and so does Father, who we find tugging on his jacket at the door, and so do all the people of Haven. Roused from our beds, everyone hurries toward the southern wall, where torches blaze and shouts like gunfire fill the air.

Father pushes through the gathered crowd of sobbing women and scowling men and screaming children, Blessing and I close on his heels.

Just outside the wall, at the meadow's edge, we see him at once. Another dead man, this one splayed and naked. Wooden stakes drive his hands and feet into the earth. His body is odd, lumpen, misshapen, but I do not understand why until Blessing turns away to be sick and I dare press closer to Father.

Tom Wickens, the butcher—the man who confessed his sins to me in yesterday's visitation, and held me hard against him— stares back at me, but with fistfuls of bloody gray rocks instead of eyes. His jaw has been cracked open, his body cut apart and sewn back together, and every inch of him has been stuffed fat with stones.

On my hands and knees, I scrub Elder Peter's kitchen floor. The smells of the supper I cooked for him linger in the air. The shirt I mended now sits folded neatly in his bureau. Amity Barrow, loyal friend and dutiful caretaker.

But in my head—my lips and tongue moving silently—I practice witch words.

I have written a summoning spell. That is, I *think* it will be a summoning spell.

Samdech, unseen, *malyodam*, *grahala*, beast, seek, *malyatzaf.*

Every few moments, I glance up to make sure Elder Peter has not noticed me muttering quietly to myself as I work. But no, he still sits on his porch just past the open kitchen door, staring sadly out at the yard and the fence and the road beyond. A watchman on patrol walks past, rifle slung over his shoulder. He raises his hand in greeting. Elder Peter does not respond. He holds his wrinkled hands in his lap, thumb worrying thumb.

An owl swoops through the dusk light, near the porch steps. The sudden movement makes Elder Peter jump. Then he bows his head and rubs his right temple.

Since Tom Wickens was found dead two days past, Elder Peter has not said much when I have visited for my nightly chores. No one has, except in whispers and prayers. Haven is quiet, but I do not trust it. I see the way they look at Blessing and me, even Father. I know those looks.

Eleven men now dead. I am not moving quickly enough. How many more will die before I am finished? How long will the people of Haven wait before those wary looks they give us Barrows turn to something worse?

I scrub harder, the back-and-forth scrape of bristles against wood cleaning Tom Wickens's stretched, stuffed face from my mind.

Samdech, unseen, *malyodam*, *grahala*, beast, seek, *malyatzaf.*

His glittering eyes in Holy House, just before he spat on me.

I scrub and scrape, glaring at the floor.

Samdech, unseen, *malyodam*, *grahala*, beast, seek, *malyatzaf.*

I have said the words so many times that they have become more than words. They are feelings inside me, a secret pattern only I know how to weave.

"Good evening to you, Elder Peter," comes Samuel's voice from the yard. The gate opens and shuts.

"Samuel," says Elder Peter, sighing. "Must you take her from me so soon?"

Samuel laughs. "Even Saint Amity needs her sleep, Elder Peter. She has already missed evening prayers for you, after all."

Listening to them, my heart jumps. It is time.

Quickly, I clear away the cleaning tools and join them on the steps. "Everything is finished, Elder Peter. I will see you tomorrow."

He looks at me mournfully. "It is too quiet without you here."

Samuel glances at me, shifting from left foot to right. "And God is pleased by quiet, for in it lies room for solemn prayer."

"Yes," Elder Peter says faintly. "Very true, my boy."

I do not like how he rubs his thumbs together without ceasing, or the sadness on his face. Something in his eyes chills me—a lostness I have not seen before. Each death these past months has aged him a year.

Placing my hand on his, I kiss his fuzzy white head.

"Tomorrow," I say firmly. "Good night, Elder Peter."

We leave him in silence, walking side by side. Then, on the road past the trees, once another watchman has come and gone, we hurry to Samuel's house and down the gentle slope of his yard. A clutch of oak trees stands there, drawing spider-web-shadows among their trunks.

Once we are well hidden, I crouch and shove my hand in the pocket of my dress, find the petals I took from my garden. The feeling of them in my sweating palm reminds me of my feet on the ground, the breath in my body, my strong bones.

Samuel peers past the trees, keeping watch. "Hurry, Amity. Remember, you must be back in your bed in one hour."

"Yes, which I already know very well," I whisper angrily. "Stop talking. You are frightening me."

He frowns at me. "You should be frightened. *I* am frightened."

But he does fall quiet then, for which I am grateful. We have argued enough about this plan.

Now I must work, and quickly.

Malice told me to come find her on my own, without help. No chasing after Temperance and Mercy, not this time. Only then will she teach me.

And I must be taught. I must learn more summoning spells—cleaner ones, stronger ones—and more about *extasia*. Book, mirror, belt, knife, key. I need them all now, before another man dies. I needed them two days ago, before they found Tom Wickens.

I close my eyes. One hand holds my petals, keeping me steady. The other presses flat against the soil.

I hope—I even dare to pray—that this will work.

Samdech, unseen, *malyodam*, *grahala*, beast, seek, *malyatzaf.*

As I begin, I feel foolish, crouching here like some animal, muttering words I am not certain mean anything.

Samdech, unseen, *malyodam*, *grahala*, beast, seek, *malyatzaf.*

The summoning words I heard Liberty use, added to my own.

Unseen, so that no one will catch me.

Beast, like those birds, or some other frightful white-eyed creature with a witch walking inside it. A fox, a mouse.

Seek. I seek Avazel and whatever secret path leads to it.

Samdech, unseen, *malyodam*, *grahala*, beast, seek, *malyatzaf.*

The words spill from my lips quietly, quickly. The feelings of them—colors, sounds, scents—climb inside me on a slow rise of heat.

Unseen. I crawl in darkness.

Beast. I gallop fast across the meadow on agile paws. Nostrils flaring, hide steaming.

Seek. I climb and climb, pushing through brambles that prick my palms.

Samuel gasps. My eyes fly open.

Hazy, swaying a little on my burning feet, my fingers tingling around my crushed petals, I meet the white, round, unblinking eyes of the hare sitting tall before me. Unmoving, unafraid. Hooked claws, leaking mouth, fur scabby and matted.

I stare at it, my head pounding. The world around me fades and quiets. It is only me and this fright, this Devil's beast.

I did it. I *summoned* this hare.

Samuel backs slowly away. "Dear God, forgive us," he whispers.

"Find your courage," I snap at him, gaze locked with the creature's. I wonder who walks inside it. Ire? Cunning?

The hare bares its fangs, then runs off into the shadows.

"Go *now*," I tell Samuel.

Samuel grabs my arm, his eyes pleading. "One hour, Amity."

For one hour, he will accompany my father on his nightly patrol around Haven. After that, I must be back in my bedroom, prayers said, sleeping peacefully. Blessing will go to Father if he comes home before I do. She will ask him questions about the Sanctificat, keep him talking, ask him to pray with her for all the dead men's souls.

Hopefully, the time they give me will be enough to find Avazel, show Malice I am worthy of her.

Samuel releases me. I run.

The hare is quick, but so am I. It seems to know the darkest path to wherever we are going—the deepest shadows, the quietest corners.

Only once does it stop, freezing near John Ames's sheep pen.

I flatten myself against the wall of his shed, holding my breath.

Two watchmen walk by, talking quietly. Rifles on their backs, torches lighting the way.

My heart pounds so fast I feel as though my head will burst. I need to breathe, my lungs burning.

The watchmen pass. The hare darts away, and I follow it to the western wall, where it disappears into the elm grove. I crash in after it, clumsy and panting, my side pinching.

Together we weave through the trees. I leap over roots and stumble over the little ravine near the grove's edge. I expect to see the wall just ahead—but instead I see only more trees. Hundreds of them, dark and tall, stretching for miles. Thicker and thicker this forest becomes, until I must turn to the side to squeeze between fat gnarled trunks. Their bark scrapes my skin. I suck in my belly, hold my breath, force my way through. The trees are growing closer, larger, rougher. They will crush me, they are squeezing out all my air—

At last, I burst free, falling forward onto a ground soft and cool with moss.

When I look up, Malice is standing over me, hands on her hips. Pale skin, black hair, red gown, broad grin. Past her are narrow white trees, a black sky, a fat scarlet moon.

"Welcome, little sister, and well done. You've got some strength in you. Come, dine with us." Malice extends her hand to me. "After that, we will begin."

21

MALICE SAYS NOTHING ABOUT THE stolen book. Instead, she leads me to a cluster of blazing fires. Dripping meat turns on a spit. Roasted carrots and potatoes slick with butter fill steaming silver pots. There is a delicious spice in the air that I do not recognize—rich, savory, a little sweet. My mouth waters.

The other women of the coven sit on stones around the fire, all of them in their bright fine gowns—including Temperance and Mercy. When they see me approach, their eyes widen.

"How did she get here?" blurts Mercy, her mouth full of food and her long red hair shining in the firelight.

Temperance puts down her pretty flowered plate, runs to me, and kisses my cheek. Warmth blooms in my belly.

"She found Avazel on her own." Temperance puts her arm around me and grins proudly at the others. "You see? *Extasia* chose wisely."

The coven watches me carefully, some of them curious, some frowning, others glaring.

I meet their eyes without fear, giddy from my triumph.

There is the woman with the deep brown skin and shorn black hair, her body draped in a gown of sunset colors, orange and red and violet.

"Hello, Cunning," I say calmly. I find the woman with white skin and hair who wears green trousers and a gold-hemmed tunic, a great white-eyed crow on her shoulder. "And Ire, good evening to you. Greetings, Furor." The copper-haired woman who spilled the wolf's guts. "Liberty, it is good to see you again." The woman with brown skin and shining black hair who cooked in Malice's hut.

I draw in a breath and claim an open stone, settling my white skirts around me. "I look forward to meeting the rest of you, of course," I say, looking around serenely, though my thudding heartbeat fills my entire body. "Thank you for welcoming me to your meal."

Quiet laughter moves around the fire. Liberty smiles softly. Ire appraises me with raised eyebrows.

"A bold little thing, isn't she?" Malice says, cackling. "Gall, Storm, Rampant, Vixen. You'll meet them all later." She waves her hand at the women I do not know. "Here, eat up. Lots to do tonight."

Liberty fills a plain tin dish and passes it to me. The thought flits through my mind that I wish I could have a flowered plate, as Temperance has—and when my fingers close around the dish, it has changed. No longer tin but fine glazed clay. Tiny blue and yellow flowers border the rim.

Temperance beams at me. "*Extasia* reads your thoughts well, Amity."

"If only she had some thoughts of her own," grumbles Mercy, glaring at my plate.

"In fact, I do." I swallow a mouthful of potatoes so tender they seem to melt on my tongue. "How do you all know about *extasia*? Who taught you?"

"I taught most of them," says Malice, settling back onto her stone with a sigh. She spreads out her legs, hikes up her skirts to air them out. "And an old witch named Rogue taught me."

"It is a power that's been known since the world was young," Cunning says, her voice soft as if in reverent prayer.

"Sacred knowledge that not even the fires of war could destroy," adds Liberty.

"And now," croons Ire, stroking the head of her crow, "we travel the ravaged wild to pass on the teachings of *extasia* to those who are worthy."

"Are there other covens then, besides your own?" I ask.

"Of course," says a pale woman with a light dusting of short black hair, shorter than a man's. Her gown is sage green and leaves her shoulders bare. "I'm Gall, by the way. I would say there are dozens of covens out there, maybe even hundreds. Don't you think, Malice?"

Malice hums into her ornate glass goblet something that

sounds like an agreement. The liquid inside is as deep a red as Malice's crimson gown.

"I'm impressed you managed to find us so quickly," says another woman, watching me with narrowed eyes. Her ruddy skin is striped with scars. One of her arms, I am shocked to see, is made of metal. Metal joints, metal fingers, as if a blacksmith has forged it for her. It moves as smoothly as my own and is polished to a gleam.

I look at the fierce blue light in the woman's eyes, her wild nest of gray hair. "You are Storm?"

She raises an eyebrow, which pulls at her wrinkled face. "Aye, child. A sharp guess."

"Tell us how you did it," says Temperance eagerly. "It took me weeks to find Avazel on my own."

"I summoned a beast to show me the way," I tell them. I catch Ire's eyes. "Was it you who walked inside it?"

She cocks her head at me. "*Extasia* said you needed me, showed me what you wanted to do. I'd say I was pissed at being made to work so late in the evening, but when the power speaks, a lady's got to listen."

The other women nod. Some raise their cups to the sky.

I frown. "Pissed?"

Mercy snorts.

"It means angry," says Temperance kindly.

"But if you really want to learn *extasia*, you have to do more than take a chance and get lucky," Malice says. Her drink has stained her lips purple. "You've got to honor the power with your word and your works. You've got to live every day in service of it. Listen to it. Do as it tells you. Speak to it only the truth."

"*Extasia* loves lies," says Ire. "Knows them backward and forward like a singer knows songs. But it doesn't like to be lied *to*."

As a daughter of Haven, I have long known not to lie. I rip a hunk of meat from the bone in my hand. The juice drips down my chin. I know what to ask next, for out of everything that has happened, this is the thing I have the most trouble understanding.

"You told me you came from other villages," I say. "Where are they? What do they look like?"

"Mostly they are villages like yours, though not quite so pretty," says Gall, with a mean little smile.

Cunning, picking her teeth with a small bone, leans back against a white tree. "Some people think there are still cities, if you walk far enough. Big ones."

"There are," Malice says plainly.

Cunning snorts and tosses her bone into the shadows.

"I've seen them," says Liberty. "There's one in the mountains down south, about three hundred miles from here. Another in the plains far to the east. There are markets and towers and farms. Most have crumbled, but others still stand."

Cunning rolls her eyes. "She's come the farthest, so she thinks we'll believe anything she says."

Liberty looks at me. "They do exist, Amity."

"And so do elves and fairies and little green men!" says Cunning.

Some of the other women laugh.

Malice does not. She finishes her drink, her eyes on me.

I hear their words, and yet my mind still struggles to hold them all in an order that makes sense. "Then . . . did God choose other villages besides Haven to save from The World That Once Was? Or are your homes full of lost wretches, not righteous enough to save but not wicked enough to damn?"

Gall narrows her eyes. "Oh, for the love of . . . Enough with this religious crap. Malice, you said she had promise."

"And she does, or else she would not be here," snaps Temperance, her hands in fists.

Mercy wipes her mouth on her pretty green sleeve. "Be patient with her. She knows nothing, just as we did. They make sure we know nothing."

It is the most kindness Mercy has yet shown me. I glance at her with a small smile, but she looks away, scowling.

"The power never lies, Gall," Malice says quietly.

The rest of the coven, even chastened Gall, answers her: "The power never lies."

For a long moment, everyone is quiet. The silence feels sacred, but my hour is nearly gone. I must be quick.

"You told me that if I learned *extasia*, you would help me save Haven." I look at Malice, hoping I look steadier than I feel. "Well, I learned something of *extasia*, and that brought me here tonight. I think you should do something for me in exchange. Something to protect Haven."

Quiet falls over this little clearing. It seems to me that the white trees circling us draw closer, holding their breath. The witches look to Malice, except for wide-eyed Temperance, who shakes her head at me ever so slightly.

I clear my throat. "Is there perhaps a spell that would build an unseen wall? Or one that hurts those who would hurt others?"

Malice, twirling a lock of black hair around her finger, lets it fall with a delighted smile. "Funny you should ask that, little sister."

She snaps her fingers. Four women rise and hurry off into the shadows.

Temperance leans forward. "Malice, not yet. I do not think she is ready."

"Oh, now, I think she is. She asked for it herself, after all. A spell that hurts those who would hurt others. It's as if she knows. Maybe she does, somehow. *Extasia* works in mysterious ways."

The delight in her voice turns my skin icy cold.

Malice rises, her scarlet gown aglow with red moonlight.

Temperance tries to protest again, but Mercy grabs her hand, whispering fiercely.

"Now comes your true test," says Malice, suddenly near. She takes my arms gently, but when I try to jerk away, she holds me fast. Her breath is hot on my temple. "*Extasia* says your name, and you have some affinity with it. Fine, very well.

But can I *trust* you? Are you strong or weak? Dauntless or gutless? This I have to find out for myself."

Two of the women return, dragging the corpse of a buck. Its chest glints with fresh blood.

Then a hoarse cry sounds from behind me.

I turn around and feel as if all the bones have been sucked out of my body.

The other two women who left the circle are now pulling toward us a naked man with only one eye.

22

HIS BODY IS TOO THIN, his cheeks hollow and his bones close to pushing out of his skin. One of them has, a bone in his left arm. He is covered in blood both fresh and dried, the whole right side of his body scabbed and crusty. Ire and Storm, the two witches carrying him, drag him inside our circle and drop him beside the dead buck.

My blood rushes and roars inside me, and my palms begin to sweat. The man moans, drool dripping from his mouth. All those snapped bones, that broken skin. He hardly looks like a man anymore.

Then I remember that I have lungs and legs and fists, all of them strong and whole here in Avazel, and rise sharply to my feet. What remains of my meal falls forgotten into the mud.

"What happened to him?" I lurch toward him, but Mercy and Temperance grab me.

"Be calm, Amity," Temperance pleads.

"What have you done to him?" I shout, trying to rip free of her. "Let me help him!"

"He calls himself the governor," Malice tells me, pacing around the man. "He sent Furor away from her home and her children, and the only crime she'd committed wasn't a crime at all. She'd told the truth about his cruel fists, you see. That's all. She told the truth about what her husband did."

Furor, her copper hair bound with flowers, stares at me with tense shoulders and a fierce jaw. She looks ready to flatten me if I move wrong even once.

Malice straddles the deer's corpse and takes the knife Gall offers her. "No one ever punished the governor for beating his wife. No one ever does. So it falls on us here in this coven to do it. We've dragged him along with us for quite some time now, but I think tonight is the perfect time to end his story. And just think, little sister—if he were not here with us, if he were far away, even then, he would feel these cuts. He would fall bleeding from his velvet chair, and not a soul would know why. Watch and learn. Feel the air as I work, how it burns and snaps with power."

The man, bruised from head to toe, turns to look at me and parts his cracked lips. He bleats, his mouth too swollen for words. His missing eye is a knot of flesh, and the shaking hand he stretches toward me is quilted with scars, three of his fingers mere leaking stubs.

Malice spits on him. "The power never lies."

"The power never lies!" the coven answers.

"*Zohil*," she cries, "*caelata-rem, oshisa, belevorah!*"

Then Malice drags her blade across the dead buck's shoulder.

The man screams. A red gash opens on his left shoulder, just as there now gleams a red gash on the buck's own. Malice slices her knife down the buck's right shoulder. Another peels open on the man, from his shoulder to his breastbone. It is as though a sinister mirror stands between them, man and beast.

Forming a tight circle around them, the coven repeats Malice's spell. "*Zohil, caelata-rem, oshisa, belevorah!*"

Even Mercy and Temperance say it on either side of me, Mercy spitting the words like sparks from a fire. I pull at the hands holding me back, screaming for Malice to stop.

But her blade moves swift as a darting fish. Howling her spell over and over, she cuts and cuts. She carves four thick lines into the buck's belly. A mass of violet and red and pink organs, glistening and plump, spill out along with a wash of blood.

The man writhes in the dirt, gasping and twitching, for now four jagged lines have cut his torso into quarters. I see his spurting heart and white ribs. Blood bubbles out from his lips, his nose, his ears. Yellow pus leaks from his single eye. His teeth turn black and fall from his mouth.

These are no mere cuts. They bear the wrath of all the chanting witches in this wood.

I scream until my throat hurts. "Please stop, you are killing him!"

"Yes, and with great delight," says Malice, and then, with

one strong swipe of her blade, she opens the deer's throat.

The man's choked cries quickly cease as a red sheet pours down his chest. Soon he is a sodden pile on the forest floor.

In the silence following his death, Avazel seems to hum, as if something monstrous lives within it and the man's blood is sating its appetite.

Malice stands over her kill, red drops scattered across her skin like freckles.

And suddenly I understand. I see the ruin of this man on the ground before me and feel as though I am newly born, opening my eyes for the first time—light, color, sound, touch. Movement.

Heat.

Home.

For a single moment, I wish I were there, hidden in my garden, alone and safe. Petals kissing my skin, dirt cool against my cheek.

Then I tear away from Temperance and Mercy with such force that they fall forward and hit the ground hard. I run at Malice, a vicious cry bursting from my throat.

"Vanuriisa!" Malice hisses, swinging her arm. She does not strike me, but something does, something sharp and hot. It catches me across my chest and sends me flying.

I lie on my back for a moment, gasping for air, then push myself up and snarl at her, tears in my voice, "It was you."

Malice stares at me, eyes wide and face pale. Something has surprised her. I smell smoke, and a strange sweet perfume.

Gall rushes at me, murder in her eyes and a knife in her fist.

"Do not touch her," Malice snaps. "Don't anyone touch her."

"How did she do that?" someone demands. I think it is Storm. "The girl uttered no spell!"

"Everyone be quiet!" Malice roars.

"You, *all* of you!" I push myself to my unsteady feet. "You killed them, didn't you? It is *you* who have been killing the men of Haven!"

"That's what we do, little sister. We travel this land and hurt those who hurt others."

"Jeremiah Heath had hurt no one!"

"Neither did Furor, or Cunning, or Gall, or any of us. And yet our skin is bruised and scarred, and our nightmares hold the terror of what has been done to us."

Malice's voice is a quiet thin line. "They hate us, Amity, and they hate you too, and so does the world they have made. The world then, and the world now. So I feel no remorse for doing what I must to take back a little of the power that has been taken from me, and from my mother before me, and hers before her, and so on and so on, back to the beginning of time."

"You lied to me," I whisper, like some tricked child. "You told me your power was beautiful."

"It is."

"You told me you would help me save my village!"

"No, I told you I would help *you*." Malice smiles. Some of the other witches laugh. "I just didn't say how. And I do still want to help you. I want to help you wake up."

"But you told me there was no Devil here!"

"Ah. Now, that *was* a lie." Malice begins walking slowly toward me. "What, do you think such power simply sprouts up out of the ground? That you can mutter a few words and use it for free? *Extasia* is a gift from the Dark Prince himself. Serve him well, pledge your loyalty, sate his appetites, and you can use his power to your heart's content." Something like pity softens her face. "*Extasia* is not always cruel, Amity. You saw that yourself."

I cannot listen to her any longer. I whirl on Mercy and Temperance. "You knew about this?"

Their faces tell me all I need to know—Mercy's defiant sharp jaw, Temperance's downcast eyes.

I follow her gaze to the ground.

A carpet of flowers spills across the dirt, flowers that were not there moments ago. Blue, white, yellow, pink. Bright green leaves, tender and new. They start where I stood, trapped between Mercy and Temperance, spread across the clearing in a path of brilliant color, and finally stop where I did, when Malice hit me with her power.

Staring at them, bile rises in my throat. I know those flowers. Yellow arnica and tiny pink roses. Daisies bobbing their white heads. Lavender hollyhocks, blue larkspurs, golden irises, cheerful bluebells. Winding green vines with moonflowers opening their white mouths against my legs.

I have grown these flowers. Some bloom even now in my

garden at home. Others will show themselves later, as the weather warms.

I scramble away, uprooting the blossoms nearest me. "What is this? What have you done?"

"What have *you* done, is the question," says Malice quietly.

"No. *No*."

"Wake up, little sister. You've been asleep for too long. Listen to what I say, and listen well."

I clap my hands over my ears. Some distant voice in my head tells me to do as she says and listen, that this is what I wanted—to find the Devil. And now, here he is.

But I ignore that voice. It sickens me. All I can think of is the body of Jeremiah Heath, and Tom Wickens, and Clarence Woodworth, and Benjamin Aldridge, and the seven others who died. The wives and children and parents in mourning. Samuel's frightened question in the meadow: *What if I am next?*

"I am not one of you," I rasp out. "I am no sister of yours, no Devil's daughter."

Laughter spills across the circle. Ire's bird caws and flaps its wings.

"Believe what you will," Malice says, "but I see the truth clear as day. No girl of God can conjure flowers from the earth. No girl of God can call upon *extasia* without even a single spell word on her lips." Malice comes close, takes my chin hard in her hot bloodied hand. Never have I seen so many teeth in a smile. "I smell the mark of the Devil on you, Amity.

Extasia has spoken and spoken true. He has chosen you for his own, same as he did me."

Frantic, I try to twist out of her grip.

She flings me free, her face smooth and hard. "I know you stole my book, Amity. It called to you, didn't it?"

I sob, too furious to say anything but, "No, no, *no* . . ."

"And why would a witch's book, full of witches' names and witches' spells, call to a girl of God? Wake up, little sister, or else this power he's given you will grow and grow until you shatter. You can't do this alone. You need us. You need *him*, and so do we."

I turn and run, crashing through the unholy flowers I made and into the trees beyond.

"Let her go!" Malice calls out. "Let them talk to her."

Someone chases after me, their footsteps light and swift.

But mine are faster, and with each one comes a word, an awful new prayer writing itself in my mind.

Book. Mirror. Belt. Knife. Key.

Daisy. Hollyhock. Larkspur. Bluebell. Rose.

Jeremiah. Tom. Clarence. Benjamin. The dead man with only one eye.

23

WHICH OF THEM HITS ME, I do not know. One moment I am running, and the next I am lying on the ground, my face mashed into the dirt and my shoulders tingling as if struck.

I recognize the feeling of the nubby root under my hand. Its sour, bitter scent stings my nostrils. I tear away a piece of it, push myself to my feet, and spin around.

Mercy catches my left arm, Temperance my right.

"Let go of me!" I scream, twisting hard, but *extasia* must be aiding them. Their hands are like iron.

I fall silent and glare.

"Are you quite finished?" Mercy snaps.

"You have been letting them kill our people," I say, my voice deadly soft. I pin Temperance with my eyes. "Why?"

"Because they deserved it."

"Mercy, hush!" Temperance lets out a sharp sigh. "I know it seems terrible, Amity—"

"It is more than terrible. It is *evil*. You have been aiding servants of the Devil! You have been helping them kill our people!"

"And *our people*," says Mercy, "have been hurting us for years. And before us, others."

I stare at her. "What are you talking about?"

"The visitations? The saintly trials? The vile things confessed to me in the House of Whispers?" Mercy's eyes narrow. "What they did to your mother?"

If my arms were not trapped, I would strike her flat. "Do not dare speak of my mother."

"You asked me a question. I answered."

"Jeremiah Heath, all of thirteen years old? And Benjamin Aldridge, who had never in his life spoken ill of anyone? *They* deserved death?"

"Jeremiah Heath was a mistake," Temperance says quietly, "and I was furious with Malice for it. We both were."

"But Benjamin Aldridge sought me out every visitation," says Mercy, "and every time he found me, he struck me so hard I bled. One blow was all he needed. He was that strong. It was a game. He always rushed for me. He wanted to be the first. He hit me, and then he laughed."

I think back to the visitations I attended, looking for a memory of Benjamin striking Mercy in such a way, but I cannot find one. 'Tis true that Benjamin was strong, but I cannot imagine him reveling in someone else's pain. Dutiful, yes, but not malicious, not brutal. Other men delight in the violence of visitation. Not the Aldridge boys.

"He struck you, just as he was supposed to," I say, though the words sound suddenly feeble, which makes me so angry it hurts, a sharp pinch in my chest. "Everyone is supposed to visit their sins upon the saints."

"And does that not seem unfair to you?" Mercy snaps.

Her words remind me of my own bitter thoughts after visitation, how I cursed Tom Wickens's name. "It is in the Sanctificat!" I say harshly. "It is God's command!"

"Please, quiet your shouting," Temperance says, looking over her shoulder. "We do not want to draw the others near, not until we have spoken among ourselves."

"And you." I glare at my old friend. "You also think those men deserved to die?"

She looks at me with the wide, frightened eyes of someone lost in the dark. "I do not know."

"Yes, you do," Mercy says, clearly surprised. "You told them about Tom Wickens and what he did to Amity at visitation. You wanted him to die, and he did."

Temperance looks between us helplessly. "You do not understand, Amity. My bleeding has begun, and I must hide it from my father and brothers, from the elders. They do not look so hard at my bedsheets when there are men dying all around them." She shakes me a little, desperate. "I cannot marry

Elias. I do not love him, nor do I want to bear his children!"

So it was all true, what I saw and heard in the elm grove. How impossible it seems that Temperance and I loved each other once, that I ever allowed her to drag her fingers through the dirt of my garden.

"Tom Wickens did as he ought to have done," I say slowly, very low, reminding myself as well as them. "They all did. How dare you ask for him to be killed in my name. How dare you trespass against God's word and hide the fact of your blood."

Temperance blinks, her tears spilling over. "I did not want violence, even as afraid as I am. I simply wanted to run away, Amity, I swear it. I asked Malice to leave; I begged her to take Mercy and me with her. We could not survive in the wild on our own. But she will not do it. She needs sixteen men, she says, before the Devil will come, and she has worked too long and too hard to stop now, not until it is finished—"

Mercy releases me and tugs hard on Temperance's arm. "Quiet!"

"Sixteen men?" I edge closer to them, my thoughts racing. "Sixteen men to summon the Devil? Some sort of ritual, then. And with Tom Wickens dead, now Malice has killed eleven and needs only five more. Is that the way of it? Or does the one-eyed man count among her dead?"

Temperance rubs her wet cheeks. "No. Malice says the men must all be of the same village. It makes for more powerful grief and fear, she says, and this pleases *extasia*."

"Temperance, be quiet," Mercy says harshly.

"The coven has traveled far and tried many rituals. Nine men, three men. Bleeding spells, crushing spells. Nothing has worked. The Devil remains hidden. But now—"

"*Temperance,*" Mercy hisses.

"No, I will not be quiet! She ought to know. Haven is her home, same as ours."

"And what will Malice do, if she does indeed summon the Devil this time?" I ask.

Mercy and Temperance glance at each other. Even Mercy now looks uneasy.

"We do not know," Temperance says. "She will not tell us."

"I see." Then I take a breath, shove the nub of bloodroot into my mouth, bite into it, and gulp it down. I have not written a spell for this, but nor did I for those flowers, and yet there they were, spilling freely out of the earth.

Take me home, extasia, I pray, and hope to God it works.

Temperance cries out, and Mercy grabs for me, but I am already gone.

Darkness rushes past me. Heat scorches my throat and races down my legs. My skin prickles as if stuck with a thousand needles, and my body bucks.

Then I stumble forward onto new ground that rises up out of nothing and open my eyes.

I am in the true woods near Haven, at the edge of the trees, where the meadow's grasses thin. In the distance stands our village's dark wall, and I am so relieved that my lungs crack open and a great sob bursts free.

Something plows through the brush behind me. I whirl to see Temperance running out of the gloom. Our fine Avazel clothes are gone. We wear our white nightgowns, our cloaks and boots, our bruises and our saintly marks.

"Amity!" cries Temperance. "Wait, stop!"

I run. I have never run so fast in my life, and if it is the Devil's power that gives me this strength, well, then, for these next few moments, I will embrace it.

Malice said this thing awakening inside me would frighten me, that *extasia* would consume me if I did not learn it proper, but nothing has ever frightened me so much as the hard set of her face when she opened that man's throat.

Panting, my side aching, I run without a thought in my head except for *home, Father, help.*

A sharp heat stings the back of my left thigh. My legs buckle; I fall hard to my hands and knees. I look back to see Temperance cradling a small flame in her hands. Despite everything, a thrill of awe washes over me. Temperance has summoned *fire.*

The second sacrament of darkness.

But I am too wild with fear to stop and think about sacraments and relics. I want to be at home. I want my garden, my father, my sister, my Samuel.

I push myself up and run.

"Amity, wait!" Temperance cries. "Stop! *Please!*"

Her fire hits the back of my arm, then my left shoulder, but still I run, pushing my legs as fast as they will go.

The wall is near, the watchmen's torches burning bright. Temperance and I race through the tall grasses, the bobbing blue catmint, the pale pink milkweed, the yellow coneflowers. I cannot turn, I will not turn. If I do, if her eyes find me, she will ensnare me in some witchery, she will drag me back to Malice, and they will make me write a spell that will kill a man with flowers.

Then Temperance screams, and I turn back without thinking.

Two watchmen in the tall dark grass. One has tackled Temperance to the ground. The other stands with his gun at the ready. They must have been patrolling the meadow, looking for some villain come to kill another man, and Temperance's fire brought them straight to her. She struggles to rise, but one of the watchmen punches her back down, and she bleats a pained cry.

I stumble back, blinking hard, breathing hard. This is a dream, and soon I will wake. Please, God, please let it be a nightmare. Tonight, this week, this entire winter past.

But then I knock into something tall and hard, and when I turn around with a frightened shout, I find my father standing there with his long coat and gun, Samuel and three other watchmen standing behind him.

I grab on to Father, hide my tears in his chest, but he says nothing, he does nothing. When I look up at him, I turn cold, for there on his face is the same fury he wore during those long weeks before my mother was run out of Haven. All that anger, now pointed straight at me.

"What have you done?" he whispers.

I do not know what to say. Horror sits heavy on my tongue. I glance once at Samuel, who looks as though he might faint with fear. "Father . . ." I whisper.

He shakes me a little, his face twisting. No love there, only fury. "What have you *done*, Amity?"

And then I hear Temperance somewhere behind me in the dark, laughing a horrible wheezing laugh.

"No, no, no," she says, quietly, "no, no, Elder Thomas. No, it is me you want. Not her."

We all turn to face her. She stands tall, her arms held behind her by a grim-faced watchman—Zacharias Rutledge. He is a young man, and handsome, just old enough for his post, and he shakes Temperance to shut her up, but she will not do it. Blood runs down her face from where they have hit her, and she is sobbing and laughing too, her body seized with some unholy madness come straight from Avazel. She looks nothing like the friend I have known.

"I am the one who has seen him," she says. "I tricked your daughter from her bed."

My father steps in front of me. "Him?"

Everything grows still. The songs of the meadow bugs drop to silence.

Temperance smiles behind the bloody streaks of her hair.

Something changes then. The air grows hot and snaps, as if it holds an unseen fire.

❖❃ 173 ❃❖

Already, I know that feeling.

Extasia.

Temperance mutters something too quiet for me to hear. Lilting words. Sing-speak.

There is not time for me to even shout a warning before Zacharias Rutledge begins to scream.

He releases Temperance and staggers back from her, slapping his legs, his belly, his arms. First slapping, then clawing, his screams turning wild, for a great wave of darkness is rushing up his body. At first I do not understand what it is, but then the other watchman standing near him cries out and hurries off, his gun forgotten, and then I see. I see, and the ground falls out from under my feet. I see, and my skin turns to ice.

Up Zacharias Rutledge's body crawl hundreds and hundreds of creatures—spiders and snakes, beetles and worms. They wriggle, they bite, they scurry. They crawl under his clothes and they swarm over his face and into his mouth and they burrow under his skin. He chokes and gags. He falls to the ground, and soon I cannot see him, not his skin or his clothes, for he is covered in these creatures, he is filled with them.

And beside him stands serene Temperance, white-eyed, wearing a lamb-sweet smile.

She has a way with animals, Malice said.

My father shoves me behind him, quick as lightning. Samuel catches me with his warm strong hands.

Then Father raises his rifle and fires.

Temperance falls.

The creatures scatter, but it is too late. Zacharias Rutledge lies swollen and twitching and dead in the dirt.

The other watchmen rush forward, their own guns raised.

"No," says my father, and they stop at once. He towers over Temperance's body. She moans, clutching her side. "Do nothing else to hurt her."

Then he turns to look back at me, and I shiver, my body stiff and cold even with Samuel so near.

"When she burns," says my father, "she will be alive to feel it."

AND SO THEY DID. THEY burned her, with all of Haven gathered around to watch. But I do not like to think of it.

The elders' seconds tied the ruined body of Zacharias Rutledge to a table inside the House of Woe, then tied Temperance's body tight atop him. This was so she would be forced to breathe in the stink of the man she'd killed while the flames grew and grew and grew around her.

Samuel was one of those who helped tie her down. He threw me a wretched look afterward. He knew she had once been dear to me, and he had never before been made to put a living body in the House of Woe. Maybe if I had not run from Avazel, Temperance would not have run after me, and Samuel would not have had to bind her wrists, and she would not have died.

Somehow, Mercy snuck home to her bed without being seen. The elders and their seconds went to fetch her, and Silence too, and then tied all three of us to great wooden poles thrust into the soil near the House of Woe. Temperance's brave lie saved me from the fire. Father believed her, and me, but I still was made to watch and listen. She was quiet when they tied her down. She was quiet until the flames caught her, and then she screamed, and I heard quite clearly how fast her screams turned from girl to animal.

But I do not like to think of it.

Four gray women flew through the smoke while she burned, their mouths black and gaping. They circled the House of Woe, long thin arms dragging on the ground like plows. They screamed as Temperance screamed. So desperate was I to cover my ears that I scratched my fingers bloody on my wooden post.

"Hello, there," whispered Silence beside me. A bruise on her cheek, her damp flaxen hair clinging to her jaw. She trembled, watching her gray storytellers fly. Frightened or glad or maybe simply tired—I could not read her voice.

I wondered if Mercy could see them too, but I did not dare look at her, too afraid of what I would find on her face.

I crouch in my garden the next day, listening to the hammer-and-nail sounds of the House of Woe being rebuilt atop Temperance's ashes. Above, the clear sky is as blue as the new House of Woe will be.

Surrounded by green, I think of the fire cradled in Temperance's hand as she ran after me. She wished to stop me, or protect me, or protect herself and Mercy and Malice, or drag me back screaming to Avazel, or all of those things. Awful sounds I am afraid to let loose sit like knives in my throat. The stolen book lies open by my toes, and I stare at it until my eyes fill with tears.

When Temperance first began practicing her fire spell, did she ever think she might be crafting the very thing that would kill her?

As we scratched out letters in the dirt together all those years ago, did Temperance ever fear me? Even for a moment, even for a single breath?

It seems that she should have.

That evening, Blessing finds me in the garden and sits quietly beside me as I hunch over the book like a beast over its kill. She holds her knees to her chest. I wish she would not. She looks too small that way, too young and fragile. It frightens me.

"Did you sleep at all last night?" she asks me.

That question does not deserve an answer.

She tries again. "Supper is almost ready. Father is washing up."

"Thank you. I will come soon."

Moving closer, Blessing peers at the book. I can hear the little frown in her voice. "Maybe you should put that away for a time. You need rest."

I fix her with a burning glare. "I cannot rest. Did you not

understand what I told you? She needs only five more dead men to finish her ritual. Four, if Zacharias Rutledge can be counted. If I do not work faster than her, if I cannot stop her, more people will die!"

"I understand," Blessing says quietly. She has gone pale, her mouth thin with fear, but her hand on mine is as warm and soft as ever. "How can I help?"

The gentleness is too much to bear. Fool that I am, I do not deserve it. I look away, my eyes burning. "I simply need to work. Any moment, the coven could come for me and punish me for Temperance's death."

"But Malice told you *extasia* has been telling her your name," Blessing says after a moment, so used to the strange word now that she no longer stumbles over it. "Would she not spare you, if only for that reason?"

"Maybe," I mutter. "I must hope so."

Blessing says nothing else, rubbing gentle circles on my back. The feeling unties some of the horrible hot knots in my shoulders.

"I need to see Samuel," I say quietly. "I need help reading this book. I need to learn how to summon fire."

Malice thinks she needs sixteen dead men to find the Devil.

But I need only four more relics.

After supper, Samuel walks me to Elder Peter's house for my evening caretaking. I must bite my tongue to keep silent about the book.

Tonight, for the first time this spring, Elder Joseph is sitting outside his house, his bad leg resting on a stool. Despite his leg, he sits with sprawling ease, as if daring the Devil to come for him. I stumble a little. All these years and months, and still the image of his naked body pinning my mother's naked body to my father's bed is as vivid as it ever was. A nightmare that will not rest.

As we walk by, his eyes follow us, hawk-like. I swallow hard, my mouth full of an awful moldy flavor. His daughter Rachel blows on her thin little flute at his feet, but when we near, she stops playing. She stands and backs away toward their front door. Her face darkens with hatred.

And Elder Joseph—well, he grabs his cane and follows us all the way to Elder Peter's gate. Whistling cheerfully to himself, as if he is merely out for an idle walk. Each time his cane thumps the dirt road, my stomach jumps.

"He is protecting us," Samuel says quietly, as if to comfort me, and then turns to wave at Elder Joseph in greeting.

"He is *watching* us," I say through gritted teeth.

'Tis a violent relief to step inside Elder Peter's house. I look out the window, my knees weak. Samuel meets Elder Joseph on the road, hands in his pockets. They begin slowly walking away, talking pleasantly as if it is any other day, as if Temperance has not only just died, as if Elder Joseph was never, not once, in my parents' bed.

I close the door and sag against it, squeezing my eyes shut against sudden fierce tears.

Elder Peter hobbles in from the next room, sees my face, and draws me into his arms. The embrace is so welcome and dear that I let out a shuddering gasp.

"When will it end?" I whisper. "When will Haven be safe again?" One of many questions storming inside me, but the only one safe to say aloud.

Elder Peter pulls back to look at me, his withered hands trembling against my shoulders.

"I ask God that question every night, child," he says, "and I have not yet heard an answer."

I wish he had said nothing at all, for there it is again: that lostness on his face, that terrible, terrible sadness.

Temperance looked that way too, in Avazel, when I asked her if she thought the men of Haven deserved to die.

Lost. Shrinking. Like a trapped rabbit, helpless and afraid.

The next evening, Samuel and I take a longer path to Elder Peter, one that keeps us far from Elder Joseph's house. The road grows still as we pass. Stern faces peer out of windows, doors close quietly. Despite my father's assurances, they must wonder if Temperance can be believed. Did she truly steal me away that night? Or did I go well and willing?

John Ames, finishing repairs to his sheep pen, straightens to watch us. He has pitied my family through everything. He comforted me during visitation, lets Blessing help with his lambs. He says little but smiles easily.

Not tonight. Tonight he watches Samuel and me with a

frown, his hammer held in a tight fist.

Sarah Abbott hurries her three children inside before we reach her house. And there is Tabitha Grainger, and Willow Dale, both staring out of their windows, and there is Jacob Farthing, and beside him his betrothed, Dorothy Prower, coming in from the fields for supper. Jacob tells her to hurry up. When she does not walk fast enough for him, he yanks her behind a tree, and there comes a thud, a muted cry, and then nothing.

Nothing, truly. Tabitha Grainger closes her curtains and does nothing, and I do nothing, and Samuel does nothing, though his jaw is tenser now. Once, someone would have stopped Jacob, I think. Saints are for beating, and saints alone.

But now we are all thinking the same thing, I know it: maybe, if the daughters of those long-ago women who ruined the world are beaten hard enough—not only the saints, but every sister, mother, aunt, niece—then God will be pleased and start protecting Haven once again.

Maybe if Jacob Farthing saw me coming at him with a fist full of summoned flames, he would leave Dorothy Prower alone.

Quickly, I banish that thought from my mind. I unclench my hands. We keep walking.

Elias Holt, who was betrothed to Temperance, walks onto his father's porch and watches us approach, fists balled and eyes red from crying. I hold my breath as we pass him, as Samuel nods a greeting. Elias is so still I think we are safe, but then he rushes out onto the road and comes around to stand before us.

We stop at once. "Good evening, Elias," Samuel says quietly.

At first Elias says nothing, ignoring Samuel. Instead, he glares at me, his face cold with fury. I should cast my gaze to the ground, make myself small, but I am fixed to this moment and its danger, the lines of my body flushed and tense. In my mind, I begin reciting the summoning spell that called the white-eyed hare to me, with one word changed. This time, I do not seek Avazel. No, I need something to drive Elias away from us. I need protection from that hard light in his eyes.

Samdech, unseen, *malyodam*, *grahala*, beast, defend, *malyatzaf*.

Will it work if I do not utter the words aloud? I have to believe it will. I summoned flowers in Avazel without a word. Today I will summon a beast.

Then Elias says, his narrowed eyes still fixed on my face, "Careful, Samuel. The Devil lives in that one, same as her mother. Everyone knows it, even if they are too afraid of her father to say it aloud." Elias looks up and down the road, noticing the people watching from their homes.

An ill feeling crawls over me, like tiny hot-cold feet that leave clammy tracks behind. The feeling says, *Hide, girl*, but if I ran now, Elias would follow me. Instead, I silently repeat my spell, lowering my eyes to his boots. I must appear contrite.

Then Elias shouts for all to hear, "I know what you really think of the Barrow family! I know you see the truth of what they are, just as I do! But you are all too cowardly to speak up."

He turns back to us, then mutters, "Look at me."

I hesitate, hating the sound of his voice. A mistake. He grabs my face, forces it upward.

"Look at me!" he shouts, tears trembling in his eyes.

Samuel spits angry words I cannot quite hear, for my head is hot and roaring, anger I have never felt rushing like fire under my skin, anger that makes it difficult to breathe. Samuel moves quickly in front of me, but Elias pushes him away. "How is it fair that your betrothed still lives and breathes while mine is dead?" he whispers. I know that anger in his voice, that grief. Since Temperance's death, I have felt it too.

Samdech, unseen, *malyodam*, *grahala*, beast, defend, *malyatzaf*.

Again and again, I hurry through the words, pressing my tongue hard against my teeth. I might be a fool to do this, but now that I have started, I cannot stop. Will it work? I must know. I *ache* to know. This fire rising up my spine—where will it go? What will it find?

"I hope she ruins you," Elias says, stepping closer to us, "same as she did Temperance, same as her mother did Elder Joseph. I know it will happen." On his face curls a tiny cruel smile. "She may look like her father, but do not be deceived. She is her mother's daughter, and the Devil likes whores best of all."

Samuel lunges at Elias, but Elias is faster, taller, stronger. He shoves Samuel hard to the ground. I stumble away, Elias stalking after me. Samuel springs up, yanks Elias back by his shirt, swings his fist to punch him. It lands on Elias's jaw, but not squarely. He grabs Samuel's collar, roars in anger, readies his own fist—and then, down out of the sky swoops a bat, then another, and three more. Five white-eyed bats, fangs as long as my thumbnail, wings as long as my forearm.

Shrieking, they swarm around Elias, then around Samuel and me. The boys shout and scurry away, batting at their hair and clothes. I do the same, screaming in fear though my whole body blazes with triumph. My spell called out, and the coven answered. Perhaps they are not angry with me after all, or else the power compels them to help me even so. I wonder: Is it Ire alone flying inside these bats, or is someone helping her?

Samuel holds his arm around me as we hurry down the road. From behind us comes the flap of bat wings and the frightened cries of everyone who stood there watching, waiting for Elias to strike me. Some of them praying for it, I would guess.

When we turn the corner, Samuel says, panting, "Was that you? Did you summon them?"

"No," I lie. He looks too frightened and pale for the truth. "The coven must have been watching us and decided to help."

I hope I am right. I hope my screams sounded real to all my watching, wary neighbors. Perhaps I was a fool to be so bold. That shake in my voice, the quake in my belly as we run, the hot howl of blood in my ears—I name it fear, shame, regret. But I know even as I think the words that they are wicked lies.

⚚ ⚚ ⚚

I stare at my fingers and try again.

"*Babacael,*" I murmur, and rub my thumb against my middle finger—a gentle, quick snap, only a slight brush of sound—and as I do this, I think of fire. Not the hungry inferno that devoured Temperance, but something smaller, tidier. In my mind, I see the little palmful of flame she held as she chased me.

Nothing.

I try once more, insistent. "*Babacael.*"

Blessing watches, kneeling by the door. If Father stirs, she will know.

Shadow, hiding under Blessing's bed, growls and hisses each time I try a spell word. Infernal cat. I will put her outside if she grumbles any louder.

I sigh and mark a line through *babacael* on the list Samuel wrote for me. Today in the House of Whispers, during his weekly confession, he hurried through the book's pages, found each instance of the word *fire*, and scratched out for me every nearby spell word in a tidy, ordered list. The quickness of his pencil left me reeling. I watched each stroke with a hunger that did not abate with my supper.

He also found a bit of writing in the book that surprised me:

The fewer words one uses to call upon extasia, *the more powerful will be the answer.*

So I try again, and again, each time with a different word, or two words, or three. Three saints left alive, three words to

⚚ 186 ⚚

make fire. Any more than that feels wrong to me now. I used seven words to summon that hare, and Malice used five words to kill the one-eyed man.

But I did summon those flowers, those bats, with no spoken words at all, and *extasia* has been whispering my name in Malice's ear, maybe to mock her. *This girl*, it might say, *is more powerful than even you.*

I smile a little, let out a soft short laugh.

At the door, Blessing shifts. She has been there for hours, and yet she is still wide awake and patient, uncomplaining. Love swells in me so fiercely that my eyes burn, and when I look back to my book, rubbing my face with my fist, my gaze falls at once upon two of Samuel's words. They are words I have not yet tried, not as a pair.

Malagsat. Malagzaala.

The sight of them fills me with rightness, as if I have looked down upon Haven from a bird's height and finally spotted my own house. Ah, there it is. My roof, my garden, my gate.

I draw in a shaky breath, clench my fingers around the sweaty petals in my palm. Power of the Devil it may be, but I need it.

Extasia, I think. *Hear me.*

Shadow growls the loudest yet, her eyes round and yellow in the dark.

"Shadow!" hisses Blessing. "Stop it!"

"*Malagsat*," I whisper. "*Malagzaala.*"

I snap my fingers as Temperance did, and that little hot

brush of skin on skin sparks, at last, a tiny white flame.

Blessing gasps, but I hardly hear her. As I watch the fire—*my* fire—dance above my fingertips, a great bloom of warmth unfurls in my chest, and for the first time in what feels like an endless age, I smile.

25

THIS HOUSE OF WOE MAY be fresh and new, its wood only just cut and sanded, but I can still smell the fire that killed Temperance three nights past. As I step inside, into the cool still dark, I swallow a smoky tang that makes me want to scrape my tongue raw.

There is the new wooden table upon which the dead are placed. Or the living, in the case of Temperance. The bleeding and barely alive, only enough to feel the fire.

Such agony is too immense for me to imagine. Hearing the elders speak of Hellfire is one thing; this is quite another. Tears fill my eyes as I look at this windowless dark room, the table, the dirt floor scattered with the twigs and brush I brought in from the meadow. This is where Temperance spent her last living moments.

"I am sorry," I whisper. An odd thing to say, and I know it.

She killed people, or else stood by while others did the killing, and tried to tell me it was good and right.

But I cannot judge or ignore any feeling that comes to me this night. *Extasia* does not like to be lied to. So the witches said, and though they themselves are liars, I think this, at least, is true. The Devil lies, but he is prideful and would not enjoy being fooled.

So I kneel for a moment with my hand flat against the dirt and let my grief rise as it will.

"I am sorry, my friend," I say again. "I did not know this would happen."

In the dirt, I write the letters, my fingers not so clumsy as they once were.

S

O

R

R

E

E

"Hurry up, Amity!" Samuel whispers from outside. He hides just beyond the single narrow door.

I breathe in and out slowly until my tears have dried. He is right. I must hurry. Every four days, in the middle of the night, Samuel works a watchman shift by the second wall, the barrier of wire and wood that snakes through the meadow. This half hour is his time to rest, eat, drink, relieve himself, help his friend sneak through the dark. In half an hour, at three o'clock, if he is not back at his post, someone will think the worst. They will run for the elders and ring the bells, and when they find him, he will have to craft a believable lie, and dear gentle Samuel is a terrible liar.

Kneeling in the dirt, I push my left hand into my pocket and clutch the petals I brought from my garden. Soft and sweet and familiar, they calm my hammering heart.

I raise my right hand, ready to snap.

What does it mean, if a girl uses the Devil's power to hunt the Devil? Is she then damned herself, no matter how noble her reason?

I shake my head, bite my lip. *Think, Amity. Keep your mind sharp and clear. You do not have time to fret or doubt.*

Look at that table, built upon Temperance's ashes.

Imagine how afraid she was, what her final thought might have been before the fire caught her.

My head roars, a buzzing hive. Something rises inside me, and rises, and rises on a thousand-thousand angry wings.

"*Malagsat,*" I whisper harshly, crushing my petals. "*Malagzaala.*"

Then I snap my fingers.

A flame erupts at the tip of my thumb. Tiny and proud and bright brilliant white.

No time to think. I coax the flame into my palm, then hurl it at the wall.

It catches at once and spreads fast, faster than I thought it would. *Extasia*, it would seem, is eager tonight. Good. So am

I. Hungry flames spill across the floor, leap for the rafters.

Soon I am surrounded. Coughing into my sleeve, my eyes watering, the air already too hot to bear, I fumble around on the floor, careful of any stray flames. Past their roar, I can hear Samuel yelling in the distance—not for me, for that would give me away, but for his fellow watchmen. He is simply a good dutiful boy who spotted flames in the House of Woe.

Everything inside me—blood, bones, guts—screams at me to leave, run, save myself. The House will soon fall. My flames are hard workers. Tireless.

But I cannot leave until I find it. The second sacrament of darkness is fire, and it will give me what I want.

I crawl with one arm, hide my face with the other. I claw through the dirt, digging frantically. The roof buckles, then collapses. With a sharp cry, I scramble under the table. Falling embers catch my feet. I shake them off, bite down hard on my tongue.

The fire's heat makes everything shimmer—the walls, the table, the floor. Smoke chokes me, burning my throat, and in that blackness before me, I see a face that is not a face. A gaping mouth with a silver glint deep inside it. Long body, long arms, long fingers clawing at the dirt, but the dirt does not move, for the gray woman's digging hands are not flesh and blood. They are smoke, or storm clouds, or the foul breath of the Devil.

I have no choice but to trust this awful creature.

I lurch out from under the table, tear at the dirt where the gray woman just was. Mud wedges under my nails, smoke burns my throat, and then my fingers hit something hard and hot. I grab it, wrench it free.

A small round mirror, scorching hot, gleams in my filthy hand. Unlike Father's mirror, this one boasts an ornate silver frame of flowers and vines.

Book. Mirror. Belt. Knife. Key.

Skin. Fire. Bone. Blood. Palm.

I laugh through my coughs, tears streaming down my cheeks. I did it. *I did it.*

A shrieking howl rises just beside my ear. I jerk away from the sound and fall back to see the gray woman looming over me, tossing her head like a panicked horse.

Her howl tells me plainer than any word could: *go.*

I stagger to my feet and stumble through the smoke toward the door. Once outside, I gulp down great blessed mouthfuls of air. But I cannot stop and rest, or someone might spot me. I pray desperately that they have not already and run along the path Samuel showed me, down a little hill and through a wet ravine where the grasses grow high.

Shouts of watchmen come from behind me. I come out of the ravine and see a dozen of them running toward the House of Woe, a blazing beacon in the dark meadow. My flames have completely consumed it, and my poor aching chest, burning from the smoke, swells with a pride I do not even try to diminish. I know I will remember the sight of my fire for as long as God sees fit to let me live.

I spoke to *extasia*.

And *extasia* answered with glad fury.

With the bells ringing and everyone out of their houses to see the fire, I am easily able to sneak home. Blessing sees me coming through the garden and climbs out the window, a pail of water at the ready.

"Has he gone?" I whisper.

"He left as soon as the bells began," she tells me. "I ran out, asking him what it meant. I told him we were frightened—had another man died? He told me to stay here, that we should lock the doors. He does not know you were gone."

She glances at my hand, which clutches the mirror. Her eyes light up with awe. "You did it. It worked."

I nod, hiding my smile. I know how much she has worried, and how much Samuel will until he knows I survived the fire.

But there is no time to comfort her. In the night air, I strip off my ruined dress, bury it in the thickest corner of my garden. Shivering, my teeth chattering, I clean my face with a damp rag while Blessing soaps and scrubs my body, wets and combs my hair.

We work in brisk, busy silence. Then, as Blessing hides the bucket and kicks dry dirt over the fresh patches of mud, I gulp down water to quench my burning throat, tuck the mirror into the tiny cloth sack where I keep the book, shove the sack into the small hole in the wall I have cut behind the baseboard, fit the board back into place, drag my bedside table back in front of it. Climb into bed. Tremble.

Blessing shoves open the window to let in fresh air. Shadow, annoyed by all our bustling, yowls and jumps out.

My sister bends over me, seizes me in a quick, tight embrace, then hurries out into the hallway. She will keep watch by the front window and see Father the moment he turns the corner down the road. I wonder if, when he steps into our house tonight, he will know what I have done. I wonder if he will smell the echo of *extasia* on his pillows.

Alone, I lie in the dark, trying to calm my breathing. I cannot stop thinking of the gray woman howling at me to run. She meant to help me, it seems. But to what end? And who is she? *What* is she? How many of her kind are there, and who is able to see them? Malice did not, that day in Avazel. Or was it that she simply did not look quickly enough?

So much else has been happening that I have not allowed these strange creatures very far into my thoughts. But they are important. That I must accept. I need to know more about them, and there is only one person I know for certain can help me.

First, though, I will visit Avazel.

Malice is on the hunt, after all. Well, so am I. And I think I know a way to slow her down.

26

When I enter Avazel the next night, the entire coven is waiting for me near their circle of stone huts, each thatched roof adorned with flowers that seem far too cheery for this tense, angry silence.

The white-eyed fox I summoned to lead me here jumps into Ire's arms, its patchy gray coat now lush and red.

"You've got some nerve, showing your face here," Ire says, "and summoning my beasts as you please. You're lucky I haven't send some wolf to rip out your throat."

I push down the fear churning in my belly. "Thank you for sending the bats. They were most helpful."

Ire hisses out a furious breath and says nothing.

Cunning, arms crossed over her chest, glares at me. "I thought you'd be smart enough to stay away."

"Or *run* away," mutters Furor, her sky-blue gown swishing around her ankles as she paces.

Liberty fiddles with the sleeves of her violet tunic, its hem stitched with tiny white flowers. "Amity didn't kill Temperance."

Gall holds a knife in her fist, its blade half hidden in the skirt of her sage-green gown. "She might as well have!" she snarls.

"Her death was the fault of her elders," Liberty insists.

I knew they would be angry, and yet it is still difficult to find my voice. Malice and Mercy stand a little apart from the others, saying nothing. Mercy's shoulders are rigid, her hands in fists. I am still too afraid to meet her eyes.

"Please, I understand your anger," I say quickly, "and I feel it too—"

The air around me suddenly snaps as if set afire. The next moment, someone slams into my side and shoves me to the ground. All the air struck out of me, I look up in a daze and see that Mercy was the one who knocked me out of the fire's path. Past her races a knot of flame. It arcs into the trees and disappears in a burst of sparks. I cannot say for certain who threw it at me—their faces are all made of stone—but I see Malice's fingers rubbing against one another and wonder, a little chill prickling my neck.

Mercy holds out her hand to help me up, her green eyes bright with tears. "We are not friends," she tells me, but then she turns to the others and says more fiercely, "but Amity is not our enemy. We insult Temperance's memory by turning on our own. If anyone here should attack Amity, it should be me, and I am not, and I *will* not." She meets the glaring eyes of each witch. "Do not do that again."

Something softens then in the air around us. Cunning lowers her gaze. Ire frowns thoughtfully at the fox in her arms, stroking its chin.

I squeeze Mercy's hand in thanks. She rips it away from me.

"All valid points," Malice says in a clear, firm voice, striding forward, "but none of them matter. *Extasia* has whispered the name *Amity* to me for months, as you all know. I believe she's meant to help us join the Devil at last. Was Temperance's death part of this?" Malice shrugs. "Perhaps. But the power wants Amity. I haven't ever defied it, and I certainly won't start now. If Amity wants to be here, then here she shall be."

Malice turns to me, a little smile on her lips. "So. Why *have* you come here tonight, Amity? Do tell us."

In her voice, my name sounds like an ugly mockery. I bite down on my tongue to squash my indignation and take a step toward the coven.

"I wanted to tell all of you that I am sorry Temperance is gone," I say, a little unsteadily. My calm teeters on a knife's edge. "We were friends once. I grieve her death. I did not want her killed. I was . . . I was angry, that night I fled, and afraid. I had been lied to, if not with spoken words, then with unspoken ones."

I fix Malice with a hard look. "I had only just learned that you had killed people in my village. How was I to know you would not kill me next? Is it so surprising that I condemned your actions and ran from you?"

Malice shrugs. "Surprising? No. Disappointing, though."

Gall laughs quietly. "I expected no better."

"Careful, Gall. It is unwise to scorn the power's choice."

Abashed, Gall glares at her feet.

"And unwise to ignore its warning," says Storm, the fleshy fingers of her left hand drumming against her metal arm. "How do we know it wants her here, Malice? Maybe it wants us to keep her away."

The moment is slipping fast from me. I step forward again, lift my chin. "I am not used to watching people be killed. This is true. What you did to that man, however deserved, rattled me. I admit that, though it shames me. But hear this: if *extasia* did not want me here, I think it would also deny me its power. Would you not agree?"

Then I lift my right hand, whisper, "*Malagsat, malagzaala*," and snap my fingers, hoping hard.

A bright white flame sparks to life just above my hand.

Liberty gasps. Storm, wide-eyed, lowers her arms to her sides. Ire's fox leaps away and runs off into the trees.

"But it takes weeks, even months, to learn how to summon

fire," says Cunning weakly.

Be bold, Amity Barrow. Show them you are not afraid.

"Not for me," I declare.

Malice simply smiles, as if she expected all of this to happen.

Mercy steps back from me, staring. "It was you. The House of Woe. *You* burned it down."

"I did," I say. "And in the flames, I found this."

I take a deep breath, reach for the sack tied to my waist, and withdraw the tiny silver mirror.

"A mirror." Liberty frowns. "What does that mean?"

Beside me, Mercy draws in a sharp breath. "The sacraments of darkness . . ."

"You remember the story, then?" I say, and then, emboldened by that look of slow understanding on her face, take from my sack the stolen book.

"Will someone please explain what's going on?" snaps Gall.

"You think you need to kill sixteen men to summon the Devil," I say, staring Malice full in the face. "Well, I can do it faster."

Malice is no longer smiling. "Explain."

"There is a tale among my people. Long ago, a girl named Abigail sought out relics of God meant only for men's use. She stole them for her own by honoring five sacraments of darkness and in doing so was able to summon the Devil. Book, mirror . . ."

". . . belt, knife, key," whispers Mercy.

I tell them the story, how with her stolen relics Lost Abigail summoned the Devil but was too weak to bear the sight of him.

"She was afraid," I say, pacing before them. My pounding heart has never been more thunderous. "The Devil saw her fear, knew she did not deserve his favor, and took her to Hell as a mere servant. She was weak." I stop, looking around at them all. "We are not."

I hold up the book and mirror. "Using the power of *extasia*, I have already stolen two of the relics. Now I need only three more."

Quiet falls for a long moment.

"That's just some story your daddy told you to keep you in line," Gall snaps, "not the truth. That's any old mirror, and that book"—she points at it, scowling—"I know that book. You stole it from Malice like a common thief!"

"But she didn't," says Malice quietly, painted red and black by moon and trees. "She took it from my shelf, yes, the first day she was here, but then she dropped it, and then I sent her home. I put the book on the table. Not an hour later, it was gone."

"It disappeared right before our eyes," Liberty agrees. "I saw it. We both did."

Ire's eyes narrow. "Why did you tell none of us about this?"

"*Extasia* works in mysterious ways," Malice replies. "Wise women know when to step back, watch, and listen."

"I called the book to me," I tell them. "I remembered the

summoning spell I heard Liberty use, and when I said it and thought of what I wanted, the book came to me in my home. It grew beneath the flesh of my back. My sister helped me tear it free."

"You *birthed* it," says Cunning, with a little nervous laugh. "Your first try at the power, and you birthed a book?"

"She could be lying," Ire mutters, but no one speaks up to agree with her.

"Skin," whispers Mercy. A faint smile touches her lips. Her red hair glows brighter now in the red moonlight, as if some inner fire has awakened within her. "'Tis the first sacrament of darkness in the story. Skin, fire, bone, blood, palm."

"*Extasia* has said my name to you for some time," I remind the coven, "and now here I am, and this is what I aim to do."

This is the moment. My entire body burns hot and cold. Beneath my dress, my knees tremble. I hope the others cannot see.

"You have traveled far and tried many times to find the Devil." My voice is clear and firm. *Father, forgive me.* I think of him in this moment, how his voice commands hundreds with merely a word. "You have fashioned many different rituals, killed many men. And still he does not come. Perhaps he never will. But he came to Lost Abigail. And he will come to me. He is already on his way." I hold up the book and mirror. "The power brought these relics to me. And the power never lies."

When Father says *amen* during worship, every soul in Holy

House says it back to him. The witches are just the same.

"The power never lies," they repeat. Even Malice does, though some of the others look at her nervously.

The sight of her hard blue eyes watching me so closely chills me to my bones.

Swallowing hard, I give the book and mirror to Mercy, then utter my spell, snap my fingers once again. My flame flickers to life before the coven's staring eyes.

"You see this fire," I say proudly. They cannot see my fear. They *will* not. I shall not allow it. "You remember the flowers I spelled to life without even a word. Give me one week to find the other three relics. Do nothing until then. The more men you kill, the more watchmen walk Haven's streets. The closer I am watched, the more difficult it becomes for me to do my work." I wait a moment, letting my words settle. Then I say, "Would you risk the power's wrath by denying me my request?"

Avazel holds its breath. The others watch Malice, waiting.

"What if this is all some scheme to trick us into sparing your people," she says at last, very quietly, "thereby ruining our ritual?"

"Then do not heed me," I tell her, "and see for your own self what the power will do. Or wait one week, allow me to prove myself to you, and revel with me in my triumph. Share it with me."

A few of the witches mutter among themselves. Malice raises her arm to silence them.

"Not so long ago," she tells me, "you wanted to save your people, and now you want to destroy them?"

I must be careful, here. I must not waver, and I must believe what I say. I think of Tom Wickens's spit on my face and his swollen rotting skin, Temperance screaming in agony, the Jamison twins kicking me during visitation, Elias Holt raising his fist to strike me.

The anger rising in my chest frightens me. It should not come so quickly; it should taste more like a lie. But I must have faith that God sees my true heart, even if right now I cannot.

I do this for Haven, I pray.

"You send your animals to watch us. And Mercy has told you much, I am certain. You know what they do, how they hurt us. Did you hear Temperance scream as they burned her? We did. *Extasia* is new to me, but anger is not." I give Malice a knowing smile. "You were not truthful with me when first we met. Nor was I with you. I think now, though, we understand each other."

She laughs once, a quiet burst of air. "And what is it you plan to do once you've got all your little relics and the Devil comes calling for you?"

This, at least, will not be a lie. "I will make certain that what happened to Temperance happens to no one else in Haven, not ever again."

Malice stares at me so long and hard that I fear my heart will burst from my chest. Beneath my fine white gown, a single drop of sweat rolls down my back.

"One week, little sister," she says at last. "Until nightfall on the seventh day. After that, this coven will resume our work, and we will not stop again." Then she comes to me, touches my cheek with the backs of her fingers. "And if I were you, I would tread carefully. *Extasia* has eyes everywhere, and so do we."

They leave me then, one by one, following Malice through the trees. Liberty pauses to give me a small smile. Ire watches me thoughtfully before turning away. Gall stalks off, scowling.

But Mercy stays, standing uncertainly beside me with the relics in her hands.

Once we are alone, I waste no time.

"How do you come and go from Avazel?" I ask her. "I saw you and Temperance that first night. You fled through the wall right under the watchmen's eyes, and yet they did not see you."

She hesitates, frowning. "I use a cloaking spell. 'Tis one of the first spells I learned. It allows me to travel unseen for a time."

Relief rushes through me. This will make things easier.

"Will you use it to take me somewhere?"

"Where?" she asks, narrowing her eyes.

"I know we are not true friends," I tell her softly, daring to touch her slim freckled wrist, "and I know your heart grieves. But if you do this for me—*with* me—it may help us find the relics more quickly."

"Which means avenging Temperance sooner."

Hearing that word, uneasiness rears its slippery head in my belly. The lies I am weaving to save my village veer perilously close to unforgivable sins.

But if the cost of saving Haven is my soul, then so be it.

"Where do you need to go?" Mercy asks quietly.

"To the Goodman house," I tell her. "I think Silence can help us."

27

THE CLOAKING SPELL MERCY USES wraps us in a flat gray feeling like the sky above—buttery and thick, smoothed over with almost-morning. The spell muffles outside noises and makes our own louder. I try to breathe more quietly. The sound of air booming through my body draws lines of sweaty panic down my arms.

We squeeze through the Goodmans' gate, which is overgrown with tangled vines. Scraps of wood, tin, and wire scatter the yard and the wild rows of its unkempt garden. We settle in the shadows near one of the back windows, and I stand on a small crate to peer inside. Not long after, I hear a sharp cry of pain from within the house. A slight crash, then another cry, then all is quiet.

I freeze, my jaw clenched tight. Those cries belonged to Silence. Mercy gives the house a look as if she would like to strike it flat, then makes for the back door, but I grab her wrist.

Mercy whirls around, glaring. "I can help cloak her."

"And what will Emmy Goodman think if her daughter disappears from under her nose?"

Then the back door opens. Silence hurries down the steps and into the yard. Face in her hands, tiny catches like scars in her every breath.

"Silence," I whisper.

She turns at once, and God save me, the look of joy on her face when she finds me—not Mercy, but me, just *me*—is a wash of gold sweet as sunrise. She rushes at me, folds me into her arms, and clings there like some blown petal caught on a thorn.

"How did you know to come to me tonight?" she says. "Dear Amity. How did you know I would need you?"

I have forgotten every word I have ever known. I can only stand on my own two feet, and hold her, and feel the warmth rising in my cheeks and my chest, and remember to breathe.

"Are you hurt?" Mercy asks sharply.

"No," Silence whispers. "No, no, no."

"But we heard—"

"Mother is not bad. You must know this. She loves me, but the years of caring for Father have worn on her. Do you see? Sometimes she gets angry. But her anger is not anger, it is sadness. It is sleep without rest."

Mercy's eyes are thin and angry. "She hits you, then?"

"No! No. She throws things at the walls. She yells. She

weeps for hours. But she never strikes me. And most days, her sadness is not anger. Most days, her sadness is only sadness." Silence's breath hitches. "Do you see? Mother is not bad."

Trembling, I cup her head, let my fingers slip into the soft flaxen world of her hair. She is so warm, her chest pounding against mine, her hands clutching my sleeves. The pictures that fly into my mind frighten me: Temperance's fingers in Mercy's hair; Temperance's fingers scratching through the dirt beside mine; Temperance and Mercy kissing in the elm grove.

Silence hiding in my garden after visitation. White night-gown, moon-silvered eyes, blood on her lip. Her voice in my hair, my flower in her palms.

I pull back from her, rougher than I mean to, and duck away from Mercy's fierce bright eyes. The raw pain on her face makes me sick with guilt. I wonder if such a wound as losing Temperance will ever truly heal—and if Mercy will end our fragile friendship should I utter even one wrong word.

We hide in a corner of the yard, a scraggly patch of brush and weeds. Mercy faces the house, watchful.

"Tell me, why have you both come here?" Silence whispers, her hands around mine. Then she tilts her head. "My voice—how strange it sounds. Hollow."

"We are cloaked," I tell her. "No one can hear or see us, thanks to Mercy."

"But not for much longer," Mercy mutters. "My strength is not endless."

Silence turns shining eyes to Mercy. "How are you doing this?"

Mercy is terse, her mouth thin. "Ask your questions so we may leave."

"Did you see the gray women at the House of Woe that night?" I ask Silence. "When . . ."

Words hang between us, but never sound. *Temperance, burn, scream, smoke.* Though the night is warm, I feel cold with memory.

"I did," Silence says gravely. "Four of them."

"I saw them too," Mercy says quietly. "In the smoke."

I turn to her, surprised. "You said nothing of this to me."

"And you did not tell me why we were coming here, only that Silence could help us."

"I did not want to frighten you."

Mercy laughs bitterly. "You think women floating in smoke can frighten me after everything I have endured?"

"How often do they come to you, Mercy?" Silence asks, cheerfully curious, as if we are all friends, and no one has burned, and no one is angry. "Do they tell you stories, same as they do for me?"

"Stories?" snaps Mercy, frowning. "I told you, I only saw them, and only that once."

I touch Silence's hand without thinking. The softness of it, the delicate splay of her bones, startles me quickly away. "Have they told you anything else since we last spoke of them?"

"Yes, in fact. Just this morning." Silence pauses. A strand of her long pale hair is stuck to her cheek. "Shall I tell it?"

I itch to pull the hair free, tuck it behind her ear. *Dear Amity*, she said.

I sit on my hands. "Please."

"And hurry," Mercy mutters. "The sun is coming."

"Once," says Silence after a quiet moment, "there was a lost girl who traveled a long broad road made of polished pink stones. She searched for home, a place she had never been. The underland, some called it. The great city, said others. She traveled with three companions. A girl with an aching head. A girl with a tired heart. A girl who feared all she saw. And at the end of the road stood a great black door wedged into the side of a hill."

Silence's words settle coldly inside me, a soft endless fall of snow that will bury me if I do not find shelter.

I had hoped I would not know whatever story Silence had heard, but I do. This is one I could tell in my sleep, for no matter how many nights I have spent trying to pray Mother out of my head, she does not seem willing to leave.

"The girl with the aching head opened the door," I whisper, "hoping that on the other side would be her home, for her feet were sore from walking, and she longed to sleep at last."

Silence stares at me. Mercy turns back to watch.

"But on the other side of the door lay a field of fire," says Silence, "so she closed the door at once."

I wish, oh I wish, that I did not know what words come next. What does it mean, that Silence knows this story?

"The girl with the tired heart tried the same," I say through my teeth, "but beyond the door was a vast forest so thick they could not press inside it. She too closed the door."

Silence shifts closer to me. My hands remain trapped under my thighs. I press them harder into the dirt.

"The girl who feared all she saw would not open the door set into the hill," Silence says softly. "They begged her to try, but she did not. She sat on the ground and wept, for she knew all their walking had been in vain, that they would never reach the underland."

"Then the final girl, the lost girl, opened the door." I struggle to hold on to my voice. "And beyond it was only more road, and on the far horizon, a speck of darkness that she knew was another door, standing in wait. The girls joined hands and began again."

Silence finishes it with me. "For they knew they had no choice but to keep walking."

Mercy stares at us, her anger gone. Without it, she looks smaller. "What is this story? How do you both know it? I have never heard it."

My cheeks burn. I scratch hard at the back of my head. A single bold fright, clawing its fear into my thoughts. "My mother told it to Blessing and me. She was always dreaming up new stories for us. I did not think anyone else knew them. I have never heard them anywhere else. But Silence has now told me two of them."

"Stop lying to me," Mercy says, shaking her head. "If you

are trying to scare me, it will not work."

Silence frowns, puzzled. "But there is no reason to lie to you."

"And why would these flying women tell you stories that make no kind of sense?"

"Do you know what they are?" I ask Silence. "For how long have you seen them?"

"Oh, I have always seen them," she says, worrying a lock of hair between her fingers. Her eyes dart to me, then away. "At least, for as long as I can remember. Certainly since I was anointed. Sometimes one will stay for months and months. Then it will leave, and new ones will come."

"But what *are* they?"

"I think they are ghosts."

Mercy looks at me, lost. "Ghosts?"

"Mother told me about them." Once again, Silence glances nervously at me. "She was a saint too, long ago. For five years she wore her hood. Elder Michael liked her. He is dead now. Very dead—he hanged himself. No one ever talks about that, but Mother did. He visited her often for confession in the House of Whispers. Mother told me she was his particular favorite. He told her ghosts are souls of those sinners who have been turned away by God and entrapped by the Devil instead. Then he died not long after that. They found him in his barn."

"I have never heard of this," says Mercy. "Floating dead sinners, drifting about and telling stories?"

The word *ghosts* makes my skin crawl with cold. "Elder

Michael might have told your mother these things to frighten her, or impress her."

"Yes, so he could do with her whatever he wished," Mercy says angrily.

"Just as he ought," I say quietly, but the words do not fit well on my tongue.

"Or he told her about the ghosts because he had seen them," Silence says, plucking a weed from the ground. "And maybe they spoke to him, and maybe that was driving him mad. So he told Mother to settle his mind, but it did not help." She plucks petals from the scraggly little weed, shrugging. "That is the story I tell myself. Stories are helpful. They show me the truth when nothing else can. I think that is why the ghosts tell them." She considers the shorn weed fondly. "I wonder if, in The World That Once Was, there were ghosts everywhere, in all villages. Or maybe 'tis only here in Haven."

A thought rises inside me on a sudden howling wind. "Do you think . . . every sinner who has died in Haven has become one of these ghosts?"

"I do not know. I try to look at their faces when I can, to see who is who, but they seldom let me get very close. I have seen echoes, though. Noses and chins and eyes. Bits of color flying across them like leaves, there and gone again. Oh, Amity!" It is as though something has burst open inside her. She wrings her hands, hesitates, and then grabs mine. "I have wanted to tell you but did not know how to do it." She takes a breath. "The gray women—I have seen your mother among them."

I stare at her in horror for a moment, then shake off her hands. Once again, Silence has stolen all my words from me.

"Maybe you should not speak of her mother right now," Mercy snaps. "Have you no sense at all?"

Silence reaches for me, but I scramble away, stumble to my feet. "You are lying," I tell her, "or you saw something you did not understand." The words sound weak, strange, as if someone else's voice is pretending to be my own. "Perhaps you mean to comfort me, but you are wrong to try."

"I should not have told you," Silence says, bowing her head, tangling her fingers in her hair. Her voice is thick with misery. "I knew I should not have told you. But it is no lie, Amity, it is what I have seen. I would not tell you an untruth. Not you. Never you."

"We must go." Cold all over, I turn my words to bullets on my tongue. No, no, no. "Mercy is growing tired from her spell." No, Silence, we shall not speak of my mother. No, Silence, you are wrong. No, Silence, if she ever did appear to living eyes through some unholy work, she would come to *me*, not you.

Or would she? After all, Silence did not do what I did those five years past. She saw nothing, she said nothing.

I hurry away, blinking back tears. I hate them. I do not deserve them, and neither does my mother.

Silence runs after us to the gate. "Wait! Amity, I . . . I am sorry. I only wanted to help. I thought it would . . . I did not mean—"

"It is nothing." I catch her hands and dredge up a smile. "Thank you for what you have said. We will speak again soon."

Tears in her eyes, Silence nods bravely and steps back from me. "Before you leave, please tell me how you learned this . . . spell? Your cloak of unseeing?"

Mercy and I glance at each other.

"Will you teach me?" Silence looks at us with careful hope. "I would like to be unseen sometimes, when Mother is sad. It seems better than just plain hiding."

Mercy softens, touching Silence's hand. "I can promise nothing, but . . . I will ask the others."

Then we hurry off, and not a moment too soon, for even harder to bear than the sight of Silence's thin, sad face watching us leave is the idea of my mother—not dead after all, but roaming the skies, faceless and monstrous, watching me, following me, remembering what I did.

ONE WEEK IS NOT LONG to find the three remaining relics, but I have no choice.

The first night after telling the coven about my quest, I stay awake for hours, practicing on twigs from my garden. Skin. Fire. *Bone.*

I do not know if crafting a spell that breaks a twig can then become a spell that breaks a bone. But what else can I do? If I knew I could *mend* a bone, I would practice on myself.

Instead, I frown at my pathetic little pile of sticks, look at the new list Samuel wrote out for me—all the words he found near the many instances of *bone* in Malice's stolen book—and try again.

"*Samhaasyo, rahasa, larinalim, das!*" I whisper.

The twigs gathered at my toes go flying across the floor, scattering like spilled grain. Out of all the words I have tried, that arrangement feels best, but a quick glance tells me all my twigs are still in one piece.

A wasp's nest of rage drops and bursts open inside me. The angry little stingers go flying, ripping their way up my arms and legs and burrowing into my cheeks, and I am crawling out of my skin, so burning hot that I cannot bear it anymore—

I grab the book and fling it against the wall.

The loud *smack* booms like thunder.

Blessing, having fallen asleep at her post by the door, jerks awake. She stares at me, eyes wide, and we hold our breaths, waiting to hear Father's footsteps in the hallway.

But the quiet does not break, and an hour later, then two, Blessing has once again fallen asleep, her head leaning against the door, and I am still working, crackling with the remnants of my anger. They zip and dart inside me, tireless and buzzing, firing my mind clear.

The idea of sleep seems impossible, and as long as I am working, as long as I am angry, I cannot think of anything else. Here is the book, the list, the twigs, my devoted sister, the crushed petals from my garden that fill my pockets and litter the rug and remind me of my own two feet on the floor. There is no room in my mind for more than that.

And yet some quiet inner voice buried deep within me manages to whisper that the wise thing to do next would be to seek out a gray woman—a ghost—and ask for help. I should at least try. I have spent hours crouching here. The sun will soon rise, and all I have done is scatter twigs across the floor and frighten the wits out of my sister.

But what if I look too hard into one of those gaping black mouths and see Mother's face staring back at me? What if she speaks to me? What would she say?

I do not intend to find out.

Six days left for me to find the relics.

The House of Knowing is a large square building painted a somber gray, the windows small and high. As an elder's second, Samuel has a key that lets us inside. He keeps it on a chain around his neck, under his shirt. In a small door near the building's rear, he inserts the key, turns it, hesitates, looks over his shoulder.

I bite my tongue, brimming with impatience.

Then he opens the door, pulls me in after him, and shuts it behind us.

We stand in thick silence in a small dark hallway with a low ceiling. We wait and listen but hear nothing, only the slight hum of the shimmering cloak I have spelled around us. The faint sound is more like a feeling—a watchfulness, as if we are being spied upon, though we are entirely alone.

That I had to witness Mercy crafting this spell only once before creating it myself should frighten me. It means *extasia* is far too eager for me, or else I am farther down the road to Hell than I thought.

Most likely 'tis the second reason. After all, a godly girl

would be frightened by what I have done.

But I am not frightened. The cloak is solid, strong. A blanket of warmth. A feeling of pleasure unwinds inside me, like a vine stretching to feel the sunlight.

I did this.

Samuel lets out a long, slow breath. "This cloak you have made. Can you . . . put it away?"

I raise my eyebrows. "Do you want someone to find us?"

"No, it is only that . . ." He rubs the back of his neck. "It feels strange against my skin. It is too tight. My head hurts."

My impatience bubbles again. "The sooner we finish this, the sooner you can take me home and rid yourself of this cloak you so hate."

"I do not *hate* it, I simply—" He sighs sharply. Things have been strange between us since Temperance's death. We seldom look straight at each other. I know he helped light the fire that burned her. He knows that the same power I practice is what Temperance used to kill Zacharias Rutledge.

He does not know everything, though. For instance, the true murderers of Haven's men. No, of that he remains ignorant, and he will continue to. I will not tell him, not until I am finished. Perhaps not even then.

Particularly if I am in Hell on that day. A place good Samuel will never see with his own eyes.

"I do not have keys for every room in this house, Amity," he says quietly. "The elders' private rooms, the attic."

"Surely not everything is locked away?"

"There are books in the library, which any elder's second may use."

"Take me there."

In the dark, he looks at me. Waiting.

I bite my tongue, struggling not to snap at him. "*Please*, Samuel."

Library, he calls this large room, filled floor to ceiling with shelves stacked high with books. Not even Malice's hut held so many. Samuel finds a candle in the corner, a tinderbox and flint beside it, and soon the room is lit in soft gold.

At once, he begins searching the shelves. As I watch him scan the stitched and painted words, my insides curdle darkly. If I could read all these words myself, I could have taken his key and come here on my own.

"I do not know quite what I am looking for," Samuel admits after a few moments, his voice hushed. "What is the word again?"

"*Ghosts*," I answer. "The spirits of dead sinners. I need to understand what they are, where they come from, if they are any danger to my work."

"Ah, yes. Tall dead sinners, floating through the air, with gray arms as long as trees."

I bristle at the tone of his voice. "Are you saying I imagined what I have seen? That my mind is spinning lies?"

He slams shut the book he had been reading, an enormous thing bound in red-dyed leather. "I am risking much by helping you, Amity—tonight and all nights."

"Yes, we both are, and we do it for Haven."

"Are you certain that is the only reason why you are doing this?" He turns toward me. The candlelight makes him look older, turns his face harsh and angry. "Because it seems to me you are enjoying these new tricks you have learned. You have an appetite for them."

"The only hunger I feel is the desire to save our people!"

"No, Amity, you hunger for *extasia*!"

The anger on his face makes me step back toward the door. I have never seen him look at me this way, not in all the years we have known and loved each other. This look frightens me. A slight sensation of falling leaves me unsteady.

Samuel would not betray me to the elders after all. Would he?

He stares at me, blinks, then looks away as if ashamed, his jaw working.

"I will keep looking here," he says. "There is a second library down the hall, where a small stool is kept. Can you please bring it to me? The shelves here are high even for me."

"Of course." I am glad to leave him, glad to be alone with the sound of my horrible pounding heart. In the hallway, I lean against the wall, a hot pressure building behind my eyes.

Then—voices. Footsteps.

I stiffen, look left down the hallway. I see a door pulled to, a line of light beneath it.

We are not alone in this house. I should get Samuel and run.

But something tugs me toward that room and the quiet voices within it. 'Tis the same feeling that brought me to

Malice's book on the shelf two weeks ago now—a tightness in my chest, a hum in my ears, a hot flush through my body. Not bad, not good, but more good than bad.

Extasia.

I follow the power's path to the door, hold my breath, peek inside.

First, Elder Peter. My gentle, frail friend. He crouches, reaching for a book on a low shelf. His face twists in pain. I nearly move to help him. He knows very well he should not strain his back like that.

Second—

My breath catches in my throat.

Elder Joseph stands above him, gray hair hanging loose in neat waves, gray tunic buttoned at his wrists. He leans on his cane and smiles, watching Elder Peter struggle without offering to help, and this would be enough to make me hate him, even if he had never lain with my mother.

But then he jabs Elder Peter's hip with the end of his cane, which sends my friend falling to the floor with a pained cry.

"You lose your balance so easily these days, old man," says Elder Joseph kindly. "Too easily, some might say, for an elder meant to inspire his people with strength and vigor." He clucks his tongue. "Perhaps it is time to hang up your sash for good."

This time, my anger does not burst open. It simply *is*, presenting itself to me with a sudden calm fire that illuminates everything I must do and raises the hair on my arms. I flush hot to my fingertips.

"*Samhaasyo, rahasa, larinalim, das,*" I whisper.

Then there is a horrible snap, a pained, strangled cry, and Elder Joseph falls to the ground. His bad leg—never fully healed from when my mother broke it—is bent at an awful angle. I see blood, torn skin.

Bone.

I hurry back to Samuel, still encased in my spelled cloak. Elder Joseph's howling will bring someone running, and soon.

Samuel stands frozen at the shelves, an open book in his hands. "What is that?"

"Elder Peter and Elder Joseph have had a disagreement, it seems," is the only thing I can think of to say. Samuel's mouth thins, but he does not argue. If my cloak fails and we are caught, it will be the end of everything.

Hidden by *extasia*, our breath deafening inside the cloak's thick shell, we run.

—

Five days left.

Dutifully, I sweep Elder Peter's kitchen floor.

I had hoped breaking Elder Joseph's leg would be enough to satisfy the sacrament, but no particular belt has shown itself to me, and hours of practicing the spell in my bedroom have yielded nothing but a pile of twigs that refuse to snap.

Sitting on the porch steps after my chores are finished, waiting for Samuel to escort me home, I hear soft footsteps shuffling out to join me.

I look up to see Elder Peter in his sleeping clothes and long woolen robe.

I scramble to my feet. "I thought you were asleep."

"Sit, sit," he tells me, waving me back down. With a great sigh, he settles into his favorite chair.

For a moment, all is quiet save the songs of bugs and night birds, the whisper of wind through the trees.

Then Elder Peter says softly, "'Tis a great shame what befell Elder Joseph."

At once I am full awake, my whole body drawing tight. "Indeed. What misfortune, to have so badly hurt the same leg twice."

"I was there when it happened. One moment he was standing tall, the next he was on the floor, his leg snapped nearly in two."

I swallow hard. "Gracious."

And then he says nothing more until Samuel arrives at the gate with a wave and I rise to leave.

His hand catches me by the wrist. Those sad eyes looking up at me, watery with age, chill me utterly. Never have I seen an elder look so frightened, nor so resigned. As if he has seen the end and accepts it, is even glad for it.

"There is great evil afoot, Amity," Elder Peter whispers. "I sincerely hope you will stay safe."

I hardly speak to Samuel as we walk home, my thoughts lingering on Elder Peter's porch. *There is great evil afoot*, he said. What does he know? What does he suspect?

Most puzzling of all is this: Could he have somehow seen me in the House of Knowing? Does he wonder if I was the one who hurt Elder Joseph? I do not see how, but some creeping fear I cannot ignore settles between my shoulder blades, making me restless.

And if Elder Peter does wonder this about me, if he even thinks it possible, why has he said nothing to the elders?

Why does he keep my secret?

Four days.

In the early morning hours, I wake from a fitful sleep to see Blessing climbing through our window, skirts hiked up to her thighs. A piece of straw hangs in her hair, and a red mark on her neck fills me with a twisting dread.

She sees me staring, claps her hand over the mark, presses her lips tight.

I say nothing, simply turn away from her and squeeze my eyes shut.

Whatever trouble my sister seeks, however she manages it without spells to aid her, it is none of my concern.

I have no worry to spare for her mischief. My own is more than enough.

29

THREE.

Hidden in a spelled cloak by Silence's back door, I wait and hope in the darkness of deep night, my hands full of flowers, my pocket full of words, my arms and legs restless and sore.

Maybe seeing my friend will calm me. Maybe the time away from practicing my bone spell—which could very well be useless unless I find someone else's leg to break—will do me some good.

Or maybe three more days will come and go, I will return to Malice with nothing, and the roads of Haven will run red with fresh blood. Her ritual will work as no other has before, and the Devil will come, and I will have failed utterly.

This chain of thoughts leaves my insides itching with frantic laughter. I need to sleep. I cannot possibly sleep.

The Goodman house is quiet tonight. When Silence comes

out at last, she hums to herself, hangs up washing in the dark. An odd nighttime chore, but then, so are mine.

At last I find the courage to near her, bringing her into my cloak with a soft whisper of sound.

She turns around at once, beaming at me. "Hello. I wondered when you would next come visit me."

The sight of her melts me—those wide blue eyes, the long pale hair framing her face, even the stitched scars poking up from her collar. All the bunched-up worries inside me open with a sigh.

If my hands were not full, I think I would touch her cheeks, cradle them like eggshells in my palms. I wonder if they are as soft as they look.

"I have been wanting to talk to you about what I said when you were last here," she says carefully, but I wave her quiet.

"We will speak of that another time," I lie. "Tonight, I cannot stay long. I brought you two gifts."

One, the flowers. I press them into her hands—sky-bright bluebells, roses with the thorns scraped off.

Her eyes shine. "Thank you, Amity. I—"

"No, wait. There is something else." From my pocket, I unfold the three pieces of paper I tore from Malice's book. I try not to look at my crude handwriting, so much clumsier than Samuel's.

"I want you to have these in case anything should happen to me and I have no time to teach you properly," I tell her.

"They are spell words, like the ones Mercy and I use to make our cloaks."

"The cloak of unseeing," she whispers, awestruck.

"Yes. Those words are here, and others too. Words for unlocking doors. My reading is clumsy, but Samuel taught me well enough to sound out the letters slowly. I searched the book for everything that might be useful. In case . . ." My eyes and nose tingle. I swallow the lump in my throat. "In case you ever find yourself locked somewhere you do not wish to be."

Silence looks at me gravely. "Amity, what is wrong? What will happen to you that you cannot teach me these things yourself?"

I look away from her. She might see in my eyes what lies ahead for us all, and I cannot bear the thought of frightening her.

"The power you will use is called *extasia*," I tell her. "It . . . It is not a godly power, I must warn you. But I think it will help you if you need it, as it has helped me. When you say the words, you must think of what it is you want, form a clear picture in your mind. I find that holding petals from my flowers in my palm or pocket helps me remember who I am, where I come from. They pin me in place so the power cannot take me too far away. Do you understand?"

"Amity—"

"You must practice where no one can see or hear you," I press on, my tears rising fast. Here I am in this yard of weeds, so near to this girl who not long ago was a mere saint, who has become so many things that I do not understand. And in three days, what will happen? Will I see her after that? Will I see anyone at all? "And you must tell no one what I have said to you—"

"*Amity.*" Silence drops the flowers and turns me gently. "Look."

I do, and I see a gray woman, tall as the Goodman house itself, drifting near the gate. Very still. Very dark. Her long arms touching the ground like the legs of some strange ladder.

One of them she raises to point down the road.

A feeling touches the back of my neck, slow and creeping. I do not want to go to her, but I must. I know I must. The power tingling in my palms tells me so. When *extasia* speaks, a girl should listen.

Nearing her—this gray woman, this *ghost*—I look up, and up, and then to the side. Whatever her face might show me, whatever truth lies in the cave of her mouth, I refuse to see it.

"What is it?" Silence whispers, coming up behind me. She offers up a single flower. "Do you need our help?"

I follow the dark line of the ghost's finger to the tall red barn that belongs to Uriah Brinsley. Adam's father.

For a moment, I cannot feel the ground under my feet. One of the glittering black flies that swarms inside the ghost's mouth swoops down and bumps against my brow.

My bile rising, I turn to Silence and say quickly, "This is not fair of me to ask of you. 'Tis dangerous, and I am sorry, truly.

But will you go to Mercy's house and fetch her, bring her to the Brinsleys' barn?"

Silence nods solemnly. "I am really quite good at hiding," she tells me, and then she tucks that little blue flower behind my ear, which makes my chest ache so sharply that I bring Silence's hands to my mouth and kiss them.

Then we are hurrying down the road, the ghost and me, my cloak hiding me from the eyes of the patrolling watchmen—two, four, six of them. Three pairs, stalking the streets. Rifles and torches, quick cutting eyes. Panic swirls in my throat, at the clammy backs of my knees. I should never have sent Silence away. I wish I knew how to move a cloak from one girl to another, but it is too late for that.

The ghost and I, we are at the Brinsley barn. All is shadowed and quiet, the barn narrow and tall. Bright red in daylight, now dull and gray. Its high windows stare, waiting for me.

I find a small door and open it, and when the ghost lowers her tall, tall body next to me and cranes her long neck to peer inside, I make a terrible mistake. I glance left and see, in her buzzing, gaping mouth, a rim of bright silver, and I realize that glinting thing I have often seen in her throat is a bell, stuffed down deep.

I gulp down a sharp, sick feeling. There is no time for sick feelings. Inside, the barn is dark, the only light a small golden glow in the far corner, past the horses asleep in their stalls. I duck through the door, look back over my shoulder.

The ghost, the bell-stuffed woman, is gone.

I move softly through the barn, toward the golden-lit room where tack is stored. I kneel. Slow, as if sinking into water. I peer through cracks between the wall's wooden planks. The barn's very own hidey-hole.

Inside the room, a small lamp sits on a crate, and beside it, panting in the hay, is my sister, her nightgown rucked up about her hips. Beside her is Adam Brinsley, who has stared at her for months, whose mouth has marked her skin. His hand moves between my sister's legs, his shining red face mashed against my sister's neck.

She moves against him, her body rocking. Adam's does the same. Small strangled noises come from both their mouths, and when my sister lets out a sharp cry, Adam's hand flies up to cover her mouth. He smiles, and so does she, past his fingers.

I lean hard against the wall as I watch them. I should run, but something pins me here, some fluttering question that warms my thighs. Adam removes his shirt and lets it fall to the hay. How long and broad his gleaming back is, its lines shifting like bound cords. I stare, my head hot and spinning.

Adam shifts, showing me my sister's bare legs, and at this I turn away, flushed with shame. My legs catch on each other, and for a moment, as I fall hard onto the ground, I lose my grip on the cloak.

Their noises cease. I hold still as a deer in the meadow.

Then I hear Adam say, "Do not worry, Blessing. No one is here. Only the wind."

"That was no wind," says my sister. I hear her rustle in the hay.

"The horses, then, moving in their sleep."

"No, no, I . . . I must go home. I'm sorry, I . . . Please walk me home, Adam."

Adam's voice hardens. "No. You promised. You will stay here with me."

I press my face once more to the wood.

Adam is atop my sister, his hips holding down her hips, his hands pinning her arms.

"Let me go!" she cries, pushing at him. He covers her mouth and shoves her hard into the hay. She claws at him, but he dodges her and slaps her twice. His face has gone dark, Adam Brinsley, and when he speaks, his voice is wholly changed from the one I know. A new man, sweating and furious.

"You whore," he spits at her. "You said you would lie with me. I have waited *months* for this. I will wait no longer."

"Someone will hear us," whispers my sister, her eyes wide. She twists away, and he strikes her for it, then pushes her hard into the hay and, with his free hand, reaches for the brown belt holding up his trousers. He yanks them down, baring himself. My sister sobs, kicks at him, but he wrestles her flat.

Whatever anger I have felt before in my life, it is nothing next to this. I can see only red and black and gold, a whirl of colors. They pound up my arms and down my legs, and against my eyes too, like stars bursting open, and they say *no*, and shout *no*, and howl *no*.

In my mind, a picture of the black mountain rises on a hot rushing current. When the world was new and boiling, and the Devil traveled far and wide to choose his home, that great black rock thrust up through the earth and tossed fire, lighting his path.

Now I am the thing that tosses fire.

A flitting shadow draws my eye up. A dozen ghosts skitter along the rafters, their heads whipping from side to side, their long bodies trailing like angry snakes. From their mouths pour horrible harsh sounds, like the howls of those baying hounds that chased my gun-shot mother into the woods. I long to cover my ears, but my bones, my booted feet on the ground, the fists pounding in my chest, they all scream that the sounds are meant for me—and that the more of them I hear, the stronger I will become.

I find the woman with the mouth full of black flies and the bell-stuffed throat. She points at nothing now. She simply watches and waits.

For me.

A power inside me bursts free.

And the power never lies.

"*Extasia*," I whisper, a greeting, and then I tear into that lamplit room on feet that have cooked in the world's oldest fires.

30

When I rush toward Adam, he turns and gapes at me. Good. Gape and gulp. Be afraid.

I lunge at him, grab his hair and arm, and pull. My nails mark him with his own blood. Together we tumble back into the hay.

Blessing scrambles to her feet with a sob, and now Adam is above me instead. His face twists into terrible shapes. Beneath his hard body, I suddenly feel the truth of my own smallness, and my flooding fierce anger loosens its grip.

Adam strikes me, hard. My head spins. A great white pain bursts open between my ears. My lips are salt-sharp with blood.

"You vile creature," spits Adam. His belt hangs loose, and when he strikes me again, black spots bloom before my eyes, but even so, I see it. A miraculous thing.

Book, mirror, *belt*. And there it sits at Adam's hips. My hands ache to hold it. Adam Brinsley's belt.

Ablaze with understanding, I cannot help but laugh.

"Stop laughing," Adam growls. With every few words comes a new blow. "Were you watching us, Amity? Were you watching your sister and wishing it was you instead of her? I would sooner bed a dog."

A dark night spreads fast across me. I see thick red spots and the sharp thin knife of Adam's smile. If he hits me once more, I think I shall die. My face is wet, and if I still have a body, it is lost to me. I can feel only the hot pulsing places where Adam's hands have struck me. I reach feebly for his hanging belt. If I can only grab hold of it, tug it free, maybe someone will help me. God or Devil, whoever is listening.

But then Adam's weight lifts away. My ears ring as if bells have been struck over and over inside them. I push myself up and open my eyes, and then I see them—Mercy and Silence, each of them holding one of Adam's arms. Mercy's red hair gleams with lamplight, and Silence's cloak is tied at her throat with a tidy white bow.

Adam is strong, but Mercy is a witch, and Silence will be soon, I think. After all, she can speak with ghosts, and in this barn her eyes are burning bright with a fire I know well. Malice will love her. And if she does not, she will when I tell her to.

Adam twists his body and breaks free. He kicks Mercy against the wall. Silence staggers back.

I hope the ghosts writhing at the ceiling keep us cloaked from the world beyond this barn. My sister, my Blessing, clings to the door frame and watches them, her tear-streaked face alight with wonder. Knowing she can see them too is a balm to my wounds.

I rise to my feet and swallow the blood pooled in my mouth, loath to lose any precious scrap of myself to this revolting beast of a man. I draw in a ragged breath, then whisper harshly, *"Samhaasyo, rahasa, larinalim, das!"*

Adam's legs snap, both at once. Two twigs broken in half. He collapses with a howl, his useless feet dangling.

I reach out for the others and thrill when Blessing grabs my right hand and Silence my left, Mercy scrambling to her other side.

"Samhaasyo, rahasa, larinalim, das!" I say again.

Adam flies across the hay-strewn floor and slams into the wall, his left arm bent sharply around his back.

Soon the others join me—first Mercy, then Blessing and Silence. Hesitant, clumsy, then steady, then eager. Four rising voices, becoming one.

"Samhaasyo, rahasa, larinalim, das!"

Adam's body twists against the wall, knotting itself smaller and smaller into impossible shapes.

My lips swell from his cruel hands, and my sight is spotted black and red, but the mark carved into my chest is afire with power, a pulsing sharp-edged heat. It runs true down to my fingers and then courses through them to Silence's hands, and then her pale bowed head, and Blessing's golden one, and then to Mercy, fierce beneath her firefall of hair.

"Samhaasyo, rahasa, larinalim, das!"

Adam's jaw cracks open, his skull splinters.

Then he is no longer screaming.

For a moment, we stand over him, breathing hard. I wait for some stab of guilt to pierce me.

It does not come. All I can think of is how he threw that terrible, furious look at my sister and trapped her beneath the claw of his body.

Some booming distant noise rings in my ears. The echoes of his fists.

I am glad he is dead.

"We have to move quickly," Mercy says, the first to pull away.

Blessing wipes the tears from her cheeks with shaking hands. "To Avazel?"

"I did it," breathes Silence, staring at her fingers. Then she looks at me, wide-eyed. "Is this how you make the cloaks for hiding?"

I do not answer her, too stunned for words. My bleeding face pulses with swells of pain. Only a short while ago, I was giving her flowers.

Mercy grasps Adam's knotted arm, and Blessing takes the other, her mouth thin and bitten, her body swaying. I almost tell her to go home, but if she did, someone might catch her, and even if she made it there, what then? All this time she has helped me practice the power, and now she has touched *extasia* herself. She will have questions; she will be curious. Turning her away now would only put her in danger, not protect her.

What have I done, bringing my sister into this? First those long nights keeping watch in our bedroom as I worked, and now this. What will become of us now? The question settles like a brick in my aching head.

Mercy spells a cloak around us. No one says another word as we carry Adam's body past the quiet horses watching from their beds. I wonder if beasts such as they can see through witches' cloaks.

Dawn is rising. Soon the people of Haven will wake to tend their fields, light their fires, feed their animals. We hurry, ghosts roiling at our feet. They crawl fast, cleaning away blood and footprints with long sweeps of their shadowed arms.

Our muscles shake and burn under Adam's twisted weight. We must stop several times as we hurry across the meadow, panting and sweating, before hauling him back up again. Not long after we enter the woods, into which the watchmen chased my mother long ago, the dark gray trees change to white, the brown soil to colorful moss, the white moon to red.

We let the body fall, and ourselves with it.

I tremble in the dirt. My head feels cleaved in two, and my eyes stream tired tears, but it is not for Adam that I weep. 'Tis for myself, for I have killed, and so has my sister, who huddles in the mud beside me. When I reach for Blessing, she touches my fingers. Avazel has healed her hurts, banished her bruises. She is whole and with me, her Avazel gown a blue as rich and deep as a crisp autumn sky, a crown of curling green leaves on her head, and I am not sorry, I feel not at all sorry, I will never, not once, feel sorry.

Mercy is the first to raise her head and see the wolves coming through the gloom.

She hisses through her teeth. We rise to watch them come—a pack of six wolves with thick shining coats. Their eyes are dark—creatures of Avazel, yes, but not in service of the coven just now. No, these beasts of the witch-realm are coming of their own will. We move away and let them sniff Adam's body. There are five small pups and one enormous she-wolf, larger than any wolf would be outside Avazel. We are quiet as they feast, and when they have gone, trotting silkily away into the white trees, there is nothing left of Adam but his mangled head and small gnawed bones and his long brown belt, gnawed and wet.

I hold the belt in my slick hands, listening to the song of *extasia* rushing through my tired bones. Then a twig breaks, and Malice and the coven step out of the trees to circle around us. They say nothing, their faces solemn. No one looks at me unkindly now.

Malice kneels close to look at me, then the belt. Then she nods slowly.

"Now what, little sister?" she asks.

The answer comes to me as I stare at my hands. Humming

extasia draws pulsing red pictures in my mind—the wall of Haven, the roads down which we carried Adam's body, my garden, my house, the carved-out spot where the book and mirror live. The book. The *book*. Now I understand what Samuel read. A list of names, crossed out.

And a list of new ones beside them. *Furor. Storm. Gall. Rampant. Liberty.*

Names that were given, and names that were chosen.

I laugh quietly, my tired limbs trembling. The book is *there*, but I need it *here*.

"*Malyatzaf, samdech, grahala, malyodam*," I whisper, twisting my fingers in the moss beneath me.

Extasia obeys quickly, its fires stoked by what we have done. My body seizes, twisted all over in fists of power. I gasp and choke, drop flat to the dirt. Blessing hurries to me with a cry, but someone clever pulls her away just before I begin to cough. Not skin tearing open this time, but something else. Heat punches me in the gut like a kicked foot, then slides fast up my throat. I gag, my body jerks, and then I vomit black bile into the dirt near my fingers. A pile of it, thick and glistening.

And then as I watch, panting, my eyes watering, the steaming bile congeals, shaping itself anew. Soon Malice's stolen book lies there before me. Dust on its cover, its pages browned. When a wind comes, the papers flutter like stirred leaves.

Through bleary eyes, I smile up at Malice. "Now, we write our names in your book."

"I should say so," Malice says with a smile. "You've earned it."

She rises to her feet, steps back to join the others. In silence, they wait and watch. When I open the book to the pages of names, then dip my fingers in the ruin of Adam's body, my sisters gather near. Silence holds Blessing close, and Mercy glares at the coven, crouched and feral, as if daring any of them to come closer.

First I write my saintly name. Amity, daughter of Thomas Barrow. With the tip of my bloody nail, I draw a line through the letters, as the other witches have done before me, and write a new word beside it. The jagged red letters spell out the feeling that has been growing inside me, sly and tireless, for weeks now, for months, for years—since my anointing, since I endured the humiliation of the saintly trials to wash away the stain of Mother's sin, since the day I first saw her writhing beneath a man who was not her husband.

Perhaps I was born with this feeling, chosen by the Devil even before I took my first breath.

RAGE.

A new name, fresh-born and glistening. A word I have heard Father shout from the altar on many a worship day, and now it belongs to me.

I pass the book to Mercy, who descends upon it with fierce attention. MERCY, she writes first, with my help—and then beside it, she writes another word, thick with spikes.

VENGEANCE.

Then it is time for my sister to add her name. Her face is dry and her eyes are clear. She pulls the book into her lap, writes her name as I tell her, then strikes a line through it. She pauses, thinking. There is a proud jut to her jaw. Those nights she twisted quietly in her bed or lay in the hay with the boy she thought might wed her, the tears she wept for me after visitation left me marked by Haven's fists. My tenderhearted sister, who wailed for hours the day our mother died. The word she writes is the bright red of popped berries.

HUNGER.

She turns to me, laughing nervously under her breath, and holds tight to my arm. Her mouth is thin, pinched. Even here in Avazel, some signs of what has happened remain. There are shadows under her eyes that I have never seen before. I know the fists that put them there, and when I think of the broken body to which those fists belonged, I feel sick and glad and defiant all at once.

Then there is Silence, so quiet and grave, in a long black gown that floats about her legs like smoke. Her white hair hangs before her eyes as she bends over the open book. I hear the coven whispering about her. *Two new girls*, they say. *Girls who kill as well as any learned witch.*

Pride swells in me as I watch her write, her hand following my whispered instructions. I have brought them a clever girl, a girl strong in power, though she has not before tonight known its name. She writes in shaking red the word SILENCE. Her eyes glittering with tears, she crosses it out, smears it angrily, and writes beside it a bold new word.

SORROW.

Then she lowers herself to the ground, plants her fists hard upon the earth, draws in a ragged breath, and wails.

These are not the quiet tears I have seen her weep before. This is her ill father, her despairing mother, her lonesome, cheerless house. This is the howl of Widow Heath, her dead son in her arms.

The coven cries out with her, matching her ragged sobs. Ire's black bird takes to the sky, shrieking. Storm throws back her head, her metal arm gleaming, and sings harsh words I have not yet learned. But I want to know them.

I must know.

I *will* know. All there is to being a witch, both kind and cruel, I will know it, for I understand now what will become of me. After what I have done? After what I have seen and heard and thought? No, God will offer none of His light to me, and a great peace floods through me as I understand this. I was born to a Devil-touched woman, and the path of my life has brought me here at last. When I find the final two relics and call the great darkness to me, I know now that I will do it in triumph, godless, with only my sisters in power to help me. And whatever strength the Devil grants me, I will use it to protect myself and my own. No one will ever hurt my sister again. No one will ever again touch us in anger.

The thought leaves me calm as a windless winter night, clear and still and sharp. I am tired, more tired than I have ever been, and yet for the first time in my life, I am truly awake.

"We are saints not of Scripture but of fire," I whisper into my sister's golden hair.

"We are saints of flesh and bone," says Hunger. We open our arms to Sorrow. She moves into our embrace, her quiet eyes locked on mine.

"We are saints of the moon and the stars," she says. She turns her face up to the red moon and closes her eyes, a smile softening her face. I ache to draw my finger along the pale line of her jaw.

Vengeance takes my head in her hands and places her hot brow against mine. Perhaps part of her will always despise me for Temperance's death. And yet here she is, looking straight at me. Saint Vengeance, saying firm and fierce against my cheek, "We are saints of blood."

The coven encircles us, their hands joined, their voices hissing and whispering and weeping and singing—in joy, in fury, in mourning. We are a knot of girls within them, a fist of women.

I shut the book upon our names, clasp it in jubilation to my breast. Malice comes toward us and holds out her hand to bring me to my feet, but I do not need her help, not this night. I am not afraid. I am not ashamed. I am not the girl I once was. I am a saint. I am a witch.

I am Rage.

III

may your eyes see much

31

THE COVEN STUFFS US WITH hot food. Afterward, as the others rest and practice their spells, Mercy and Silence and I huddle in a grove of trees.

No. Those are not their names.

Mercy is now Vengeance. Silence is now Sorrow.

And Blessing, my own beloved, is now Hunger. In a nearby clearing, she sits beside grinning Ire. A red fox has curled up in my sister's lap with its white eyes closed, and Ire's crow hops across the moss to her, tame and chirping. Beautiful except for those strange Avazel eyes.

Ire claps her hands and rubs them together. "You have a talent with animals," she announces. "Just as Temperance did. Next time you come, once you've rested, I'll start teaching you how to slip inside their furry little minds and make them cleverer than they ought to be. How to command them as you will."

Hunger strokes the red fox's back, her brow troubled. My eyes fill as I look at her. She has always been a beauty, but here in Avazel on this night of bones, she is splendid. In Haven, her face never shines as it does now. In Haven, Father thinks he will someday find a man for her to wed—not Adam Brinsley in body, but perhaps someone like him in heart, and she would be trapped in her husband's bed instead of a barn.

But Father is wrong. That will not happen, not ever, not unless Hunger wishes for it to be so. Once my quest is complete, the relics in hand, my soul bound to the Devil's service, I will make certain of it.

"It seems wrong to order them about as if they have no minds of their own," my sister says. "Should I not first ask for their consent?"

Ire boasts a brilliant grin. "Good girl. That's exactly the right question to ask."

I watch them, silently saying our new names over and over and rubbing my fingers with the pad of my thumb. Vengeance. Sorrow. Hunger.

Rage.

I wonder if the other names will soon fade from my mind. Will I forget what my name once was, that saintly name I so longed for? How much else will I forget, or rename, or feed to the wolves?

All of it. The words are there inside me. Maybe they have always been, and it is only with my new eyes that I can see them. *I want to rename all of it.*

"We should agree upon what to say when we return," Sorrow whispers. Liberty, the gentlest in the coven, at once took a shine to Sorrow and has woven a few thin braids into her hair. Sorrow wraps one of them around her finger until the end softens and curls. "We must all tell the same story."

"Or we could simply burn Haven to the ground," says Vengeance. Muttering her own fire spell too quietly for me to hear the words, she snaps her fingers, which summons a sparking flame. "We have killed a boy. If we go back, they will see the truth of that on our faces. If we leave, they may never stop hunting us."

I shake my head. "We must return. I still have two relics to find."

My fingers itch to hold the book and belt, which I have sent away with a summoning spell said backward. A clever idea Liberty gave me—instead of bringing them to me, bid them go home, hide themselves away with the mirror behind the baseboard in my room.

I know they are there safely—the power tells me as much when I close my eyes, and ask, and listen—but I will not rest easy until I see them with my own eyes, and maybe not even then. Maybe not even after all five are mine at last.

Maybe, for a girl such as me, there can be no such thing as rest.

"We can find the knife and the key out here," Vengeance continues, "in the woods and the wild."

"But the story of Lost Abigail belongs to us," I say quietly.

"All the relics showed themselves on Haven's land, or on Haven's people."

Vengeance squares her jaw. "It may not be the same for the knife and key."

"But it seems likely, does it not?" says Sorrow.

I have told her everything—my quest for the relics, the sacraments of darkness, the book and mirror and belt. When she asked me what I will do when the Devil comes, I told her I would fight him with God's blessing and banish him, cast out all evil from our home, or else offer myself to him in exchange for Haven's safety.

But now, sitting under this fat red moon with Vengeance's furious words in my ears and Adam Brinsley's blood crusted on my hands, I am embarrassed by those feeble words.

What will I do when the Devil comes?

I dig my fingernails into the soft rich soil, watching my sister pet the red fox with a new sadness in her eyes.

'Tis a simple answer: I will demand from him the protection we deserve, no matter the cost.

"Three relics were found in Haven," Sorrow is saying. "Why should the fourth and fifth not be the same?"

Our eyes meet—softly, like the warm press of two hands—and then she looks away, hiding behind her tangled hair.

Vengeance leans closer, her eyes piercing me. "You know what they think of you in Haven. I heard about Elias Holt, and he is not alone. Over the past week, I was called to the House of Whispers many times, and all the men who confessed to me spoke ill of the name Barrow. They see your anointing as the beginning of a new dark age. How did Elder Thomas convince the others to anoint one of his girls, they say, after everything her mother did? Has he made a pact with the Devil? Exalt and protect his daughter, and in return, he lets the Devil feed on thirteen of our men? Once they know Adam is dead, the elders might assign watchmen to guard your house, make certain you do not go sneaking about. Maybe one will stand outside your window. The wall will hold thirty men at night instead of twenty, and all their eyes will be searching the dark for anything peculiar."

A curl of smoke from one of Vengeance's spelled flames floats before her freckled cheeks. "This is the home you wish to go back to?" she whispers.

She has rattled me, but I refuse to let her see it. "It is."

Vengeance pushes herself back from me. "Then you are a fool."

"Haven is not all bad," Sorrow whispers into the seething quiet. "Not everyone there is like Adam Brinsley."

Vengeance glares at her. "True. There is also your mother, who does not hit you now but might someday. Your father, who would not stop her even if he were well."

Sorrow closes her eyes.

"Vengeance, stop it," I say quietly.

She counts on her fingers. "There are Fanny and Hetta Jamison, who like to corner me at visitation and hit my chest until I can hardly breathe. There is Elder Daniel, who during his confessions sometimes undresses so I can see 'the wretched picture' that is his sinful body."

"And there is Samuel Aldridge," I snap at last. "And Elder Peter. And Granny Dale and John Ames. And my father too. Kind, godly people who do not deserve your wrath. We need not hurt them. We need only hurt those who hurt us. An eye for an eye, nothing more."

Vengeance scoffs. "And your father is not a dealer of pain? Saint Rage the Foolish. He could have stopped it, you know. Your father could have said Elder Joseph was a liar, and the other elders would have believed him, and your mother would still be alive. But he did not. He chose to condemn his wife to death. He chose to torment and then discard her."

My stomach lurches as if I have suddenly lost my footing. "She lay with Elder Joseph. They were both wed, and she lay with him many times."

"And for this she deserved to die?"

"She broke his leg. She poisoned him, tried to kill him."

"Yes, just as we killed Adam Brinsley. But your mother died for fighting her attacker. We do not have to. We can ruin them."

"Her attacker?" I press my fingertips farther into the mossy dirt. "She tempted Elder Joseph into her marriage bed. Then she grew afraid of being found out and tried to silence him."

"Do you really still believe that? After all you have seen and done? After all the years of loving your mother, those long hours she wailed out her story to the night air while tied to her post in the square, you still believe them, not her?"

I stare at her, breathing hard. Avazel glitters silver with my furious tears. Sorrow's hand finds mine and squeezes gently. I cling to her. The truth is, I no longer know what to believe about anything. I should never have followed Mercy and Temperance all those days ago. If I had not, I would be my old self still, a content and godly girl.

And yet, now I cannot imagine walking through the world without the taste of *extasia* on my tongue.

"My mother was weak," I say, forcing out the words. "She let the Devil in without a fight and went mad for it. I will not go mad. I will give myself to him and in exchange demand ever more of his power."

"Rage, please, you are frightening me," whispers Sorrow, her gentle touch as cool and smooth as a river stone, securing me to the ground.

Vengeance laughs, paying us no mind. "I have long envied your mother, you know. I have tried for years to let the Devil in. I have prayed for madness to set me free of this place, and since meeting the coven, I have prayed that their ritual will be the thing to do it at last. But instead I am now stuck here with you, a girl who denies the truth even as it lays itself bare before her." She looks at me in disgust. "Once you possess all the relics, will you have the courage to do what must be done? I had started to think you might, but now I cannot be sure."

"Watch me," I say fiercely, my harsh voice tearing out of me like a knife.

Vengeance stares at me, startled silent. Something changes in her face, shrinking her. A little flinching fear.

"Problems, girls?"

We look up as Malice comes near. She holds my sister's hand and settles beside us in a cloud of red skirts. Hunger scoots toward me, rests her head on my shoulder. With her on one side of me and Sorrow stroking my hand on the other, I am able to come back to myself. My heart slows and calms, though the air around me pops, as if I am more fire than girl, my every breath a spark.

"Rage wishes to return to Haven," Vengeance says quietly, her voice not so vicious anymore.

"Of course she does," Malice says. "She has a knife and a key still to find."

"Yes, but—"

"Listen, for years I have tried to call the Devil to me and failed. And now we've come to Haven. I studied *extasia* for months before I could do even half of what you girls can do." Malice looks at me, her bright blue eyes hard as stones. "The power brought you here for a reason, and the power never lies. You will find those relics. I will make certain of it."

"And our bargain?" I ask. "Only three days are left in the week you promised."

"Yes, so you had better search quickly."

"But what if it takes longer than three days, now that Adam is dead?" Hunger says quietly. "Everyone will be watching us."

"It wasn't *my* decision to kill him," Malice says calmly. "I thought I already made this clear. Once your week is up, my coven will return to the work we were doing before. I can't trust that you'll succeed, after all, no matter how many flashy tricks you can do."

She speaks so carelessly, as if it is nothing at all, what we have done, what is still to come. I think of Hunger's frightened cries, the shadow of Adam's body darkening the hay upon which she cowered, and clench my fists. "Given what has happened this night, you should grant us more time."

Malice snorts. "You're a funny one, Rage."

"If you do not, once I find the knife and the key, and the Devil comes, I will turn whatever power he grants me against you."

Her smile freezes, a small thing that does not reach her eyes. "That would be extremely unwise."

"Killing people will not help us in our search!"

"Odd that you should say so, since you yourself just murdered someone."

A little lash of shame hits me, the first I have felt. I shove it aside. "Adam was hurting my sister, and then he was hurting *me—*"

"I didn't say you were wrong. Just stating facts. Now." Malice waves me silent and addresses us all. I bite my tongue. I may yet need her in the days to come.

"What you need before you go back," she says, "is a good story. Something to convince your people that you've done nothing wrong. Something to turn their eyes elsewhere and keep you safe."

Vengeance hisses out an annoyed breath and crosses her arms over her chest.

"But what story would they believe?" Sorrow asks softly. "When they find out Adam is dead—"

"You must think like a witch. Avazel gives us what we need when we need it, as you've seen. Clothes and food and tools. You need some time to rest and plan and practice what you'll say until you can say it without thinking. Avazel will give this time to you. Then you'll return home. You'll tell them about us, the horrible women in the woods. You'll show them your wounds, your bloody clothes, and spin a wild tale. Tell them we wanted you for our own, but you fought us, and your bravest men must go find us, or else we'll come for you again and again. And while your men go off chasing shadows, hunting for witches they'll never find"—this she says with a crooked grin—"you, little sisters, will pray hard. You'll pray often. You'll pray in the bright sunshine where all can see you."

"And with their attentions scattered," Hunger says, "we will search for the final relics."

"I do not see how," says Vengeance sharply. "Once we return, they might very well lock us in our rooms."

"I have the utmost confidence you'll find a way," Malice says, rising easily to her feet, "talented girls that you are."

I catch that look on her face before she turns away, that little secret smile. Our cat, Shadow, looks just the same after she fills her belly with mice. The sight freezes me. Does Malice think she will somehow find the last relics before I do? Does she want us to return to Haven so we will be watched, leaving her free to steal my relics, take my quest from me, and claim all the Devil's favor for her own?

I feel sick at the thought. She would not do such a thing. She *could* not. *Extasia* would not let her. *I* will not let her.

Once Malice is gone, Hunger says quietly into the silence, "What if we left? We could forget the relics altogether and travel far from here. The coven says there are other places in the world, yes? Well, we could find one, a safe place, and begin there anew. All of us."

"Run away?" Sorrow twists her fingers in her lap, her face drawn and pale. "But what if we find nothing? What if we are lost to the wild? What if we follow a road paved with pink stones and find a door, but beyond the door is only fire?"

"What?" Hunger says. "What road?" Then she frowns, her gaze distant. "I have heard that before somewhere . . ."

I pull Hunger closer, rubbing my thumb against her palm in a quiet panic. I have not told her about the stories Sorrow has heard from the ghosts, or even what the ghosts might be. She thinks they are simply some tool of *extasia*, dark creatures that guard and aid us.

I will do whatever I must to keep her thinking that way. The only thing worse than the thought of Mother still being in the world, even if only dead and floating, is the thought of what truths she might whisper to Hunger when I am not there to hear them.

"A safe place," Vengeance says, her voice flat. "You truly

think there is anywhere in the world that would treat us kindly? You think there is anywhere safe besides the spaces we make for ourselves?"

Hunger does not answer that, nor do I. Instead, I turn away from Vengeance, draw my sister closer to me, and bury my face in her hair. The night is beginning to wear on me, its weight like stones pressing my shoulders into the earth. I feel Sorrow settle on my other side, curled up against my back. I reach behind me, under my hair, to find her hand resting near my neck. I crook my finger around her tiniest one and hold on tight.

Somewhere far above in the canopy of white branches, birds begin to sing, their cries strange and eerie. As I slip into sleep, I try to think of what a safe place would look like, what it would feel like to step inside it—how many rooms the houses would have, what the people would pray for, what flowers would grow in their gardens—but I am too tired to picture it. Instead, my shapeless dreams roar red with the blood I have spilled, or have yet to, though whose blood it is I cannot say, and I am too afraid to look.

32

WE WAKE IN THE ELM grove, scattered under the trees. Above me, beyond the black branches, a dim gray sky. Early morning. When I swallow, my mouth tastes sour and my throat feels raw. A knife in my head strikes fast and sharp.

It tastes as though I have swallowed bloodroot, though I do not remember eating it.

When I touch my lips, they bloom with pain. In Avazel, the hurts from Adam's fists vanished, but now they are back, though not so terrible as before. My face is swollen. My fingers come away red with blood. Hunger has a mean bruise on her face where Adam struck her.

But the true strangeness comes when I look at Vengeance and Sorrow. When we left the Brinsley barn and fled to Avazel, they were well and whole, but now there are scratches up and down pale Sorrow's arms and legs, as if a creature with thin sharp claws has torn her flesh. Beneath Vengeance's red hair, her left eye is black and violet, and she cannot fully open it.

"What has happened here?" whispers Vengeance. She clutches herself and breathes thinly, as if her ribs are bruised, and I wonder if Malice kicked her. Or was it Gall, or Ire?

"Did we sleep?" asks Sorrow, staring at her cut-up limbs. "I do not remember falling asleep."

"It was the coven," Hunger says, low. "They hurt us, to help the lie."

My skin prickles. I think she is right. Malice said we must tell a good story, and now here we are. Did we lie there unaware in Avazel, spelled asleep, while the coven kicked and struck and cut us and then shoved bloodroot into our mouths?

Vengeance stares miserably at nothing. "They would not do that to us. We are their *sisters*."

"Perhaps only when it is useful to them," I mutter, pushing myself to my feet just as a shadow peels away from the elm branches above and drifts down.

My heart seems to stop, jarred silent with fear. It is her—the ghost I know with the mouth full of flies. She braces herself against the ground with those long arms like poles and tilts her head to the side to stare at Hunger, who watches, trembling, in her torn nightgown. Then she reaches for my sister with her long, thin arms—too long, too thin—and opens her mouth wide, and there it is, that bell. A silver smile jammed deep in her throat.

My heart is a hammer and anvil. It clangs and hums against my bones. The gray woman moans a low, sad note like the beginning of a song, but I do not want to hear it, nor see her face, nor have her anywhere near my sister. Looking at her, hearing her, makes it hard to breathe. Sorrow said she has seen echoes of things in the ghosts' shadows—noses and eyes and bits of color. My mother's face. And if that is true? What words might she say for all of us to hear?

I jump to my feet, spring at her wildly, wave my arms, punch the air.

"Go away!" I cry. "Leave her! Leave us!"

Then a bell rings through the silent morning—an elder's bell, soon joined by its brothers, and last of all the higher, shriller bells from the wall. The sounds jolt me. I look again, and the ghost is gone.

Sorrow's wide blue gaze catches my own. I grab Hunger's hand. Even Vengeance looks afraid.

A woman shrieks in the distance. Soon after, the cries of others rise into the air. Haven is waking up and finding another of their sons gone.

Hunger squeezes my hand. "We must go to Father. Now, before they realize we are all gone too and make their own story."

"Do we understand what we must say?" I ask, looking around at the others. Vengeance gives a sharp nod. Sorrow swallows hard, her restless hands turning at her waist. I wish there was time to comfort her.

Instead, I hurry toward town, the others close behind me. Thanks to Adam Brinsley and Malice and her coven, none of us has to pretend to limp.

Near Holy House, a murmuring, teeming crowd has gathered. A quick glance tells me nearly all of Haven is here. Silver-haired Granny Dale, wrinkled lips pursed in consternation, pushes her way closer to whatever is happening, four small grandchildren clinging to her nightcoat. Elias Holt glowers at everyone, both hands tight around the barrel of his rifle. Tabitha Grainger whispers frantically to her daughter, Hannah, who is for some reason sobbing into her apron.

At the heart of this chaos stands my father. And at his feet kneels Hester Brinsley, Adam's mother, and behind her stands Uriah Brinsley, Adam's father. In Hester's red arms is their dog, a mean cur with a bitten ear and a knife stuck in his chest.

No, not a knife. A white branch from Avazel.

The sight of it shakes my every bone.

"My son!" Hester Brinsley is a thin woman, pale and wild-eyed, with long hair in dark waves. She wails at my father's feet, shoves her dead dog at him. "My son is not in his bed. We cannot find him anywhere. When we went to look for him, we found this on our steps! *This!*"

I draw in a long round breath. *Tell your story, Rage Barrow. Do it now, and do it well.*

I push forward through the crowd. My fear has shoved my heart high in my throat, and I am tired, dreadful tired, and my face tingles with the echo of Adam's fists, so when I open my mouth, a horrible cry bursts out. I do not have to pretend my distress.

"Father! Help us!" I throw myself toward him, but before I can reach him, Elias Holt crashes into me, whacks my arm hard with his rifle, and knocks me flat.

I lie on the ground, gasping. The fall has knocked new pain into my wounds. I feel around in my mouth with my tongue, but I have not lost any teeth. Not yet.

Immediately, two men yank Elias away from me. A few of the elders spread out, hands raised to calm the shouting, shifting crowd. Samuel rushes over to help me sit, along with Willow Dale, one of Granny's younger daughters. She was one of the women who took my inconsolable wailing sister home the day Mother died. But I do not want her or Samuel. I want Hunger, Sorrow, Vengeance.

I reach out, searching for them, trying to blink the black spots from my eyes. A soft hand finds mine. I know those fingers. I squeeze them, pull my sister close.

"Since she was anointed," Elias roars, struggling against the men who restrain him, "four men have been executed by a great evil, their bodies abused and defiled! Jeremiah Heath, Tom Wickens, Zacharias Rutledge, and now Adam Brinsley, all in less than a month!"

"Peace, my son," says Elder Peter, who has hobbled over to stand between me and Elias. "Yes, the Devil has his claws around our home, but that is no cause to attack our own."

Elias's face screws up in furious disgust. He spits at Elder

❖ 265 ❖

Peter's feet. "And what do you know, old man? You limp around for years, not an inch from death, and this is supposed to protect us from the fires of Hell?"

Angry mutterings rise from the crowd. Everyone surges closer, barely held back by the elders and their seconds. Frantically, I search the faces surrounding me, looking for my father. But instead I find Elder Joseph, smiling smugly, leaning hard on his new crutches and doing absolutely nothing to help.

I am glad to see that face I hate, those thick waves of gray hair. Out of everything that happened all those years ago, for some strange reason, I remember his hair most of all. How fingers could sink into it and grip tight and tug. But now, that bandaged leg of his reminds me of something else—what I have done, what I *can* do—and dulls some of my throbbing pain.

Rage. With each pulse of my pounding head, my name rises higher and higher inside me until I can almost see the blazing letters. *Rage, Rage, I am Rage, and the power loves me.*

Samuel shoots to his feet, pointing at Elias. "How dare you disrespect the elders! They have the ear and favor of God! To curse them is to curse Him!"

"Blasphemy!" someone shouts in agreement.

"God sees all, God judges all!" comes another enraged cry.

"Silence!"

My father's voice rings out, a crack of lightning splitting the world into quiet pieces. He moves through the crowd. Everyone parts around him, but it is me he looks at. All of me. My cuts and bruises, my swollen face.

Samuel and Elder Peter and Willow Dale give him room. He kneels before me, calm as a bedtime prayer.

"Tell me plain, Amity," he says. "Who did this to you?"

His soft voice pops me open. Real tears come, exhausted and angry and afraid. This lie will be easy.

"The women," I say through my tears, "the wild women from the woods, they took us from our beds! They beat us, Father, they tore at us! They had long claws like wolves instead of fingers!"

I fall forward, and he catches me, and the feeling of his strong arms holding me up makes me cry harder. The others follow me, and oh, they are clever, my girls, they are cunning liars. Hunger clings to our father's side, sobbing into his shirt, and Sorrow and Vengeance kneel beside him, beseeching. We are a piteous sight, to be sure, and when I glance around at the people of Haven, I see a staring crowd gripped by sudden, horrible fear. Even Elias Holt looks spooked.

Father holds my shoulders. "Slowly, Amity. Tell us what happened."

I whimper, pushing down my sobs. "The women, the witches in the woods. They stole us from our beds."

"Witches?" Father asks.

I look up at him, at everyone. I wait until I can feel their every held breath. "Wild women who worship the Devil."

The crowd gasps, curses, spits, shouts, weeps. A din of frightened disbelief. Beyond my father, Elder Joseph is no longer smiling. Elder Peter has closed his eyes as if in pain.

"They took Blessing and me first," I continue quickly, my fingers nervously wringing my father's sleeve, "and then Mercy and Silence. They dragged us from our beds with arms like snakes and stuffed our mouths with foul cloth so we could not call for help. They flew us, Father, they *flew* us out over the wall on white branches and hid us with their cloaks so we would not be seen. And in the woods . . . in the *woods* . . ."

I let my words break and fall. Hunger speaks next.

"They told us to sign their Devil's book, Father," she whispers harshly, "but we did not. We *would* not. I had never seen such a thing as this book, so dark and terrible, but I knew it for evil, and I would not touch it. They struck me, and still I would not. The Devil's book can only be touched by one who wants to touch it, they told us that."

"They brought us Adam," says Sorrow in her thin quiet voice, crouched at my father's feet. "They cut upon him while we watched. They said to us, sign the Devil's book, or we will claim this boy for our own."

Hester Brinsley wails anew. Uriah Brinsley, Adam's father, sits down in the dirt, looking blankly at his hands.

"We would not do it," says Vengeance. She huddles on the ground with her arms crossed over her chest and shivers, her hair wild about her face. "We knew it for an evil trick. We longed to save Adam, but we could not exchange our souls for him. We could not!"

I touch my father's face with shaking fingers. The tale has been told. Was it told well enough?

"I do not think we were wrong, Father," I say, "and yet my heart grieves for Adam, that he must live now in the woods with those women. They will make him their own, they said, they will . . ."

I cry out and bury my face in my father's shirt. For a moment I think, *Ah, here is the safe place I tried to dream of. Here in my father's arms.* But then I think of the truth hiding behind our lies and Vengeance's words from Avazel—*He chose to condemn his wife to death. He chose to torment and then discard her*—and no matter how hard I try to push all of that away, the safe feeling shatters and abandons me. Once I was a girl named Amity who would have felt her father's embrace and been purely, cleanly glad.

That girl, it seems, is truly gone.

"They told us they will keep him alive for many long years," I say through my tears. "They told us they will not let him die, even if he begs for it!"

My words stir the people of Haven into a frenzy. They shout for the elders. They fall to their knees and cry out for God. Hester Brinsley drops her dead dog and collapses. Everyone scatters away from her. She crawls to my father, pushes us aside, grabs his trousers.

"Please, sir," she cries out to him, "please, you must save my boy! Go to the woods and find him! *Save him!*"

Father looks at me once more. I cannot read his face. The lines around his eyes, mouth, and brow betray nothing, and a cold, quiet terror takes root in my belly.

What if he does not believe us?

"Brave men of Haven!" he cries, turning to address our people. "One of our sons has been taken by dark forces, and we must trust that God will protect his soul until we can reach him. Who among you is brave enough to ride out with me and bring him home?"

Many men punch the air with their fists and yell their assent. But not everyone. Elias Holt shakes off the men holding him and stalks away. Several others follow him, including Elder Joseph, aided by his second.

"Take them to Holy House and wait for us there," Father tells Elder Peter quietly, with a quick glance at us girls. "Lead prayers and read from the Sanctificat. Reassure them." He clasps Elder Peter's shoulder with a small smile. "We will return with Adam before nightfall."

Elder Peter nods but says nothing. His brow shines with sweat as he shuffles toward me, aided by his second. A boy named Timothy Williams, young but strong, who stares openly at my wounds. Other elders call out words of hope—*Gather with us, let us all come together and sing praise to our Lord, let us pray with such joy in our hearts that the Devil will run from us in fear!*

The crowd breaks apart. Some follow Father to gather weapons and horses. Others storm away, muttering, glaring back over their shoulders.

Everyone else drifts along with us, holding hands, muttering prayers. Someone helps dead-eyed Uriah Brinsley to his feet. Someone sits with wailing Hester. Someone takes care of the dead dog.

I do not dare look at Elder Peter as he leads us toward Holy House. What would he see in my eyes if I did? Some glimpse of the truth? The girl who sweeps his floor and cooks his suppers has killed a boy and would do it again if she had to.

There is great evil afoot, Elder Peter said.

He was right. And it seems that evil is me.

33

When night falls, all of us gathered in Holy House, our throats raw from praying, hear the sounds of horses' hooves, baying hounds, shouting men. Getting louder, getting closer.

I raise my head too quickly from its bowed position. My body aches a little less than it did this morning, for Elder Peter made sure we were tended to—Hunger, Vengeance, Sorrow, and me. We have bandages and ointments, water and a little food. But my head still reels as I stand up. Everyone rises, looking to the doors. Hunger hooks her arm around mine.

I glance quickly at Vengeance, but it seems she is better than I am at hiding fear. She looks concerned but pious, placid. She is a saint and has been praying all day, just as she ought to, and all will soon be as it should.

And Sorrow—her eyes are clear as pale stones in shallow water, her smile serene. She murmurs the Woman's Prayer over and over, not stopping even now. She has been reciting it all day. A small circle of women huddle around her, clutching her skirts, hunched over in prayer. Their soft unbroken refrain has wormed its way into my bones. I can feel the words crawling inside me like busy ants.

Wherever you step,
whatever you seek,
may your tongue hold still,
may your heart live meek.

I clench and unclench my fists. *Gather yourself, Rage Barrow. Be calm and look sharp. You are a witch, not a child.*

The doors of Holy House boom open. My father is the first one through them, striding straight toward the altar. Behind him, solemn and twitchy, come Elder Daniel, Elder Wyatt, their seconds, and several watchmen, all of them sweaty and dirt-smudged. Their eyes find me and the saints, my sister. They stare hard. They stare right under my skin.

Only Samuel does not look at me, his fierce gaze trained dutifully upon my father. Has he found out the truth? Or is he merely protecting my secrets? Maybe if he looked at me, his eyes would betray what he knows.

With all the strength left in me, I hope that is true. *Please, Samuel. Stay with me for only a little while longer.*

Father's gaze travels across the room. He lets the silence grow until the air draws so taut it feels ready to burst. Then, without a word, he holds up a brown cloth sack for all to see, reaches inside it, and draws out, by a chunk of matted dark hair, the mangled head of Adam Brinsley.

Holy House blows apart into screams, hoarse cries, wild wails from the children. Desperate shouted prayers, furious demands soon lost in the uproar. None of these are as awful as the sounds of Hester Brinsley. She pushes herself toward the altar, howling and sobbing, animal in her grief, and reaches for the head of her son.

But my father is pitiless. Without one word of comfort, he returns the head to its sack.

"Thirteen men of Haven have now lost their lives to evil," he says, his solemn voice blotting out all other sounds. "And in the woods today, as we searched for Adam, we saw even more signs of that evil."

"What did you see?" several people call out.

"Unholy creatures," one of the watchmen yells. John Britteridge—wild-eyed, shoulders hunched, thinning brown hair plastered to his forehead. "Deformed beasts with white eyes and forked tongues."

"Darkness came, and our torches went out," calls out old Moses Eaton, his eyes full of tears, his voice cracking. "No matter what we did, we could not relight them!"

Listening to them, I quietly panic. How should I hold my face? How frightened should I look? How serene? Hunger turns into my sleeve with a soft cry. I could shake her, I am so afraid. Will they believe her distress? Is it too much?

"We rode in circles for hours," mutters Calvin Fletcher, drawing a shaking hand over his face. "Something chased us, something that howled. But we could not see it."

"I saw it!" James Turner pushes forward, climbs halfway up the altar steps. "I saw curved horns. I saw wings spread out on either side like a great fearsome bat!"

"You saw a stag or an owl and let your fear run away with you," Samuel says firmly.

James turns on him. His smile is thin and mean. "Trying to protect your girl, is that it? Trying to make us think there is nothing to fear, that all the men who have so quickly died since Amity's anointing mean nothing? Well, I know what I saw."

"Something foul lives in those woods," mutters John Britteridge—and then he points a savage finger at my father. "What will you do to protect us? What *have* you done? Nothing!"

Cries of agreement sweep through the room. Some people crowd toward the altar. Others hold them back, shove them away. John Ames grabs James Turner by the collar and yanks him off the altar steps. James swings wide with his fist, but John easily dodges him, then knocks him flat.

Someone shrieks, "Let me pass! Let me through!"

My bile rises. I think that was Hester Brinsley.

"Calm yourselves!" Samuel cries, spreading his arms wide. "Listen to your elders!"

"Enough."

My father's voice cows them all into silence.

I wonder how many more times he will be able to do so.

"You are correct, John Britteridge," he says after a tense moment. "Something foul lives in those woods. Something evil lives *here* in Haven, among us. And we have not done enough to protect you."

Father gestures at the elders nearest him. Elder Peter leans hard against the holy table, his face drained of all color. Elder Joseph watches unhappily from the shadows like some skulking rat.

"For this negligence," my father says, "we ask you to forgive us. We are God's disciples here on Earth, but we are still merely men. We are imperfect. We feel fear, just as you do, and sometimes that fear means we do not act when we should. But there is a reason God left only us here in Haven alive after The World That Once Was fell."

Father lets those words settle in the air. The fear inside me is making me reckless. I want to scream at them all that they are wrong. We are *not* the only ones. There are cities, towers, governors, witches. A world of others. Now that I know this, it seems impossible that my fool neighbors do not.

Though here in Holy House, it is all too easy to doubt everything the coven has told me. Servants of the Devil would do that, would they not? Confuse me, muddle my mind with untruths to slow my quest?

My head pounds with something like malevolence. I need to rest. I need to *think*. But this I know: if anyone in the coven has lied, I will find out. When the Devil comes, he will tell me everything and whisper to me what punishment would be best.

"Unlike the dead of that fallen world," my father says, "we can see the wrongs of the past, the mistakes, the poor choices, and learn from them, and continue on with even greater strength. We have done it before, and we will do it again."

The crowd shifts. I see people nod—Samuel, Moses Eaton, John Ames, Sarah Abbott. A few cries of *amen* scatter through the room.

"We have not protected you well enough, precious children of God," Father continues, his voice rising with each sentence. "But that ends tonight. God tests us. We will accept every trial with love in our hearts."

"Yes!" cry the people of Haven.

"Amen!"

"Hear us, oh Lord!"

"The Devil hunts us," Father cries. "In answer, we will raise our voices ever louder to God!"

The room swells with sound—bellowed cheers, calls to God, praise of God.

My back is drenched with sweat. I force out a scratchy, "Amen!"

"Believe me, my neighbors, my friends—this night begins a new era in Haven!" Father calls out. "From this day forth, doors will lock at dusk, and all must remain in their homes unless accompanied by an elder, a second, or a watchman. Anyone who trespasses outside after this time will be held in the House of Sighs until they have fully understood their crime and satisfied the elders with their penitence."

My heart sinks. It takes everything in me not to look at Vengeance in dismay.

Book. Mirror. Belt.

Knife. Key.

How will we find them now? Under such rules, the strangeness of *extasia* will be clear to anyone nearby unless we take excruciating care—and in two days, our time to search will end.

Father raises his arms before anyone can object. "Now, hear me! I know this may seem severe, even unfair. But I ask you this—did God choose us because we are weak?"

"No!" the crowd cries as one.

"No," Father agrees, "He chose us because we are people of sacrifice, of vigilance. And so we shall honor His vision! We—your elders, your watchmen, who put themselves in harm's way to guard you—will search every home in Haven. We will ask questions. We will look into every heart, consider the fortitude of every soul. Young and old. Anointed and not."

Then he looks straight at me. "No one will be spared from these efforts. Not even your elders or their families."

Fear drops down my throat, so bitter and scorching I feel sick. That cold, unfeeling look is the same one he gave me the night he caught me running from Temperance in the meadow. As if I am my mother born again.

His whispered name sits on my lips. A plea. An apology.

I nearly confess and ruin everything. *I killed Adam Brinsley, Father. The relics are hidden behind the baseboard, Father.*

Hunger pinches my arm.

I grit my teeth, turn my saintly gaze to the floor.

"Evil is cunning," Father says, "but it lacks the wisdom of God. Its path is strewn with tokens of wickedness for those who search hard and well. And so we will. We will root out whatever evil lives here and strike it forever from our lands—but first!"

And in that pause, I hear what will come next. I have dreaded it this entire day.

"We shall have a visitation," Father cries, "this very night!"

The people of Haven cry out in elation. My body clenches up tight, all my cuts and bruises screaming in protest.

"As we have always done," Father says, "in times of both joy and despair, we shall take comfort from our saints. Though they are only three, they remain symbols of what has come before and what shall never come again. And the saints themselves," says he, turning his back on me, "may be cleansed of whatever evil touched them in those dark woods that claimed Adam Brinsley's life."

Then he tears Hunger away from me, and the crowd surges forward. No oil tonight, no ceremony or prayers. The people of Haven do not want more prayers.

They want only this.

I look for Samuel, for my father, Hunger, Elder Peter, but find only the scowls and grins and fists of my frightened people.

My throbbing head whirls, pulling my thoughts inward and twisting them. The white trees of Avazel. The pile of twigs scattering across my bedroom floor. The etched words above Holy House's doors—CONCORDIA PER DOLOREM. Harmony through sorrow. Sorrow, Sorrow. Where is she? Where is Vengeance? But they are already gone. Someone tears a bandage from my forehead. Someone drives their fist into an open cut. The pain is so blinding that I gag and fall over, which makes those nearest me laugh.

Lying flat, black spots in my eyes, I look up to see Hester Brinsley looming over me. Her fist is red with fresh blood— mine.

Beyond her, the shadows split apart and take a new shape. My ghost, with her fat mouth of bell and flies. Gladness spills through me to see her there, thrashing her long gray body in the shadows as if to see me hurt is to feel hurt herself.

I reach for her with a trembling arm. I dare to look straight into her mouth, searching, seeking.

Hester Brinsley smacks down my arm. She grabs my hair, brings my ear close to her mouth.

"You hold lies inside you, Saint Amity," says Hester, tears rough in her voice, "and I shall not rest until I find them."

34

THE NEXT DAY, FATHER TAKES me to the House of Whispers. Samuel has requested a confession.

Only yesterday, I would have been glad for the chance to see him. But this morning, as soon as the words left Father's lips, the scrap of peace I had found during my short night of sleep tore itself to shreds.

Samuel wants a confession—his own? Or mine?

I try to think of what I will say, how I will defend myself, how I will lie, but my exhausted thoughts are slippery and cross, impossible to order. With each step, my wounds throb quietly with pain.

During the walk, Father talks of nothing. Little things, pleasant things. As if he was not holding a head without a body yesterday. As if I am not limping and terrified beside him, pious and contrite in my ribboned yellow dress embroidered with blue flowers.

"What a beautiful day God has blessed us with," he says. "We shall have to thank Him for it during evening prayers."

Is it beautiful? I suppose. Blue sky, bright sun.

Dead boy. Knife and key, somewhere, and two days left to find them. Less than two, truly—what remains of this day, and then all of the next.

"Yes, Father," I say quietly.

"I thought tonight we might also read from the Sanctificat," Father says. "The Book of the New World. A story of Haven's first days to remind us how far we have come."

"Yes, Father."

Haven buzzes around us. With the elders' new rules, the daylight is even more precious. People stop in their gardens to watch us pass. They let their arms fall and stand beside their hanging laundry. They stop playing with their brothers, lean close to one another, whisper.

Father does not seem to mind, but I know he does, deep in his heart. Nothing about our family has been what he thought it would be. I think of the four painted girls holding hands in Hunger's and my bedroom. Two blank faces, two smiling ones. Again and again and again. Father on his stool, Mother standing on a chair. Painting girls, painting lambs.

I blink back tears. Would a house like that feel safe? Four daughters, all of them saints. A father, a mother. Both alive, both happy. The Barrow name still bright and shining.

"You conducted yourself well during last night's visitation," Father says at last.

I look over at him. At the same time, he looks at me. I watch his eyes travel over my bruised, swollen face. A shadow of something passes over him. A softness, there and gone.

"Thank you, Father. I . . ." I lose my voice, look away. My mouth draws tight with anger. Last night's visitation was short but fierce. Not once did Father step in to lead a prayer and offer me a moment's rest. I wish I could grab his shirt and shake him and ask him why. I wish I could show him my power, snap a fire to life right before his eyes, and watch him quail.

But there is the road before me, footstep after footstep. I clasp my hands at my waist. "I wish always to make you proud."

Elias Holt sits on the fence outside the smithy, sweaty from his work as an apprentice. As I walk by, he spits on me. All he dares to do, I suppose, with Father beside me. A huge hot fleck of it hits my cheek. I let it drip freely. Soon I will walk at the Devil's side, and I will remember this feeling well.

Father does nothing to admonish Elias. Of course he does not. Why this surprises me, I cannot say. Weeks ago, I would not have expected it. I certainly should not expect it today.

And yet, somehow I have come to expect new things. I have come to want more than I should be given.

Inside the House of Whispers, I sit rigidly on the bench beside Samuel. He watches the floor. I watch him—his handsome pale brow, his troubled dark eyes. The quiet is monstrous. It has a beating heart.

"You have to stop," he says at last.

Relief leaves me weak. He is not accusing me of anything, not today.

"I cannot stop," I tell him. Calm. Unafraid. That is not a lie, but this is: "I have to save Haven."

"Thirteen men and boys now dead. Adam torn apart by God knows what. You bruised and hardly able to walk. And this is saving Haven?" I open my mouth to protest, but he pushes on without me. "Four men have died since your anointing day. Four men in one month. 'Twas a good thing you tried. Noble and brave. But clearly it is either angering God or pleasing the Devil, or both."

"We cannot know that," I argue. "God sends trials to those who aim to fight for Him. And perhaps the Devil is lashing out because he is afraid of me. After all, I have three relics now. Only two more, and then he will have to face me at long last."

Samuel goes very still.

"Amity," he says, so quietly it frightens me. "You did not tell me you had found the third relic. The belt?"

I grip the edge of the bench to hold myself up. What do I say? All my words and wits are gone, and in their place a wild bird of fluttering panic.

"Yes," I whisper. "The belt."

"But when I last saw you, before Adam went missing, you said nothing of it."

"I . . . I forgot to tell you."

"Or you found the belt between then and now."

My thoughts scramble. I did not expect this. Foolish girl; I should have. Samuel's mind is sharp. What false story can I tell him? I need more time. I need to return to the safety of my bedroom and *think*.

I am silent for too long.

Samuel rises and steps away.

"Adam," he whispers. "Adam Brinsley."

A heartbeat, a second heartbeat, a quivering pulse in my throat. I open my mouth, but nothing comes out.

Samuel's face falls open with sadness. "You killed him."

The how of every lie I have ever told falls out of my head. I fumble for words, but I have used them all up.

Samuel turns from me, drags a hand through his hair. "How dare you? How *dare* you, Amity? You never told me you would kill to find these relics!"

Finally, my feelings land on something—anger. The burn of it comforts me, clears my head.

"You should have guessed," I snap at him. "Skin, fire, bone, blood, palm. This is a quest of sacrifice and violence."

Samuel is pacing, his movements more and more frantic. "If I had known this would happen, I would never have agreed to help you. I would have dragged you to the elders that very first day!"

"Samuel, please listen—"

He whirls around, angry tears in his eyes. "Amity, Adam

did not deserve to die."

"You were not there. He was going to hurt Hun— He was going to hurt Blessing."

"And so you decided you would be the one to cast judgment on him? You alone would choose his fate?"

"Blessing asked him to stop. He would not listen. He beat her, and he beat me." I point at my face. "I did not give myself these bruises!"

"He was with Blessing, you say."

"Yes, in the barn. They were . . ." I clench my fists, nails into palms. "They were lying together. My sister wished to stop. He would not."

Samuel looks aghast. "Your sister was lying with him. She agreed to lie with him, and then she wished to stop."

"As anyone might wish to stop eating, or drinking, or wish to stop sitting and stand up instead! What if I told you I was no longer hungry, and you kept shoving food into my mouth all the same?"

"That is different, Amity."

"How? Tell me."

He looks away, but I will not allow him to hide. I rush around to stand before him. "Tell me!"

"Because she is a girl unwed," he bursts out, "and yet she chose to lie with Adam. She chose lust over virtue, when that is one of the very things that brought The World That Once Was to ruin!"

Now I am the one to step back from him. My Samuel, my

gentle Samuel. I hardly recognize my friend. I do not know that voice. I hardly know my own.

"You think she deserved to be hurt by him," I say quietly, slowly, each word a steep hill to climb. "That she should have borne his fists without complaint."

Samuel looks at me as if I have truly lost my senses. "Yes, Amity. As the Sanctificat explains. You know this. You have always known this. It happened just last night, at visitation. I saw Hester Brinsley hit you, and you did nothing. You accepted it beautifully, just as you ought to have done. Why should your sister have done any different?"

And he is right. I did what I was taught to do, and so did he. He watched them strike me and thought, *Yes, that is correct.*

I could choke on my disappointment. I could weep fire for a thousand years.

"I should have known you would think such a thing," I whisper. I laugh a little, astounded at what I am about to say. But I *will* say it. He has hurt me, and I will hurt him. Kindness is for girls named Amity. "Mercy told me Benjamin always sought her out first at visitation. He hit her so hard it drew blood. He wanted to be the first man to mark her. It was not devotion; it was cruelty. He hungered for it. All this time I thought you gentle, kind, and good. But I suppose that beneath the kindness, you are just the same as he was."

The silence between us then is the worst thing I have ever heard. I lift my chin against it.

"I love you, Amity," Samuel says at last, looking away from

me, his face half in shadow. "I have loved you always, even now, and I will not tell your secret, terrible as it is, because I know your heart is true. But you will stop this quest *now*. No more relics, no more visits to the woods. You will do as your father tells you and let the elders do the rest."

Then he does look at me, his expression so fierce that I know he speaks true.

"Do this," he says hoarsely, "stay home and stay quiet and forget this quest, this power, that damned infernal book—and never, *ever* talk about my brother again—or I will tell the elders. I will tell them everything."

He gives me no time to say another word. He opens the door, waits for me to limp out into the sun, and walks me home. Samuel lightly kisses my cheek at my father's porch, as every good boy does for his betrothed. Then he leaves me to walk inside, past my sister cooking in the kitchen, down the hallway, and into my bedroom, where, as loudly as I dare, tears streaming down my face, I scream furiously into my pillow for the friend I have just lost.

35

THAT NIGHT, MY BACK AGAINST the house, knees hugged to my chest, nightgown on, feet bare, I sit in the dark in my garden, holding very still.

For the hundredth time today, I consider uttering a cloaking spell. The thought of Sorrow being trapped inside her desolate house makes my insides clench up. If I were cloaked, I could visit her and Vengeance, see with my own eyes that they are well, that their wounds are healing. Hunger could come with me. We could, all of us, run. Run somewhere. Run *anywhere*.

But for the hundredth time, I decide against it. I cannot leave Haven before I have found the knife and the key. And I cannot find the knife and the key if my cloaking spell fails and I am locked in the House of Sighs for being caught outside after the elders' curfew.

Instead, I sit and watch the watchmen.

A dozen of them patrol the streets of Haven, their torches bobbing up and down like fireflies in late summer. Another nine have been assigned to guard the elders' homes.

I do not know who circles my house tonight, and I do not care. He is nothing to me, neither man nor beast. He is simply a shadow carrying torchlight, passing around the yard, around my house, and back again. My garden grows so thickly along our fence, a solid wall of flowers, that I cannot see him and he cannot see me. I hear his boots on the ground, fading away, then coming back. Once, he unbuckles his trousers and relieves himself, a hot stream of liquid hitting our fence and trickling down.

The sound makes me seethe, but there is no time to ponder whether there is a spell somewhere in Malice's book that will turn a man's piss to fire, because here comes Shadow, trotting proudly out of the weeds. She carries something in her mouth.

I hold my breath. I moved too quickly the first time, perhaps an hour ago, grabbed for the mouse before Shadow was close enough. She ran off with it still dangling from her jaws.

But it seems this time she appreciates my stillness and cannot resist showing me her conquest. She drops the mouse at my feet, then flops onto the dirt, bends around like a sideways moon, shows me her belly.

My pounding heart pushes heat all the way down my limbs, granting me a lightning quickness. I grab the mouse by its tail, scratch Shadow behind her ears—blessed killer that she is—and crawl back through the window, wincing as I bend my tender limbs. Carefully, quietly.

Hunger is awake, of course. My own tireless watchman, sitting patiently by the door.

"Anything?" I whisper.

She shakes her head, inches a little closer to me. "She found one?"

I nod. "The most useful creature on God's green Earth."

Reverently, I lay out the mouse before me on the floor. So tiny, still a little warm, only a bit mangled by Shadow's teeth.

A giddy thrill twists in my chest as I bring out the book from its hiding place. Samuel would hate that I am doing what he asked me not to do. He would be furious. If he spoke true this morning, he would run to Father and tell on me.

But Samuel is not here, and if I have not found the knife and key by tomorrow's end, the week Malice gave me will be finished. Malice will start killing again, maybe even someone I love, just to show me she can, and already the fear in Haven hangs thick as smoke in the air.

I cannot let her win. The Devil is mine, not hers. *Extasia*'s whispers said *Amity*, not *Malice*.

Staring grimly at my little dead mouse, I scatter petals across the floor. *"Vanuriisa,"* I hiss—the word Malice used that day in Avazel on the buck and the one-eyed man. 'Tis the first on my scrawled list of spell words. Each one appeared near *blood* in Malice's book, which I cannot look at without thinking of Samuel and aching with furious grief. I hope the memory of our lessons fills his sleep with nightmares forevermore.

The word said, I hold my breath and wait.

Nothing.

I crush one petal under my right foot, another between two fingers. Thinking of my garden, my flowers, the earth beneath them, my feet on the floor, the mouse's scrubby little hide, the cuts Malice made on the dead buck, I try again. My fingers bloom with heat.

"Vanuriisa!"

The mouse's dead body jerks slightly. A thin cut opens near the top of its left back leg.

Near the door, Hunger yelps and claps a hand over her thigh. Shakily, she draws up her nightgown. A thin bloody smile cuts across her white flesh.

I stare at the wound in astonished horror. I had thought that if it worked, the power would cut *me*. That was my intent, the thing I held in my mind. Not Hunger, never Hunger. I drop my petals and hurry to my sister, but she waves me away, her mouth thin.

"Keep trying," she says tightly. "'Tis only a shallow cut."

My eyes fill as I settle once more by the book, the mouse. She is right—only a shallow cut. It will heal quickly, and no one will see it and wonder where it came from.

And yet my clammy hands still shake as I mark through *vanuriisa*. Too dangerous, with Hunger here. I shall not utter it again.

I move to the next word, and the next, practicing each one until it rolls easily off my tongue.

Camliad.

Vauldaph.

Iallay.

Nothing. For hours, nothing. The mouse grows cold, Hunger's eyelids grow heavy, and I could scream with frustration. One more day, only one more day, and after a night of tireless work, I am no closer to finding what I need.

When there is time to try only one more spell before Father wakes and chores begin, my eyes land on the clumsiest of all the words I wrote out. How I despise the sight of my ungainly letters, etched with awkward care and none of Samuel's deftness.

Weary, my voice hoarse, I whisper, "*Grozixniila.*"

And then, easily, silently, the mouse opens. Like streams of rainwater on a window, thin rivulets of blood rise on its body and join together and trickle to the floor.

My joy is ferocious, a heat that spills through my entire body. The sun rising all at once, bright and boiling.

Hunger, now fully awake, sits up straight and grins. "There it is," she whispers. "That is the one."

I blow out a long breath, smiling at the mess I have made. A rooster crows. The world outside our window is a downy gray.

Dawn has come. Only one day remains—this one. And between this moment and nightfall, the hours are far too few.

36

THE DAY SPILLS THROUGH MY fingers like water.

In a quiet frenzy, I pray with Hunger and Father in the morning, eat breakfast, scrub the kitchen floor, do the washing, say midday prayers when Father comes home after a meeting with the elders, scrub the hallway floor and stare out the front window at the watchmen marching by—up and down the quiet streets—as everyone hurries to finish their work by sundown.

One of them paces around and around our house. Ten times. Twenty. He pauses to rest, shifts his gun from one shoulder to the other. Paces again. Even in daylight, we Barrow girls are not to be trusted, it seems. Today it is James Turner, his face sullen but wary.

I pause in my cleaning, peek out from behind the flowered white curtains Mother made.

My heart pulses in my fingertips. I know the word to

say—*grozixniila*—the word for bleeding that *extasia* seems to prefer I use. And only a few hours remain to find the knife and key, and being trapped in this house as the sun crawls across the sky means I am forever swallowing a desperate scream.

Maybe . . .

My fingers twitch against the curtain.

I could try it on him. James Turner. I could do it right now, make him bleed, hope the knife appears soon after, grab it, grab the other relics, grab Hunger, run. The final sacrament of darkness: *palm*. Maybe my hands clasped around my sister's, terror binding our palms together, will be enough to summon forth the key, and it will be done. Such luck seems unlikely, but if I can only bring us all safely to Avazel, perhaps I can bargain with Malice for more time, flatter her, plead with her, keep her somehow content until I do find the key. And then witches and relics, all of us together, will call forth the Devil at last.

But when James Turner strides by the window, I duck in sudden fear and start my cleaning again, shoving my brush against the wooden floor so hard that I feel the bristles in my teeth. When I have finished, I am panting, flushed hot, crawling with anger. I need help, guidance, from someone I can trust, and since the creature I seek has not shown herself to me, not since visitation two days prior, I shall have to find her myself.

I throw the brush into its bucket and hurry into the kitchen, where Hunger stirs a pot of boiling potatoes. She has been quiet all day, tense and pale.

Soon I will stop hating myself for drawing her into this

mess of mine. Soon the Devil will come, and we will be safe at his side.

"I am going to try something," I tell her. Each terse word feels feral in my mouth. "In the garden, before Father comes home." I put up my hand before she can speak. "Do not follow me or ask anything else. If he comes home earlier than he ought and asks where I am, you will tell him you do not know, and it will be true."

Hunger glances fearfully out the window at the reddening sky, then nods.

"I love you," she tells me as I walk out the kitchen door. I wish I could stuff the words back in her mouth. I do not want to think about love, not right now.

Blazing with purpose, my eyes fixed on the far side of the yard, I shove my left hand into my pocket, which I keep filled with fresh petals. No doubt, no hesitation.

"*Ziirdagras,*" I hiss—a word I found in Malice's book, a word I liked the look of, woven as it was into a scratchy drawing of trees that seemed somehow familiar. Peering closer, I found letters among the branches. *Ziirdagras.* I have never uttered the word until now, but as it falls from my tongue, I clutch my petals, and with all my strength, I imagine the white trees, the red moon. I charge into the thickest corner of my garden, and I do not stop even when the thorns prick me and the vines grab at my ankles, not even when the fence should stop me.

Two steps, five, twelve, and my foot lands on the mossy forest floor.

Alight with triumph, I spin around and search the black Avazel sky, the shadows drawn by the white trees, the roots and their hollows.

"Where are you?" I shout. "Show yourself!"

Stillness. A distant wolf howls its song at the red moon.

I plunge into the trees, walking so quickly it seems my feet will soon lift off the ground. Here in Avazel, my skin is whole, my bruises gone. The paths leading here are many, in this desperate moment, I dare to hope for a life long enough to find all of them.

"You come to visitation," I cry out, pushing past branches, stomping through thickets. "You scream with Temperance as she burns, you show me the way out of the fire, help me save Hunger, float and fly and stare, and yet *now* you disappear? You show yourself to Sorrow, but not to me?" Climbing over a huge fallen log draped with moss, I choke out an angry little sob. "I know why. You are angry with me. You blame me. Well, I blame you! I did not choose the things you did! I was but a child, and now I am a child no longer, and I need help. Do you hear me? Or do you come only when you wish to, never when I wish it? *Where are you?*"

I stumble to a halt, hands on my knees. How far have I walked? The soles of my bare feet burn, as do my lungs, and yet the Avazel skies are quiet, the shadows still and faceless. No ghosts here, not today.

"I will not say your name," I mutter, wiping my face. "That is what you would want, but you shall not have it."

Bleary-eyed, I look up to search the wood once more, only once more before I lose my courage—and see a clearing that was not there moments ago. At its heart stands a pool of water. Around it grow soft gold grasses, thin pale trees, thick snowy brambles tipped with red berries. The black water matches the dark hollow places behind my eyes. Its stillness is that of deepest sleep.

"Rage?" Malice, looking harried, pushes through the tangled white thicket at the clearing's edge. The branches snag on her skirts. She has to shove with all her might to get through them, as if they do not want her here.

"Damn, girl," she hisses, shaking out her dress. "What are you shouting about? You've spooked everyone. What is—"

Then she stops, her gaze frozen on the pool of black water.

"How did you do this?" she asks quietly.

The look on her face chills me. "Do what?"

She approaches the pool slowly, as if she fears it will rise up and drown her. She crouches beside the water, staring for a long moment, then looks up, dazed, and beckons to me. Only hours are left in this day. I dare not refuse whatever *extasia* chooses to show me.

I kneel beside her, dig my bare toes into the mud, and try to find the solid steady feeling my garden gives me, the soft warm green of all the things I have grown. Then, holding my breath, I peer into the black water—but I see only myself, and Malice, and nothing else.

"It's a scrying pool," Malice whispers. She draws her

hand through the air above the pool, but the water does not ripple. "An elusive tool, and powerful. If she's lucky, a witch can look into its black waters and see things no one else can. A scrying pool has shown itself to me only once, years ago, and when I looked into it, I saw nothing."

After a moment, her mouth hardens. "Same as now," she says bitterly. Then she looks at me, her blue eyes narrowed. "I suppose it isn't here for me. Lean in, little sister. What does the water show you?"

I cannot move my body for fear. This pool is an open mouth in the earth. If I peer inside it, I will fall and never reach the bottom. But beyond Avazel, the sun is setting fast.

I lean out over the smooth dark water and look down.

Once my eyes hit the water, a cold so great it burns shoots from my fingertips down into the dark deep. As if I have dropped a stone into its depths, the water shivers and changes, but though I see colors and shapes, I can make no sense of them. There is gold and brown, then white and red.

"Ask it a question," urges Malice beside me. "Calm your thoughts. Don't waste this."

I have many questions, and yet I ask only the most pressing one. Two relics remain, and thus far I have found them in the order spoken in Lost Abigail's story. I have no reason to think this will change. To find the key, I must first find the knife.

Where can I find the knife?

I say it without moving my lips. Instead, I press my hands into the dirt and think it. Chest burning, thighs clenched, fingernails filling with mud.

Then comes the answer. The water's colors shift into a familiar shape—my sister, eyes still and staring, skin bleeding from a hundred knife cuts. Bare arms drifting, bobbing, in the cold endless black.

37

W_RENCHING_ MYSELF BACK FROM THE scrying pool, I let out a horrible sound—part scream, part sob.

Impossible. *Impossible.*

This water must be lying. Not even the Devil would be cruel enough to require that the next sacrament of darkness—blood—be carried out using my own sister.

But then comes the memory of that cut on my sister's thigh, smiling across the room at me, and I think, yes, yes, of course, the Devil is entirely that cruel. Perhaps I should have expected this all along.

Malice is saying something, but I do not wait to hear what. I push away from her, slap her back when she comes too close, and run. Where, I do not know. Just *away*, crashing through the tangled white brush like some crazed animal, gulping down whining, frantic breaths. I fumble for the petals in the pocket of my white gown. Avazel has been kind enough to leave them there.

"Ziirdagras," I gasp out, and duck under a low white branch, then stumble out into a different light—sunset over Haven, the sky the same as it was when I left. Not yet nightfall. My legs shake with relief. Avazel granted me precious time. Father may not have even realized I was gone. But then I blink, steadying myself, and see the elm tree near Elder Peter's house, which seems to lean more to the right every year.

My fear must have broken my connection with *extasia*, or displeased it. This is not my garden. The power has thrown me out on the other side of town.

Voices and footsteps send me scrambling for the elm tree. Its huge gnarled trunk is a decent hiding spot. I catch my breath, press my trembling fingers into the bark, then peek around.

A ways down the road, three elders in gray tunics, their seconds in blue, and two armed watchmen gather at someone's porch steps. A lantern, a torch. I narrow my eyes, squinting through the fading light. 'Tis Sarah Abbott and her two boys, her husband, and her mother, all standing on the road. Waiting as the elders go inside to search their house.

The sight frays my already-thin nerves. They are searching every home for signs of the Devil, just as they said they would. And what do they think they might find? My mind races through all mentions of the Devil I can recall from the Sanctificat. A shed serpent skin? Tracks left by cloven hooves?

I think hard, trying to remember if I properly put the cut piece of baseboard back over the hole in the wall. Did I move my bedside table back into place? What if they search our house while I am gone, with only Hunger there to think up a good lie?

Hunger. My *sister.* The sight of her dead body floating in the black water comes back to me, and I sink to the ground, hand clapped over my mouth, and squeeze my eyes shut. No, *extasia.* That I will not do. That I *refuse.* Not my sister. Not even for you, Devil. I would rather cut my own self to pieces than see any harm come to her.

I push myself up, my knees wobbling, and wipe my face so hard it hurts my bruises. I must go to her now. I should never have left her. I look back at the Abbott house. Their backs are to me. If I run home now, I might make it unseen.

Then a light passes through the shadowed place farther down the road where several trees stand close together, near the Brinsley barn. I swallow hard, my hands clammy and cold. Floating in the air, the light moves left for a time, then sinks to the ground.

Something rumbles deep in my bones, rolling forward again and again. I think of a stone being pushed across the earth. It moves faster and faster away from me, tugging at my breastbone, and I must follow it, I must find out where it leads. There could be a knife at the end of it, a knife wearing my sister's name.

I have no choice, and I have no time.

I run toward the light, past windows glowing gold beyond their closed curtains, past Tabitha Grainger's tidy garden and the Farthings' yellow house and Granny Dale's sprawling green cottage, and then I turn the corner, where I stumble to a stop.

Hester Brinsley sits in the dirt outside her house, beside her fence lined with flowers—posies and bluebells, nodding yellow-and-black susans. Beside Hester is a thin candle in a brass holder. Her dark hair flies wildly about her face and down her back, and her wet red nightgown sticks to her front. Her eyes are white, all their color gone. She grins at me, or maybe at nothing.

And in her lap and on the ground before her, spread out all around her like the petals of a torn flower, is her husband, Uriah Brinsley, cut into a hundred shining red pieces.

38

I SEE HIS HEAD AND the two dark places where his eyes once were. I see his ribs and toes, all his plump insides glistening in piles.

Hester lifts a piece of him toward her mouth. My stomach twists and heaves. She means to eat it, I know it; she means to tear into it with her own teeth.

I rush toward her, knock her flat against the ground. We tumble, and I land on a scattered pile of something, wet things, hard and soft things. A hand torn from its arm, pieces of flesh and bone I cannot name. I cry out and scramble away.

Hester turns on her hands and knees, her eyes white and her mouth stained red. The air quakes around her, hot and reeking with the smell of blood. Those eyes of hers, as bright and unblinking as Ire's birds—someone has spelled her. Ire? Malice?

She crawls fast toward me and strikes my temple, a tender place still bruised from Adam's fist. The sudden swoop of pain fells me. I crumble with a sharp cry. Hester grabs my hair and lifts me up and spits upon me. I twist myself loose, but she grabs me and slams me to the dirt. I push hard, wriggle free of her, and stumble away.

"You will not take him from me!" Hester cries, huddled on the ground. She scoops the ruin of her husband into a neater pile. "My boy, my Adam, he will be safe here with me!"

Her harsh voice splinters. It is her voice, and I could swear it is another's too. She stuffs her mouth and starts to chew. I could think of some spell to stop her, maybe, if I could think at all, but those awful wet sounds are driving everything out of me except the urge to run.

"Dear Lord," Hester mumbles, "keep him safe inside my belly, right where he came from. No one can touch him there, not if he's there in my blood, no, not even the Devil."

My sight wavers, the world a blur. I race down the dimming road and through Elder Peter's gate. At his porch, I grab the rope of his elder's bell and pull hard. Its clanging din will soon bring everyone to the streets. Where are the patrolling watchmen, the elders searching the Abbotts' house? I look around, tugging wildly.

Elder Peter comes out in his nightshirt, coat, and boots. His hair, white and already slept upon. When he sees me spattered with blood, he hurries over as best he can, helps steady me.

"What's happened?" he says at once.

I point down the road, my arm shaking. "Hester Brinsley has killed her husband," I tell him. The lie comes quick. "God spoke to me as I said my evening prayers, and I snuck out and found her."

Elder Peter stares at me. All the color has left his face, and there was not much there to begin with. But then he nods and touches my arm.

"Take me to her," he says firmly.

I do, though walking as slowly as we must makes me want to scream. Other elders' bells have taken up the call. My neighbors rush out of their homes and down the road. I wave them on, screaming for them to hurry. Black-bearded Elder Wyatt gets there first, along with his second, Patrick Dale. They grab Hester Brinsley and drag her away from the ruin of her man. She is beastly, fighting with wild shrieks. She claws and bites and tears; she kicks at their faces and scratches at their eyes.

"My boy!" she screams at them, her milky eyes leaking milky tears. "I must hide him! I must keep him here, where no harm may come to him!"

Father pushes forward through the crowd, Hunger just behind him. Her worried eyes find me at once. I shake my head frantically at her. *Stay there, stay back.* And then it happens all at once, too quick for me to shout or move. Hester grabs Father's knife from his belt, lunges straight for me with a piercing shriek.

"She did it!" she cries, the blade flashing. "It was her!"

But before the blade can find me, it finds someone

else—Elder Peter, who shoves me out of the way and stumbles into Hester Brinsley's path. The knife sinks into his gut, and his little surprised grunt of pain seems to shake something loose in Hester. She stops, stares, rips the knife out of him, and watches him fall, her mouth agape. The rest of us stare in shocked silence.

Then, with a laughing mad sob, Hester turns the knife around and thrusts it into her own belly—smooth, fast, as if she has been practicing for this all her life—and falls forward into my father's arms.

39

WITH THAT, MY BREATH SLAMS back into me. "No," I whisper, still frozen, and then my knees give out. I am on the ground beside Elder Peter, lifting his head into my lap. "No, no, no," I whisper, and someone takes hold of my arm—maybe Hunger, maybe Samuel—but I shove them away and snarl over my shoulder, "No!"

Elder Peter groans, his eyelids fluttering. He lifts a hand to my cheek, hooks a trembling finger into my hair. His mouth opens, closes, opens again. I lean closer, listen hard.

"Forgive me, child," he whispers, and then his body slackens. He slides a little, sagging onto the dirt.

I shake my head, sobbing over him, smoothing back the sleepy tangles of his hair. "No, please, no . . ."

Then stronger arms, one at each of my elbows, pulling me back. They unhinge me. I whirl around, kicking and twisting.

There is Elder Peter's second, Timothy Williams, and Elder Wyatt, and Elder Daniel, all of them kneeling beside my friend, closing his eyes, bowing their heads. Someone in the crowd around us begins to wail, quickly joined by several others.

"No, let me go! Leave him alone!" How dare they touch him? How *dare* they lift him from the ground as if he were a mere sack of grain? "Elder Peter! *No!*"

Someone slaps me. I fall silent, gasping for air. Father is there, holding me hard by my left arm. Past him is Hunger, her face wet with tears—and Samuel, standing protectively near us, his rifle in hand. Our gazes lock, but I cannot tell what he is thinking.

I try to push words into my eyes. *I did not do it, Samuel. This is not my fault.*

"Come with me," Father says. He looks past us, whistles sharply, then starts storming down the road, still gripping my arm. I stumble to keep up. Hunger and Samuel hurry after us, and Elder Malcolm and Elder Phillip, and several others—John Ames, Moses Eaton, Calvin Fletcher.

"Where are we going?" I say, gasping.

"Home, before any of them have a chance to kill you too," Father mutters. "Though your grief for Elder Peter might have saved us. Tell me what happened."

"God spoke to me as I said my evening prayers," I answer. The lie tastes sickly sweet, like overripe fruit, but I have to say it, I have to find the words. "He told me I should hurry and tell no one, for there was danger near. I did not know where to run, but I prayed and listened, and God led me to the Brinsley plot. I tried to stop Hester, but she struck me. I ran to Elder Peter's bell and rang it."

But after that, I can say no more. Not even my father's great strides can outpace the crowd rushing after us.

"More, Elder Thomas!" Fanny Jamison calls after us. "Not one killed this night, not two, but *three!*"

"Did you do it, Saint Amity?" roars Elias Holt. "Did you cut up Uriah Brinsley?"

"No Barrow girl should wear a hood!" cries Jacob Farthing.

The words come faster, louder, until I cannot tell apart the voices.

"Take her hood! Take her hood!"

"Bring her to Holy House!"

"How much more death will your family bring upon us, Elder Thomas?"

That voice I recognize. Sharp and rough, more pleased than angry.

Elder Joseph.

We reach our house, and not a moment too soon. The shouting crowd rushes toward our porch, right on my heels as I stumble up the steps after Father. He wrenches open our door, shoves both Hunger and me inside, then bursts back out, points his rifle at the sky, and fires three times.

The sounds crack and echo like thunder. I hear the shuffling, stumbling steps of our pursuers scuttling back to the road.

I drop to my hands and knees on the hallway rug, drag

myself to the window. Hunger whispers my name, begs me to sit still, but I push her away, grip the sill with shaking fingers, and pull myself up to peek out.

Around our house, two crowds have gathered—one facing the house, pressing as close as they can, furious and glaring, the other surrounding our porch, facing the others with guns raised. At least a dozen watchmen defend us, as well as several of the elders' seconds and Elders Malcolm, Phillip, and Ezra.

But not Elder Peter.

I heave against the wall, hearing over and over in my mind the squelch of Hester Brinsley's blade—my *father's* blade—sinking into his gut. Was this the blood sacrament? Is that the knife I need?

No, it cannot be. I did not commit that violence. Or did I? I failed to find the knife and the key in the week Malice gave me, so she did what she swore she would, and now it is nightfall on the seventh day, and now Uriah and Hester and Elder Peter are dead.

Then my father begins to speak, his voice the clearest I have ever heard it, the strongest, the most beautiful. He stands to my right, on our porch. The lines of his face—his nose, his jaw—fill me with an aching, desperate love.

"I know you are frightened," he says. "I am frightened too. But we cannot allow fear and anger to—"

"How strange it is," calls out Elder Joseph, "that whenever something dreadful has befallen us this past month, your daughter is somehow tied to it."

Murmurs of agreement sweep through the crowd. Some raise their torches, their guns. Desperate, I search the crowd for a white head, a spill of red hair. Sorrow, Vengeance. What must they be thinking? They must be terrified, wondering what will happen next, what they should do, what *I* will do. If only I knew; if only I could speak to them.

"You forget yourself, Elder Joseph," shouts Samuel from the steps. I blink, wipe my face, try to pay attention. His back is to me, but I would know those brave wiry shoulders anywhere. "You speak to the High Elder of Haven!"

More shouts surge up from the crowd—my name, my father's name, my mother's name. Defending us, condemning us. A confusion of anger that pulls my chest so tight I can hardly breathe.

My father raises his arms, then his voice. "I will remind all of you that 'twas not only my decision for Amity, my daughter, to be anointed a saint of Haven. 'Twas the decision of all the elders, after many days and weeks of conference and prayer."

A pause. The silence settles. My father knows, more than anything, how to command a crowd with his voice.

He steps forward, lowers his gun. "These curses you hiss, these accusations—do they mean you doubt your elders, and thereby doubt the word of God? Well, for that, as I have said before, I cannot blame you. I too look in horror upon what has happened this night. Hester and Uriah Brinsley. Elder Peter. All of them struck down by evil none of us can begin to fathom, for only God our Lord can see the full truth. But I can tell you this—your elders will continue the work we have begun. We will not rest, we will not sleep, until we have searched every house, shone light into every dark corner, frightened every beast of evil from its den. And until then . . ." His voice trails off. I see his jaw working, how the torches of everyone gathered glitter in his eyes.

"Until then, I offer you this: a public penance. Is it my family, my wife and daughter, who have brought evil into Haven? I do not think so. I pray it is not so. But until we know this for certain, I must atone, for it is under my watch that Haven has suffered so profoundly. I hope that this act of attrition appeases God, and I will do it here, now, before all of you, so you can see with your own eyes that no one is spared from the justice of God—not even me."

The air is heavy with a waiting hush. There is the lowing of a cow, the call of a bird, then silence.

The door opens, admitting my father. He does not look at us, Hunger and me, huddled near the window, but I can see him well enough. His haggard face looks wrenched open, every line on his skin carved deeper, and my chest clenches from loving him. I hold my breath as he enters his bedroom, then returns with a long slender cord coiled in his left hand. He returns to the porch. Kneels. Removes his shirt and gives it to Samuel. Turns so that everyone can clearly see what happens.

Hunger grips my arm hard. I sink to the floor. I cannot look.

Silence for a time, and then a horrible lashing sound. A slap of sharp to skin, followed by gasps of surprise, muted shouts of awe. They cannot believe what they are seeing. Thomas Barrow, High Elder of Haven, half naked and repenting right before their eyes. Laying his shame bare for them to gape and gawk at.

Then it happens again, that lashing sound, and Father lets out a low, sharp groan.

Hunger claps her hands over her ears and runs toward our bedroom, keeping close to the wall so no one outside can see her flee. Shadow scampers after her, tail high and happy.

I stay right where I am, breathing in rhythm with that cracking sound, that hiss and slap. I have not heard it in years, not since the spring when Mother died. For weeks after that day, my father whipped himself every night so that in the morning, the people of Haven would see his shirt soaked in red. The shame of a man who had wed a poisoner, an adulteress, a liar.

A strange peace comes over me as I sit and listen, my hands pressed flat to the floor. My gown, wet with Elder Peter's blood, and Hester's too, clings sticky to my chest, but my pockets still smell of flowers. I take a petal, bury my nose in its silken little cup, breathe deep.

I did this.

Hiss, crack.

I did this, and I would do it again.

Adam Brinsley.

Hiss.

Elder Peter.

Crack.

Hester Brinsley. Uriah Brinsley.

Hiss.

Zacharias Rutledge.

Crack.

My father's muted cry hits the window, but I listen with dry eyes.

Hiss.

Maybe there is still time. Uriah and Elder Peter make fifteen men dead and one woman. But it is sixteen *men* Malice needs, and if I move quickly, perhaps I can still beat her to the Devil, and Father will never wear that look on his face again, never feel pain again, and whatever knives hunt Hunger will never find her.

Crack.

Malice needs to kill only one more man to finish her ritual, but I still need two more relics to finish mine, and now the sun has set.

Crack.

Malice's cunning is great, but my will is even greater.

Crack.

I cannot stop, will not stop, until this is done.

40

THAT NIGHT, I WAIT UNTIL everyone has gone home. Father has shut himself in his room, Hunger has cried herself to sleep, and the watchmen are circling our house. But I have *extasia*, and it muffles my steps as I climb out the window.

My garden is quiet, my mind clear. I hurry toward the far corner, its piles of green and blooms. *"Ziirdagras,"* I whisper, and the power opens a hidden path to me. Green becomes white, nightgown becomes dress, moon turns red. White-eyed birds watch me from the trees. A few minutes of searching leads me to Malice sitting on a fallen white tree, skinning a hare and humming cheerfully to herself.

"I saw you coming," says Malice, her eyes on the naked creature hanging from her fist. "Thought I'd meet you half-way." Her eyes flick up at me. "You seem troubled."

I am breathing hard, sharp all over with the rising heat of

my anger. I want to say a thousand things.

"You hurt Vengeance and Sorrow after we signed our names in the book," I tell her. "You did something to make us sleep, then cut on them and kicked them while they were not awake to stop you. You fed us bloodroot against our will."

"Of course," Malice says, still deftly working. "All of that was to help you craft your story. And they believed you, didn't they?"

"Barely," I say through gritted teeth. "You made Hester Brinsley think her husband was her son. You whispered some spell to her that made her think he would be safe if only she ate him."

Malice rests the hare in her lap and sits back to look at me. "Well, your week was up, or at least near enough. It was time for me to get back to work."

"But why her? Why Hester and Uriah? They had done nothing. They had only just lost their *son*. And . . ." No, I will not cry, not even for my friend. Not now, not in front of Malice. I am not sad, I am not grieving, I am *angry*. "And Elder Peter. He was kind and gentle. He was my friend."

Malice laughs. 'Tis a patient sound, but not particularly kind, as though I am a bad child throwing a fit on the floor. "Sweet Rage, with those fierce little fists and those red cheeks. You're much prettier when you're furious."

My chest coils tight and hot, like a fist clenching to strike. I speak through my teeth. "Why them? Tell me."

"I saw what Hester did to you during your last visitation. It made me extremely angry. And may I remind you, she raised that boy Adam. And look what he did."

"So you decided to hurt her in return."

"It's not only men who hurt us, you know. Hester Brinsley is not absolved simply because she's a woman. And if I could rid us of her husband? Well, good riddance. Adam was his boy, too."

"But Elder Peter—"

"Elder Peter is the worst of the three," Malice snaps. "I didn't set out to kill him, but what beautiful, blazing luck. He added to my count, and now I need only one more. And some friend he was. He held great power in your village, and what did he do with it? He hurt people. He sat back and let everyone hurt *you*. Maybe it pained him to watch you beaten and groped and humiliated during your visitations, but did it pain him the thousand times before that, when other girls endured the same?"

To that I have no answer. I stare at her, remembering the horrible hollow lostness of Elder Peter's face these past weeks. As if he had seen something terrible and had only just now begun to understand that the terrible thing was him.

Malice, watching me closely, nods in satisfaction. "You see? I know you understand. You killed Adam, didn't you? He hurt your sister, and you hurt him. Hester hurt you, and I hurt her. There are many things you can do with anger, but I've found none of them are as powerful as that. We are the same, you and I. We are dealers of pain."

It is as though she has slapped me. I step back, my head

ringing. "You are wrong. Your killing is selfish. I was protecting my sister."

"And I was protecting myself and my own. It's the same thing, Rage. And didn't it feel good to crush the bastard's bones into a knot? Wouldn't you do it again in some other barn, to some other boy who won't listen to your sister when she says no?" She smiles a little. "I think you would."

And she is right. Staring at her, her words sinking into me like stones to the bottom of a river, I know she is right. A roaring heat floods my body, head to fingers to toes. Feverish, faint, I scramble for something to say. "You do not know what I saw in the scrying pool. My sister is in danger, and what you did might have made that danger worse."

"Ha! Rage. Darling. We are always in danger. Everywhere we go. No matter what we do."

"But you must have known that by killing the Brinsleys, everyone would watch me, and Vengeance, Sorrow, and Hunger, even more closely. They burned a saint not so long ago. My father cut open his back earlier this very night, in plain view of everyone, to keep them from storming our house and killing me." I clench my muscles, trying to hold back a storm of tears. "You knew that could happen, and you did it anyway. You do not care about us at all."

Malice sighs. She stuffs the skinned rabbit in a sack and rises to leave, muttering something I cannot hear.

"What was that?" I hurry around to block her path. "What did you say?"

She lifts her cold eyes to mine. "I said, you are *weak*. If I were in your place, I would've found those relics weeks ago. I wouldn't have rested until they were mine. And yet here you are, still searching, still sniveling and cowering, coming out here to yell at me about hurting *Hester Brinsley*?"

Indignant, I choke out a few words. "And Jeremiah Heath. And Benjamin Aldridge. And Elder Peter."

"Yes, yes, and so on, and so on." Then Malice steps closer, her blue eyes blazing. "These people will never change, Rage. Your people. My people. Cunning's people, and Gall's, and Ire's. They'll never stop hurting you, or your sister, or your friends, or any of us, unless they're so hurt themselves that they fall to their knees and beg to be spared. That's the only way it'll work, little sister. We've tried everything else. We've tried kindness, we've tried mercy, we've tried education. The women in the before times, they did all of that, but it was too late. I won't make that same mistake. Will you?"

When I do not answer, struck speechless by the savage light in her eyes, she looks me up and down, her lip curling.

"You don't deserve to meet the Devil," she says at last.

Then she leaves me standing among the white trees, alone and aching under the still red moon.

41

THE NEXT DAY PASSES IN wretched stillness. Father left early, ruined back and all, to meet the other elders in the House of Knowing. Elder Peter will be burned in the House of Woe tomorrow. Watchmen are in the streets, circling our house.

And Hunger and I are inside, doing nothing, waiting for something, *anything*. I am stuck inside my own thoughts, inside my own useless body. I practice my spell again when Shadow finds another mouse, and the blood rises easily, spills onto the floor. I scrub it away. Without a body to use it on, there is no purpose to the spell, no purpose to *me*. I have become trapped inside my own quest, and the only way out is to kill again, but I do not know who it must be or if I can do it.

Malice would say, *Of course you can. You already did it once. Why not twice?*

"Only to protect my sister," I whisper. And Sorrow, and

Vengeance. My father. Samuel. I seek the Devil to protect them from harm, and to seek the Devil, I must harm others in their stead. Like Malice, I am a dealer of pain.

I know this is right. It is the only way forward I can see. We have been hurt, so now I will hurt. But those words sit askew inside me, crooked as my own clumsy letters.

I start to pace. The men skulking outside pace all day, all night. Well, I will too. I kick the bloody mouse under the bed. Shadow, kept unjustly out of the bedroom while I work, stops her pathetic meowing and knocks over the broom standing in the hallway. The sharp smack of the handle hitting the floor makes me jump. Everything makes me jump. Everything could be something come to kill my sister.

"Shadow!" Hunger scolds. She is cooking supper. I smell roasting vegetables, the golden sweetness of baking bread. "You horrible cat. Go outside!"

The kitchen door opens and shuts.

I watch Shadow bound up the garden fence and out. Lucky thing. If she is frightened, annoyed, bored, she can run off and go somewhere else. If she wanted to leave, she could. If she disappeared, no one would run after her. If she is hungry, she can eat. If she maims, if she kills, if she attacks her attacker, no one thinks anything of it. 'Tis natural. A creature with a will, using it. What is more godly than that?

That night, restless and angry, tense with worry I cannot push away, I fall asleep late and wake up even later to see, of all things, Sorrow, outside my window in her nightgown and a dark cloak bordered with pink embroidered flowers. Her hair a tangled mess, pale as a dove's belly. Her smile beaming.

When she sees that I am awake, she beckons me outside.

I hurry to the window and open it. "What are you *doing*? You should be at home! If they catch you—"

"But I have been practicing the words you gave me," she says. "The unlocking spells. The cloak. I think I am rather good at it. I came all the way here, and no one saw me. I missed you and thought that if we were quiet and cloaked and in your garden, we could talk and no one would see. I have practiced every minute I could find. Are you proud of me?"

Proud? I stare at her. I cannot stare at her enough. The sight of her in my garden, surrounded by my flowers, so close to my bed, robs me of all sense.

"Well done, Saint Sorrow," I manage at last, and her sun-bright smile cuts me to the meaty quick.

She looks past me, smiles. "Hello, Hunger."

My sister, now awake, gives me a groggy smile. "Do not worry. Father is asleep. Haven is quiet. I will keep watch. Go."

Yes, Haven is quiet. Too quiet. But the night outside is warm, the bugs are singing, the breeze makes my flowers nod *yes*, and the moment I take Sorrow's hand to climb out the window, all the clenched-up bits inside me soften.

We must walk close together for me to stay inside her cloak—and she spoke true. 'Tis a strong thing, a shell of cool supple air around us that moves as we do but never breaks.

The outside sounds fade away, leaving only my breathing, her breathing, our feet in the dirt.

She leads me to the back corner of the garden, where the flowers grow thickest and where *extasia* opens its path to Avazel for me. But I utter no spells this night.

Sorrow is spell enough.

We crawl into the green, ducking under vines heavy with honeysuckle, and when we settle in the little hollow there, so buried that we can no longer see the world beyond my flowers, Sorrow reaches for me, hesitates, then opens her arms to me with a shy smile.

"I did miss you," she says, her wide blue eyes so careful, so hopeful. Her slim pale arms, still bearing their cuts, are almost too tender a sight to bear. Here she is, battered same as me, reaching for me so gently that all the fear and anger inside me rises up as warmth, buzzes in my cheeks, spills out of me in quiet tears.

"I missed you too," I tell her, and burrow close to her, clutching her nightgown and listening to her pounding heart until I find my breath again. She says nothing, only strokes my hair softly. I am grateful. What could she say about all that has happened? There is nothing left to say that I haven't already thought, wept, wished, raged about. I am tired, and she is too, and we are here together, and for this moment, that is enough. We, in our little green corner, are enough.

As if she hears my unsaid thoughts, she says quietly, "I know we must find the knife and key, and soon. That is important.

That is foremost. I keep dreaming of it—all the relics, and the Devil come to see us. No one will dare hurt us then. Not even my mother. I know all of this. It frightens me, but I know it, and I welcome it. You say it must be done, and I trust you. Truly, I trust no one else." She sighs a little, and I listen, rapt, to her every breath.

"I will not miss visitation," she says softly. "I would like to forget the word entirely. I would like to forget what it feels like when they hit us. But tonight . . ." I hear her chewing her lip, just above my cheek. "Tonight we are here with the flowers. I think they like you. They are especially pretty this night." She touches a delicate clutch of yellow arnica. The very same flower Samuel gave to me the morning of my anointing. "Don't you think so?"

My eyes burn. I am quiet for a time, listening to the world. With each soft pull of Sorrow's fingers through my hair, my body tingles as if tiny cottonwood seeds have blown across my skin. I dig my toes into the dirt, shift my weight, and my knee knocks gently against Sorrow's.

We grow very still. I breathe shallowly, then move away, rising up onto my elbows. Slow, careful. I do not look at the place where the collar of Sorrow's nightgown has opened, all the white softness underneath. I do not, I will not.

But then the wind knocks gently against our little cave. A few petals fall from the flowers overhead—yellow, white, pink—and settle in Sorrow's tangled hair. One lands upon her nose. She laughs, and I do too. It has been so long since I have laughed with real joy in it. Without thinking, I move closer to her, and still without thinking, I lean low, and lower, my face so near hers that if I spoke, my mouth would brush her cheek.

I hold myself still as glass. I can feel my heart in my fingertips; I can feel my heart in my cheeks, sticky with drying tears; I can feel my heart in the place where our thighs touch. Sorrow watches me, her chest rising and falling with each soft breath.

Then she releases that lip she keeps biting, lets out a little frustrated cry, and reaches for me. The sound cracks open an egg of light in my chest. She pulls me down gently into the dirt beside her. Our legs tangle, half bare. Wild longings peal open inside me, clear and clamoring as bells. To clutch her gown and wring it in my hands, to wind my fingers in her hair and use those knots to bind her to me—but she has said nothing, has asked me for nothing beyond this nearness. I wait, then, in fear, my nose and mouth full of green scents I love, fresh and ripe with growing. Her body is marked with hurts, and so is mine. I would not blame her if the thought of yet another person's touch made her want to crawl out of her skin.

But then she presses her face against my neck, her lips gentle on the hollow of my throat. My toes curl into the dirt.

She whispers, trembling, against my skin, "Is this right?"

I nod and slide my arms around her. She hooks a leg over mine and draws me close, hips to hips. A nervous breath of laughter blows hot against my ear. I kiss her brow, I kiss her temple, where her hair is slick and soft, I kiss the turn of her nose. Bee and flower. Lock and key.

"I did not know kisses could be so kind," Sorrow tells me, and then puts her mouth upon my cheek, and then in my hair, just as I did to her. She is so warm and gentle beside me, kitten-soft. I kiss the tender place where her lashes meet her cheeks, the delicate spot behind her ear, the turns of her wrists. I linger on her darkest bruise. If only a kiss could heal a hurt. Maybe, if I live past these dark days, I can make such a spell.

"May I keep touching you?" she asks, her eyes shining.

"Yes," I tell her. I wish to tell her that forever. I close my eyes and lay my head against her neck. She wraps me in her arms, and I feel supple and loose, as if the thing that was my body has fallen away and all that remains is light, twisting, blooming.

Neither of us knows what to do, where to touch. All I know is what Hunger does in her bed some nights, the noises Father and Mother used to make in their bedroom, the noises I heard Mother make when I found her with—

No. *No.* Not this night. Not here. Not now.

I hide my face in Sorrow's hair, shift a little so that my leg slips between hers. My thighs are hot, my chest is hot, everything is warm and aching. I move against Sorrow, rocking slowly. With each press against her leg, a new warmth blooms inside me, travels all the way to my toes.

"Is this right?" I whisper. My voice is shaking.

"I think it must be," she says. Her fingers fumble at the hem of my nightgown, grazing my hip. The touch of skin to skin makes me jerk against her. I cling to her more tightly, lock my legs around hers. I feel her panting hot breath in my hair, how her hips move under me. I find a lock of her hair and kiss it. My nightgown has rucked up so high I can feel the damp earth rubbing against my legs, and now I see why Hunger moved as she did when I saw her squirm in her bed. Now I see so many things.

The warmth rising under my skin bubbles, boils, melts me. It rises and rises, then spills over, flooding down my body. I cry out and shake in Sorrow's arms, her hands clutch my gown and my hair, she whispers against my cheek the name I chose in Avazel, over and over, and we move, and we move, miraculous and gasping, until the soft black and gold that fell over my eyes lifts away.

Then Sorrow whispers into the hot still silence, "Rage, look."

I lift my head from her damp shoulder and see that all around us shiver mounds of new flowers glowing with starlight—Anne's lace and milkweed and primrose, daisy and blue columbine and piles of sweet honeysuckle. Purple and pink and white and gold, they glow with me, with us, with *extasia*. Just as in Avazel, I have grown flowers without meaning to— but this time, they grew out of neither anger nor fear.

For a long while, I cannot look at Sorrow. The ache inside me is a rosebud, tight and tender. A sadness, or a gladness. A relief. Everything in the world is here, inside me, between us, beneath us. I sob a little, quietly, and laugh too. My damp arms are speckled with dirt, and Sorrow's are the same, her hair spilled cream against the earth.

Amity would tell me I should feel ashamed. I should feel vile with sin. The Sanctificat says a girl should lie with no girl, nor a boy with a boy, nor an unwed woman with anyone.

But I—Rage—feel no shame. I feel light and open, as if I could push off from the ground and rise forever. As if I could open my mouth and drink my fill of stars.

A great and gentle quiet falls over us. I turn on my side, touch Sorrow's hair. In the shivering petals of my witched flowers, she kisses my hand, her cheeks pink and damp. "We are still friends, I hope?" she says to me.

"We are still friends," I tell her, my voice soft. I trace the twin silken arches of her pale brows. "That has not changed. It never will."

She sighs and smiles, closes her eyes, turns her face up to our ceiling of flowers. Never have I seen her so at ease, so liquid and lovely. No fear, no sadness.

"Once there was a girl," she says, dreamy, half asleep, "who came upon a boy with pointed ears and a clever quick smile. He hopped from tree to tree, nimble as a bird, with fur on his arms and hooves on his feet."

I frown. The last things I wish to think of just now are my mother or any of her stories, but Sorrow's voice is sweet and lilting, and I want more of it. "Another ghost story?"

"Yes, I meant to tell you. They told it to me just this morning.

Three of them, floating about my room. I do not think I shall ever grow used to how frightful they look. Do you know this story? Of the clever boy?"

"Yes, I do." Maybe if we say the rest of it quick, we can stop this, talk of flowers instead, or of nothing. Kiss again. My cheeks burning, I continue the story. "The girl followed him, chasing his shadow on the ground, for he was so high in the trees. At last, the girl came out into a meadow vast as the sea. She watched the boy chase fireflies, which he shut up in a jar."

Then Sorrow says, "The girl cried to see the trapped creatures and begged the boy to stop. 'But, ah,' he said with his clever grin, ''tis the only way to the underland, for their glow will light the way. Do you see?'"

"He pointed to a river," I say next, shivering, for memory brings my mother's voice far too close, "where beneath the rushing water, thousands and thousands of lights and colors and shapes drifted, painting pictures the girl could not see. 'But how do I get there?' she cried."

"'First,'" whispers Sorrow, "'you must find a light of your own,' the clever boy said, sticking out his tongue and holding the jar just out of the girl's reach. 'Then you must simply think happy thoughts, and they will pull you down below!' And then—"

Sorrow falls quiet. For a moment, I think she has heard a watchman's footfall. Has her cloak faded? Has someone heard us? I hold very still.

"The underland," Sorrow whispers.

"Do you hear something?"

"No, no. The *underland*." She turns to me, fully awake, her eyes wide and clear. "The stories your mother told you. The stories the ghosts tell me. Not all of them speak of the underland, but many do. In the stories, the girls search for the underland."

Suddenly, as her words sink into me, the world grows too loud and too quiet both at once. I sit up slowly, my heartbeat roaring in my ears.

"You think it is a message," I whisper. "You think they are telling us where to find the final relics."

Sorrow glances west. Past my garden, the fence, Haven, the wall, a distant tall shape stands dark against the stars—square and fat, like a giant thick tree wedged into the earth, its branches cut clean off.

The underland, the *underland*.

And where does the Devil live?

Under the black mountain, we have been taught. The mountain that sits upon the fires of Hell.

"It cannot be," I whisper, and yet the tingling slow feeling spreading through my limbs tells me it can. By now, I know that feeling well. The power is speaking to me, and the power never lies.

"Maybe your mother knew this without knowing what she knew," Sorrow says quickly. "Maybe the Devil was speaking to her always, and she told you what she heard because she could not help herself, but she did not understand it, and neither did you."

Yes, that could be. She could have welcomed the Devil into her thoughts long ago, just as she welcomed Joseph Redding into my father's bed. I hold myself very still, my fingers lightly tingling. I do not know what to think, what to feel. That my mother could have known this for years, that she could have wanted to help me with some mysterious thing while not knowing why or how, makes me unbearably, breathlessly sad.

"Or maybe they were only silly stories dreamed up to make me smile," I say.

"But then why would she tell them to me? Why would any of them?"

"I do not know the ways of ghosts. It could mean nothing."

Sorrow gently takes my hands. "It could mean *everything*."

Then, suddenly, her grip tightens, her eyes widen. She hisses my name in warning.

I whirl around, expecting to see some watchman pushing his head down into our green cave—but it is not a watchman. 'Tis worse than that.

Beyond our cloak, our little shimmering shell, flickers a snapping field of orange, yellow, red. Growing closer. Growing hotter.

Fire.

42

For a moment, I cannot move, cannot breathe, cannot think.

My garden is on fire.

Someone has set my garden—my mother's garden—on fire.

Who did it? I will kill them. Malice? Elder Joseph? Elias Holt? Samuel? The Devil himself? God, feeling wrathful? Whoever it was, I will find them. I will hunt them down and tear into them with my teeth.

Anger cuts through me like the knife I seek, slicing away all the new softness Sorrow made.

"Run," I tell Sorrow. "Spell your cloak again and run home." She starts to protest, the fire painting her skin gold. I allow myself to touch her cheek. We cannot let them find you here. Run, *now*."

She hesitates, her mouth tight and thin, then mutters a few quiet words—her cloaking spell, I think—crawls away toward the fence, and disappears. Her cloak slips down my arms and legs, down my back, like warm water receding, and then it is gone.

I hold my breath and duck out of the flowers before the flames can catch me, hiding my mouth in my sleeve as I did in the House of Woe. I run for the kitchen door just as Father steps out of it in his tunic and red sash, gun slung over his shoulder, knife at his belt.

"My garden," I scream, coughing from the smoke. The yard is wreathed in growing flames, orange eating green, and it is climbing so high, so fast, that I know all is lost, and my heart shatters. Men run beyond the fence, shouting to each other. Water comes flying. Someone bursts through the gate with a bucket. I race for the water pump, grab a pail of my own—but Father seizes my wrist, hauls me inside.

"Wait, no! My flowers!" I try to pull away. "Father, I want to help! Let me *go*!"

"'Tis over, Amity," he says, not looking at me, dragging me through the house. "I can protect you no more."

His words rake me open. Whatever anger I felt, whatever strength it gave me, flies away. I stumble, suddenly cold even though the fire nearly cooked me.

Our front door stands open. On the steps, Hunger screams and sobs, trying to twist her body free of Samuel, who holds her fast with both arms, pinning her back to his front. When she sees me, her screams grow crazed. "Amity! Father, do not do this!"

"Keep her here," Father says sharply to Samuel. "Try to quiet her, if you can."

He hurries me down the steps, past Hunger, who reaches for me, weeping frantically. Samuel watches us go with such hard, miserable sadness on his face that a sudden wave of fear punches through me, nearly knocking me over.

"What is happening?" I ask Father, but he does not answer, and it is only now, the world showing itself to me in jagged surges of panic, that I see the crowd surrounding our house. It seems everyone in Haven is there, all of them shouting and pumping their fists, raising their torches and guns, throwing rocks at our windows.

And beyond them, a body hangs from a long wooden post thrust into the dirt.

Elder Joseph, mouth gaping, eyes wide and staring. A set of large antlers has been fixed to his head and strapped into place with thorny vines. All across his naked body, sewn on with thick black thread, are patches of bloody deer hide. A quilt of skin and skin.

Malice. *Malice* has done this.

And that makes sixteen.

A vile chill rips through me. She did it. She finished. And I am here with nothing but three useless relics, and my garden is ablaze, and Hunger is screaming my name, and Sorrow, Sorrow—I hope she is safe at home. Not here, not watching this.

Father shoves me before him, gripping my shoulders hard.

I squint against the light of all their torches and wish I could cover myself, my thin filthy nightgown, but I dare not move. I know I will not find Elder Peter but search desperately for him all the same, my eyes filling up fast. He would help me. He would come forward and talk of peace, give me time to think, give me time to find *extasia*.

Or would he? Malice would say. *He hurt people. Some friend he was.*

"People of Haven," my father calls out. "My brothers and sisters all. Sixteen men and one woman—the good wife Hester Brinsley—have now met violent ends on our sacred soil. Evil is among us. Evil *walks* among us. This I have never denied. I have prayed to God about it. I have begged Him to help me understand, as have all your elders. We have enforced new rules to keep you safe, searched your homes for the Devil's mark. I have mortified my flesh until I bled on the steps of my own house, hoping this act of repentance would please the good Lord and offer us some respite from this tireless violence. And none of this has helped us, for now another elder is dead."

The crowd bursts into angry shouts and jeers.

"And your daughter killed him!" someone cries.

"Or else she helped the Devil do it!" yells someone else. "Just as she did the others!"

I cannot see their faces, cannot tell apart their voices. They are faceless beasts, shouting my name, screaming for justice.

The light of their fire flickers across Elder Joseph's ruined body. Has anyone put out the fire in my garden? I try to turn around and look, breathing too hard, sweating all over.

"I hear you!" my father calls out. "I hear your anger, your fear, and I feel it too! Now." He waits for them to quiet, though there is still a rumble of discontent. The people of Haven are a growling creature, waiting for the right moment to pounce.

"The anointing of a saint is a thing most holy," Father says. "God speaks, your elders listen, and we anoint as He tells us. Even I shall not dare to break that holy covenant with our Lord. But I shall show Him that I understand His anger and that I shall repent as I can, as will my daughter."

He pauses. The growling creature leans close, eager for more. A wriggling feeling breaks loose in me. I shift, try to jerk free, but my father's grip is too strong, his fingers like iron talons. Antlered Elder Joseph stares down at me. The firelight draws a smile of shadows across his face.

"To help cleanse this evil from our home," Father says, in that voice unbreakable as the sky, "my daughter Amity shall remain in the House of Sighs in solitude, in contrition, until such time as we, your elders, and God above, who deigns to speak to us, decide that she is pure, untouched by evil, and may return to life in Haven . . . or that she is indeed fallen, irredeemable, and should be driven out into the wild, as was her mother."

The crowd boils over with a great howl. Torches and shovels

338

are thrust into the air. Some people fall to their knees with hands clasped, muttering fierce thanks to God, to my father, to all the wise elders. Some shout my name, curse it. They spit at me as Father pushes me down the street. Six watchmen circle us, shoving away anyone who gets too close.

"Yes, walk with us, my friends!" Father calls out, his voice triumphant, unworried. His stride is steady. "God is pleased to see such zeal from you!"

The sound of his voice shakes some sense back into me. A squall of fear shrieks through my skull—not fear of the House of Sighs, nor of the thundering crowd, but a fear for my sister. I have told neither Sorrow nor Vengeance what I saw—Hunger, knife-carved and dead, floating in the scrying pool's black water. With me gone, my sister, my own dear one, will be alone, unguarded. And Malice has killed her sixteen men. Even now, in Avazel, she and the coven might be dancing with the Devil.

"Father, please, listen to me," I mutter, trying to turn to him as we walk, "you do not understand what you do. *Blessing*, Father, she is in danger—"

He strikes me so hard with the back of his hand that stars burst behind my eyes. I stagger, stare up at him in disbelief, but he does not let me fall. Behind us, several people laugh. They throw clods of dirt at my head, my backside. They chant the Woman's Prayer louder and louder as we hurry west through Haven.

Wherever you step,
whatever you seek,
may your tongue hold still,
may your heart live meek!

Then I see the House of Sighs—a small square house of faded black, sitting alone in a clearing near the western wall. No trees to shade or shelter it. No flowers adorn its door. Small, at first sight. Hardly more than an outhouse. But the main rooms are belowground, hidden and unknown. My mother slept here for a month before they chased her away with gun, horse, and hound. 'Tis a place for thieves, killers, adulterers. Sinners who go down there seldom live for long.

I dig my heels into the dirt. "No! No, Father! You cannot do this!"

He grabs my arms, lifts me off my feet. I kick and scream at him, swing my fists uselessly. His brow is sharp, his dark eyes flat and unreadable. He does not smile—he is not happy, but he will do this thing nevertheless.

My body is ringing with terror. I could call on the power, maybe, but then what? I am not strong enough to make a spell that would stop all of them at once, and if I cloak myself, if I run and disappear, they could turn on Hunger next, or Sorrow, or Vengeance. A path to Avazel will do me no good; I do not think I should unleash Haven upon the coven or the coven upon Haven. Not right now, with everything in such confusion. Any unnatural thing I do might swiftly bring down anger upon the people I love.

Grozixniila. The blood spell. *Extasia* would no doubt be pleased if I did it right now, in front of everyone, but I will not kill my father. I imagine how Malice would grin as I stood over his blood-soaked body, how satisfied she would be.

No, I will not kill him. I know he is afraid. I know he loves me. But I will fight him. I am a girl gone mad. I twist my body so hard it leaves me dizzy. Some bold soul reaches out from the mass of people pressing close around us and smacks me hard on the ear.

Black-bearded Elder Wyatt unlocks the door. A small room, no windows, and steps leading down into darkness. Down there, I will feel the weight of the earth above me. Down there, I will be of no use to my quest, my friends, my sister. Frantically, I think of the spells I wrote for Sorrow to practice. One was a spell for unlocking doors. But what are the words? I cannot think, I am breathing too fast, too hard.

I claw at my father, wrench myself around in his arms, and scream my sister's name as loud as I can. In my panic, I shriek, "Hunger!" Her name crackles through the air.

We begin down the stairs. Father shakes me. "Stop that, Amity. Be quiet, be calm, and this will be easier."

And I do—not to please him, but because as we descend, the air grows too thick and damp to breathe. The weight of it presses on me like a giant hand. Its fingers grip my skull; its palm crushes my shoulder blades. Down you go, Saint Rage, into the deep, deep dark.

At the bottom, a little hallway. No metal bars here, as I have heard, but instead two heavy wooden doors that will shut me away into blackness. One room is empty. The other, on the left, is mine.

It happens so quickly. Elder Wyatt unlocks the door, Father pushes me inside, something is muttered—my name, a prayer, a threat, I cannot say—and then the door is shut and locked, and I am alone. Alone in the House of Sighs. All dark, no windows.

I listen to their footsteps climbing back up the stairs. The door above opens. Far away, muffled, I hear the cheers of my neighbors, their triumphant cries, their stamping feet. My father's faint voice, leading a prayer. Then the House's door closes. Silence.

In the dark, I crawl. I measure the room with my shaking hands. Stone floor, stone walls. Maybe ten feet each way. I measure it four times, then five, ten, because if I keep crawling, keep moving, keep thinking, I will remember how to breathe again.

But soon my knees give out. My arms buckle. I find a corner away from the door and claim it, huddling on the hard cold floor. Hours pass. Or minutes? Days? No sunlight to mark the time, and no sound now that the doors are closed and locked. Did they already burn Elder Peter's body? Have I been denied that moment of farewell?

I listen hard. Maybe I will hear a dog bark, a child yell to his friend. Maybe if I hold my breath, I will hear the whispers of *extasia*, telling me what to do.

But I hear only the weight of the earth, the silence so complete it swallows all sense of my own body. I could be a beetle, having lived its short life, lying down to die. That is why it is the House of Sighs—sighs of woe, sighs of regret. The final sighs that come before death.

As I drift into sleep, a single, small hope comes to me.

The ghosts. *My* ghost. She has helped me before. If I think of her, if I call her, if I say her name at last, will she come?

I draw a picture of her in my mind. Towering body, black mouth, silver bell, mouth of flies. I have not once said her name aloud. Not to Hunger, not to Sorrow, not to myself. Not even in Avazel when I yelled for her, searching the shadows for her horrid face. To say her name is to think it. To think it— really, truly think it—to look at the word straight on and give it life, is a thing I have not been able to endure.

But here in the dark, tears squeezing out of my eyes, it does not feel so frightening to say it.

"Mother," I whisper, "help me."

IF SHE HEARS ME, IF anyone hears me, they do not come.

I wake to the same silence, the same heavy weight. I sit up and whisper, "*Malagsat, malagzaala,*" my voice cracking, but when I snap my shaking fingers, only the same empty darkness greets me. I try to gather my thoughts and find the power, listening for the heat and hum and will of *extasia*. But my head aches, my heart aches, and my scattered mind will not stop spinning, and I cannot find anything. I can barely find my next breath.

And what would fire do for me, even if I could calm myself enough to summon it? Fill my lungs with smoke until I die choking in my own cell, as my flowers died in their garden? Burn the House of Sighs down around me? Maybe my ghost would come and lead me out, as she did in the House of Woe, but she has not come yet, and she may never come again, now that I have dared to say her name and ask for help outright, even after everything that happened five years ago. Even after everything I did. Everything I said and did not say. Everything I am and am not. Witch. Saint. Good. Evil.

Daughter. Traitor.

I find the door, yell for my father, beat on the wood until my fists are so tender that I give up, weeping. Not from the pain, but from a sharp, vivid anger. What is happening up above? Would I know it if my sister were in danger? Would I feel her pain as my own?

I curl up on the floor, holding my aching stomach. I tell myself the scrying pool was a lie. Some deception made by Malice to frighten me. A trick, some witchy mischief. Hunger will be fine. She will live a long and healthy life. She will forget that her sister rots beneath the ground. She will remember her prayers and forget Avazel, forget *extasia*, forget every dark thing she has learned from me, and at the Devil's side, I will protect her always.

I tell myself this story many times, fold it over itself again and again until the words feel worn and soft inside me. Comforted, I sleep.

I wake when a cool breeze touches my feet and open my eyes to see something I at first think must be a dream—Sorrow is there beside me, lit by a faint light. A flame, held in Vengeance's palm. She stands at the open door, looking fierce and frightening.

"Sorrow?" I whisper, reaching for her face. "Is it you?"

She presses my palm against her cheek. "Yes, Rage. We have come for you. Those words you gave me to study, for cloaking and unlocking? I practiced. I know not if I read them proper, but the words I did say were all of them right and mine. I think *extasia* must like me, for I am now really quite good at unlocking. And locking—you must simply say the words you choose in reverse order and put your thoughts backward too. I think I like those spells even better than the ones for cloaks. They are playful. They scamper in my mind like little pups."

Then her face darkens. "I locked Mother in the closet. She tried to put me in, but I did it first. Oh, and worry not! We have the relics." She turns, shows me the cloth sack slung across her body. "Hunger showed me where they were, before . . ."

She trails off, looks away, and suddenly I am cold all over.

"They have your sister," Vengeance says, her voice tense, her red hair bound in a tight knot. "Your father has called a meeting. All the elders are in Holy House, and Hunger is with them. Something will happen soon, though I do not know what."

She hesitates, looks around the dark room. Fist clenched, eyes bright with angry tears. "I am sorry we did not come sooner. Everyone is watching us, and we thought that if they caught us working with the power, they might kill us, or you, or maybe hurt Hunger. I am so sorry, Rage. We only just now got away."

Sorrow helps me to my feet. I hold her hand tightly, and

with my other hand I cup Vengeance's head, bring her brow to mine.

"You have done well, sister," I tell her. "I am not hurt."

She smiles, tears shimmering on her lashes, and between the three of us rushes a warm swift current, binding us together, bolstering us. My thoughts settle. My limbs feel stronger.

We run up the stairs and into the grass beyond the House of Sighs, they in their boots, me in my bare feet. Every window I see is black save for those of Holy House, and as we near that building of worship, I hear a scream, a sharp high sound that quickly breaks off.

I stumble. Even as a scream, I know that voice at once.

"This way," says Vengeance, her hand firm on my arm, holding me up. She spells a cloak, and we hurry toward the back of the building, away from the watchmen guarding the front door. Here there is a smaller door, plain and locked. Sorrow murmurs her spell and smiles happily as the door swings open. We race downstairs into dark cool rooms where oils and sacred cloths and festival bowls are stored. Wooden boxes are stacked high, marked with words I do not know.

Hurrying past them, we find another staircase, narrow and steep. We climb carefully, for the wood creaks. I want to scream. Too careful, too slow, too many moments passing too quickly.

At the top, we come out into the great gold hall of Holy House, near the back of the room, where our door stands hidden in shadows. Across the room from us, stairs lead up to a high room of prayer and conference for men who are grown and wed.

And here I stand, cold hands tight around my heart, cold fingernails carving furrows down my legs, as I stare at the altar, where my father, in his long white robe edged with yellow flowers, in his red elder's sash, raises his arms high over the table before him, upon which lies my sister, naked and bound.

The six other elders stand in a circle around the altar. Robes on, hair combed, eyes bright as they watch.

I grip the door frame beside me. I cannot quite believe it as I watch my father bring down his long knife. I cannot quite believe it as he cuts a shallow line between the breasts of my sister, his daughter, down to her soft white belly.

She screams at the touch of his knife. Her body jerks as much as it can with her arms and legs tied. She tries to twist away, but my father's blade comes down again. A slash down her left arm, another down her right. Shallow cuts, but deep enough to burn like fire. She screams and screams, but I know, as does she, that no one will come.

Elder Wyatt, his smile grim, watches with glittering eyes. Gray-headed Elder Phillip murmurs prayers under his breath.

My father raises his arms, red-tipped knife held in one hand.

"With this knife, I offer the blood of my own to you, my Lord," cries my father. "I am unclean!"

"He is unclean," murmur the elders.

"The Devil has touched my wife and now my daughters, and through them, he has touched me!"

"Clean him," cry the elders in their circle. "Save him!"

"In my pride, weak with love, I did not act when I should have. I showed mercy when I should have shown strength. Forgive me, my Lord!"

"Forgive him!"

"I have atoned," says my father quietly, his reddened eyes gazing somewhere else, somewhere far away, "and yet still I cannot escape the grasp of evil. My wife."

"His wife," whisper the elders.

"My daughters," Father says, his voice wrung out.

"His daughters."

"Father, stop this, please!" my sister screams, her face soaked with tears. "Why are you doing this? Stop this! I love you, Father!"

But our father, his face shining with sweat, says nothing. He closes his eyes, his face serene, and lowers his knife once more to my sister's chest.

Her shrieking wails turn wild. She twists so violently that Elder Daniel and Elder Wyatt have to hold her down, one at each arm, as my father cuts.

There is a high howling sound in my ears. I cannot breathe, I cannot think.

My father wets his lips. "Only with this sacrifice of blood can I be made pure once more."

"Amen," say the elders.

"Only by giving up my own flesh and blood to Him, as He did for us, will He forgive me for the weakness that has brought me to the Devil's door."

"Amen!" cry the elders.

"First, my youngest," he says, and only once does his voice crack, unsteady. "Next, my eldest."

Someone shakes me. Vengeance, with embers for eyes. "We must use your bone spell. *Now.*"

"On all of them?" I whisper weakly.

"Are we strong enough for that?" says Sorrow, beneath my father's shouted prayers. Her hand is slick around my own. "What if the spell does not catch all of them? They will kill us."

Vengeance looks ready to knock Sorrow to the floor. "Are you a witch, or are you not?"

"There must be another way."

"Each moment we delay is another moment closer to her death!"

I stand caught between them, staring and frozen. I must kill my father or allow my sister to be killed. I must be a saint or a witch, and yet I am both, and I am neither. The bone spell. I think I could do it, I think I could snap my father's arms off. Frantic, I think through the words—*samhaasyo, rahasa, larinalim, das*—but they do not feel right. Something does not feel right; something feels just beyond my reach. Hiding. Waiting.

I look to the rafters, desperate for the sight of ghosts—but we are alone, we girls, and no help will come for us.

Then there is a great crash from the far side of the room and a sharp, angry cry.

Samuel, a shovel in his hand, tears down the stairs from the men's prayer room. He runs toward the altar, too fast for the astonished elders to stop him.

Samuel rams into my father, slams the shovel hard against his back. Father's legs buckle. He falls with a sharp groan, and there flies his knife, spinning silver across the floor toward my toes.

Samuel raises his shovel to strike again, but now the other elders are upon him. They grab him and throw him to the floor. They pound him and kick him and knock away his shovel. Elder Wyatt grabs his knife from where it lies on a low table, and Elder Phillip holds Samuel up by his hair to bare his throat.

Suddenly, I understand. A clear white light bursts through me, sweeping me clean, warming me from skull to heel.

A mere step away, my father's knife trembles, the blade tapping fast against the floor's wooden planks.

Book, mirror, belt, knife, key.

Knife.

Dead mouse. Dead buck. Dead man. That smiling red cut I made on Hunger's thigh, the one I did not mean to cause. I have never tried the spell again after that. It was not the time, then.

But it is now.

Am I strong enough for this?

As if in answer, a feeling of calm courses through me, hot and steady.

I grab the knife, turn quickly to Vengeance. "Do you remember when Malice cut upon that deer, and then the same cuts appeared on Furor's man? The governor? Malice said that even if he were far away, she could make him bleed."

Vengeance understands at once. Eyes gleaming, she shrugs off her cloak and loosens her collar's ribbons, baring her neck and shoulders. Her arms prickle with goose bumps.

"I will get Hunger," Sorrow whispers, standing ready beside me.

"Do it," Vengeance says in her rough hard voice, and I do. I raise my father's knife, hiss out the word—*"Vanuriisa!"*—and slash a line across Vengeance's shoulder.

Elder Phillip cries out, drops Samuel, clutches the bright fresh wound on his shoulder. Blood leaks out from between his fingers.

I cut twice more, once each on Vengeance's freckled arms.

Elder Wyatt drops his knife and falls, his own arms spilling red.

"Deeper," Vengeance says, grinning hard as she watches them.

I obey, cutting again and again, bringing every elder screaming to their knees. Now their blood joins my sister's, decorating the altar. If Vengeance feels pain, she does not show it.

Sorrow hurries back to us, my sister in her arms. She has

wrapped Hunger in her own cloak, and my sister clings to her, crying quietly.

"Run to the elm grove, and hurry," I tell them. "We will follow you, and I will summon us a path to Avazel."

Where, perhaps, the Devil waits—not summoned by me, but by Malice. What will she have him do to us? What will he think when we arrive with four relics and not yet five?

I open my mouth, a wordless warning on my lips, but Sorrow and Hunger have already hurried away.

A sudden cry from the altar splits the air.

I turn, feeling wild, knife raised.

'Tis Samuel. Father has found him and is beating him with angry red fists. I stare at this man who made me, his face so cruel and sharp beneath that fierce black brow I have loved. It would be better if I could look upon that meanness and not see my father's face at all. If the meanness had eaten him up, swallowed him whole, and left nothing I knew behind—that I would prefer.

But I see him plainly. There he is, my father. He put me in the House of Sighs, and he cut upon my sister, and now he beats Samuel, his own second, with no pause for breath.

I glance at Vengeance.

She wets her mouth and grins. "Do it."

If only I had a dead mouse to cut on, again and again, until no blood was left inside it.

I think I would do it, even with these furious tears building behind my eyes. I think I would kill my father.

Instead, I slice my knife across Vengeance's chest—a little deeper this time, to make the hurt hit hard.

She cries out, buckles against me. I hold her up with one arm and watch, with a dark thing turning inside me, a feathered blackness like one of Ire's crowing birds, as my father falls, clutching his chest. He looks up, finds me watching him, and his face goes slack with shock.

We run to Samuel and help him rise. His breathing is ragged, but his grip is still strong. He whispers my name, the word slurred. A tear slides down his bloody cheek. I heave him tighter against the side of my body. Boy in one arm, girl in the other, knife clutched in my fist.

And then all of us, saints and Samuel, we run. The guards outside Holy House try to stop us—they shoot at us, grab for us—but with our fire and our cloaks and the swiftness of *extasia*, they cannot touch us. Through Haven we fly, and once inside the elm grove, I find Hunger and Sorrow hiding, gather everyone as close to me as I can, and whisper harshly, "*Ziirdagras.*"

Extasia answers. The power buzzes around us, an angry swarm that lights up our limbs and the sleepy old elms. We run, limping, gulping down air. Dirt turns to moss, black trees become white. And just before we disappear fully inside Avazel, I hear it, a thousand miles behind us, no doubt rung by one of the watchmen who failed to catch us—the piercing urgent clangor of a single angry bell.

BLACK SKY, WHITE TREES, RED moon.

Samuel steps away from me and falls, unable to bear his own weight. He huddles in the moss, shaking. I crouch beside him to see the worst of it, because it seems Avazel has chosen not to take away his wounds. Blood drips from his nose and mouth, the flesh already swelling from my father's fists. I remember well that pain, the tooth-rattling blows Adam dealt me.

Then there is a sudden outcry, a storm of noise. I look over my shoulder to see Ire's black birds spin up into the sky, their screeching calls filling the air. Cunning marches out of the trees, her sunset gown floating around her legs. Furor, vines of red flowers trailing from her hair, holds two crooked knives as long as her forearms. With her metal arm, Storm swings a thick white branch, ready to crack someone's head.

I push myself to my feet and step in front of Samuel. Behind me, Sorrow and Hunger press close—Hunger in her deep blue gown, Sorrow solemn and pale as snow, wearing a long black dress with loose flowing sleeves. She holds the bag of relics close to her chest.

Vengeance laughs quietly to herself in the dirt, the blood from her wounds seeping into her green dress. Perhaps not even Avazel can heal wounds made by a spell.

Or, I think, Malice has told the Devil to let us bleed.

And there she is, pushing through the others to stalk toward us, her face so twisted with anger that it takes everything in me to stay right where I am.

"How dare you bring him here?" Malice says, stopping just short of striking me. "These woods are ours!"

"He helped us save Hunger," I tell her. "You will not hurt him."

I am not afraid of her. I am not afraid of anyone, not even the Devil. I stand tall, thinking quickly. Maybe, even if his loyalty is already tied to Malice, I can offer him the four relics as a gift of appeasement until I can find the fifth.

"Please," Samuel says hoarsely, pushing himself upright, "if you grant me the mercy of a few moments, I can explain—"

"Finish that sentence and I will tear your tongue from your throat," Malice snaps.

My sister steps forward. Her wounds, I am glad to see, have faded. She puts her hand in mine and lifts her chin. "Samuel stopped my father from killing me."

"He gave Rage time to make her cuts," says Sorrow.

Malice looks at Vengeance—dripping red arms, sharp bright smile. "Reckless cuts. You have skill but not finesse, not yet. You could have killed her."

"But she did not," Vengeance says, her tired pale face triumphant. "I would take even more cuts if it meant I could see the elders keep squirming on the floor."

"Can you heal her?" I ask.

"Avazel will, eventually," Malice says sharply. "Spell-made injuries simply take longer to heal. Until then, there are things we can do to help the power along."

"And . . ." I swallow hard. I must ask, no matter what the answer might be. "Where is he?"

"Where is who?"

"The Devil." I pause. "You killed sixteen men. Your ritual is finished. Have you not summoned him yet?"

The coven is silent. Ire watches us with blank, tired eyes. Gall furiously wipes her cheeks.

"It didn't work," Malice says at last. All the anger has left her voice. She looks away, her jaw tight. "Once again, it didn't work. We killed. We said the spells we've written and rewritten and rewritten a thousand times. We felt the power listening—but nothing answered."

Then she sees the knife in my hand, still wet with Vengeance's blood. Her eyes brighten, lifting to mine. "Is that the knife? *The* knife?"

I brace myself. "It is."

Behind Malice, the coven stirs, their faces alight with hope.

"Then we'll get to work at once," Malice says. "You'll need to write your own summoning spells to find the key, of course, but we'll help you bear the load."

Liberty offers hopefully, "Maybe you can tell us the story of Lost Abigail again. The words might point the way, offer inspiration."

"Excellent idea. First we'll eat, tend to Vengeance, and then—"

"I will do nothing until you promise me you will not hurt Samuel," I say firmly, "and accept that he is under my protection."

A terrible quiet follows my words. Hunger squeezes my clammy hand.

Malice says nothing at first, then steps sideways to peer at Samuel. I feel him tense, hear his ragged breathing.

"So he helped you," Malice says. "I don't think that's enough. I don't think that earns him his life."

"I have all but one of the relics," I remind her, struggling to keep my voice steady. "I have found them quickly, far more quickly than you have killed your men, and I will find the final relic, the key, very soon. And since the Devil has not come to you, I may be your only way to find him. It would be unwise, then, to deny me this favor. The power brought me here, as you have said yourself, and the power never lies."

"The power never lies," the coven repeats, and Malice too. She glares at me, her eyes keen.

"He will be named a traitor for what he has done," I press

on. "By fighting the elders, he has given up his place in Haven."

"And you think he should be rewarded for this?" Malice asks. "You think he should be spared for one night of heroism?"

That look she throws at me—even with my father's knife in hand, I flinch. "I do."

"And where was brave Samuel during all the visitations of his life, when innocent girls were brought before him and he was told to touch and strike and curse them as he pleased? Did he ever say a word? Did he ask questions of his elders? Did he think for even a moment that maybe this is not what should be done?"

I know the answers, and so does she. So do we all.

Samuel steps forward, a crack in his voice. "I am sorry, truly. I . . . I did not understand."

"Oh, I see, you didn't understand! That makes everything better!" Malice looks around at the coven. Many of them laugh.

"I spoke with Amity a few days ago," Samuel says. He sways a little, and I long to steady him, but if there is any hope of mercy here, I think he must do this on his own. "She said things I did not understand. Doubt as to the wisdom of our elders' teachings. Defiance in the face of laws upon which Haven was built. At first, I was angry. I did not understand what she meant. I thought she was wrong. I thought she had lost her way. But then . . . I kept thinking. I watched her garden burn. I watched her father lock her away."

Samuel looks back at me then, his eyes bright with fierce

tears. He laughs a little, helplessly. "Amity, I feel lost. 'Tis difficult for me, all of this. I admit that. I do not know what to believe or what to do next. But I think I understand now why you were angry at me that day. When I said your sister deserved what Adam—" He glances at Hunger. His face crumples and takes my heart with it. "I was wrong. I am so sorry."

Malice watches in stony silence. "That's not enough, boy. That will never be enough."

Part of me thinks she is right. I know all Samuel has seen and done and not done—but if she kills him and I let her do it, I will be no better than the elders I left bleeding in Holy House. Malice said we are the same, she and I, and perhaps some of me is, but not all. I was like Samuel not so long ago. We all were. I saw and did nothing. I wondered but asked nothing. I was taught prayers and said them all, word for word. I did not understand. I did not have to.

And this is my friend Samuel, after all. Samuel, who has been as good and gentle a boy as I have ever seen, who listens well and gives me flowers and tries—I truly believe—tries to do what he thinks is right. Did he not do so just tonight? He hid in Holy House, knowing what the elders might do. He tore himself away from everything he has known and put himself between them and my sister. He did not know that Vengeance, Sorrow, and I were hidden in the shadows, and still he tried to help, all alone. He is my friend, and he was wrong, and he is also good, and I was wrong and good too, and I am furious with him, and I love him, and he does not deserve to die.

All of these things are true.

But I know these words, if I say them, will do me no good. Malice's face tells me that, plain as day. She is too angry to listen. Maybe someday. But not now.

"He may prove to be valuable," I tell her instead. "He is a second to the elders, and he knows things about Haven that I do not. Spare him for that, if not for me. It would be foolish to get rid of him now."

Malice looks at me coldly for a long moment. Then she says, "Rest, then, until morning. All of you. We'll tend his wounds, see him to health. And then we'll get to work. I've waited a long time to meet the Devil, Rage. I won't wait much longer."

Once we are alone, Sorrow helps Vengeance to her feet, and Hunger and I help Samuel hobble through Avazel behind Liberty, who does not seem as angry as the rest of the coven. She settles beside a tree and gathers her tools, begins preparing medicines. She smiles at me when I kneel beside her, and as she tends the wounds of my dear ones, I help her in silence. I find the leaves and roots and berries she tells me to, and I cut and mash them. She fetches a bowl and clothes, and Hunger brings a bucket of water from a nearby stream. Vengeance, her eyes heavy, rests her head in Sorrow's lap. The light from Liberty's fire flickers across Sorrow's hair.

My chest aches to look at her. Here in Avazel, we are safe, at least for the moment, but how long will that last? If only we could return to that little green corner in my garden, where there are no stabbing fathers or stabbed fathers, where there is no anger or unkindness. But my garden is dead, and Father is my enemy. Beyond that, nothing before me is clear.

Eyes burning, I wet a cloth and begin cleaning Samuel's face. It seems the right thing to do, and yet there is a bitter taste in my mouth as I do it. Part of me wants to leave him to mend his own hurts, or even step aside and let Malice do whatever she likes.

Part of me wishes I could take him into my arms, and cry into the thick brown hair I have known all my life, and tell him everything I am feeling—all the good, all the bad, all the anger gnawing on my bones, and all the questions I cannot answer.

Samuel watches me. "Amity, thank you."

"That is not my name," I tell him flatly. I see in his face that he wishes to ask me, *What is it, then? Your true name, Amity. What is it?*

But he says nothing, and I am glad.

I am not certain anymore what answer I would give him.

45

Not two hours later, I wake among the white trees to a dreadful stillness. The air presses against me, heavy and thick, like the presence of someone lurking around the corner.

Samuel and my sisters sleep not far from me, curled up in the leaves. Liberty sleeps sitting up in the roots of a nearby tree. Her head lolls, her lips slightly parted. At least some of the coven sleeps beyond her. I see Cunning's sunset gown spilled across the moss, her dark head still and peaceful.

All seems well, and yet the wood's strange new weight raises the hairs on my arms. A whine builds deep in my ears, far off but determined. *Extasia* is near, and the power is speaking—but I do not know what it is saying. A summons? A warning? Slowly, I find my father's knife, grip it tight.

Then I turn left and see the reason for my disquiet.

The scrying pool, still and black, sits not twenty feet from me. Around it grows soft green moss and bulbous white toadstools. Above its glassy surface, motes of dust spin slowly in the air, each tiny speck lit red by the moon.

I know the pool was not there when I fell asleep.

The whine in my ears grows louder, more piercing. All other sounds disappear, save for a strange noise—many quiet whispers hissing all at once. There are words inside them, but I cannot understand them. Too many, too fast, too eager.

They are coming from the water.

I could run. I could wake the others.

But this could be the thing I have been waiting for and working toward these long awful weeks. The end of my quest. The Devil did not come to Malice, not even after she offered him so much blood—but here I am, and here are four relics, and maybe this is how he will come to me, and he will offer me his vile hand and help me find the key himself. Maybe I need no summoning spells at all.

We have been taught that the Devil lives under the black mountain, but what if instead he lives under this water? Perhaps at the bottom of this strange black pool lies the true underland from Mother's stories.

I move slowly, as if the pool is a beast I must be careful not to disturb. I find the sack that holds the relics and slip it over my head. In my right hand, I grip my father's knife.

And then, though I truly despise the sight of it, this awful still water like a mouth in the earth, I rise and walk toward it. I must. I would be a fool to lose my courage now. My toes sink into the moss. With every step, the whispers grow louder. The whine in my ears is like a nail being dragged across glass.

At the edge of the water, I hold my breath and look down.

The pool is silent and black. Still as sleep. No images, no dead cut sisters, no gleaming Devil's eyes.

A whisper floats up from the water, a single hoarse word: *Barrow.*

I dip my foot into the cold black surface. My toes slide in, but no ripples move out across the water. The water sucks at me. I pause, draw my foot back out, my stomach turning at the wrongness of it.

This is madness, utter madness, and yet I have to try. If I do not, what then? What will Malice do? What will happen to all of us?

I squeeze my eyes shut.

You started this quest, Rage Barrow of Haven. Now you must finish it.

You wanted to meet the Devil—so do it.

I step off the grass and drop into the water.

46

AND DROP. AND *DROP.*

Cold rushes over me, into me. Cold becomes me. I open my eyes and see nothing, not even my own flailing hands. The darkness is frigid, the water thicker than water should be. I gasp and choke, sucking in water and something else too, something gritty and dry.

I have swum before in the river, in the calm little pools that collect off its banks, so I kick hard and look up toward the white wood, where the air is crisp and clean. But I see nothing—no surface, no moon, no trees above.

My lungs burn. The bag of relics sits heavy against my hip. I squeeze my right hand. Yes, my father's knife is still there. I must not drop it. If nothing else, I must not drop this knife.

I claw through the water, I kick and push, searching for the pool's edge or its floor. *Anything* but this endless choking black.

Then I see a dim gleam of light. A paleness, drifting closer.

Frantically, I reach for it. If this is the Devil come for me, then one of three things might happen. He will kill me, unimpressed with my unfinished quest, and be done with it. He will be pleased to see the four relics I offer and bid me with love to keep searching. He will sense my conflict, my confusion, the pity and grief and tenderness in me, and turn up his nose in disgust. *Where has all your conviction gone, Saint Rage?*

But it is no Devil floating toward me.

'Tis a ghost. Not mine, not my—*say it, Rage, say it, you horrible coward*—not my *mother* with her mouth full of flies, but instead a woman whose face flickers with color. I see a straight nose, a dark eye, flashing teeth. Then that familiar huge mouth returns, gaping in the dark, before the colors come back again, as if she is changing every time I blink—real, not real, here, not here, woman, ghost.

She crawls toward me, her mouth bared. Now there are teeth, now not. Now wild white eyes, now nothing.

I turn away, try to scream, and choke, gagging. Water should rush into my mouth, water should be drowning me, but this is not water.

It is dirt. Wet, black, stinking dirt.

I try to kick, but my legs do not move so easily now. Instead of water, they churn up clods of mud. My palm meets stone. Dirt. Sand. Little pebbles push at my mouth.

I force my head to turn, though movement is now nearly

impossible. The clawing woman is still behind me. She grabs my ankles, pulls hard on my legs, trying to drag me back down. And she is not alone. Another ghost slithers after her, climbing up a steep dark slope, right for us. And another, and *another*. Ten ghosts, crawling fast.

I push my head back around, gasp for air, choke down dirt. I spit and heave, I claw at this black hill like some wriggling underground creature. My fingers sink into the sucking mud. When I rip my hand free, warm wetness splatters my face. Not water, I realize, choking on the stink. Too salty, too hot.

Not water, but blood.

I crawl through it—left hand, right knife. I stab the bloody soil, drag up the impossible heft of my body, pull against the grip of cold hands. But I will not be kept in this awful place. The weight of the soil atop me is difficult to believe. It will crush me, flatten me, if I let it. Is this Hell? Some trial set by the Devil? *See if you can crawl faster than my ghosts, Rage Barrow. See if you have the courage to let my ghosts drag you down into the depths, Rage Barrow.*

But I do not have that courage. My body has become pure beast, all my frantic thoughts fixed on survival. There is air up above, and I must have it. My lungs burn, my vision blooming black. My elbows and knees buckle under me; the knife nearly slips from my hand. Cold fingers claw at my feet.

Then a coolness falls over my brow. A pocket of air forms around my nose and mouth.

I force open my burning eyes.

A ghost, but a kind one. Color moves across the maw of her face—a flash of hazel eyes, a sweet there-and-gone smile. She has pressed her gray palms to my brow and mouth. She is helping me breathe.

I gasp and gulp. Tears stream down my cheeks. My dying thoughts cannot be trusted, but still I think: I know her. I know those eyes, that smile.

Her whisper hits my sweating cheek. *Now, go.*

Quickly she crawls past me, back down this muddy slope. The ghosts behind me shriek and hiss, their hands scrabbling in the dirt—but my helper, whoever she was, is not afraid.

I keep crawling.

More ghosts come, more women with flitting faces—some that I know somehow, though in my panic I cannot place them, and others I do not. They press their palms to my brow, they bend close and touch their mouths to mine. They breathe into me, they remind me how to do it on my own, they dart past me and scream at my pursuers. Walls of black bloody dirt on either side, above me, below me, and still I crawl, still I breathe. In, out, hand, foot.

The soil is looser now, easier to swim through. I claw and shovel, I stab and drag. I still feel the weight of my sack and its relics, and I still have the knife. Slender white roots snag my hair, scrape my arms. I hack through them.

And then she comes. I know her touch even before I hear

those buzzing flies. Her palm on my forehead, the other on my mouth. And now I understand, sobbing in the dirt, choking on the blood dripping down my hair and face, now I understand what I have seen.

I remember names from the past. Names I have tried to forget. Names we have all tried to forget in Haven.

Vera Lowell. The hazel eyes and sweet smile. She stole her husband's gun, they said, and tried to run off into the wild with her three children. Thank the good Lord, my father said the day they caught her a mere mile from the black mountain. Those poor children, he said.

Sarah Miller. The dark brow, the straight nose. She accused her husband of unspeakable things. A madwoman to her bones, that one. No surprise, then, that she would hang herself.

Anna Corey. Brown birthmark from brow to ear. She was run off just as my mother was. A wicked girl, they called her. A harlot from whom no godly man was safe.

And now, my mother, helping me climb. Patience Barrow, the temptress who tried to kill Joseph Redding when he threatened to tell the elders what the two of them had done, what she had made him do. The woman who shouted mad stories of the Devil even as they chased her into the woods.

I see it now, as I crawl. I see the story of that day.

My mother ran through the meadow, then into the trees. Sobbing, panting, muttering words that had lived in her head for years, but she had no coven of her own to help her and was only just beginning to understand them.

The underland. The door in the ground. The long road to walk.

But no one would listen to her, and Joseph had betrayed her, and now she would never see her daughters again.

In the trees, a bullet caught her, then another, then a hound, then a watchman. He held her down, laughing, as did another, while a third jumped off his horse. Hardly more than a boy, I think, though I cannot remember his face. I cannot remember any of their faces, but it does not matter. They were all there, they were all men of Haven, they were all watching. This boy, he took a fat silver bell from his horse's bag—one of the ribboned ones girls of Haven sometimes give their beaus—and pried open my mother's mouth.

A hand grabs mine. Ghost hand or no, it keeps me from drowning. I clutch it fiercely, and in that slap of palm to palm, my lungs and legs and eyes burning, understanding bursts open inside me—a swollen storm cloud giving way to blessed rain and calmer winds.

Palm.

Key.

I burst through to the surface, claw the ground for something to hold on to. I gasp down so much air that I choke on it. I am soaked in so much blood I cannot see. Hands grab me, help pull me out of the water and onto the solid moss-covered earth of Avazel. I jerk in their grip, cough up wet wads of dirt. I want desperately to breathe, but I am sobbing too hard, so hard that I gag.

Voices whisper, tender and near. *Rage*, they say, and *sister*. *We are here*, they tell me. *You are safe*.

Gentle fingers clean the blood from my eyes and mouth, push back the stiff wet sheets of my hair. Palms on my cheeks, palms on my brow. I sense a warm body near me, though I still cannot quite see. My eyes show me only the black of the pool, the black of the choking earth, the red of the blood that soaks it.

I turn into this warmth, this softness beside me, and catch a glimpse of gold at last. My sister's hair. Hunger is her name. I cling to her and weep, gasp out her name, and mother's, again and again, my throat burning.

"I did it," I whisper, when I can find the words. They are ones I have held trapped inside me for years, held tight in a net of shame, but the scrying pool has torn that open, and now they gush out of me like blood. "I found Mother and Elder Joseph together. I walked into Father's bedroom and saw them many times. One day, they saw me. I did not say anything, not to anyone, I swore I would not, but it was too late. After that, Mother wanted to stop. Elder Joseph did not. She poisoned him. I saw her do it. He chased her. She broke his leg. I ran. I found Father. I told him. I told everyone."

I cling to my sister, arms around her like a metal trap. "I am sorry," I sob against her dress, over and over. "I did it. I killed her. I am sorry, I am so sorry."

I expect her to shove me away any moment now. I know she will do it. She will yell at me, condemn me, blame me, weep and wail at me, betray me the first moment she can, hate me forever and ever.

But instead, she simply rocks me gently against her. My little sister. My dearest blessing. "I know," she whispers, then kisses my head. "I have known for years, and I do not blame you, and I still love you always. Do you hear me? I love you. I love you."

She holds on to me until I can breathe again, until I have wrestled with the knowledge that yes, Hunger knows what I have done, and yes, she knew all this time, and yes, yes, *yes*, she loves me all the same. She will not leave me. She will not despise me, not ever.

I look into her eyes, cup her face with my filthy red palms. I have no words to give her, but I see in her soft smile that they are not needed. She kisses my forehead, unafraid of the blood.

"It was not your fault," she whispers, and then harder, with a fierceness: "It was theirs."

Theirs. The elders.

My heartbeat begins to slow, and at last, I look up.

We are in the mossy clearing near the scrying pool, ringed by white trees. There is the coven—Malice, Cunning, Ire, all of them. Malice stares at me, her face winter pale. Gall has fallen to her knees. Liberty weeps quietly, hands covering her mouth.

Samuel crouches before me, facing the coven defensively. Swollen and bruised, he wields a thick white branch, as if he could do anything to keep the coven away if they wanted to come at me. I choke on a little sprig of laughter. Dear Samuel.

He tries so hard, even when he is wrong.

Sorrow is here too, her arm hooked through mine, her cheek pressed to my sodden shoulder. Vengeance kneels beside us, watchful and tense. In her open palm flickers a ready fire.

"What did you see?" Hunger whispers, her blue eyes—our mother's eyes—fixed on mine without fear.

"Ghosts," I rasp, my right hand still gripping my father's red knife. "Some I knew, and others I did not, but I think—no, I *know*—they are all women who have died in Haven. Some did not like me. They wished to keep me."

Sorrow does not lift her head from my arm. She strokes my shaking left hand. "And the others? What did they do?"

Each word is like fire in my throat. "The others helped me crawl through it. They pulled me and guided me, they cupped my mouth with their palms and helped me breathe." I squeeze Hunger's hand. "Mother was there too."

Hunger says nothing. I wonder so desperately what she is thinking.

Malice speaks before I can ask, her voice tense and hopeful. "And . . . all that blood? Did . . . did you see the Devil?"

"No." I look up at her. The words come easily, as if they have always lived inside me. That time in the water soaked me with understanding. My head hurts from crying, from screaming, but my thoughts are clear and crisp as ice. "*Extasia*. That is what the blood is, where our power comes from. It comes from the blood itself. *Their* blood. Any woman who has died in this world. The more unjust the death, the greater the power in her blood. It soaks the earth, we walk upon the earth, we draw upon the blood. Those of us who listen. Those of us who can hear and see what others cannot. We hear the power, and the power never lies." I smile faintly. *"Extasia."*

Some in the coven faintly repeat my words. Others cannot find their voices. Ire closes her eyes and turns away, one of her birds fluffing its wings on her shoulder. Furor, a knife in each hand, sinks onto a mossy stone.

Finally, Sorrow says softly, "And what of the key? Did you find it?"

I look up at her, then to Vengeance, then to Hunger. I drop my father's knife and clasp the hands nearest me. The others quickly grab on, and soon all four of us are linked. A chain of hearts and bones and bloody palms.

"We are the key," I whisper. A calm falls over me, soft as a sigh. "We four daughters of Haven, who have hurt and been hurt, who have made for ourselves new names. All of us, together, we are the key."

For a long moment, no one speaks. I cannot even hear a single drawn breath. Avazel has utterly hushed itself and its creatures. In that silence, anyone who may doubt my answer does not dare voice it.

Sorrow squeezes my palm.

Hunger does the same and presses her brow against my shoulder.

Then Vengeance says, her voice very small, "So, then, what do we do now?"

"Now we do as the ghosts have told us all this time," I say quietly. "We go under the black mountain."

The coven shifts on their feet.

Malice steps forward. "To find the Devil?"

Maybe. He could live there, or he could not. I know only that whatever I saw in the pool, wherever I was, 'twas not the underland of my mother's stories. There was no door in the ground, no river of golden light. So what did those stories mean? Why did she tell them, and why did the ghosts tell them to Sorrow in the very same words, and why did *extasia* come and find me? Is all of this leading me to the Devil, as I thought it would? Or is it simply *extasia*, and the women who feed it, wanting to be heard?

I do not know the answers, but the power never lies, and right now the power says, in my dead mother's shredded voice, *Keep going.*

Everyone around me flinches. It seems I said the words aloud. My voice and my mother's.

"Keep going where?" Malice asks nervously.

I lift my tired head to look at her. "To find the truth."

IV

may your rage burn bright

47

Avazel gives us the time we need, but I almost wish it would not, that we were forced to leave at once, for I am itching to move. The black mountain awaits, and each passing moment brings to mind memories of the Sanctificat's terrifying stories—the horned creatures perched on its slopes, the vast lake of fire underground, how someday the mountain will unfold its wings and reveal itself to be a beast with jaws big enough to swallow the world.

For two days we prepare—resting, gathering weapons and supplies, practicing our spells. Samuel thinks the elders might send watchmen to the mountain to patrol for signs of evil. We may not only be going to the Devil's mountain; we may also be going into battle.

In the final hour before we leave, nearly everyone is asleep. A smart thing, to rest. But I cannot find any sort of peace. I go to the scrying pool, thinking I might hear a whisper with some wisdom in it, but the water is no longer there. Instead, there is an empty clearing, piled soft with moss. I sit where the water once was, hug my knees to my chest, rest my cheek on my knee.

Sorrow finds me not long after. "Would you rather be alone?" she asks softly. Without moving, all I can see of her is the silken black hem of her gown brushing against her feet.

"No," I mumble.

She sits beside me and sighs. For a long time, she says nothing, just fiddles with a long white lock of her hair. Then a quiet question: "What do you think the Devil really looks like?"

One of the many things I keep asking myself. "I do not know."

"What will you ask him for when you see him? What exactly?"

"To punish the people who have hurt us. To make me my very own Avazel where you, Hunger, Vengeance, and I can live all alone. Maybe Samuel too. Maybe John Ames. Maybe Granny Dale."

"Granny Dale," Sorrow declares quietly, "bakes excellent bread."

My soft laugh dredges up exhausted tears. "True to her new name, so does Hunger."

Another moment of quiet. Then Sorrow says, "You do not really know what to ask him, do you?"

"No. I did once. Now . . ."

"I will hope he can do all of those things you just said, or anything else you might think of. He must be in great admiration of everything you have done."

"Yes. All the people I have hurt. All the lies I have told." I draw in a shaky breath. "I wanted to save Haven not so long ago. I believed in the goodness of God. Then my god became the Devil. I will never forget how it felt when Adam's bones broke at my will. The gladness of it, the thrill of power. He hurt us, I hurt him. A dealer of pain, Malice called me, and I cannot say she was wrong. But now . . ." I blink back tears. "Now I do not know what to believe about anything—God, the Devil, my father, my home. What a fool I was, and still am."

Sorrow hesitates, then begins rubbing my back in soft, slow circles. "I do not know what to believe either," she muses thoughtfully, "except that I believe in you. Whatever happens next, I am glad to be here. I am glad to be at your side."

I look up at her, cheek still mashed against my knee, and smile. "You are sweet."

"And you are not alone, Rage Barrow," she says, her soft lilting voice gone quite grave. "I hope you will not forget that, no matter what tomorrow brings."

I cannot possibly sit here without touching her any longer. I sit up, gently wind my fingers into her hair, and kiss her softly, again and again, until the warmth of her touch washes away all my fear and doubt. Until I am simply a girl tangled up with another girl, kissing happily, quietly, under the silent white trees.

⚸ ⚸ ⚸

Malice summons a path out of Avazel and onto a flat grassy ridge near the black mountain. We all step through it—Hunger, Sorrow, Vengeance, Samuel, Malice, the coven, a small herd of white-eyed birds and wolves that Ire and Storm have spelled to watch over us, and me.

And the moment we step out into the world beyond the wood, everything changes.

Instead of clean faces, mud and scars. Instead of gowns and fine linens, threadbare tunics, patched trousers, ragged coats, my filthy nightgown. Storm has no metal arm outside Avazel; her flesh-and-blood arm ends at the elbow. Gall takes off her coat, and Liberty removes the long leather apron she wears over her clothes so that Hunger, who arrived wearing only Sorrow's cloak, can cover herself with something.

I look around at all of us, my heart quietly sinking. Tattered and battered, bruised and thin, the coven hardly looks like their usual splendid selves. Even with our weapons, our witched animals, if we should meet any trouble . . . well, I only hope that *extasia* will choose to protect us well.

Malice strides toward me, her long black hair now short and choppy, a belt of knives around her hips and a spelled white branch from Avazel clutched in her hand.

"Well?" she says sharply, mocking me. "You wanted to go to the mountain, and here we are. You're the key, aren't you? Now what?"

⚸ 382 ⚸

I clutch my father's knife, touch the bag of relics. Truthfully, I do not know, but I try to sound serene. "We listen. The power will tell us."

"We should not be here." Samuel gazes up at the black mountain's flat top, hundreds and hundreds of feet above us. "We tread upon the flesh of evil."

"And thank your dearest darling God for that," Malice calls out with a laugh. "We have waited long enough for this! Haven't we, girls?"

The rest of the coven yells their agreement. Gall and Storm lift their own spelled branches and hover in the air, whooping proudly. Liberty hoists her rifle onto her right shoulder. Furor spins a knife with each hand, watching the mountain with eager eyes.

Sorrow, who has climbed atop a large flat stone, points down the hills. "Look there!"

I follow her arm. Vast fields and ravines, spotty woods and two small rivers, lie between where we stand, in the mountain's foothills, and where Haven sits on the horizon. Small, faraway lights bob and cluster—the torches of watchmen on the wall. Through the stillness comes the baying of hounds.

One of Ire's white-eyed wolves tilts its head, whuffs out a quiet bark, then shakes itself. Bits of skin and ash go flying from its mottled, scaly coat.

My back itches with dread. "They are coming for us."

Samuel hurries over. "If I can borrow a gun and bring two, maybe three, of the others with me, we can take up posts below, where the hills begin, and pick off the first riders who reach us. That will give you more time."

I hesitate.

He takes my hands. That gentle touch—I know it well. "Please, trust me, and let me do something to help. I cannot undo what has been done, but I can do *this*."

I soften, cup his face in my hand. "Go, then."

I glance at Malice.

She nods once. "Liberty? Gall?" Good choices. They seem at the greatest ease with their guns. "Go with the boy and listen to what he says. His help is the only reason we kept him alive." She jerks her chin sharply at him. "Make sure that he gives it."

They go without complaint, though Gall mutters under her breath. She may mutter all she likes. I feel better knowing Samuel's sharp eyes are watching out for us.

"Well, then?" Malice says. She jerks her chin up at the mountain, then glares at me. "We're waiting."

Hunger frowns at the piles of boulders around us. "Perhaps there is a cave that marks the entrance to an underground path."

"I was rather hoping the Devil would be kind enough to simply present himself, given everything we have done," says Vengeance, coming lightly down from the air. Furor taught her to fly, and it suits her. In the wind, her red hair snaps like fire.

Sorrow stares up at the mountain, absently fiddling with her hair. "Maybe we could summon a door from the rock itself if we go closer. And if it is locked, well . . ." She turns to me, smiling. "If we are the key, then no locked door should worry us. And besides that, I wrote a spell for unlocking, did I not?"

If there was time, I would kiss her. I would kiss her all over, all over again. "That seems a good place to start."

"Agreed," says Malice, sounding encouraged. "Not a bad idea at all."

Without another word, she marches toward the mountain, Storm, Furor, and Ire right behind her—but then something shifts in the shadows ahead of them, some veil of darkness being drawn swiftly through the air.

I open my mouth to warn them, but it is too late. They slam into the darkness, stagger back with sharp screams of pain. Hurrying over to them, I smell it before I see it: the smoky bite of cooked meat.

Malice, shaking all over, turns to face me.

Vengeance gasps. Hunger's hands fly to her mouth.

Glistening red burns mark Malice's face and arms. The fabric over her chest is singed, steaming. 'Tis the same for all the others. Every one of them has been burned.

"What is this?" Malice bursts out. Gingerly, she peels the

burned fabric from her chest, revealing a red handprint.

"'Tis the ghosts," Sorrow breathes, pointing. Hunger gasps, and Vengeance laughs once, a quick, frightened gust of air.

Sorrow is right. That darkness I saw is no mere shadow; it is a line of ghosts drifting between us and the mountain. Bodies stretched tall, arms drifting ten feet to the ground.

The dead women of Haven. Not all, but some. The kind ones who helped me climb. I search their faces for the one I most want to see, but the darkness muddles my vision.

"Mother?" Hunger whispers. "Is she there?"

"I cannot tell," I say, and then walk toward them, ignoring Malice's shout of warning. I near the wall of their bodies, hold my breath, close my eyes—and step through them. Easily, as if the ghosts are not even there. I look down at my chest, my arms. I feel my face. No burns. Not even a scrape.

Hunger follows, looking up at the ghosts' faces in wonder. Then Sorrow, then Vengeance. All of us cross the line of ghosts, and beyond them the air is colder, the mountain nearer. Vengeance shivers, gazing up at its sheer black slopes.

Malice comes as close to the ghosts as she dares, clutching her burned arm. "The power never lies," she says, the disappointment heavy in her voice. "You are the key indeed. This is your land, not ours."

"And they are our people," I say, looking up at the ghosts, "not yours. Whatever is down there . . ."

" . . . it is for you alone to see. When *extasia* speaks, I listen.

And it has never been louder than it is right now. The power never lies."

"The power never lies," we all say quietly.

Malice opens her mouth, shuts it, then looks up. "What do they . . . what do they look like? Your ghosts?"

Because, of course, she cannot see them. I was right that first day in Avazel. I saw a ghost in the smoke, and Malice saw nothing. The thought makes my heart clench for what Malice cannot see, and for the girl I once was.

"They are sad," I tell her simply, because there is no time to say more. "And they are angry."

Malice smiles softly. "I know that combination well. Go quickly, little sister. Find the Devil, and find him fast."

Then she turns with the others and leaves us—me, my sisters, the ghosts. Their silent wailing faces watch us as we climb up the rocks amid the twisted trees. After a time, I look back to see them, but they have already gone.

Whatever we do next, we will do it alone.

I open my sack and drop Father's knife into it. My body is beginning to ache from this climb. I will need both hands to keep going.

"Up here!" Vengeance cries. She is already far ahead on a huge jutting rock, peering over the edge. We join her and look down. Below us, at the bottom of a slope covered in pieces of loose flat stone, is a narrow mouth of darkness set between towering walls of rock.

Vengeance looks around at all of us, her eyes blazing with triumph. She mutters a spell, snaps her fingers, summons a small fire to light the way, starts looking for a safe first step.

We say nothing. What else is there to say? We are here. So is the path.

We follow it down.

48

Soon we are deep in a tangled black land. The strange trails winding down through the mountain's stony hills are many and narrow, but the power always tells us where to go. Little spots of heat prick our palms. The weight of some presence we cannot see presses near. We come to a fork in the rocks, and I know at once which way to go, just as I know, on the streets of Haven that I have walked for so long, where every house is, every garden. Left, right, right again.

Rocks make a forest around us, tall and narrow, short and squat. The air grows cold and damp, and I concentrate on my feet, my breath, pushing away the memories of Father forcing me downstairs into the House of Sighs. With each step, I wonder if we will ever reach a bottom or if we will keep climbing down forever and ever. Maybe the path to Hell never ends.

There is so much noise inside me, all my thoughts scrambling to imagine what lies ahead. I look up only once to see the mountain looming ever higher above us. I would not be surprised if, at any moment now, it rose up to swallow the entire sky.

Then Vengeance stops, goes utterly still. My body prickles all over with cold.

She looks back at us and points at a place just ahead.

A black door, grown over with leaves and brambles, but we can see it in patches. 'Tis made not of wood but of dark metal, with nails big as eyeballs hammered around its edges. A column of flat gray boxes runs down its right side, each thick with rust. I think they must be a strange set of locks.

"A black door, set in a hill," says Vengeance tightly. "If I remember right, one of your mother's stories spoke of such a place."

"And at the end of the road stood a great black door wedged in the side of a hill," whispers Sorrow, the cold wind ruffling her long white hair.

"On the other side of the door lay a field of fire," says my sister, her hand squeezing mine. She looks up at me. "Can this be real? Is this truly from Mother's story?"

"Maybe." My tongue feels too fat in my mouth. The alarming thought that it will keep growing until it chokes me leaves me feeling slightly hysterical. We should be here, I know it—everything has led us here. And yet the sight of that door terrifies me. I hold my breath, hoping it will swing open. *We are the key.* I say it four times, my newest prayer. *We are the key.*

I glance at Sorrow. She is staring at the locks, her head tilted like that puzzled white-eyed wolf who heard the hounds.

"Can you do it?" I ask her.

She smiles faintly. "Yes, I think so."

She walks down to the door, light as a bird upon the rocks. Then she holds her hands just above those rusted boxes, closes her eyes, and mutters what must be her unlocking spell. I do not try to hear it; a witch's spell is her own creation. But I watch closely, holding my breath as she murmurs the spell again and again. The power floods out from her, warming our skin and pulling the air tight around us. *Extasia*'s hum grows louder and deeper, a rumble of thunder shaking in my chest.

Then, all at once, silence.

A small click sounds, followed by two more. I hear something like the chime of a bell, but smaller and cleaner. A strange quiet crackle buzzes in the air, and a small glass eye above the door lights up and then darkens, again and again. The eye of the Devil, blinking as he watches us?

The door swings open wide—slowly, metal grinding on metal in a steady rhythm, like a song. At last, the door clicks into place and then stops.

We peer into the blackness.

Hell is meant to be a place of fire, but the air that greets us is cold.

"There is a path," says Vengeance, squinting, "and steps."

She mutters her fire spell, snaps her fingers. The flame she holds in her palm grows, bathing us in warm light, and for a moment, I feel a little less afraid.

I step past her, my heart hammering, Hunger's slick hand around mine. Sorrow follows us, then Vengeance last of all. She does not close the door but instead leaves it open to the world above. Odd that I once thought those black rocks and brambles so fearsome.

This is far more terrible, this long slow drop into utter blackness.

The steps descend forever. Every now and then, we reach a small room, another black metal door. No knobs on these doors, and no handles. Each has a square of dark glass set in the wall above it.

We do not go near these doors. They frighten me, so still and dark, probably with unspeakable terrors behind them. 'Tis a strange comfort that the stairway to the Devil's home is in itself a torment. This makes a beautiful kind of sense to me.

At last, my skin crawling, a scream ready to burst from my throat—we stop.

We stand in a large empty room, muscles aching, lungs burning. There are no more stairs to climb down.

In this room, there is only a single door of black metal, like the ones we have already seen. No lock, no latch. Above it, a dark square made of glass.

Vengeance marches to the door, a hard grim look on her face. Her sweaty hair sticks to her cheeks and neck. She hesitates, then presses a piece of round metal stuck into the wall beside the door. We wait, breathless, but nothing happens.

"Well," Vengeance says, her voice shaking only a little, "maybe I can melt the lock."

She raises her palm, still holding its flame, but then the glass eye above the door blinks awake. Red, dark, red, dark.

The door slides open—how strange, a door that slides instead of swinging—and a cold rush of fear drops to my toes, and I think, *Ah, here it is, here he comes.* I have done what I must, and now my work is ended.

But stepping out through the door is no Devil.

It is people—four dressed in white coats and trousers, six others in gray. Hard shells cover the graycoats' faces, and they carry strange black rifles that look nothing like my father's. The whitecoats have no weapons. Their face coverings are soft, leaving their wide eyes free to look upon us.

"Don't be afraid," says one of the whitecoats, a man with gray hair and kind eyes. Behind him is a woman, her dark hair in a knot on the top of her head. Beyond them, through the door, lies a clean hallway of stone with strange sharp lights trapped in boxes of glass along the ceiling.

I step back, my mind whirling. What a strange Hell this is. Where is all the fire?

Vengeance is closest. When they reach for her, she throws her flame at them, and it lands on the gray-haired man's white coat. He shouts and jumps back from her. Then the people in gray, the ones carrying rifles, rush at us. They grab me by my arms and tear my sister away from me. I hear Sorrow cry out and look around wildly to find her.

One of the whitecoats has pressed a strange thing to Sorrow's skin—a tool of glass and metal—and then she falls into his arms, her eyes closed and her arms gone limp.

"What the hell are they?" one of the riflemen shouts. "Was that *fire*?"

There are strange hands on me, strange hands in smooth cool gloves. They are quick and strong, and in my fear, in my utter panic, a moment passes before I think to call upon the power and make my own fire.

"*Malagsat*," I begin, but the dark-haired woman in the white coat is too quick. She grabs hold of me, says quietly, "It's all right, you're safe now." Then a sharp prick stings my arm, a soft, swift blackness floods my eyes, and I am gone.

49

WHEN I WAKE, I AM in a room with white walls, lying in a bed of soft pale linens. A white door with a red glass eye above it stands closed in the corner. A small green bush in a pale brown pot sits on a narrow table against the wall. White lamps hang from the ceiling in cases of glass, and there are sounds around me—soft clear chimes like strange bells and a low steady buzz, very faint, though I see no flies, no bees.

I look down at my body. I wear a clean white gown, and I am alone.

My wrists and legs are held to the bed with thick gray straps, and I am alone.

I squeeze my eyes shut and think of my mother's voice. "Once there was a girl," I whisper, "who on a summer's morn in the meadow came upon a blue door set flat in the ground."

Then I hear a soft click and another chime. This one is

different from the others—a little higher, a little sharper. The white door opens.

I am no longer alone.

A girl enters the room, closes the door quickly behind her, then turns to look at me. She has smooth skin, a dark brown like Cunning's, and long black hair kept in many neat braids.

"I've come to help you, even though I'm not supposed to," says this girl. "But if you try to burn me like your friend did, I'll call security right away. They'll come and sedate you again, or something worse. Can you stay calm so I can talk to you? Will you do that?"

I nod.

"Good." The girl pulls a white board down from the wall. It shines softly with some strange unnatural light. "You're perfectly healthy, this says. One hundred percent normal. My name is Jaime, by the way. What's yours?"

I know not how to answer her.

Her face gentles. "If I take off these straps for a minute, will that help? You won't shoot fire at me or anything like that?"

I nod again. "I will not call upon *extasia*. You have my word."

"*Extasia*, huh? Is that what you call it?"

Once I am freed, Jaime helps me sit. Her hands are warm. I could go back on my word, use my bone spell to throw her against the wall, then run out the door and find my sister, but she seems kind. I will wait at least a moment.

When Jaime puts a blanket around my shivering shoulders,

I hold it against my chest and whisper, "My name is Rage."

Jaime brings a chair to my bed and sits beside me. "Nice to meet you, Rage. We don't have a lot of time. My mother is one of the governors here, and you and your friends have really freaked them out. No one but the governors and a few security chiefs and, like, six doctors know you and your friends are here. Well, and me. I'm an excellent eavesdropper."

"What is security?" I say, embarrassed.

"The people who keep us safe." Jaime looks keenly at me. "Do you know what year this is?"

At last, something I know. "Year one fifty-three of the After Age. It is May."

"Yeah. Okay. Well, it is definitely May." Jaime scratches the back of her head. "Do you know where we are?"

I do not know how to answer. The question could be a game of the Devil and Jaime a trickster from his court sent to test me.

But she could also bring me to Hunger, Sorrow, Vengeance. Her mother is a governor, and I know that word. Malice used it in Avazel. Furor was banished from her village by a governor who did not like that she told the truth about his beatings. The one-eyed man Malice killed.

A governor seems to be something like an elder, but Jaime said her mother was a governor, a woman and not a man, in this place where men live. I am confounded. Are they too some kind of coven? If I answer Jaime, she and her mother could help me. They could explain.

"We are beneath the mountain," I say at last. "Where the Devil lives."

Then I hold my breath, waiting.

Jaime speaks very calmly. "We are beneath the mountain, that's true. But the Devil doesn't live here, Rage. Okay, the mountain is called Devil, kind of, but forget that. This is a city called Hope. It's full of people and homes and crops and schools, all of it underground. It was dug out years and years ago."

"Schools?" I say to her. My head hurts, too small and slow to keep up with what Jaime is saying. How could this be? How could any of this be?

"Schools are places where people learn," says Jaime.

"You are lying to me."

"I swear I'm not."

"The *Devil* lives under the mountain."

"He really, really doesn't."

I drop my blanket to the floor. I am too warm now. I need air, I need sky and trees, earth and blooms—but here there is only white and glass and the one small bush sitting on its table.

"You were sent to torment me," I tell her roughly. I push myself off the bed and go to the bush. I clutch it to my belly, touch its tiny green leaves.

"*Extasia*," I whisper, closing my eyes. "Help me understand."

But I can hear and feel nothing of the power in this place,

only those accursed tiny bell chimes and my own hammering panic.

"I promise, I'm here to help." I hear Jaime rising from her chair. "Please don't do anything crazy, okay? If you throw a fit, they'll hear and come running. I've rerouted the cameras' feeds, but we have maybe five more minutes before they figure that out."

Jaime touches my shoulders and turns me. I jerk away from her. The plant falls, and the pot breaks open on the ground. Soil scatters far.

"Rage, listen," Jaime says. "I know you're confused and scared, and I'm sorry. But I don't know if they'll tell you the truth. I'm going to try to stop them before they do whatever it is they're going to do to you, because it isn't fair. You're just kids, like me. I don't care if you can shoot fire or whatever. I'm going to try, okay? My mother will listen, and I think the others will listen to her. But just in case, I think you should know. If you're going to be . . . well. No matter what, you should know the truth."

"The truth," I whisper.

"Yes. Tell me where you live."

My legs are shaking, my knees useless. Jaime helps me to the bed and holds my hand as Hunger would, as Sorrow would, and I cling to her, this girl with her bright dark eyes and strange words.

"I live in the village of Haven," I say. "Not far from the black mountain."

"Okay. And you said one fifty-three. You mean year one fifty-three?"

"Of the After Age."

"Which means . . . what?"

I stare at her. This must be a test, some trial I must endure to gain entry to the Devil's true domain. "The World That Once Was ended many years ago, but God chose us to survive and begin the world again. We, the chosen people of Haven. My father, the High Elder, he and the other elders teach everyone this is so. Only . . ." I remember those first nights in Avazel, how the coven spoke of cities, other settlements somewhere out in the wild. "Only I do not think that is right. Not anymore. I have heard things . . ."

Then I cannot speak. Jaime is looking at me with such pity on her face that I feel suddenly, awfully, very small.

"Okay." Jaime takes a deep breath. "So, Rage, here's the thing. Yes, the world ended. I mean, basically. There were awful wars over food and water and a million other things, and most people died, but not everyone. Some people made it here to Hope and started a new safe life underground. I can't believe this." Jaime looks away and shakes her head. "I thought we were the only people left, and this whole time, you were living right over our heads, basically, and no one told us. They must have known. The sentinels must be able to see you from the upper decks."

I find my voice slowly. "You say there were wars, and that many died."

"Far too many."

"Was it because of the women?"

Jaime frowns at me. "What women?"

"The women of The World That Once Was. Were they why the world came to ruin? Because of their deceit? Their defiance? Their lust and their weakness?" I swallow down the sick, screaming feeling in my stomach, the feeling that tells me the answer Jaime will tell me, the answer I already know. "Because they were touched by the Devil?"

For a long moment, Jaime is quiet.

Then she says, with a dreadful, gentle softness, "No. It wasn't the fault of women. It was everyone's fault. We all messed up. Women aren't evil, Rage. Is that what they've taught you?"

I cannot answer. My head pulses black and red. I lean over, one hand on my knee, the other clutching Jaime's hand, and she says nothing, blessedly, nothing, only strokes my fingers with her thumb until I can breathe again. A word comes to me, showing me the way.

"City," I say. "You said you thought Hope was the only city left in the world."

"That's right. Some super-rich people built it in secret and went underground with their families. Don't even get me started on how messed up my ancestors were."

Now I can tell *her* a truth. It is unkind of me, this urge to shock her, to ruin her understanding of the world as mine has been ruined, but I cannot help myself. "You are wrong. There *are* other cities beyond even Haven. Liberty told me she has seen them. There is one in the mountains down south, she said, and another in the plains to the east."

Jaime goes very still. "Who is Liberty?"

"A witch from far away."

"A *witch*?"

"None of them are from here. They hail from other cities, they have traveled far—"

Then, a noise from the door. Jaime jumps to her feet and spits a word I do not know.

The door opens. Through it steps a woman I think must be Jaime's mother, the governor, for her skin is just the same brown. The same dark eyes, the same black braids. She wears a long pale shirt to her knees, gray trousers, dark boots.

She looks at Jaime, closes her eyes as if suddenly deeply saddened, then opens them to look sorrowfully at me.

Jaime moves to stand between us. "Hi, Mom. Rage—this is Rage, by the way, one of the girls who's been living in a god-damn *cult* right over our heads. She tells me there are other cities besides Hope. One down south, in the mountains, and another out east. Probably more than that?"

She looks back at me. I nod. The way the coven spoke, there are many, many more.

"Is this true?" Jaime says sharply.

Her mother does not answer.

"I thought we were the only ones left," Jaime says. "That's what everyone thinks; that's what you've told me all my life.

But I guess there's been this village sitting right up there this whole time, doing horrible things and telling horrible lies. You had to have known about that, but you said nothing, not a single thing."

Jaime clenches her fists, squares her shoulders. "Tell me the truth, Mom," she says, her voice strong but shaking. "Tell us both the truth."

Jaime's mother says nothing for a very long time. The pain in her eyes stokes in me a rising fire of fear. They stare at one another, mother and daughter, as if fighting a silent battle, and the pit of me, the deep tender pit of me, aches to watch them, even in their anger.

Then Jaime's mother turns to touch the closed door. A chime sounds from the ceiling. I hear four clicks, like locks turning. She taps a strange black band around her wrist, and the red eye above the door goes dark.

"Oh, Jaime," she says, her voice thick with tears. "I really wish you hadn't come in here."

50

JAIME STARES AT HER MOTHER with real fear on her face and takes a single step back.

"I heard you speaking to Governor Chu," she says. "I wanted to see the girls for myself. I didn't think it was right to keep them locked up with no explanation. Oh, and you don't actually have to confirm that you've been lying to me and to everyone else. I can see it on your face."

Jaime's mother rubs her brow, her eyes glittering with tears. "Jaime, you've put me in an awful position."

"I used to believe in the cities above," says Jaime, her voice now wavering a little. "That more people had survived besides just us. You told me those stories were nothing but fairy tales."

"What I told you was a kindness, sweetheart."

"If there are other cities in the world, we should be talking to them! How many are there? How many people survived the wars?"

"These questions will lead nowhere you want to go." Jaime's mother moves quietly toward my bed. "We've made a good life for ourselves here. We are self-sufficient and peaceful. Reaching out to others is too great a risk. They will want what we have. They will steal, or we will. It has happened before. It won't happen again. The first governors of Hope decided that long ago."

Jaime's mother has a beautiful voice—heavy with sadness, but rich and warm. Different from my own mother's, yet it reminds me of her just the same.

"You have watched us from your city under the mountain?" I ask. "You have known of Haven?"

She takes my hand gently, and I let her, though my body is ready to spring. "We have."

The world tilts, then stills. My breath echoes like thunder inside mc. "You have seen the things that happen there."

Jaime's mother nods. "We have surveillance equipment that can reach Haven. You're the nearest settlement to us. We keep a close eye on you."

My anger is a bramble in my throat, hot and mean and spiky.

Jaime stares at her mother. "And you did nothing to help them?"

Jaime's mother walks away, hands clasped at her lips. When

she turns back, her face is harder, less kind.

I grip the edge of my bed, my tired body aching with tension.

"Five generations ago," says Jaime's mother, "when Hope was founded and the world as people knew it was ending, part of the community split from us and chose to remain behind on the surface. They didn't want to adhere to the strict social and moral codes we have in place here. Full of fear and hate stoked by the fires of war, they created the village of Haven. It's true that our governors worried what would become of that place. But they had a city to run. If a bunch of bigots wanted to remain aboveground and live out their lily-white, neo-Puritan, misogynistic fantasies in the wild, so be it, and good riddance. Every few months, we leave them some supplies—ammunition, medicine, seeds. In exchange, they leave us alone, keep their people away." She looks at me, softening a little. "I'm so sorry. We didn't know what they would do, what they would become, and by the time we did, it was too late to stop them."

Jaime stares at her mother, hand over her mouth. The peculiar boxed lights on the ceiling shine in her eyes.

I think through her mother's words, collecting the ones that are familiar, puzzling over the ones that are not. And from these words, a truth forms. The truth my mother, and all the ghosts of Haven, wished for me and my girls to know.

There is no Devil under the black mountain.

Instead, there is a city, very close to us, where there are no visitations, no saints, no Sanctificat. Instead, schools and crops. Healers and governors. An entire underground world.

"Does everyone know this?" I whisper. "All the elders?"

"Our understanding from the intelligence we've gathered is that the only two families that pass down the truth to their children are descendants of the two men who founded Haven. Very charismatic men, the records say. And in the wake of war, the people who went with them were willing to believe anything. Even false prophets."

My mind is a blinding whirl of light. "What were their names?"

"Timothy Redding and Edward Barrow."

The room spins and darkens. I grip my knees and breathe. Jaime gently touches my shoulder. I shrug her off with a furious little sob. I wish I had never come down beneath the mountain. I wish my old friend Temperance had started bleeding years ago, before she ever thought of fleeing to the woods. I wish Malice and her coven had never come here. I wish I were a saint, pious and sweet and ignorant, sleeping peacefully in my father's house.

But I may wish those things for the rest of my life. Doing so will not change the truth.

Something shifts in the air near the door. A drifting tall darkness, a familiar black curtain of flies. Locked doors mean nothing to her.

I stare at her with a thousand questions burning in my chest and love, terrible aching love, twisting my heart, twisting my belly, twisting, twisting, tearing me to pieces. I wish I could look away from her. I wish I had gotten it wrong. She is not my mother. My mother is at home, alive and safe. My mother is in heaven, finally at peace.

But there is no Devil here, and maybe not anywhere. If that is true, then maybe there is no God, no heaven, no Hell. Maybe there are only ghosts, the earth soaked with blood, the people living above and below it.

Maybe there is only *extasia*. Hot rivers of power binding me to my sisters, binding us to our ghosts, living to dead, flesh to smoke, heart to heart to heart to heart.

Did Mother know about this underground city? Did she know the truth about the world, or did Father keep it from her as well? Were they waiting to tell me until I was grown and wed? I must know the answers to these questions. I am ravenous for them.

"What are you doing?" Jaime's voice has grown small. "Mom?"

Her mother is tapping the strange black band on her wrist. Tears are rolling down her cheeks. "What did you think would happen if you came in here, Jaime? You've talked to a girl from the outside world, and now you know the truth. And what will happen next? People will want to leave, go explore the world. Others will find us. We'll be overwhelmed.

Everything we've built will fall."

Jaime approaches her carefully. "Mom, listen, I know you're angry, but—"

"There isn't a word to describe how angry I am, Jaime. Do you think I want to euthanize these girls? Do you think I want to send my own daughter to Quarantine?"

Jaime flinches. "What? Are you serious?"

"You were compromised the moment you entered this room—"

"I am *not* getting my memory wiped. No one needs to know I was here."

"Someone would find out eventually. There are cameras everywhere, Jaime. Not even you can override everything."

"Just talk to the other governors! Make them see reason!"

Jaime's mother goes quiet, and in that stillness is an answer even I, who has only just met her, can understand.

"You don't want to talk to them," Jaime says flatly. "You want things to stay as they are."

Her mother lets out a small, helpless sound. She shakes her head, speechless for a moment. "Baby girl, listen to me. It's . . . I'm afraid of what could happen to us if everything changes. Aren't you?"

Jaime nods slowly. "Sure. But that isn't a good enough reason not to try."

A long look passes between them. Jaime's tears spill over.

Her mother cups her cheek, her face raw with sadness.

"You are stronger than I ever was," she whispers.

I can no longer look at them. Their faces are so tender and open that it crushes me. Instead, I look back to my mother, who waits by the door. Her arm, dark as charcoal, long and thin as a stretched vine, points toward the hallway.

Go.

That single word, the sight of her frozen scream, scorches my tired thoughts clear and reminds me who I am, what I can do. The power is coming back to me, and the power never lies.

I jump from the bed and run toward Jaime's mother. My feet skim across the ground, each light step a drum of power beating through my blood.

"*Grozixniila!*" I hiss, then slam my hot hands against Jaime's mother, hitting her shoulders hard.

She cries out, staggers back into the wall, and falls. Her eyes flutter shut. Blood drips from her nose, from cuts that have opened on her arms, but she will not die. I stand over her, breathing hard, listening to the hum of this cold white world. The stone above us, the little plant and its spilled soil.

No, she will not die. *Extasia* tells me so.

Jaime touches her mother's wrist and neck, looks hard at her slack face. Then she rips the black band from her arm and a long silver stem from her belt and leaves her bleeding on the floor.

Jaime grabs my arm. Her eyes are bright, but her voice is

strong. "Will she die?"

"No," I answer. "The power never lies."

"Whatever that means. Come on, I'll help you get the others. You have to get out of here."

51

JAIME RUNS WITH ME DOWN the white hall outside my room. With the silver stem she stole from her mother, she opens three other heavy white doors. We find first Vengeance, then Sorrow, then Hunger last of all, each of them in a long white gown, same as me.

Once my sister is free of her bindings, I pull her roughly off her bed and embrace her harder than I ever have. She clings to my shoulders, her grip like claws, her heart beating wildly against mine.

"I thought you were dead," Hunger sobs. "I cannot feel *extasia* here. I called for you and called for you, and no one came."

I kiss her hot brow, unable to speak.

Vengeance hurries over next, and then my beloved Sorrow. Their arms come around us both, holding tight, pressing close, until the four of us become a tight knot. Fingers digging into arms and shoulders, Sorrow's face soft against my neck, Vengeance's hot breath on my arm. I think in time with my galloping heart, *Maybe nothing else I know is true, but* this *is.*

Vengeance glares at Jaime. Her fingers rub against each other, ready to snap. "Who is that? Is she one of them?"

"She is a friend," I say, though I cannot be certain that is true. Then, as Jaime waits at the door and peers fretfully down the hall, I tell my sisters, as quickly as I can, what I have learned.

Once I have finished, they stare at me—revolted, astonished—as if I have told them that they are not alive, that they are dead, that this is all a dream.

"Father knew about this place?" Hunger whispers. She looks so small under these harsh lights, so worn out. "And Elder Joseph too?"

"Then there is no Devil." Sorrow is frightfully pale, worrying a strand of her hair between her fingers. I take her hand, press my thumb into her clammy palm.

Vengeance shakes her head viciously. "But this cannot be. He is here somewhere. He has to be. We are not alone in this quest. Malice sought the Devil too, didn't she? She longed to find him; she searches the *world* for him. When we told her about Lost Abigail, the relics, the black mountain, she believed it all to be true!"

"Malice believed the story she wished to believe," I say quietly. "The story that was told to her. The story she told herself."

"The story that brought her comfort," Sorrow says. "The

words that helped her fit all the pieces of her life together, helped her to keep walking on the road." She smiles faintly, closes her eyes. "So many stories, so many truths. So many ways to see the world."

"And the relics?" says Hunger in a small voice. "The book, the mirror . . . they mean nothing?"

"No," I tell her. "That is not true."

I glance over Jaime's shoulder, where my mother drifts closer in her cloud of darkness. She is so tall that she must bend to look at us through the doorway. Vengeance gasps sharply. Hunger lets out a tiny sob. "Mother?"

I smile softly, staring without fear into the wide mouth that is my mother's face. "Finding the relics taught us to fight. They brought us here. They brought us to each other."

"And we are the key," Sorrow says softly to herself, a small sweet smile at her lips.

"Yeah, so, I hate to tell you this," says Jaime from the door, "but all your things—those relics you're talking about, I guess?—have been locked away. And we don't have time to get them." She looks uneasily over her shoulder at the place where we are all staring. "Also, we've got to move, now. Any minute, my mother could come to and sound the alarm, or someone will find her and do it themselves. I can show you the quickest way to the surface, but it's possible security may come after you. I don't know." Jaime's eyes are bright, but she holds her face very still, as if trying to keep any and all feeling from touching it. "I'm sorry. I'm sorry about all of this."

She dries her face with her sleeve and looks away from us, back toward the room where her mother lies bleeding on the floor.

"Your father cannot be the only one who knows the truth," says Vengeance, her eyes hard as metal. "Some of the other elders must too. They know, or they wonder, and they've said nothing. Maybe others as well. Other men loath to lose their precious visitation days. Other men who love a God who loves them best." Her voice shakes with fury. She summons a flame, which snaps red in her palm. "I will kill him. For what he has done to us, for his lies, for his every deceit, I will gut your father and bathe in his blood, and then do the same to all the rest of them."

"Stop it, Vengeance," Sorrow says sharply. "You are not helping."

"But where will we go?" Hunger says, hugging herself. "After we run from here, we should run from Haven too. We cannot go home. They will kill us." She draws in a shuddering breath, her face crumpling. "Father will kill us."

I ache to hold her, I ache for all of us, I ache, I ache, I burn, I boil.

"We'll burn Haven to the ground," growls Vengeance, "and then leave with the coven. We will find every village that has lied to its daughters and ruin them. They will beg us for our mercy, but we shall never grant it."

"Okay, listen." Jaime steps between us, her palms up, silencing us. "Burn whatever you want—I wouldn't even blame you for it. But first, we seriously have to get you out of here. If my people find you, you're dead."

She leans out into the hallway, looks left, then right, then beckons for us to follow her. We do, hurrying after her in our bare feet. The floor is smooth and cold. My mother darts ahead of us, too quick to follow, a shadow always at the edge of my sight.

Once, I look back at Vengeance. Her expression frightens me, for I feel the same. Jaime's words, her mother's words, the truth of this place—it all settles inside me, spreading roots, sprouting blooms. A growing tangle of truth spitting fire from its petals. *Extasia* still, but darker than I have ever felt it, sharp as my father's lost knife. As we run through these underground rooms, fangs sprout from my mouth, and my tongue turns black. My skin grows a rough hide, and horns burst from my skull.

I imagine it, and the imagining is delicious. The Devil is not real? Well, I could be my own Devil. There would be nothing inside me then but fire and hate. The relief of that, the strength it would give me. The strength to destroy and punish, the strength to walk away.

I feel this thing, this glorious growing monster, turn and twitch inside me. If I tore off my skin, it could break free, race over the walls of Haven, and devour all it sees.

But if I do this, I may no longer know myself. In my rage, I may forget the blue of my sister's eyes, the press of Sorrow's sweet mouth on my skin. I may forget the tender parts of my heart, its softness, the meadow's green scents, Samuel's dear dark eyes, and instead know only the beast living inside me and its powerful burning appetite.

So I say nothing. I tear at nothing. My tongue is my own, my skin pink and smooth. I push down the fire crackling in my chest, mold it into a single steady flame, small but unwavering. I follow Jaime through dim hallways and metal doors, up dark iron rungs hammered into rock.

At last, we open a final door, set so cleverly into the wall that once we are through it, I can no longer see where it stands. And ah, yes, this room is a place I know, the empty room where the whitecoats pricked us. Jaime hurries us through it and then up the stairs from our endless descent.

"We were here," I whisper to her, "but when?"

"It's only been a few hours, don't worry. It's mid-morning." She leads us into another room, where one of those black metal doors is set flush in the wall. Above it, a dark glass square.

Jaime stands beside it, her face grim. "I don't suppose any of you have used an elevator before?"

Suddenly, that dark square of glass flashes red. A chime sounds, some urgent shrill bell. It pulses, then falls silent, then pulses again.

Jaime whispers something sharp under her breath. "They've

shut down the elevators. You'll have to climb the stairs, just like you came down. Use your witchiness or whatever. *Extasia?*" She bites her lip, then pulls me fiercely into her arms and squeezes. "Go as fast as you can. I know you're tired, but just fight that, okay? I've got friends who'll help me. We'll hold them off for you as long as we can, and I'll make sure to send people to Haven as soon as possible. Okay?"

Then Jaime turns and runs back down the stairs to that room below. I wonder if I will ever see her again.

But already Vengeance is climbing fast up those endless dark stairs, following the trail of my mother's long body, and Sorrow is hurrying to match her. Hunger reaches for my hand. "Rage, come! We must run!"

I grab her fingers, scramble up behind her. Mother's shadow turns our feet swift as sunlight, and Vengeance's fire lights our path. As we climb up through the flame-lit gloom, her words ring inside me.

I will kill him, she said. *I will gut him and bathe in his blood.*

Him. My father. The beast in me roars to think of him, but I cannot risk setting it free. Gutting my father, bathing in his blood—those words do not sit right in my heart, but no others come to take their place. My head pounds and my chest aches, tired and empty, raw from too many wounds. I run up the stairs in my mother's shadow and wish I could speak to her as she once was. Whole and warm and loving me.

What should I do? I would ask her this.

When I see them—the people of Haven, the elders, the

watchmen, Malice and her coven, Samuel hiding in the dark with his gun, my wounded furious father and his mouth full of lies—what should I do?

Once this day has passed, what will be left of the world I have known?

And what will be left of me?

52

When we come out of the door aboveground and into the black-rock forest of the mountain's foothills, the first thing I do is gulp down the fresh air—so crisp and cool and full of life.

The first thing I see is fire.

It bleeds orange into the sky of thick gray clouds. A storm has come, dark and roiling, blocking out the sun. A storm of the world, or a storm of witches? I hear a distant clamor of sounds—screams and shouts, the howling calls of wolves, the shrieks of birds and horses, the pop of gunfire.

We climb fast up the winding stone paths, then come out onto a flat black ridge. From there, we can see the truth of things. Not far from the mountain's foothills, the meadow is alight with flames.

Watchmen from Haven ride hard on their horses, swinging

axes, throwing knives, shooting guns. Their fallen torches are burning up the meadow.

But the witches, the swarming coven—they too have thrown fire. The earth shakes with their power, the air snaps with black lightning. We can feel it from here. *Extasia* shrieks in my ears, urging me to run. There is Malice, soaring with her white branch in hand. A man flies off his saddle, straight up into the air. He hovers there, spinning, then is flung hard to the ground. A cloud of white-eyed black birds swoops down upon a running horse. The horse screams and rears up, throwing its rider.

I stare at the violence in awed horror—the flickering orange heat of it, the long snapping shadows. Some of them are ghosts, flying to the witches' aid like enormous wailing birds. Mother hovers behind me, and the air shakes between us, as if she is eager to fight at their side but refuses to leave mine. My skin prickles with our shared power.

"What do we do?" whispers Sorrow on my left. Beyond her stands Hunger, wide-eyed.

"We fight with our sisters," Vengeance snaps. She murmurs a summoning spell, and a white branch gleaming below in the dirt—lost by another witch during the fight—comes flying to her, strikes her palm. She rises into the air, her white gown from beneath the mountain fluttering, her hair a red banner. I call out her name, but she does not listen. She dives down and is soon obscured by the fire.

We follow her, Sorrow and Hunger and I, climbing down the rocks on foot. Mother helps us, darting around our feet to guide them toward the steadiest stones. The touch of her hands is like the kiss of snow. When we reach the bottom, we hide behind a clutch of pines. From there, we stare at the burning meadow. *This* is Hell, too hot and wild to be believed. There, the silver fall of an ax. There, the snarling leap of a wolf with white eyes, its fur nearly gone, leaving only mottled gray flesh behind. A body, still and broken—Gall's, I think. My heart clenches at the sight.

I look wildly around for Samuel, for my father, for any living face I know, but all is harsh light and quick shadow. I can hardly tell one man from the next.

A horse runs past with wild eyes, its reins trailing across the ground. There is fire everywhere, and smoke, and the ghosts' darting shadows. They push the witches faster, knock them left and right, helping them dodge bullets. Very near us, a witch cries out. I think it is Cunning. A sharp squelching sound stabs the darkness, but I dare not look. I do not wish to see it, I do not wish to see any of this. Somewhere, Vengeance is fighting, and Samuel too, and maybe even my father—if he still lives, if violence has not already felled all of them.

Caught between what came before and what will come next, torn between too many choices, I look back at Mother towering behind us, and my desperate question from our underground climb returns on a whisper, like a wind come down for only me to hear.

What should I do?

I stare at the silver smile stuck in my mother's shredded throat. *Our* mother. But I am a selfish girl, and I want her all for myself. The wanting climbs up my body like chewing small fires, and with it an idea.

I turn to Sorrow and Hunger, though I cannot bear to look at my sister's face. Such a betrayal, and yet I shall do it anyway. Did my sister have to crawl through that pool of earth and blood? Did a book burst from her back? No. I will claim this thing for myself.

"Cloak yourselves and go to Haven," I tell them quickly. "If the coven gets past the wall, they will kill everyone they can. But our neighbors have all been told lies, same as we have. Help people safely from their homes. Take them to the woods and hide them until you hear from me."

"But what will you do?" Hunger asks.

"I am going to Avazel to bring back a weapon I think will help us." It is not entirely a lie, and I would tell it a thousand times if I had to. I kiss Hunger's cheek. "I will not be gone long. The days move faster in Avazel, remember? The wood and its moon give us the time we need. In what are only moments here, I will be back beside you."

Sorrow folds Hunger's hand into her own. "I will protect her with my life," she answers solemnly before I can even form the question, and I love them both so fiercely in this moment, so completely, that it hurts to look at them. Then they hurry away, and when I turn to face my mother, a blazing power roars to life inside me. I think it has been building for all my years, before I ever spoke a word. My skin flushes hot, my heartbeat booms in my ears, and I need no words to call upon *extasia*. In silence, we have made flowers together, and we will again. My garden will not be ashes forever.

I hold my breath. Inside that dizzy feeling, in its soft-spun folds, I listen for the hum, the hum, the eternal hum of *extasia* and make my demand.

A great pressure bears down on me, so hot and heavy that tears stream down my face. I am no longer girl, but fire. I am the very flames in the battle behind me, and with my hands and my will and my power, I think of the Avazel woods and hold everything still—every witch, every ghost, every watchman, every witched wolf, every blade of grass.

The world is still, flames caught mid-snap, and will not move again until I command it.

A thousand trees rush toward me, first dark, then white. Through them flies my mother, right toward me, her wide mouth opening wider than ever to show everything that wriggles inside it—every fly and color, every echo of memory and every silver inch of her bell. Her arms grow, pull at her sides, become wide as wings, and then we are one in the dark, in the deep diving dark, and together, we are gone.

53

WHEN I NEXT OPEN MY eyes, I am beneath the Avazel sky. The red moon sits full and fat in the high blue-black, a bright drop of blood.

I rise, searching the white trees, and there beneath the tallest one stands a woman in a fine gray gown, a cloak of wolf skin slung around her thin shoulders.

She is pale, as I am, with my sister's blue eyes and golden hair. Avazel has given me the gift of turning her ghostly face whole, her arms smooth and fair.

"Mother," I manage to say, my voice cracking.

"Hello, Rage," Mother says. The sound of her voice guts me. I have worked hard to forget it, and yet here it is, just as I remembered. There is a quietness about her, a stillness, like the time just before dawn, when in the darkness lies a promise of light soon to come.

I do not know how to speak to her. The words sit on my tongue. An apology. A plea. *Forgive me, Mother.* But what if she will not? What if the very request angers her and she leaves me forever?

I swallow the words, my throat painfully dry.

"Are you dead?" I ask instead. What a question. Cruel and blunt.

But she does not seem angry. She does not seem much of anything but still. "Of course."

"Did it . . . did it hurt?"

Her eyes move then, a soft flicker of memory. "I was chased into the woods. My pursuers hurt me and did what they had been taught to do. Later, I was found by wolves and eaten while there was some life left in me. Not much, but enough. Yes, it hurt. It hurt very much."

I think of how it would feel to have fangs sink and tear into me while I still breathe, how Adam Brinsley must have felt as we broke his bones and crushed him.

But I cannot cry any tears for myself or my shame, not while my mother is here, not after all she has endured. I have too many questions, and I do not know how much time Avazel will give us. Malice says it gives us what we need, but the power stretching between me and these trees and the battle on the meadow is already draining me. My lips are cracked. I wet them nervously.

"Did witches ever help you as they have helped me?" I ask.

"Since the war, there have been people roaming the earth,

looking for homes, looking for peace, looking for places to hide." My mother is so still, she could be a carving upon frozen water. "The earth has been rent open too many times, and now the blood it holds is angrier than ever. There are women who understand this, who hear and taste and smell it. Since the war, and long before that, there have been witches and covens." Her face flickers again with something like sadness. "But no, I had no witches to help me. I heard the ghosts' stories, all the dead women talking, but I was alone." Then she smiles, every inch of her warming. "I am glad you are not alone."

I cannot bear such tenderness. I grip my skirts in shaking fists. "And . . . the Devil. Where is he? Is he . . . is he real?"

Her smile turns unkind. She is my mother, and yet she is not. When I was small, when she held me and my sister close as she whispered her stories, her touch was warm, soft even though her fingers were calloused from work. But I think if she put her hand on me now, it would burn with ruthless cold.

"Once there was a mother of daughters who hoped the Devil would come to save them from their flowered prison," she says, her voice sharp with mocking, "but if he does exist, I have not seen him."

I have a hundred more jumbled questions, but I cannot order them. In my mind, there is a glittering pink road, a crown of flowers, a quiet bed, three warm heads on a pillow. Gold, brown, gold. Sorrow kneeling beside me in Holy House, in her yard, in the green glade of my garden, whispering her stories just as my mother did. A small wrinkled man in a red jacket. A black door in a hill. A river of golden lights.

A city underground.

"The stories you told us," I say. "The black door in the hill. The long pink road. The underland."

My mother watches me, waiting. I wish I could shake her, make her laugh or smile, bring some blood to her cheeks. She is even paler than the trees.

"You knew about the city of Hope, under the mountain. You knew what was the truth and what were lies."

"I wondered," says my mother, her eyes cold and distant. "I listened to the stories the ghosts told me. I listened, and I wondered. I watched the black mountain. I told you stories so you would wonder too. But I was not so quick and clever as you, my sweet girl. I was too late to understand. But when I died and found every answer I had sought, I did all I could to come back to you in whatever way was offered to me."

I fight the hot swell of my tears, my throat aching. "As a ghost."

"A messenger. An echo. A memory."

"Who offered this to you?" I say bitterly. "God?"

My mother's eyes shimmer, blue to white to blue again. "I cannot be sure. 'Tis very strange in the after. I do not think I could make you understand. Not everyone stays here, as I have. Not everyone has reason to. But I did. I had two reasons, and two alone."

Her voice is so full of sudden sadness that it cracks my chest open, leaves me raw and wriggling in the dirt. My name and my sister's. The words fall unspoken from her tongue like tiny dandelion seedlings, light as air.

Her body flickers, her color fading. "Whatever you would still ask of me, do it quick. I cannot stay here long."

I try to think. It has never been so hard to think, and the question that bursts out of me is so awful it takes my breath away. "Why did you lie with Elder Joseph?"

"I was unhappy," she says simply. "He made me happy for a time, until he did not."

"You were unhappy? Because . . . of us?"

The shape of her ripples sadly. "Not you, not my daughters. Never you."

"Are you sorry you did it?"

"That I lay with Elder Joseph? That I poisoned him? That I hurt him?"

"All of it."

"Yes. And no. More yes than no. It took me from you and your sister, and that is a regret I will carry with me for the rest of time, until I decide I can bear it no longer, and find peace in the next place at last. If there is indeed such a place for me."

"Are you angry with me for finding you?" I choke out. Suddenly, I am on my knees in the dirt. I can no longer hold myself up. "For telling Father?"

"No, Rage."

I hug my stomach, hunch over as if struck. Every breath wrenches a new sob from my lungs. I pray to whatever will listen, to *extasia* itself, to help me find my courage. "It was my fault you died."

"*No*, Rage."

"I was afraid, foolish, confused, I didn't . . . I didn't understand—"

A low rumble in the air stops me, makes me look up. Mother has tried to move toward me, I think, but something is keeping her back. She reaches for the white tree, leans heavily against it. Soon her skin will be as gray as her gown.

"It was not your fault," she says, her voice so much thinner now. "You did nothing wrong. *They* were wrong. Your father was wrong. Do you understand me? Say it."

"It was not my fault," I whisper, and though I do not quite believe them, the words pry open, deep in my heart, a door long shut, a window closed against the sun.

"Good." She gasps a little, staggers where she stands. "Hurry, Rage."

I think quickly, wipe my face with my fists. "Elder Peter, as he lay dying, asked me to forgive him."

"He was nearing the end of his life even before Hester stabbed him, and he was beginning to regret every evil he had done and allowed. He was beginning to wonder, to suspect the truth. If he had lived longer, I think he would have found it and helped you. I also think he might have felt us as he grew older. I think he might have heard the tread of ghosts."

"But he was kind to me." I cannot stop crying. "If he guessed the truth, even for a moment, he should have told me.

He should have done something!"

"Yes, you were dear to him, as I know he was to you. He was a kind man, gentle in his way, and yet he was cowardly and slow to accept the horror of what he had done, what he had allowed to happen and never thought to question. All of these things are true. You must learn how to hold them in your heart and mind at the same time."

I let out a frustrated little sob. "And if my heart and mind are not strong enough for all of this?"

She smiles. "You cannot see your strength, but I can. Others can too. Trust them. Trust me."

But how can I trust anyone if I cannot trust myself? I am a stumbling, muddled, sinful girl, rash and angry and full of thorns. What good can someone like me do in this world of lies and unkindness?

I wipe my face hard and find another question. "You stopped the coven from nearing the mountain. Why?"

A moment passes, and then she walks toward me slowly, unsteadily. Her gray feet toe the dirt, and I see a blackened nail.

"Theirs is no way forward." Her voice splinters into a dozen sharp pieces. "They are not women of Haven, like you. This was not their quest. It was yours, and you are nearly there, my girl. You are so close. You have found the truth, and now you must do something with it. Those women, the coven—they have been hurt too deeply, and now all they know is how to use their anger to hurt in return. But you . . ."

She is very near me now. She reaches for my cheek with her swollen gray fingers, and I must stand here, I must not move away, I must swallow my fear and let my mother remember what it is to touch her daughter.

"You are angry too," she says. "Good. You should be. You can use that to do what is right. But then, someday, when you are ready, you must let that anger go, or it will become all that you are. You deserve more than that, and so does your sister, and so do Sorrow and Vengeance. This life you have is precious, and now you have a chance to rebuild it. All of you overflow with possibility, with truth and light, and there is so much more for you to find inside yourselves, so much more still to see. Remember that as you decide what to do next. Protect it."

She draws soft lines along my cheeks and brow. I hold still and look upon her face, once smooth and now cracking, now peeling away in thin shreds, her mouth widening, her skin stretching around it, and I will remember this, I will always remember this, I will hold it in my heart and mind forever.

Then, suddenly, my mother cries out and staggers back from me. She groans, a wordless throaty cry, and looks away, hiding her face. Flesh falls from her body like shredded leaves. Flies buzz out from between her fingers.

I know I should not, but I hurry toward her all the same, crying out for her to wait. Shadows are everywhere, unfolding from the trees, wrapping her up too fast for me to make sense of.

"No!" she moans. "Stay away from me. Do not come near!"

She stumbles through the trees. I run after her, tripping over roots, shoving aside branches weighed down by sheets of flowers. My feet pound a frantic rhythm against the dirt. I skid down a muddy slope, hit my chin hard. Dizzy, I push myself up, and the first thing I see is my mother's abandoned wolf skin cloak. Lifting it to my face, I breathe in, but there is nothing here of the mother I remember—only fur and hide, the tang of wet earth.

I clutch it to my chest and search the trees. "But what must I do now?" I cry out.

A whisper touches my ear: *You have the answer.*

I turn, and there she is—my ghost, ten feet tall with swinging arms. When she wraps me inside them, I hear the storm of all her busy flies, feel their gleaming wings in my hair. I fall, I slide, I stumble free.

My feet touch ground hot with fire, wet with mud. The power surges at my fingertips, and the world snaps back to itself.

I open my eyes.

54

THE BATTLE LOOKS JUST AS it did before I left, the air ringing with screams and the fields raging with fire—fire that is moving toward Haven's wall far too quickly for my liking.

I find a great she-wolf wandering through the smoke, one of those from Avazel that Ire and Storm spelled to help us. If she stood on her back legs, her huge scabby body would tower over mine. Her eyes are white and clever, her fangs long and ill-fitting, poking jaggedly out of her mouth. *Extasia* still has her in its grasp, but the spell could fade at any moment. As if she can hear my thoughts, she sits quietly a few paces away, docile as I climb onto her back. Her shoulder twitches. I wrap my arms around her neck, press my body flat against hers. Her fur has nearly all fallen out, leaving her mottled skin bare and scaly. But she can still run, at least for now, and she takes me fast across the burning meadow toward Haven.

Though I cannot see my mother's ghost in the smoky air, I know she flies behind me. Her swift nearness chills the skin of my back. I can still feel the touch of her crumbling hand upon my face and cling to the memory with all the strength left in me.

As we hurry through the chaos, I see bodies lying still and dark in the weeds, most of them men. I think I see a witch, though the bloody ruin of her body means I cannot give her a name. My eyes burn from the smoke, from the long tired hours behind me. Grief and worry tie my chest into hard knots, and I wonder, if this is how it feels to be at war, why anyone in that world so long ago ever would have chosen it.

Not far from Haven's wall, the spell keeping the wolf docile breaks at last. She stops short and bucks me off her back, her eyes gone from white to black. I roll through the grass and scramble to my feet, fingers and teeth bared to fight her, but she cares nothing about me. She wants only her freedom. I watch her dart away toward the trees until the night swallows her and hope Avazel opens an easy path home for her to find.

Then I see Malice.

She fights near Haven's wall, Vengeance at her side, both of them flinging fire from their hands. Ire flies toward the wall, white branch in hand, surrounded by the few white-eyed birds still entrapped by her spell. Her scream is horrid, more dreadful than the birds' raucous cries. Liberty bends over a dead man and, as I watch, calmly pulls his heart from his gaping chest, then tucks it into a pouch tied to her waist.

I had wondered what would be left of me once this night had passed, and I wonder still, but that will come later, and I must not think of it now. Now, with my mother's words so fresh in my ears, her strength feeding mine, I know what I must do.

I run into the snapping flames. Vengeance calls my name, but I ignore her. Instead, I stand with my feet planted firm on this wet red earth, soaked with angry power, and utter a summoning spell that comes to me as easily as breathing. I say it loud, clearly, unafraid. No silent spell, this one. I need the steadiness of the words on my tongue.

"*Samdech, malyodam,* dead, fly, *grahala, malyatzaf,* ending."

From the sky and the smoke, the ghosts of Haven fly as *extasia* commands, my mother leading them. They pull Ire from her birds; they drag Liberty from her heartless man. They seize Malice and Vengeance by their arms and heave them away from their kills. They tear away the watchmen's rifles and hold the men themselves still.

Vengeance is the first to understand it is my spell restraining her. She howls with anger, her red hair clinging to her like wet weeds. But the ghosts hold her fast. For this short while, seized by dead shadows, the coven stands tame. They can do no spells; they cannot even search the mud for stones to throw.

"Let me kill them!" Vengeance fights hard against my mother's dark arms. "They do not deserve our mercy! Release me! They lied to us! They lied, and they hurt us, and they must be punished! Rage! Stop this, let me go!"

But Malice is quiet, watching me carefully, her skin singed and soaked. I do not know what Vengeance has told her, but maybe by now she knows of Hope. Maybe, she thinks, Rage Barrow will speak to the elders, and then, *then*, once she has her answers, once she has told everyone the truth, *then* she will let us finish what we have begun.

No, Malice. That is not what will happen. Not this night, not ever. Not while I still live. I stand in the blood of those who have died. I have seen who lies, who fights, who torments, who flees, who cowers, who learns, who helps. And now, with my mother's words smoldering like cinders inside me, I know my own heart and mind as I have never known them before. All these long weeks of death and secrets, of not knowing who I am, what I am, and now—now I understand. Or at least I am beginning to.

There is so much more for you to find inside yourselves, my mother said, *so much more still to see. Remember that as you decide what to do next. Protect it.*

My power is my own. I will not give it to those who hurt me.

I take a deep, shaky breath. For my mother, I will try, and for myself, and for everyone I know who has been denied the truth. They deserve the freedom I have found. They deserve a chance to atone, to remake themselves, and so do I.

A quiet has fallen upon these fields. The fires called by the witches fade to smoke, and when I look around at the men left alive, all of them bloody and staring, I find him at last—my father, limping toward me, his hands tied with a rope held by my dear brave Samuel, who himself is bloody and mud-soaked.

I bite down hard and keep my face calm, but my battered heart barely stays whole. Samuel is alive, and so is my father. I am relieved, I am glad, and yet part of me—some horrible, cowardly, selfish part of me—wishes Father had been killed while I was elsewhere, or had been driven away, or had simply dropped dead from a sudden illness. I would not have to look at him then. I would not have to face him ever again. I am a fire that wishes only to rest—but here comes more kindling, and a poker of iron, and a wind whipping up my sparks. The power speaks, and I must answer.

I stare right into the keen dark eyes that match my own. Not flinching, not showing him anything I do not wish for him to see.

Father waits, his face as stony as mine.

"I will meet with you," I tell him, "and all the elders. While we talk, there will be peace, though I cannot say if we will keep it afterward. I do not wish for any more bloodshed to happen this night, but if you should hurt me or any of my friends, I will release my coven, and they will come for you without mercy."

My father's face drips with sweat and ash, the nearby flames flickering in his eyes. I think of how I have pitied him, and loved him, and feared him, and how all of these things remain true even now, even after all he has done. I think of the goodness I saw in him when I was a child, his careful fingers painting chains of girls across my walls, his laughter in the kitchen when Mother was still happy, and how later I so fiercely longed to save him from the disgrace of what she had done.

At last he says to me, "Very well, daughter. We will meet and talk of peace."

Smooth as the skin on my wrist is his voice, thin as the place where my blood pulses.

Once, I loved that voice. I was soothed by it, I prayed with it, I listened in awe as it held all of Haven rapt.

But now, though I ache to, I do not trust it, not even for a moment, and that suddenly seems the saddest thing of all.

55

AN HOUR LATER, WE ALL stand in Holy House—my sister, Sorrow, my father, and I. The other elders who still live—Elder Daniel, Elder Wyatt, Elder Malcolm, Elder Phillip. Elder Ezra has died in the fight. Malice, Ire, Liberty, and Vengeance have refused to join us. The ghosts hold them outside, guarding them and Haven from each other. Samuel stands at the doors with his gun, keeping watch. So does John Ames, I am heartened to see, and Timothy Williams, Elder Peter's second, and three other young men. Samuel's friends.

We are not so alone as I feared we would be.

I set my jaw hard and face my father—hands clasped before him, dried blood darkening his lip. Untroubled, serene. If he closed his eyes, I might think him in solemn prayer.

I glance once at Hunger and Sorrow. We have all agreed upon what I will say. Hunger nods, her mouth set.

I take a deep breath and begin. "I know what lies beneath the black mountain," I tell my father. "We have been there, to the city called Hope. Sorrow and Vengeance and Hunger and I."

Black-bearded Elder Wyatt—he who held down my sister as my father cut her flesh—blinks in astonishment. Elders Daniel and Malcolm look at each other in utter confusion.

My heart sinks. I hoped at least one of them would know the truth, that Father was not the only one. Somehow that would have been less of a blow.

Elder Phillip frowns. "Amity, who are these people you speak of?"

Of course—he does not know our chosen names.

"The witches of Haven," I tell him.

"Hunger," says my father. "Sorrow." He looks at Sorrow, then at my sister. I wonder which of them he thinks is which. Then his eyes find me once more. "And you are?"

I meet his iron stare with my own. "Rage."

His mouth moves—a tiny smile. He says nothing.

"For years, you have lied not only to us but to all people of Haven," I tell him. "You have told us tales of the Devil. You have told us that we are the only people in the world and that saints must always stand at the altar to atone for the sins of women past. That they were the destroyers, those who brought The World That Once Was to ruin."

I pause, heart pounding in my throat. 'Tis not too late to run. I could send away the ghosts, bring the elders to Malice and Vengeance to do with as they will, abandon Haven to its fate, and then I could run to the woods and past them, far away. I could leave this place with one hand around Sorrow's and the other guiding my sister and not face what lies ahead.

But not so long ago, I was like my neighbors. I questioned nothing. I prayed and condemned and believed as I was taught. Should I not give them the same mercy I would have liked some other angry witch to give me?

My mother told me to trust her, and I will.

She said I have strength in me. So I will use it.

I tell the story of my trip underground. The city of Hope and all who live there. Timothy Redding and Edward Barrow, who built Haven and taught its people the prayers of the Sanctificat.

"You have lied," I tell my father, "to all of us."

A ringing silence follows my words.

Elder Malcolm rises to his feet, his brow furrowed. "Thomas, is this true? Tell me it is not."

My father's stillness snaps. "Oh, Malcolm. As if you would want it any other way. As if any of you would." He glares at all of them—Elder Phillip, who is quietly crying; Elder Daniel, stone-faced; Elder Wyatt, who points at me furiously.

"She is merely trying to exonerate herself," he says. "She means to turn the blame from herself onto you, onto us, just as the women of old did. Destroyers, all of them. Liars and whores."

I ignore him, speaking over him, though his words make

my stomach churn. If only I could spell his jaw shut. But he does not deserve even a lick of my power, not unless I have no other choice.

"You are not blameless," I tell them. "None of us are. But I do not wish to punish everyone in Haven." A lie. Part of me does wish I could punish them all, one by one. The flame of my anger is fresh and hungry, and I am not yet ready to let go of it.

But I think of my mother's words, of my furious redheaded friend, and press on. "No, vengeance is not the answer. Instead, I want us to reclaim our home. I want us to look at what has happened and what we have done with our eyes open wide, so that we may then rebuild what has been broken, and keep what has remained dear and good."

I take a step toward the elders. Merciful as I am, certain as I am of what I must do, I admit I am pleased to see them flinch—though my father remains a mountain, his face hard and closed. I remind myself to breathe and watch the others instead.

"And so we will forgive you," I declare. I let the words fall. The elders gape at me. Even scowling Elder Wyatt looks surprised. "Everything you have done to us, and to all those before us, and the things we did to each other while in the grip of my father's lies, we shall forgive. Anyone who asks for mercy for what they have done, and renounces it, and pledges to never do it again—to move forward in truth and kindness, and to help Haven heal from the lies upon which it was built—will receive forgiveness. The witches will leave you in peace, and life in our village will begin anew. You will tell everyone the truth of what the world once was and what it is now. We did not choose to be born here. We did not choose the stories you told us while we listened with love from our cradles. But we have a choice now. We can choose to live differently and to give ourselves and those who come after us the life, the home, they deserve."

My throat is dry from the smoke I have breathed, my voice tired and hoarse, my stomach clenched with fear. But when I look at my sister's face, and Sorrow's beside her, I feel a little less weary, a little more like the girl I am becoming.

Father's face is calm, his ashen black fingers held still at his waist. I think of my mother crumbling in Avazel; waiting outside Holy House, voiceless and dead, holding Vengeance steady; running across the meadow to the woods, naked and afraid. Hunger, bound and bleeding on the altar table. My dark cell in the House of Sighs.

I dig my nails into my palms. "Well? What say you?" I ask my father, I ask all of them, and then wait, sick-hearted, for their answer.

56

AFTER A LONG MOMENT OF silence, my father begins to weep.

In my amazement, I can only stare, thunderstruck, as he walks slowly toward me, his arms outstretched. At the altar's steps, he falls to his knees and raises his hands as if to offer praise to me instead of God.

"Daughter," he says, his voice choked with sadness, "how I have wronged you."

Never have I seen my father weep so openly, not even in my family's darkest days. But now here he is, sobbing at my feet. He reaches toward Hunger and me both, as if to gather us close.

"It was to protect you," he says through his miserable tears. "My father and I, and his father before him, and Edward Barrow himself—we all knew of the ways of those below the mountain and meant to keep you from them. They would not allow our ancestors to escape belowground with them. They left them here, in this untamed land, to grow crops from nothing, to build homes from nothing. Such cruelty! And these are the people you wish to call your own?"

A bell of warning rings inside me. I hold myself still, wishing he would stop crying. The sound is horrible, and I have no interest in his tears or his lies. Before he hurt Hunger, before he imprisoned me, before I understood the full truth, I would have been moved to see him weep—but that time, that girl, is gone.

But before I can decide how best to quiet him, there is a flash of silver, quick and sharp.

Extasia snaps hot against my ribs, awakening the beast in me. Horned and horrible, with its tough wrinkled hide and its jaws wide with teeth, it tears out of me at last, howls its tired grief, gnashes its yellow fangs, and I am this beast, and this beast is me.

Swiftly I dart to the right and dodge the knife my father holds. It was meant for my heart but only cuts under my arm, and with a burst of anger, I knock it from his hand. He cries out and clutches his fingers, all of them shining with fresh red burns. Then he gazes up at me, his face slack with fear at last.

My heart breaks to see him look so pathetic. I should have known he would do this, that he would try to silence me and protect this world of untruths he has built. Part of me, I suppose, hoped even now that I was wrong about everything.

But I am not. That look on his face as he tried to kill me tells me everything I need to know. He will never do as we ask. He will fight to his last breath to stop us, and too many people will remain loyal to him. His eyes flicker toward his dropped knife, toward me, and back again—still wondering, perhaps, if he could try again to stab me.

"Then I cannot save you," I tell him calmly, fighting back tears, "and I shall not mourn you."

A lie. Of course I will mourn him. I will try not to, and hope that someday his memory will fade and no longer hurt me, but until then, I will have to live with this grief inside me.

I mutter my bone spell—"*Samhaasyo, rahasa, larinalim, das*"—and the power obeys at once, grabbing my father by his ribs and skull and flinging him back against the wall. He drops to the floor, utterly still. He is not dead, not yet, but I hope he will not wake again.

I walk away from him. My knees shake, my chest is tight with trapped sobs, but I do not look back.

"Will you pledge to do as I have said?" I ask the other elders sharply. They nod, their faces full of horror and confusion, and even as I hate them, even though I will forever remember that they thought it right to tie my sister down and cut her, I pity them too. Would the Amity of old have done the same? Would she have held the knife to Hunger's breast?

I cannot answer that, and am glad I do not have to.

Sorrow and Samuel lead the elders out of Holy House. When Hunger and I are alone, I summon fire with my muttered spell and throw knots of flame at the walls, the chairs, the altar itself. The fire grows quickly, stronger than any flames I have ever made—roaring, a sucking yawn of heat consuming Holy House with an eager appetite. I look once more at Father's prone body, the flames snapping near his heels. Then I take my sister's hand and leave quickly, the choking heat chasing us away. I close the doors firmly, then stand for a moment with my back to the world.

Hunger squeezes my fingers and says fiercely through her tears, "You did what you had to. A man who tries to kill his daughters is no father and deserves no mercy. I love you. Do you hear me? *I love you*, forever."

I grip her hand tight, grateful for her strength, and face the people of Haven who have gathered around us. Sorrow is near, and Samuel, and the elders. Beyond them stand my neighbors by the hundreds. I swallow hard, swaying a little. It is as though I have begun floating out of my body, my bones so desperate for rest that they can no longer hold on to themselves.

But this moment, more than any other, is one I must face with every scrap of courage I can muster.

"Today marks the beginning of a new era in Haven," I cry out, raising my voice over the roar of the flames. "In the days to come, my friends and I, and your elders, will tell you everything that has happened and everything that will happen now. You will be safe, and you will be cared for. There will be no more fighting and no more deaths. I promise you that. We will rebuild, and we will forgive, and we will learn new stories and new prayers. We will look at the things we have done and accept them, the good and the bad. We have lived our lives broken without knowing it, but now that we know, we must work together, all of us, to mend the hurts we have done to each other and to ourselves."

I pause, trying to find my breath. Soon I will need a quiet room all to myself. I cannot hold back these tears forever. Looking around desperately, I find Sorrow. She has tucked a flower behind her ear, a wild primrose plucked fresh from the ground.

The sight of it, the love shining in her eyes, keeps me standing.

"But if you do not do these things," I continue, "if you choose violence and lies and cruelty, if you refuse to listen, you will not be spared, as my father was not." I gesture to Holy House, let the horrified cries of those watching wash over me. Yes, I killed him, and I will have to live with it. The girl I was is dying with my father, and someone new will emerge from her ashes. What will her name be? What will she say?

Higher and higher the flames rise, until all of Holy House is alight with fire. I hear the crash of wood, the spit of glass. I cannot say why no one watching tries to attack me. Maybe on this raw night of death and endings, they can hear *extasia* for themselves. Maybe the power has given them a warning, and they are wise enough to listen, even if they do not understand.

Behind me, huddled in the dirt, the elders pray and weep.

I wonder if they weep for my father or for themselves.

I wonder if they have ever wept for me.

57

Days pass, and Haven is quiet.

The elders spread the word about what happened to my father—what we offered, and how in return he tried to kill me. Malice, Ire, and Liberty collect the bodies of their dead and leave that very first night, along with Vengeance, to lick their wounds in Avazel. My father's death has satisfied them somewhat. Even Malice seemed a little afraid of me, not quite meeting my eyes as she told me they meant to leave for good.

"This land is cursed," she said quietly. "As soon as we're well enough, we're leaving."

"To continue your search for the Devil?" I asked.

She lifted her chin in defiance, her blue eyes ablaze beneath her messy cap of short black hair. It still startled me to see her so unkempt. In my mind, she will always be as she was in Avazel—red gown, long hair, glowing with happiness and might.

"Your Devil may have been a lie," she said quietly, "but mine isn't. He's out there somewhere, waiting for me to find him. I won't rest until I do." She looked away, her shoulders sagging a little, her face tired. "I mean, without that belief," she said quietly, "what do I have left? Not a lot. Not very much at all."

I did not plead with her to change her mind; I knew that breath would be wasted. Instead, I gently took Vengeance's hand.

"And you?" I asked her. "Will you stay with us?"

She did not answer. She hid her face and stalked furiously away at Malice's side. The ghosts, including my mother's, escorted them to the woods, helped them carry their dead. A shattered, limping coven flanked by towering shadows. I watched them all until they disappeared, giving my tears time to dry up.

Will I see Vengeance again? Or was that our final goodbye? When will the ghosts return, or will they? I fretted in miserable silence for hours after they left. I should have asked my mother to stay and speak to Hunger at least once, just the two of them, but everything happened so quickly, and now I have no answers, nor the time to wonder. I hope Mother returns, and soon. Until then, there is so much work to do, so much road ahead of me to travel.

Fear is the thing keeping the peace in our village. We bring bodies back from the fields and burn them—not in the House of Woe, for there are too many, but instead under the open sky. Then we scatter the ashes in the meadow, singing hymns to honor the dead and praying for their safe journey to God's kingdom. I am no longer certain I believe in such things, but it is a comfort to sing the old songs, even knowing what I do now. So much has changed and is changing; like Malice, I cling to whatever familiar things I can find with quiet desperation.

As we work, clearing away the ruin of Holy House and burning our dead, the people of Haven watch me like fearful rabbits.

Samuel hardly ever leaves my side, sleepless with worry for me. The surviving elders' seconds, I am relieved to see, remain fiercely loyal to him and work hard to show him that they can be loyal to me too. It helps to have him near; the fact of a man supporting me makes it easier for people to understand my authority. In their minds, I am simply a messenger; Samuel is the one truly in power, whatever I may say.

I am too tired to be angry about it. Let them think that, if it makes this time of change easier. I am neither afraid of nor insulted by my neighbors. I have hurt them; they have hurt me. They know what I did to my father and what I could do to them. They know that without me, the witches might have burned all of Haven to the ground.

And in some of their eyes, confused and somber as the air

is these days, I nevertheless see a curious light. A brightening. A wary awakening, brewing with questions.

There is no Devil, they have learned, and beneath the black mountain, there is a city. It was not only women who destroyed The World That Once Was; it was everyone. There are other people in the world—many others—besides those in Haven. What does this mean? Are we not God's chosen, then? Do they truly believe everything Sorrow, Hunger, Samuel, and I have told them? Will they continue to, once the worst of their fear has faded?

As I work and sweat, as I lie awake at night listening to Samuel pace our porch, ever watchful, I wonder what is happening in Hope. If Jaime's mother recovered, if she reconciled with her daughter. What questions do they struggle with in that underland of theirs? Are they much the same as ours?

Mother told me that I was dear to Elder Peter, and yet he never questioned the cruelties he was taught and dealt cruelties himself. Both things are true. I must learn how to hold them at the same time.

The elders taught us lies, even if in their minds the lies were true. If they ever questioned the rightness of the Sanctificat, they no doubt hurried past the thought, considering it a sin. I have done the same myself hundreds of times. Everything we knew was built on falsehoods—and yet I still mutter Small Graces to settle my mind, and they are a comfort I am loath to discard.

Both things are true.

Holding so much at once feels awful. I wonder if it does for Jaime too. Her mother lied to her and would have let us be killed—and yet she is her mother, and Jaime no doubt loves her as I did my own. Her mother felt sorry for us; her mother condemned us. She was kind; she was cowardly. All these things are true.

Do these contradictions feel as awful to Jaime as they do to me?

When I do manage to sleep, my mind draws many pictures, of Mother and Father, and of Elder Peter, and of the witches who died. Cunning, Gall, Storm. But when I wake, I can remember nothing of what they said to me in these dreams or even if they were alive or dead. My nights are full of ghosts.

I am weary of smelling smoke.

A few days after Father's death, I cannot sleep and instead go outside to find Samuel on the porch. The night is quiet. Even the bugs seem subdued, the watchmen's torches on the wall dim and tired.

Everyone is tired. Haven itself feels like an echo of what it once was.

I try to feel glad for that—this is what I wanted, to rebuild anew what had been built on lies—but it is difficult to remember what gladness feels like. It is difficult to feel much of anything.

I sit on the top step, watching Samuel pace with his gun. "You do not sleep enough."

"Neither do you," he replies, with a tiny wry smile. "Bad dreams?"

"Not tonight." I wait for a moment, trying to order my words. "I have a question."

He stops pacing to lean against the porch railing. "Ask it."

"You knew nothing about Hope. That is true, is it not?" He opens his mouth, but I rush on before he can speak, staring at my hands. "You were my father's second. And yet you did not know?"

"No. I promise you, Rage. Maybe someday he would have told me, but he never once said a word."

I blow out a relieved breath. I already knew this; Samuel is a terrible liar, and he would not have been able to pretend shock at learning about Hope. But I needed to hear him say it.

"I have been thinking about that myself," he says quietly, looking out at the road. "If I *had* known, what would I have done? If I found out later, once we were wed, would I have told you? Or would I have done as your father did, and everyone who knew the secret before him, and said nothing?"

We fall into silence. I think I know the answer to his question, but I keep it to myself. I have no wish to hurt him.

"I like to think I would have told you," he says at last. "The feeling that sent me to Holy House the night they hurt Hunger—I like to think that same feeling would have shown me how and when to do what was right."

Or, I think to myself, he would have been like Elder Peter.

Kind and gentle, a lover of flowers. Wondering about what lurks in the shadows, but too afraid to look. Comfortable with his power and afraid to give it up.

But I keep that to myself.

"What was the feeling that sent you to Holy House?" I ask him instead.

He is very quiet.

"Samuel?"

"Love." He looks over at me. "Love for you, Rage."

I continue staring at my hands.

"All these weeks—how fearless you were, how you protected Hunger. The things you said to me that day in the House of Whispers about her, and Adam, and my brother . . ."

"I am sorry for that."

"Do not be sorry. I needed to hear those things. They woke me up, Rage. *You* woke me up. And once awake, I finally understood that what the elders were doing was wrong. I had to stop them." He blows out a slow breath. "I did not ever imagine their wrongs would be so plentiful or rooted so deep. But I am glad I know now."

I do not know what to say, how to show him I am glad for the change in him, but also sad and angry that it took him this long—that it took *me* this long—to see the truth. I wonder if my heart will ever again know peace.

After a moment, he clears his throat. "Do you love me?"

And there is the question I had hoped he would not ask. "I

do. But not in the way you love me, I think." I finally look at him. How dear he is, my tireless guard. His hair is a mess, his brow grave in the lamplight. "Does this grieve you?"

"Yes," he says simply. Not angry, just speaking plain.

"Half the girls in Haven are in love with you, if not more."

"Maybe someday that will make me feel better."

"Samuel—"

"Do not worry, Rage." He glances over at me with a small, sad smile. "We will always be friends, you and I. At least, I hope we will."

He holds out his hand, and I take it, rising to my feet.

"Will you forgive me for taking so long to understand what is right and what is not?"

"I did not understand that myself, not so long ago." I think back to the girl I was only a few weeks past—trembling with excitement to receive her saintly hood—and marvel at how much has changed.

He blows out a long breath, looking out over the road. "It will take so much time to make everything right," he says quietly.

"Yes," I say, wilting a little as I think how true that is. But then I remember Jaime's words, and I smile. "But that is no reason to stop trying."

He nods, his brow knotted in earnest thought, and I almost reach out to touch his cheek fondly but stop myself. My broken heart breaks a little more; I cannot do such things anymore, not if I do not love him. It would be too unkind.

Instead, I stand there for a while in the quiet night air and take comfort from the nearness of him, my oldest friend, steady and serious beside me.

58

ONE BRIGHT AFTERNOON WHEN THE sun is high, little Timothy Williams—Elder Peter's former second—comes for me with news from the wall. Someday, perhaps, we will no longer have need for so many watchmen and a huge guarded wall. But for now, with our world so fraught and fragile, these things help my people feel safe, and I will not take that away from them.

I am in my garden when Timothy comes. I have tilled the charred soil behind my father's house and am starting anew. Hunger and I dig rows for seeds. We cover them with dirt and mutter over them the new spells we have begun to write—spells to help the blooms grow, to strengthen their roots. *Extasia* seems delighted to be put to work for the love of blossoms. My whole self feels lighter with my hands in the dirt.

I sit back on my heels and wipe my brow. The day is warm. I am not yet used to the newborn summer.

"What news?" I ask Timothy.

"There is a girl," he says, looking straight at me with shining eyes. We both loved Elder Peter, and so there is a bond between us. He is not so afraid of me as the others are. "A girl such as I have never seen. She waits for you at the wall, and others wait with her." He squints, remembering. "She said she is from Hope."

I rise swiftly, Hunger just behind me. As we hurry out of the garden, I remember to squeeze Timothy's arm in thanks. Later, once the day is done, I shall go to his house and thank him properly for all his steadfast help. His parents should know that I am no fiend, or that at least I am at present a tame one.

Beyond one of the doors in the western wall stands Jaime with ten others—men and women, some as young as she and I are, others older. They wear strange bulky clothes, as they did under the mountain, and keep their faces partly covered. When Jaime speaks through this covering, her voice comes out strangely. Distorted, as if her voice is fighting through sheets of rock and river.

"I can't stay long," she says, "not this time. But I wanted to tell you." She looks at the people standing around her. "Everyone, this is Rage. Rage, these are some of the people of Hope who helped me oust the governors. Lots of change is happening down below, and I want to tell you all about it, but our doctors say we should only stay aboveground for an hour, max. Our bodies have zero resistance to whatever might be up here.

Who knows?" She places her hands on her hips. Though I cannot see her smile, her eyes crinkle. "It's possible you gave me some kind of horrible disease and I just don't know it yet."

I stare at her. "Oust?"

"Oh." Jaime looks past me into Haven, where many have gathered to watch us fearfully. "I guess it's kind of like what you did here? The people who ruled in Hope, they don't rule anymore. We do."

A shadow moves across the part of Jaime's face I can see. I know that shadow well. These past days, it has become the companion of my sister and me, but it seems to like me most of all.

"And your mother?" I say to Jaime. "She lives?"

"She lives." It is all Jaime will say. "And your father?"

There are so many things I could say. "He tried to kill me."

Jaime laughs. I do not mind it. I know what she means by it. "What a pair we are."

She looks up at the sky, at the white clouds spread across the blue. She lets out a sad sort of breath, heavy and wistful. "Can we come back soon? I would like to."

"Yes, please do. And soon."

This makes her smile. Then she places in my hand a wrapped parcel and says, "This is for you, but don't open it around anyone else, okay?"

I promise her I will not, and as I watch her people walk across the meadow, back to the mountain I once feared, I think of times to come. I think of a day, a calm day with sun and a breeze, when I can sit beside Jaime and listen as she tells me everything that has happened in these dark days, everything that has hurt her, and then tell her what has happened here.

The thought is a small comfort, but I hold it close to me even so. I press her gift to my chest and stand by the wall, watching Jaime grow smaller and smaller. That way, if she turns, she will still see me, and perhaps she will feel a little less alone.

59

Two weeks after Father's death, I walk the wall in silence. Some of the watchmen nod as I pass them. Others shift and cringe away. At least none of them glare at me, or else they wait until I have walked on. Feared by most, loved by few. I wonder if that will ever change, if I will ever feel entirely comfortable at the elders' table, even with Samuel there beside me.

Atop the wall, above my old hidey-hole, I stop and look out at the woods. The moon is a sliver; I can see very little. But even dim as they are, those distant trees make tears prick my eyes. How easy it would be to spell myself a cloak and run into the woods and not once, not ever, look back. I would not have to rebuild anything or untangle any lies or look out for anyone but myself.

I grip the wooden railing, close my eyes, and imagine it.

A soft breeze lightly touches my nape. When I turn, I find

Vengeance, a long white branch clutched in her fist. She lands in silence on the wall. Her red hair is molten in the torchlight. The watchmen nearby cry out and flee when they see her.

"Peace," I tell them, raising my arm. "She is not here to harm us."

I glance at her, raise an eyebrow.

Her frown deepens. She shakes her head a little.

Relieved, I look with envy upon her soft leather boots and rough woolen gown. She is dirty and wild and smells of Avazel—the tang of forest berries, the scrape of leaves, the cool crisp air.

"Are you . . . well?" I ask.

Her sharp stare pierces me. "Well enough." She nods past me. "I came with your mother. She wants to take Hunger to Avazel, speak with her alone for a while." At last, her face softens. "I know very little of ghosts, but . . . I do not think she has much time left before she will have to leave for good."

I look where she points and see the tall dark shape of my mother's ghost drifting through Haven toward my house. I swallow down the urge to yell after her—*No, Mother, take* me *to Avazel*—because this time belongs to Hunger, as it should. If I never see our mother's face again, I will try to be content. We spoke the words we needed to speak.

Turning back to Vengeance, I consider reaching for her hand, but she stops me with a single hard shift of her eyes. "The people here will leave you," she says. "You must know this. They fear you, and once they learn ways to leave and still survive, they will. They will roam the wild with their Devil and their Sanctificat, their holy words, and they will build another Haven somewhere far from here."

I have thought of this—of course I have. "Some may. Not all. And if they do, that is their choice. At least they are alive to make it. At least I have told them the truth, to do with what they will."

"And those people below the mountain. If you think they will love you as we could have done, you are a bigger fool than I thought."

Her voice cracks with sadness. I know she will not understand, but I try nonetheless. "Vengeance. I could not let you kill them all."

"You could have," she says, soft and angry. "It would have been easy. We could all be far from here now, happy and wild and free, and we could find other villages turned rotten by wicked men and do the same there. We could spend our days in Avazel and our nights among the stars with birds at our backs. You could have let us kill them, and who would have grieved their deaths? Not me. I would have been glad to live in a world scorched clean of their poison."

She draws a shaking breath. "I despised you, but then you became my sister, our bond forged in fire, and yet you chose this place instead of me. You chose Haven instead of us, your true family."

"And before you met the coven, when this was all you knew, what would you have thought of some witch come out of the

❦ 465 ❦

sky to kill you? With no warning, no reason that you could understand?"

Vengeance looks away, her fists clenched, and does not answer.

"I think you would have wanted someone to tell you the truth first," I say quietly, "and then give you the choice of what to do with it." I wait a moment, then reach for her. "Vengeance, please. Come back to us. It is not so bad here, and the parts that are, we will work to make right. You are so strong. You would be able to help so many."

She jerks away from me. "Malice and the others have only waited because I begged them to. I told them you would come, and Sorrow and Hunger too. I told them to wait a while, only a little while."

"I killed my father," I whisper to her. "I told them the truth of the mountain. All of these people—I told them a horrible truth. How could I say those things and then run from them? How could I stand and watch them burn?"

"They watched us burn before. They chased us from our home. They beat us and took from us. I could help them? No, Rage. Now I help *myself.*" Vengeance drops her branch and grabs my shoulders, the grief bright in her eyes. "You have done enough for them. Would they have stayed here for you? Would they have spared you from the fire? So there is no Devil here, maybe not anywhere. Malice thinks there is, but I am not so certain. But there *is* a Devil in the hearts of men, and there shall always be, no matter how hard you work to change it. With us, with *extasia*, you can search the world for that Devil and bring him to ruin again and again. You can do *good* with us."

I step away from her, my tears turning the world to stars. "I can do good here. I must try to help them, as I would have wanted someone to help me."

She turns away with a sharp cry of frustration, finds her branch. I grab her hand. "Wait. Promise me this. Wherever you go with Malice and the others, whatever new witches you bring into your family, try to think of what has happened here. How much wrong was done with fists and knives. How much good was done without them. Think of how you would wish to be remembered."

Vengeance hisses a little in disgust.

I shake her, gently. "Promise me you will at least think about this, and urge Malice to as well." Remembering my mother's words, I whisper, "You are angry. Well, I am too. But at some point, we must let that go. We deserve that kind of peace, Vengeance."

She stares at me, biting her lip. "I promise I will think on your words," she says tightly, "but I can promise no more than that." Then she seizes me and kisses my cheek once, hard. She holds me against her, beating heart to beating heart, and then, branch in hand, steps off the wall into the air. She does not look back at me, not even once.

I watch her fly and hope that someday I will do so again.

60

In the morning, restless and sleepless, I take shelter in my garden. My spelled tangles of roses and honeysuckles and daisies and bluebells are the only things that brings me true, untroubled comfort. Beneath them, in that shadowed green place dappled with pale sunlight, I lie in the dirt, curled up like a child. I do not cry. I have cried enough. But I ache in all the places where I have ever been hurt. I press my fists against my chest, and I wait for a peace that will not come.

Then a gentle hand lifts my head from the ground.

Sorrow has come, my beloved one, with a tender kiss for my brow. Hunger is just behind her, carrying a plate of fresh bread.

Suddenly ravenous, I grab for a slice, tear it in half, and watch the steam rise.

Hunger smiles. "I thought you might be hungry. Not sleeping will do that."

I can barely look at her. There is a new quietness about her, a peacefulness, even though her eyes are swollen from crying.

"You spoke with Mother?" I ask her around my mouthful of bread.

"I did."

I swallow with some difficulty. "What did you say?"

"We spoke of many things, one of which was how to get you to eat and sleep."

Sorrow laughs a little. I smile and say nothing. Later, maybe, Hunger will tell me more; maybe not. Maybe she wants to keep those moments with our mother to herself. I would not blame her. We should claim what we can for ourselves, especially now, when so much is strange and new. When so much has been taken from us.

We sit quietly, eating. The silence is a balm; the bread warms me. Sorrow braids her long pale hair and then works it loose and braids it again, and as she does, she hums a song. Her legs are warm against mine. She wiggles her bare toes.

Hunger clears her throat. I catch her looking at Sorrow, pointing at something with her eyes. Sorrow sits up, throws her braid over her shoulder.

"Hunger and I thought of two things last night," she says after a time. That voice light as air, that sweet voice I so love. "One to tell you, one to give you."

I say nothing. Bread or no, if they think they can cheer me, they are fools.

"First, we thought there may come a time when we are no

longer needed here," says Sorrow.

"Once things have settled," Hunger says, "and once the old ways have truly died."

"And when that day comes, maybe we could go into the wild, just the three of us. Our own small coven."

Hunger's voice grows eager, her eyes shining. "We would see cities, and fly over new lands, and find other truths that need to be found and shared."

I think over their words in silence, then push myself up and look at them. Hunger beams at me, tearing into a fresh slice of bread with great satisfaction. Sorrow smiles, brushes dirt from my cheek, and then leans in to kiss me so softly that I melt into her, press my face to her hair.

"We could find other Havens," I say quietly. "Other Hopes."

"We could," Sorrow agrees, "or we could stay here, or we could come and go as birds do. Summers here, winters there."

Hunger sets her plate in the dirt and moves close to take our hands in hers. "But whatever we do, we shall do together."

I smile a little. "Three witches."

"Wild women," Hunger says with a little grin. "Seers of the unseen. Weavers of *extasia*."

Sorrow draws slow circles up and down my arm. "Tellers and keepers of stories. Truth seekers."

I hold on to my dearest ones and think of my mother's tales, of those girls who traveled the long pink road and found a door at the end of it. And beyond that another door, and after that another—but maybe, behind one of them, they someday found home. My mother's story, as she told it, ended before anything so happy could be found.

But now her story has become my own, and maybe that right door, wherever it stands, is now mine to find.

"Now," says Hunger, "our gift."

From her skirt pocket, she withdraws the book in which we saints signed our names. Malice's book, which I suppose she gave up for lost. It was this Jaime brought to me at the gates, wrapped neatly in cloth.

Sorrow opens the book, holds it open for me. I turn past the page marked with my name, and then Vengeance's, and Hunger's, and Sorrow's, all of us. Old names struck out. New names written in blood.

Then I come to the page on which Hunger and Sorrow have written their gift to me. For these last weeks, in every spare moment, we have all been practicing our letters, but they have both spent long hours at it, far longer than I have, and now I understand why.

With their help, I read the gift once, slowly, and then again. I read it until the words are carved into me, until I know I shall never forget them, no matter where I fly.

Hunger sighs happily, resting her head in my lap. Sorrow leans on my shoulder, her hair smelling of blooms and skin and salt. Of the things that are still yet to grow and the things that have lived and died.

"I heard you whisper it one night after supper," says Sorrow. "I came to the kitchen and saw you bent over this book at the table. I watched you write and heard you say these first words, here, but then you stopped."

"I couldn't think of what came next," I whisper. "The right words were hidden from me."

"That first bit is yours, of course. But Sorrow and I, we did the last part." Hunger turns to kiss my sleeve. "I hope you do not mind too much."

We sit quietly as the morning rises beyond the leaves. Sun and clouds, a singing bird, blooms opening to the sky. Together we read the prayer our fathers taught us, the prayer all girls of Haven learn—the Woman's Prayer—only now it is our own. Rewritten, remade. Our tongues learn the new words; our voices stamp them into our bones. It is our prayer now, and our daughters', and it will forever be.

Wherever you are,
whatever you fight,
may your eyes see much,
may your rage burn bright.

V

there have always been
witches

FOR THE PAST FEW WEEKS, every time it's been my turn to go to the surface for acclimation, I've seen a fox with white eyes.

This being the first ever fox I've seen in the actual world and not in a storybook or data file, at first I thought this was just what foxes looked like now. The world ended, after all. Biological weapons, chemical weapons, any kind of weapons you could think of, plus whatever other crap we'd dumped into the oceans and soil for centuries before that. It wouldn't have surprised me if whatever foxes had made it through that just had white eyes now.

At first, I didn't tell anyone. This was *my* fox, my little gift from the outside world. It seemed precious to me, significant. It found *me* every time I was aboveground, and I wanted it all for myself. Everything is chaos in Hope these days as the new councils—including me—restructure our government. People are trying to wrap their heads around the fact that *we are not alone*, which feels like it should be said with spooky music in the background or something. Some people are taking it well. Others are very much not. I'm in meetings and assemblies and looking over duty rosters from the moment I wake up until the moment my head hits the pillow.

I didn't think keeping the weird fox to myself was too selfish, then.

But the fourth time I see it—its scabby gray coat, its mouth overfull of spiky fangs, its unblinking white eyes—I decide it's weird enough that someone else should get a look at it.

I find Lee sunbathing on one of the flat black boulders surrounding the mountain. It's what they do every time their acclimation slot rolls around. They just lie on the rocks, close their eyes, and sprawl out so their limbs get as much sun as possible.

I climb up on the boulder and ruffle Lee's curly brown hair. "I hope you took a heaping dose of SunBlock."

"Of course I did, responsible councilperson that I am," Lee says sleepily. "I must set an example for all my impressionable followers."

I glance over my shoulder. Sure enough, the fox is still there, sitting only a couple of meters away from me. Watching. Waiting. But for what?

Even though the midday sun is blazing, a little chill skips up my arms.

"So, I'm sorry to barge in on your sun time," I say, "but

you've got to see this fox. It keeps following me."

Lee has slept with a stuffed fox since they were a baby. Their eyes open. "Seriously? Where?"

"Over there." I point at the fox, but Lee, sitting up, looking all around, just frowns.

"Not funny, Jaime."

"I'm not kidding! Look!"

I point right at the fox, lock my eyes with its creepy white ones, but even though Lee is definitely staring at the right spot, they just shake their head. "There's nothing there, Jaime. Maybe *you* didn't take enough SunBlock."

My little skipping chills become big stomping ones.

I force out a weak-sounding laugh. The fox is definitely still staring at me. "Guess it was just my imagination. I'll leave you be." I glance at my watch. "Only fifteen minutes left until reentry, by the way."

Lee settles back onto the boulder. "Just don't let it bite you. Might be radioactive or something. You'd turn into Fox Girl." They pause. "Actually, maybe do let it bite you. That would be excellent."

But I'm hardly listening anymore. The fox has started trotting away, and I think maybe if I can get close enough, I'll be able to see it a little better, figure out exactly what it *is*.

I jump off the boulder and follow the fox through the rocks and the stubby mountain pines until the rocks become tall grass, scattered with wildflowers and buzzing with bees. The trees elongate—leafier, less crooked—and the deeper into them we go, the faster the fox runs, until I'm racing after it as fast as my legs can carry me, which feels disappointingly slow. Apparently, all that cardio conditioning in Hope's gleaming fitness facilities is nothing compared to actual cross-country fox-chasing.

A little cramp in my right side makes itself known, screaming at me like a red alert: *Warning, Jaime, you've gone too far!* That's when I look back over my shoulder and nearly fall on my face.

The mountain is gone. The meadow is gone. The *sky* is gone.

Instead, white trees crowned with glossy black leaves and long sheets of white flowers stretch in every direction, as far as I can see. The ground is damp black soil, piles of pink-and-green moss, tangles of white roots. The sky, black. The air, suddenly cool and crisp. No sun anymore, just a huge red moon.

The sudden change in the world around me is so disorienting that I lose my balance and have to sit down, shaky-kneed and sweating all over. I hold my head, dig my fingers into my temples. Pinch my arm, lightly slap my jaw. This is a dream. Or heatstroke? Radiation poisoning? *Did* the fox bite me? Is this the beginning of my transformation into Fox Girl?

"Snap out of it," I whisper, shaking my head, blinking hard.

But when I open my eyes and look around again, it's all still there—this endless forest of white trees, eerily lit by the red moon. The fox is gone, and I seem to be completely alone.

Then something shifts in the air behind me, like I'm sitting in a quiet room and someone has snuck in behind me.

I turn around, and immediately my skin prickles all over with thunderous, nauseating fear.

I know that pond wasn't there before. I *know* it—as much as one can know things for certain when one starts vividly hallucinating, that is. I slowly rise to my feet and walk toward it, trying to step as softly as possible. If I'm too loud, will this creepy black pond rear up suddenly like some kind of monster and devour me? That feels entirely possible.

"Hello?" I whisper. The pond, funnily enough, does not answer.

But . . . it's almost like it does, actually. I don't hear words, but I hear something. I *feel* something. I should run away from this pond, but I can't, and I don't want to. The compulsion to get closer is like the urge to kick up and find air when I've sat too long on the bottom of the pool, desperate for a moment of peace and quiet. I can't *not* breathe.

I can't not look into this pond.

Golden stalks of grass, green moss, and tiny white flowers ring its perimeter. I crouch at the pond's edge and look down.

Staring back at me is water so still that I might as well be looking into a flat plane of polished dark glass. There's my reflection—brown skin, black braids, scared-shitless eyes.

I blow on the water. Nothing. No ripples.

I reach for the surface, hesitate, then dip my finger in. It slides right into the water, which, yes, does feel like water, albeit a really weird sucking kind—but again, no ripples. No movement, not even the slightest displacement. It seems the laws of physics do not apply to this pond.

Then something moves beneath the surface. The tiniest flicker of something, a fluttering ribbon of color.

My fingers tingle in the moss, as if heat building deep underground is rising up to meet me. A reasonable person would get out of here as fast as humanly possible.

But I'm too curious. I'm Alice, and this is the rabbit hole.

That worked out fine for her, right?

I lean over the water's edge, lower my face until it hovers just above the surface, and hold my breath.

Please don't eat me, creepy pond.

It doesn't.

Instead, it shows me something I don't understand. Deep below the water, creatures teem in the dark. Tall, skinny people—way too tall, way too skinny, to the point of being quite obviously inhuman—that seem composed not of flesh and blood but of shadows. Drifting, jagged darkness with huge screaming mouths instead of faces. The word *ghosts* comes to mind, and once it's there, I can't stop thinking it. There are dozens of them down there, maybe hundreds. I try to count, my eyes watering, but it's impossible.

They're everywhere. And they're angry.

They dart around like big fish feeding on smaller fish, fast and unpredictable. Swarming. At first, I think maybe that's it—this is a pond where ghosts live, and it just happens to be their lunchtime—but then something changes. The ghosts pull apart, then hurry back together. Pull apart, come back, over and over, and in the middle of their buzzing little underwater hive, something is growing. Something darker than they are, darker than the water. Like an absence of absolutely every particle of light that exists. A hole opening in the fabric of the world.

They're not eating, I realize, my heart pounding a panicky rhythm in my ears.

They're *making* something.

It takes on a shape, but not one I recognize. A long neck with a huge triangular head, spindly spider legs, wings snapping out for miles on either side. Then something shifts. That awful enormous head, so alien and *wrong*, like something out of a sci-fi movie, snaps around—and I know without a doubt that with whatever eyes that thing has, it's looking right at me.

I scream, push myself away from the pond, and scramble back across the moss. Then I hear a twig crack behind me and whirl around.

A white girl wearing a gorgeous ivory gown comes out of the trees, her long brown hair falling in waves to her waist.

I blow out a shaky, relieved breath. "Rage. Wow, hi. I didn't . . . I haven't seen you in . . . I'm so glad to . . ." I wipe my face with a shaking, dirty fist. I didn't realize until now that I was crying. "What . . . what is this place? What is *that*?" I point at the pond.

"This is Avazel, and that is a scrying pool," she says gravely.

She comes over and sits next to me, rubbing my back. That makes me cry even more, but for some reason, I'm not embarrassed to cry in front of her. "You saw something inside it?"

"Yeah, I would say so." I hug my arms over my chest, feeling very cold and very scared and very full of regret that I chased that fox. "I saw this fox, and it was so weird looking, I had to run after it like a moron, and—"

"I hope it did not frighten you," says Rage, looking concerned. "*Extasia* has been whispering many things to me of late, one of which is your name. I wanted to make certain you were well and safe. Spelling an animal to be my eyes and ears is useful for such things." She pauses, then says quietly, "I did not want to spy on you. But I worry about you. I think that whatever happens next, you may be a part of it. I promise I did not tell the fox to bring you here, not yet, but it seems *extasia* wanted you to come."

I stare at her. I should think she's crazy, but the same thing that pulled me toward the water, tugging on my bones like some primal homing signal, is telling me she's not crazy at all. "So it's true, what you said. You really *are* a witch."

She smiles a little. "And it seems you are too, one with great talent to be awakened. The scrying pool does not show itself to just any witch, and even among those who find it, not every witch can see what it has to say."

I am putting little pins in every other word she's saying. Witches, scrying pools, spelled animals. Me, a witch? Awesome? Not awesome? No idea. Fine. We'll come back to that later. "So, what did I just see in there? There were . . . *creatures*, flying around like bats, and it looked like they were building something."

"You saw what I did, then. The ghosts, and their creation." She frowns, her gaze somewhere far away. "Not all the ghosts I have met are kind. Some are angry, very angry, and I wonder . . . Perhaps they are building something—"

"A weapon?"

"—or awakening something."

That raises all the little hairs on my arms. I grit my teeth for a second to keep them from chattering. "Awakening *what*?"

"I suppose there might be other powers in the world besides *extasia*," she murmurs, frowning thoughtfully. "Something ancient, lying dormant. *Extasia* is neither cruel nor kind. It has no allegiance except to those who can use it. And not everyone who uses it has peace in their hearts." A little shadow flickers across her face. "I was chased by such ghosts not long ago. They had no kindness left in them. Only anger."

"So what does this mean? You think now they want revenge or something?"

"Perhaps." Rage shakes herself a little, then stands, all in one fluid motion, and it's only then, as I admire her gown, that I realize I'm no longer wearing my acclimation suit. I look down, my mouth falling open. My dress is a million shades of blue—royal and peacock, periwinkle and cerulean. Sleeveless with a high collar. Form-fitting bodice, skirts falling around my legs like waterfalls. It's exactly the kind of dress I'm always drawn to when I browse the archives for old fashion editorials.

Rage holds out her hand to me, her eyes a little worried but her smile kind. She radiates solidity. She is here in this forest, and nothing will hurt me while we are together. In this place, I'm safe. That I somehow know without question.

"Come," she says. "We have work to do."

I pause for maybe three seconds. Something tells me nothing will be the same after this. But since when have I ever shied away from adventure?

I take Rage's hand, hold on tight, and rise.

acknowledgments

The idea for *Extasia* was born during a conversation in an airport parking lot, during which Diya Mishra and I spoke about a patron saint of rage. Thank you, Diya, for the inspiration.

I'm grateful beyond expression for the support of my friends, my family, and my partner, Ken, who have kept me sheltered and anchored during even the fiercest storms.

Claudia Gabel, my editor, demonstrated endless patience, boundless insight, and really quite startling brilliance as we worked on this book over the past few years. Victoria Marini, my agent, has been my guide and champion in more ways than I can articulate here, and her zeal for my work continues to delight me. To both of these extraordinary women, I am forever thankful.

Finally, the team at Katherine Tegen Books has once again helped me usher a book into the world with exceptional skill and care. Thank you to Katherine Tegen, Stephanie Guerdan, Joel Tippie, Shona McCarthy, Louisa Currigan, Veronica Ambrose, Vincent Cusenza, Clare Vaughn, Shannon Cox, Aubrey Churchwald, Amy Ryan, and Shae McDaniel—as well as copy editor Alison Cherry and cover artist Diego Fernandez—for your hard work and your dedication.

READ ON FOR A VISIT TO SAWKILL ROCK

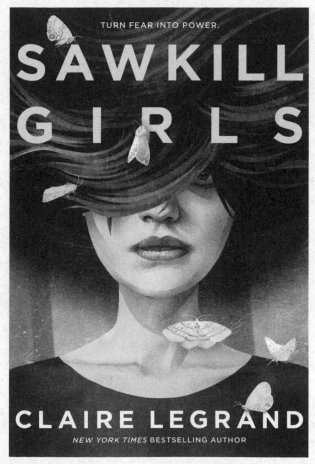

TURN FEAR INTO POWER.

SAWKILL GIRLS

CLAIRE LEGRAND

NEW YORK TIMES BESTSELLING AUTHOR

EVERYONE KNOWS ABOUT THE ISLAND of Sawkill Rock:

The silly old legends of its healing waters, which are impossible to altogether dismiss when one considers the people of Sawkill themselves—their hard white teeth and supple limbs. The brazen, easy way they walk and shop and love. Their flagrant indifference toward life beyond the Rock, and their deft handling of even the bleakest tragedy: *Oh, what a shame that was*, they say, and bow their shining heads for a moment before gliding on, untroubled.

The beauty of the Rock's rolling horse farms. Groomed flanks that gleam in the pale Atlantic sun. Grass like a glossy carpet that blows and shimmers, even at night. Especially at night. Black trees, wind-curled and water-bitten.

The houses like palaces, old but solid-hewn, gray and white and shingled. Sprawling and manicured. Careless and dignified. Old money: the taste of it sits on every tongue like a film of stale sugar.

The way the dark, rough sea bites up the shoreline. How the winds on the eastern side groan like old-time beasts turning in their sleep.

Come for a while, reads the sign at Sawkill's ferry dock, *and stay forever.*

The Rock has always hated that sign.

MARION

The Accident

These are the things people said to Marion Althouse after her father died:

Oh, God. You poor girl.

Marion, I'm so sorry.

What a loss.

What a terrible, terrible thing.

Your mom. Jesus, I just— I can't imagine.

How is she doing?

What about Charlotte? They were always so close,
those two.

If you need anything, you let me know. Okay?

I'm here for you.

You're such a rock. You see that, right?

They're depending on you.

They're lucky to have you. Blessed.

Marion, you're so strong. How do you do it?

How did she do it?

It was a good question.

Marion asked herself the same question that first morning: *How do I do this now?* There had been *before* October thirteenth of last year, and, now, there was *after*.

After David Althouse crashed his car coming home from a late night at the office, so tired he probably couldn't see straight, ready to lay down his bones by the light of dawn.

After some drunken scum-of-the-earth asshole took the mountain turn too fast, and her father was too exhausted and distracted, Marion assumed, to react in time.

After his car crashed through the guardrail and over the cliff, careening into rocks and plowing into a tree before coming to a still, smashed stop.

After the previously mentioned asshole drove away in a panic, maybe crying and shaking, too spineless to own up to their crime, leaving her father to die in the remains of his ruined fifteen-year-old Toyota.

After all that, this is what people said more than anything else:

I'm sorry for your loss, Marion.

Her loss. As if she'd misplaced her car keys.

When people said that, a part of Marion wanted to slap them, knock the cards and casseroles out of their hands.

I'll tell you what I've lost, she wanted to say, and then open up her chest so they could see the hollow pit where her heart used to live. It was stuck in a state of collapse, this pit—a tiny, organ-shaped singularity, sucking down the bleeding ravaged bits of who she used to be.

But Marion did none of this.

She accepted their bland sympathy and uncertain smiles, tucked the wrapped food into the packed fridge, sat by her mother to make sure she didn't sneak pills, and held Charlotte when she woke up sobbing.

She was Marion Althouse: devoted daughter and trusted little sister.

She sat alone on the bench outside the restroom on the ferry, arms full of everyone's purses, while her mother vomited in the toilet and her sister flirted with a boy who drove a Lexus.

She was a rock. A blessing. A good, steady girl.

She did not give in to rage or self-pity. Not ever.

Not once.

"There it is!"

Charlotte leaned against the deck railing, the wind whipping her honey-brown hair around her face.

"Don't lean out too far," said Marion. She sat on the polished black bench across from the railing and held her mother's gloved hand tightly in her own, anchoring it in place on her lap.

Charlotte, seventeen-nearly-eighteen, glanced back with a magnificent roll of her eyes.

"*Marion*," she said. "Honestly."

Marion, sixteen-nearly-seventeen, agreed. Since birth, she'd been a bit of a fusser—something she'd prided herself on, if only because it drove Charlotte batty to have Marion always chirping at her shoulder—but since their father died, her ability to nag and worry had skyrocketed to a whole new level.

Really, what did anyone expect?

There were only three Althouses left now, two and a smudge on their mother's bad days. You couldn't know which day would be the last one, and you couldn't trust Charlotte not to lean out too far or run too fast or fall in love too easily, and you couldn't trust their mother with pill bottles or sharp objects.

So Marion didn't. She held their purses and followed doggedly behind their every flighty, stumbling step.

"It looks amazing out here." Charlotte pulled out her phone to snap pictures. "It's like this . . . this *thing*, perched out there on the water. A beetle. A monster. Some magical lost place."

Marion would have preferred to be napping in their car's back seat, not talking to anyone and not looking at the rocking water and, maybe, not waking up.

But her mother wanted fresh air, hoping it would settle her stomach, and Charlotte refused to sit around being boring— God, *perish* the thought of Charlotte Althouse ever being accused of such a thing. So Marion sat without complaint and watched Sawkill Rock approach on a sheet of gray waves.

The island really did look like a *thing*. Black and solid, craggy. A little bit fearsome, a little bit lonely. That part didn't bother Marion, though. She would have lived on a barren dusty rock with no horses or people or yachts tied up at the docks, if she could have. Just her and Charlotte and their mother, a little clean white cottage, a pebbled path down to the water for sunbathing. That's all they needed—quiet, and one another. To be left to themselves for a while. No constant doorbells and phone calls. No more sympathy cards.

The salt-specked wind surged past them. In Marion's grip, her mother shivered.

Marion glanced at her and took stock: Pamela Althouse. Eyes fairly bright, observing the deck, the passengers, the water. Shoulders not so stooped as they could be. A small smile tugging at her lips as she watched Charlotte snap selfies at the railing.

Smiling was a good thing. Their mother, for now, was not in danger. Not of sneaking off, fog-brained, to unearth a knife. Not of rummaging through Marion's luggage for the hidden medicine. Marion could relax.

What a joke.

Marion had never been good at relaxing, and now, *after*, she was even worse at it. Her mother had often teased that Marion was born with ten lives' worth of tension knotted in her shoulders.

My little rock, her mother would say. *My grave little mountain*.

"Having second thoughts?" Marion gently nudged her mother's side.

"Not at all." Her mother breathed in, her eyes falling shut. "The sea air is invigorating, don't you think?"

"It's definitely cold."

"This is just what we need. A change of scenery. New faces, new roads."

A familiar litany. Marion nodded. "You're right, Mom."

"I'm excited to meet the Mortimers, aren't you?" Her mother squeezed her hand once, gently, before releasing her. "Such lovely people, on the phone. They breed award-winning Morgans. I told you that, right?"

"Yep." A hundred times. "They sound great. Real down-to-earth types."

"I thought you'd like them," her mother said with a little nudge. "A family of women who keep their mother's surname, generation after generation? Men that come and go, and never stay in the picture? A matriarchal dynasty." Her mother smiled a little. "Isn't that your thing, darling? Girl power and all that?"

Marion rolled her eyes. "Mom. No one says 'girl power' anymore. That being said, the surname thing is kind of cool. But . . . then there's the fact of their filthy rich–ness."

"Oh, Marion. Don't be a snob." Her mother clucked her tongue, fumbled with her zipper. When her fingers began to shake, Marion took over and zipped up her mother's jacket to the neck. "The Mortimers are good people," said Mrs. Althouse, her voice muffled in her scarf. "I have a sunny feeling about this. Val, their daughter. She's Charlotte's age. Did I tell you that? I'm sure I did."

At the mention of Val Mortimer, Marion looked away, down the ferry deck, to the rows of parked cars. Their faded blue station wagon, rust lining the wheel wells, was a plucky little weed in a garden of Range Rovers.

"Yeah, Mom," she said quietly. "You told me about Val."

Actually, Marion had looked up Val online, because Marion wasn't the type to let things remain uninvestigated. That's how she found out that Val Mortimer was just the kind of bright-smiled, gorgeous, damaged girl to whom Charlotte would easily attach herself. Last year Val had lost a friend—a girl their age whose death had gone unsolved, her body never found.

So Val and Charlotte had both suffered losses. Both had, presumably, endured the endless cloying condolences of friends and neighbors. Both were carelessly, shockingly beautiful—long limbs and perfect noses and poreless pale skin. Lips that curved just right. Their online lives a parade of endless friend lists and beaming, perfectly filtered photographs snapped at parties, bonfires, dances, football games.

Marion was holding out hope that Val Mortimer would be too much of a snob to befriend the housekeeper's daughter. Charlotte was hard enough to keep track of on her own, without someone like Val in the picture.

"Selfie time!" Charlotte sang, flinging herself down on the bench beside them. Before Marion could protest, Charlotte had pulled them all close and touched her phone.

"Lovely," she declared, turning the screen so Marion and Mrs. Althouse could see. "That's us. The Althouse girls."

Marion leaned in to take a look.

Yes, that was them all right:

Charlotte. Pink-cheeked, windblown hair falling in wisps around jewel-blue eyes. Worn parka framing her face in faded red nylon.

Mrs. Althouse. Dark, graying hair. Tiny lines of grief, new and alarming, etched around her eyes and mouth. Her zipped-tight jacket making her look small and squashed.

And Marion. Pale and serious. Dark-haired, gray-eyed. A near-copy of her mother, if not as old and tired. Awkward, though. Not quite smiling. Looking not at the phone but rather out to sea.

"It's all right, he won't bite. You can come say hello, if you want."

Marion had been trying not to stare at the police officer and his gleaming horse but had failed miserably.

She glanced up from her phone. "Oh, that's okay. I'm good."

"His name is Nightingale. He's fast but gentle." The officer smiled at Marion, his dark-brown face wind-bitten and clean-shaven. "I'm Ed Harlow, by the way. Sawkill Rock's police chief."

Ah, yes. Marion recognized him now, from an interview about Val Mortimer's dead friend.

"Marion Althouse." Marion shrugged back at the station wagon, packed full of everything they owned. She did not let herself think of the house they had sold—the house of her father's life. The house of her father's memorial service.

New faces, new roads. A change of scenery.

"Oh, right. The Althouses." *Ah.* There was the awkward, sympathetic smile. "Moving into the Mortimer cottage, right?"

"You know about that?"

"Small island. News spreads fast."

Marion glanced behind her, at the market into which her mother and Charlotte had disappeared to buy groceries for the night. She had claimed seasickness from the ferry ride so they'd let her stay behind by the car. A rare shirking of her duties.

Really she felt fine, stomachwise. It was her head that was the problem, and, weirdly, the soles of her feet. Since leaving the ferry, they smarted awfully, like she'd been running barefoot for ages and had scraped them raw on the concrete.

Besides, she wasn't sure she could bear the cramped lights of a grocery store at the moment, nor the curious eyes of new neighbors upon her.

Marion slipped her phone into her pocket, absently rubbed her throbbing left temple. "He's a really pretty horse."

"He's one of the Mortimer Morgans."

She placed a hand on Nightingale's sleek neck. His coat was the rich brown of a dark roast.

Despite her headache, she had to smile. "He's beautiful. Aren't you, boy?"

At her touch, Nightingale flinched. He twisted his neck around to whuff at her back and then stamped his foot against the parking lot; the impact reverberated up Marion's legs to settle like a swampy knot in her belly.

"Want to ride him?" Chief Harlow's aviator sunglasses mostly hid his eyes. "Just around the parking lot."

Marion touched her right temple. The headache appeared to be shifting back and forth between the lobes of her brain. "What, like a pony ride?"

Chief Harlow laughed, adjusting his tan cowboy hat. "This fellow is no pony."

"Well." Marion played with Nightingale's coarse mane, trimmed short. "I guess so. I mean, I've never ridden a horse before."

"Never? Well, then." Chief Harlow laced his fingers together. "Put one foot in my hands, then push up and swing your leg over the saddle."

"Jesus!" Marion hissed, fumbling to get her leg over Nightingale's back. "It's really high."

Nightingale pawed the parking lot asphalt with one hoof, then another.

"Don't worry, I've got him." Chief Harlow gestured with the reins. "Lean forward a little, pet his neck. Talk to him."

"Hi, Nightingale," Marion muttered, rubbing her hand up and down his neck. "Hi, boy."

Muscles quivered beneath her fingertips. Nightingale snorted, then shifted to the right and sharply flicked his tail.

"He seems nervous." A spike of fresh pain behind Marion's eyes threw her vision out of alignment for a solid two seconds.

She gripped Nightingale's mane, convinced she was about to slide to the bottom of the world. "Is that normal?"

Nightingale tossed his head, giving Marion a good view of the wild whites of his eyes.

A sick, cold feeling dripped down her arms. "He's freaking out. Is he freaking out?"

Chief Harlow frowned. "Hey, boy, hey, what's going on, huh?"

Nightingale backed away, lashed his head from side to side. The reins flew out of Chief Harlow's hands.

Marion tightened her legs around Nightingale's belly. Her headache careened from temple to temple, and then the pain zipped right out of her head and down her spine, got caught somewhere in her lower back, and exploded.

She cried out and lurched away from the pain, but it was everywhere, it was inescapable. Her fingers tingled sharply. "I want to get down, all right?"

"Hey! Hey!" Chief Harlow's whistle pierced the quiet parking lot.

"Get me down!" Marion could barely hear herself over the panicked roar of her blood. "Do something!"

Nightingale reared up, let out a neighing scream. Chief Harlow stumbled back, fell hard on his tailbone.

A whip of something cold smacked across Marion's shoulders, like the wind had suddenly picked up and sharpened. Marion tasted ocean echoes, the grit of wet sand, the earthy tang of close-growing trees. Her feet were on fire, and so was her head, and so were her palms against Nightingale's trembling neck.

He reared up with a savage shudder. Marion grabbed his mane to keep from sliding off.

"Marion!" came Charlotte's panicked shout.

But this horse would wait for no sister. It was out of its head, though Marion couldn't imagine why. Rabies, maybe. Something had spooked it. A snake?

Nightingale bolted.

With each slam of his hooves against the hard ground, Marion imagined her father tumbling over the cliff, his head smashing against the car over and over until there was nothing left.

ZOEY

The Snoop

Thora had disappeared seven months ago, and they'd never found the body.

No one had any answers other than the usual litany: you kids shouldn't run around on the cliffs, they're too dangerous, haven't we told you that a million times?

Zoey had had just about enough of pretending she was okay with this.

She didn't think, generally speaking, people were allowed to wander in off the street and go snooping around the police station like they owned the place. But Police Chief Harlow was in charge of things, so Zoey Harlow could do what she wanted to do.

It was the one paltry joy of living on Sawkill Rock alongside its army of gleaming people, with their smooth, untroubled faces and their sweat-stained riding jodhpurs and their cars that cost more than Zoey's house.

Rosalind, sitting at the front desk, offered Zoey an oatmeal-raisin cookie and nodded at Zoey's notebook. "What're you writing today?"

"Haven't decided yet!" Zoey replied. Which was true. She *hadn't decided yet* since Thora died. Her half-filled notebook remained half-filled. The only thing to come out of Zoey's pen over the past few months besides schoolwork were doodles of farting unicorns.

She rounded the corner, parked herself in the staff lounge, showed an old scrap of a poem to her father's nosy deputy, and doodled flatulent mythological creatures for a half hour. When the place had emptied out for lunch, Zoey retrieved her dad's office key in her pocket, crept through the quiet hallways, unlocked his door, and slipped inside.

Her heart raced. She'd been in this office hundreds of times since moving to Sawkill two years ago. But she had never entered it without her father's permission—and *definitely* never with the intent to snoop.

Zoey crept around the desk, opened the six desk drawers, leafed through papers. The office was immaculate—no surprise there—but that meant she had to go slowly, make sure she put everything back exactly where she'd found it. Ed Harlow was the kind of guy who'd flip out—mostly good-naturedly—if someone misplaced a single book.

He'd told her once, *The world is a crazy place, Zo. I like to keep my part of it as neat as I can.*